MY GOOD NAME

By Miranda Shisler

ISBN-10: 0-9965619-7-8
ISBN-13: 978-0-9965619-7-6

mirandashislerbooks.wixsite.com/mirandashislerbooks

kathleenkirtlandphotography.wordpress.com

This book is a work of historical fiction. But it is more history than fiction. The two people you are about to meet did live and love, and their story did go something like this.

Grandma and Grandpa live with Jesus now. This is my offering, a keeping of a promise, a token of love and gratitude for the legacy they left behind.

This story is dedicated to the people who inspired it, John and Nellie, whom I miss with an affection that doesn't lessen though the years keep piling up. I promise to honor my good name as you did, the name we both share—the name of Christ. And I'll love like you loved. For just as Sister Beulah always said...

Love makes the difference.

Prologue

Ollie's fist pounded against the paneled door. Summer rain fell over him in sheets, soaking him to his core as he guarded the precious package snuggled against him inside his jacket. He felt the newborn startle.

"Hold on, dearie. Dad's going to take care of you." He peeked inside his thin coat to see the glint of innocent eyes staring at him in complete helplessness. His throat swelled with emotion. His daughter was just a few hours old and so tiny. It wasn't her fault. It certainly wasn't her fault. If only Beulah...

"Ollie? Something the matter?" The door opened and a young woman from their church eyed him with concern. "Did Beulah have the baby?"

"That's why I'm here," he said slowly, his voice sticking in his throat. "The baby is born and Beulah is... ill. She can't take care of her. I know it's asking a lot, but would you take little Nellie Mae and nurse her alongside your own baby for the night?"

He saw the surprise flicker in her eyes at the personal nature of his request. Her eyes darted to his jacket.

"I suppose so," she said slowly. But Ollie wasn't sure she'd really take the baby until he gingerly brought the tiny one from her hiding place. The rain splashed against her brand-new skin and made her cry. The young woman uttered a sound of dismay and reached for her. "Of course I will." She said stoutly. "You tell Beulah to feel better and know her little one is safe."

"Thank you. God bless you." Ollie's tears mingled with raindrops as the door closed, and he was left childless on the front stoop. How he loved his babies. How he treasured holding them close and singing them a song. Two beautiful daughters and one strong son had joined their family in quick succession, all without incident. But then the loss of their third daughter had hit them, not even a year before. Little Marjorie had been stillborn, and Beulah hadn't been quite the same since.

This little girl had come early, surprising them all, but the bigger shock came when his wife, Beulah, took one look at their newborn and began to cry. Screamed, really. Begged him to take her away. She'd turned her face to the pillow and shut herself away from the little life so recently removed from her own body.

"Not the best introduction to the family, little Nellie," he said with sorrow. The sound of the name he'd given her felt strange on his tongue.

He stood on the stoop, knowing he must return to his wife and family. She couldn't care for anyone now, not even herself. His feet resisted his command to move.

What was happening to his family?

Helen paced the house, rubbing her sour stomach. Her eyes focused on the calendar hanging on the wall. April. The buds were barely opened on the trees, and her little one wasn't due to arrive until summer began knocking on the door. She sighed and wondered how much longer she could stand feeling so poorly.

She stepped toward the kitchen counter and picked up an apple quarter before it began to brown. She nibbled on it. Apples were the only thing she could stand to eat. Good thing there were plenty on the tree out back. But she made a face and set it back on the counter. Not today.

She returned to her pacing. Her hand fell over the slight bump on her abdomen. She looked down and could easily see the toes of her shoes. This baby would be small.

The pains began suddenly after dinner that night. Her husband, Henry, had just returned with the midwife when a tiny squalling boy entered the world.

The midwife shook her head and clicked her tongue. "He's the smallest I've seen, Mrs. Hagaman. I wouldn't get your hopes set high on this one." She washed and weighed him. "Three pounds."

Helen glanced at her husband who had joined them in the bedroom to view his firstborn. He didn't smile. He folded his arms over his chest and shook his head doubtfully. "He's too small."

The silence was thick in the room. Finally, the midwife took a deep breath and smiled. "You never know. He's small, but he's carrying on like nobody's business. Maybe he'll surprise us. You take him and nurse him now. Give him the best chance you can."

Helen's hands shook as she received her tiny son. He was just a bit of life between her fingers. She ached for the love that swelled inside her chest. "I don't have a crib ready," she said absently as she watched his eyes struggle to open, his lips smack awkwardly as if he were trying them out.

"All you need for this handsome fellow is a shoebox." The older woman took one from the side of the dresser and lined it with a blanket. She took the baby and set him inside. He fit with plenty of room. Helen smiled at the same time a lump formed in her throat.

After the midwife had gone, Henry sat down on the edge of the bed and sighed. His features were solemn. He didn't look her in the eye. "No sense in giving your heart to a babe that won't make it."

3

MY GOOD NAME

He left her alone without a word of naming or holding his new son.

She fought the tears, knowing Henry wouldn't approve of them. She stared into the fathomless infant eyes blinking and watching her carefully. Sizing her up, was he? She could see it. This one was no weakling, regardless of his size. He had spirit.

"Are you daring your mama not to care?" she whispered.

She brought him to her breast. "Welcome to the world, Johnny."

One

Mountain Grove, Missouri
July, 1930

"Daddy! There's a burning cross in the yard with ghosts standing all around! Is it Jesus? Did he come with the saints to take us to heaven?"

Nellie Mae's older brother called, summoning her from a deep sleep. She lifted her head from the tousled sheets, damp with perspiration. The window above the bed she shared with her sister was open in hope of a slight breeze to dispel the stifling summer humidity. She could hear voices just outside.

She sat up, her heart racing. The scent of wood smoke clung to her throat. Was the house on fire? Had Jesus accidentally set their house on fire when he came in glory with the risen dead?

"Emma Jane!" she whispered loudly and pushed her eight-year-old sister's shoulder. "Jesus came back!"

Emma Jane shot up in bed and stood to peer out the window. "That ain't Jesus, Nellie Mae," she said, her tone edged with fear. "It's the Klan."

Goosebumps rose on Nellie's skin. She stood up next to her sister to see. Imposing white figures in long robes stood around a

5

blazing cross directly in front of their porch. Masks covered their faces. Nellie could feel heat emanating from the cross.

She immediately began to wail. One of the Klan members looked their way. "Ollie Thomas! Come on out, and we won't hurt your kids."

Emma Jane grabbed Nellie and put her hand over her mouth. "Shush now. You'll get Daddy in more trouble."

"What do they want with him?" Nellie managed around her tears and the salty taste of her sister's fingers over her mouth.

Emma Jane shushed her again. "Quiet. I want to hear."

"You're not going to hurt my kids." Nellie's father stepped onto the porch. She heard the creak of weathered wood as their dad stepped down the stairs and stood before the Klan. "I'm sure even a horde of fools like you know better than that."

"We get what we want, Thomas," the man in the front spoke in a deep, intimidating voice. He sounded like he was trying to disguise his actual voice.

"Why are they trying to hide who they are?" Nellie Mae asked, glad her sister's hand had dropped from her mouth. Emma Jane didn't answer.

"I've told you before. I won't tolerate you bothering folks around here. You leave the Hollises be. They ain't hurting anyone living up on their mountain." Nellie's father didn't sound a bit scared. She was glad he was so brave, but she was worried, too. She'd overheard her parents talking about how the Klan down south killed black folk. How they'd thrashed a Catholic because he drank wine. They'd run Jewish immigrants out of town. She didn't want any of those things to happen to Daddy.

"It's not just you standing up for them Negroes," the masked man said. "Word has gotten round your woman stands up in church and speaks to the men. It's not natural."

"My wife is none of your business," Nellie's father said calmly.

6

"They won't beat him, will they?" Nellie moaned and wrung her hands. "What if they kill him, Emma?"

"Hush now!" Emma Jane shook her. "Daddy knows what he's doing."

"We won't tolerate it, Thomas," the man continued. "Next time you'll get more than a warning. I can't guarantee any of these good folk won't be back to teach you a lesson about standing up to the Ku Klux Klan. You watch your back now."

The Klan members filed away in somber procession, leaving on horses and automobiles that had been left out on the road. They left the cross there to burn out. Daddy stood and watched until it was only smoking embers.

Nellie heard her father sigh. "Beulah," he called to their mother. "Get the babies ready to travel. We'll have to move out tonight. Lou, now you come help your daddy."

Nellie's mother stood in the hallway, pacing back and forth as she tried to soothe the fussy baby. Eight-year-old Lou moved past her to help his father. Little Will held her leg and whimpered.

"Opal, come take the boys," she called to Nellie's oldest sister, who was twelve. Nellie knew her mother wouldn't question her husband's instruction for even a moment. "I'm going to pack some things. You girls get together your clothes and schoolbooks. Don't bring anything you don't absolutely need."

Nellie took her schoolbooks with tattered edges and her doll and her dresses and stuffed them into her pillowcase. She looked longingly at the blocks and pretty dollhouse her father had made them for Christmas, but she knew she'd never convince her mother they were necessities. Sometimes people had to make sacrifices for the greater good, Mother always said. Sometimes what was right was more important than what a person wanted.

And more than anything, Nellie wanted to do what was right and good and please her mother.

They ended up on a mountain farm, ten miles outside of Willow Springs, Missouri. Sharecroppers had recently been evicted for failing to make a profit, and the owner told Ollie he could stay there free of rent if he kept up the farm and took care of the animals.

"I know you have your job in town at the Chevrolet garage," Ed Beckett told him. "I'll understand if you want to keep looking for a place."

"No problem there, Ed," Ollie laughed. "I got a passel of kids ready for those responsibilities. Even the littlest are already good helpers. Besides, beggars can't be choosers. I need a place to go tonight, and I remembered you saying in church Sunday you needed to find new tenants."

Daddy made more than good on his word. He took Opal, Emma, Lou and Nellie out to the barn and showed them how to milk the cow and care for the horses. Nellie needed help from Opal, but she managed to do her part as best as she could. Daddy took them through the fields and explained how to pull the weeds around the wheat and oats. He taught them how to care for the chickens. Mother devised a rotating schedule where everyone took a turn doing everything they were able to handle.

Nellie didn't mind the work. Though she was young and the work was difficult, she liked contributing to the family. It made her feel valuable. When Mother set them to work planting a huge garden meant to feed their family, but also to can and provide for local folk in need, Nellie willingly worked alongside her mother as she planted seed and weeded and harvested potatoes and carrots and corn.

When the weather turned cold and the work of harvesting and canning was finally over, Nellie was given the winter job of milking the cow in the mornings, though Dad went with her and helped her until she was old enough to handle it herself without spilling the milk. Dad woke her before the sun rose. She learned quickly if she dawdled in bed he'd come into the room with a glass of water and a spoon and pour cold water on her face.

How she hated that miserable, cold walk to the barn with that freezing steel bucket banging against her legs! How she hated sitting in that barn next to that cow while the wind blew right through her. Goosebumps covered her skin and her teeth clattered together as she milked the animal as fast as her little fingers could manage.

But she was glad to do something to earn her place.

Nellie heard her father whistling *Springtime in the Rockies* as he rode down the lane on Clyde, the younger quarter horse he rode to work.

"Dad's home!" she announced to the household. The clamor began as everyone raced outside, hoping to be the first to greet their father.

Dad had a particular light in his eyes that day. Nellie immediately knew he had exciting news. She pulled on his hand and jumped up and down in expectation.

"Who wants to go to the circus?" he asked, slapping the newspaper with the Hagenbeck-Wallace Circus ad against his knee. Everyone cheered in response, even Nellie who wasn't quite sure what a circus might entail.

Dad leaned close with the paper and showed Nellie the picture. "We'll go after supper and watch the parade. They have lions and elephants. Can you imagine seeing one up close in real life, Nellie Mae?"

"Will they eat me?" she asked, nervous at the thought.

He laughed. "They're trained to behave. But don't get too far away from me or an elephant might just step on you." He tousled her hair and laughed again. It was a jolly sound that filled Nellie near to bursting with joy.

After supper, Mother scrubbed their faces until they were red and raw, brushed their hair until it shone and made them put on their Sunday clothes.

"You honor your father's good name and act respectable," she warned as she sent them off like a line of ducklings behind their father to the horse and cart. They waved to her as she stood on the porch with the baby and two-year old Manny, who seemed quite miffed that he hadn't been included in the invitation.

The promised parade both delighted and terrified Nellie's senses. She was sure a lion directed his roar at her, and that he wished he could devour her for supper like she'd devoured her rabbit stew. The lions and tigers were followed by smiling women in skimpy costumes and beautiful ostrich plumes worn like long wings that draped from their shoulders to the ground behind them.

"Look somewhere else, son," Daddy said in a low voice to Lou, who was unabashedly staring at the women with an open mouth. "Watch the clowns."

They all loved the antics of the clowns. One ran back and forth to either side of the road, passing out flyers and bowing to the ladies. He came close and handed a flyer to Dad. Nellie stared at his face painted white with a big red smile around his mouth. She'd never seen anyone with a painted face and bright costume before. She wanted to touch her finger to the oily colors and see if she could smudge them away, but she didn't think her father would approve.

"Thank you, boy," Dad said with a smile.

"Call me Red!" The boy shook his hand. After the young clown ran away, Dad watched after him with interest.

"Wonder what a young lad like him is doing working the big top," Dad said, more to himself than the children. "Seems he should be home helping his parents."

The circus dazzled Nellie Mae's young mind. On the way home

she stared at the still night sky, her senses full. She smelled the fresh popped corn and saw the lights flash in her vision as elephants, larger than life, ambled in front of her. Lions' terrifying roars echoed in her ears and her heart beat fast whenever she thought of the high-flyers gracefully soaring through the air. She was sure she'd never see such wonderful things again. She yearned to be able to return to any given moment of the night and repeat the experience. Or at least have a picture or a film to remember it. Wouldn't that be something?

A tug of sadness pulled away some of her euphoria. Why did fun times have to end? Why couldn't they always go to circuses or swim in the blue hole or sing songs on the front porch while Daddy played his harmonica? Why did nothing good last forever?

"What's the matter, little Nellie Mae?" Dad glanced at her in the back of the wagon from his place next to Opal on the buckboard. He lazily flipped the reigns against the horse's rump. "Didn't you like it?"

"I sure did like it – so much," Nellie replied mournfully. "But I can't figure why we don't just keep having fun all the time. Why do we spend so much time doing chores and running away from bad guys?"

"That's an interesting question," Dad said, thoughtful. "I guess – the truth is – the sad parts of life are because of sin."

Nellie pulled the wagon blanket closer around her shoulders, shivering. She didn't know what to make of her father's answer, but she felt the telltale prick of guilt. She knew what he meant by sin. She was forever doing things she knew were wrong. She threw fits. She tried to get attention. And all the while, she knew very well she was sinning against the Lord by doing so.

"I'm sorry," she said softly. Dad didn't even hear her words over the sound of his contemplative whistling. He started singing quietly to himself, the words of a hymn.

Holy, Holy, Holy! Though the darkness hide Thee,
Though the eye made blind by sin Thy glory may not see,
Only thou art holy; there is none beside Thee,
Perfect in pow'r, in love and purity.

Perfect. Something Nellie Mae would never, ever be.

Nellie dreamed of clowns laughing in her face. Elephants dancing around her, closer and closer until their giant feet stepped on her leg and trapped her. The clowns changed into the KKK with long white robes, laughing at her with their garish red mouths, holding blazing crosses close enough to burn her skin.

She woke up crying for her father.

"Hush now, Nellie," her mother called from the kitchen. "Dad already went to town. Get on out to the barn and milk the cow."

Her mother didn't sound angry. She never raised her voice except on rare occasions when she seemed to lose all control. Maybe she thought to calm Nellie by not reacting to Nellie's tears. Nellie swallowed them back until her head ached with tension. If her mother could keep from crying most of the time, Nellie figured she should as well.

She got up and dressed before heading in the direction of the barn.

"Running a bit late this morning?" Dad asked when she came into the barn. She stopped short, surprised to find him there and worried he was mad, but his eyes twinkled and she knew he was only teasing her. Then her eyes fell on the form of the young man asleep on a hay bale.

"Who's that?" she whispered.

"You don't recognize him without his clown suit and makeup, do you?" Dad set a thermos of coffee on an overturned pail next to the boy, who snored softly.

"The clown?" She took a step closer, swinging her metal pail against her legs. "What's he doing here?"

"I found him in town this morning, sleeping on a bench in front of the garage."

Nellie moved closer and poked the boy in the chest. "Is he sick?"

"Never you mind about that. Do your chores."

Nellie gave the young man another long look before she set about her task of milking. The cow glanced tolerantly at Nellie as she chewed her cud and swished her tail.

When Nellie was nearly finished and was about to call to her father for help carrying the bucket, the young man began to wake up. Dad went and sat next to him, opening the thermos of coffee and pouring some of the steaming liquid.

"What's your name, son?"

The boy blinked hard. His eyes were bloodshot. When he spoke, his voice was hoarse and quiet. "Uh, Red. Red Skelton, sir."

"Where'd you get your drink?" Daddy asked. "This town is dry."

The young man smiled sheepishly, but Nellie could tell the smile only covered the sadness underneath. "Found some moonshine, sir. Asked around."

"How old are you, Mr. Skelton?"

Red took a sip of the coffee. "Sixteen, sir."

"Where are you from?"

"Vincennes, Indiana, sir," the boy said. Nellie's ears caught the familiar name.

"Aren't you from around there, Dad?" she asked. Dad nodded.

"Still have family there." He looked at Red. "Why aren't ya at home helping your mother and dad?"

"My dad's dead, sir. Died a couple months before I was born. I think my mama's relieved to have me out of her hair, to be honest with you. One less mouth to feed, sir. And I send her my earnings.

Every penny."

"Except the pennies you spend on bootleggers' wares, that is," Daddy reminded him.

"Gave him free tickets to the circus," Red said impishly. Nellie leaned against the pole and swayed her full milk can as she watched him curiously.

"Son, I know you're trying to make the best of a life that's dealt you rough. I know it's tempting to drown your sorrows in drink. But God has better for you, if you'll let him lead you. He's got a good plan. He'll help ya get past the vices."

Red sighed. Nellie felt sad at the hopeless gesture. "I know, sir. I know I need God. But I have a hard time trusting. I ain't there yet."

Dad patted his shoulder in understanding. "Don't wait too long, son. God's way is much easier than the path you're treading."

"Thank you, sir," Red said as he stood up, unsteady. "I'll remember your kindness and advice. I will."

"I hope you will." Daddy stood with him and shook his head. "The door of my house is always open to you. And if you go home to Indiana, you look up my wife's brother, Jeff. He's a good man who'll look out for you, especially if you say you know me."

"Thank you. I'll do that, sir."

Then the young man disappeared over the misty hill, headed in the direction of the circus tents. Daddy whispered a prayer as he went on with the chores in the barn. "That old sin nature, Nellie Mae," he said with a sigh, though she didn't think he was really talking to her. "How it clings to a soul. Makes it nigh impossible for us to reach the Lord."

Then how on earth are we supposed to reach him? Nellie wondered as she headed back to the house, shivering. Her chest tightened with the familiar feeling of panic.

Would she ever be good enough?

Two

Willow Springs, Missouri, 1941

It was hot. And Nellie Mae hated to sweat.

She swung her songbook back and forth across her damp face as she heard the soft sigh of her sister next to her. A quick peek around the crowded sanctuary told her that many were willing to brave the heat to hear Sister Beulah speak her mind.

A negative emotion Nellie couldn't quite put her finger on swirled in her mind. Not an unfamiliar feeling for sure; she'd felt its icy grip on many occasions in her nearly sixteen years. She forced her gaze back to the woman everyone called Sister Thomas, who stood to the side of the pulpit and preached her heart out.

Her mother.

Emma Jane sighed again. Nellie knew what she was thinking, and if she were being honest, she thought it too. *Mother isn't really speaking to people; she's just nagging them.*

But she gave Emma Jane a small nudge of reproof anyway.

She didn't know what she'd do without Emma Jane, honestly. She loved her older sister desperately. They had developed a sort of comradery, even if Emma Jane was the rebel and Nellie Mae was always trying to do her best. Nellie hated the thought of Emma Jane up and marrying her beau in the fall. That would mean both sisters had been stolen away by their men. What would become of Nellie Mae? It wasn't as if she was going to find any wonderful man to steal her away anytime soon. She wished for another sister closer to her age. Nellie thought of Marjorie, the sister who had been lost at birth. Would that God could send Marjorie back! But she reminded herself that Mother wouldn't approve of thoughts about Marjorie. Whenever she was mentioned, they were encouraged to look to the future, not the past.

She took to fanning her face once again as she felt the extra measure of heat in her cheeks for her rebel thoughts. She looked out the window. The tiny country church overlooked the valley and community of Willow Springs. It had been standing in this spot for quite a few years, and it was obvious. The floorboards were loose and squeaky. The old windowpanes only revealed a clouded haze even when they were shined with plenty of elbow grease, and Nellie Mae knew it to be true from personal experience.

But there was a loveliness as well. The familiar smell of old, musty songbooks and aged wooden pews wiped clean with vinegar and orange oil. The echo of her mother's strong voice reverberating off the walls and striking her listeners straight in the heart with the Word of the Lord.

If only she didn't nag so much.

Her mother knew how to call forth sinful souls. Just a few weeks prior nineteen souls had walked the aisle to repent during her revival preaching. Nellie Mae had shed tears and prayed over them just as a dutiful church member should, even as she secretly wondered if she should have been the twentieth soul.

She remembered the first time she'd felt God's call. It was in a camp meeting when she was eight. She'd felt like she was being carried to the altar on an invisible wind. She had fallen on her knees and asked the Lord to forgive her many sins. Vanity.

Discontentment. Selfishness.

Mother had been so happy. Had Nellie Mae ever seen tears in her mother's eyes before that night? Mother was as calm and even as they come, except when she was fire and fury.

When Nellie was twelve, she got to wondering if it weren't her mother's forgiveness she'd been seeking and not the Lord's. She went forward again … just in case.

She'd done the same many times since. The guilt would creep up on her so heavy she didn't know what else to do. Could God forgive all those hidden places within that got so full of frustration and dark thoughts? Just knowing God could see into her brain made her blush with embarrassment.

"…we pray in the holy name of our Savior, Jesus… Amen."

Nellie realized she'd been so buried in thought she'd missed the end of Mother's talk. She knew for certain she'd hear how timely it was and what a blessing to many folks.

She walked up the aisle to the door, enjoying the sound of her high heels tapping against the hardwood. When she felt the burst of fresh air and mountain breeze, she took a deep breath and sighed.

Emma laughed. "We're always so happy when church is over."

Nellie frowned until she was sure they were out of hearing distance of their mother, who was deep in conversation in the front with a woman who had come up to speak to her. As soon as she saw she was safe, she couldn't contain her energy anymore. She giggled, kicked off her heels and ran toward the tall trees that towered around the little stone church building as if they sheltered it from the elements, their lofty branches swaying like protective arms.

"Looks like Nellie Mae wants to be chased!" Nellie heard a male voice call. She looked back and saw two of her friends following her, Bill Lyons and Henry Adamson. She laughed and ran until the fallen pine needles pricked the bottoms of her feet too many times. When she stopped, Bill came up and grabbed her arm, whooping like he'd won a prize. "Looks like I get to walk Nellie Mae back to church."

"Maybe you should carry me back – I think my feet are bleeding!" She leaned on his arm for strength as they headed back up the path.

A twinge of guilt made her wonder if it were proper to let Bill hold her hand. But, after all, Mother always reminded her that she herself had been married a year younger than Nellie was now. So, if Mother thought Nellie was mature enough to be married, maybe she was old enough to hold some boy's hand until they reached the top of the hill and returned to the crowd of worshippers.

"You're so pretty," Bill said so only she could hear.

She scoffed. "You're blind as a bat, Bill Lyons."

Emma Jane hated when Nellie put herself down, which was often. *Nellie Mae, you must be the prettiest thing in all creation,* Emma would say with a bit of wistfulness Nellie surely didn't understand. She supposed big sisters were supposed to say things like that. Didn't make it a bit true.

"You're coming to town again for high school in the fall, ain't ya, Nellie Mae?" Henry caught up to them and asked breathlessly.

"Why, for sure! Where else would I go?" Nellie was glad of it, too. She'd had her fill of the one-room schoolhouses led by teachers with hardly any more training than herself. She'd spent most of the school day last year teaching the little ones to read instead of doing much schoolwork on her own. She got to thinking the county should start paying her as well.

Mother wasn't much help. The law said children must attend school until they were sixteen, and she already had all sorts of plans for Nellie Mae the moment she turned the fateful age.

"Mother, I thought I'd finish high school," she had dared to reply. She was loathe to start arguments, especially with her mother. They had learned from an early age never to talk back to her. But learning was important to Nellie. Not only for its own sake, but for the sake of finding a dynamic different from her home. At high school, she'd been admired. Followed. Appreciated. For the first time in her life, she was special and not just another set of work hands. School was another world, and she relished the differences more than she'd ever admit to her parents.

When they got to the top of the hill, she tugged her hand away from Bill. She hurried back to Emma Jane and her shoes as her sister watched her with amusement. Nellie hoped she wouldn't get an earful from her parents later.

But sure enough, that afternoon she was made to sit on the narrow sofa in the front room. She folded her hands in her lap and waited for the lecture. Outside she heard the hollering of her brothers scuffling in the front yard. They'd talked of going to the swimming hole if Mother relented. Nellie wanted to go with them, so she determined to be sweet and repentant as her mother said her piece.

"Nellie, you're getting older now. We think it's time you take on more responsibility."

Nellie nearly choked. *More* responsibility? She bit back the sass that her tongue wanted to say. *I know, I know, you already had a child, ran a home and supported a husband at my age. I have no idea the value of hard work. I don't appreciate how easy my life is in comparison.*

Nellie Mae wished she could remind her mother of all the work she did. She tended small children for widows so they could work. She nursed elderly after falls or illness. She sat with the bereaved. What in tarnation had she missed? Mother was certainly not one to let her children be idle. Nellie knew she was to be about the Lord's business. Mother was apt to pull them out of school to send them on such missions, from the time they were twelve or so. Nellie wondered if her oldest sister Opal had married so young just so she might have a break. Her older brother might have headed off to war for the same reason.

She bit her lip to keep the smile off her face.

"It is unbecoming for a young woman to run wild with the boys," her mother began in a starched tone.

Nellie felt guilt's stranglehold on her heart. "I wasn't running wild, Mother. I just took a jog down the hill and hurt my feet on the pine needles so the boys–"

"You were holding a boy's hand in full view of the congregation." Her mother interrupted.

"Yes'm. But it was only Bill and Henry. They were just foolin'." Nellie almost left it at that, but she couldn't resist asking the question her conscience insisted she ask. "Is hand-holding with friends a sin?"

It was her father who answered after a moment of awkward silence. He came and sat next to Nellie on the sofa. His smile relaxed her, and she felt reassured even before he spoke.

"Nellie Mae, we know you're a good girl. We know you wouldn't do anything to dishonor our family. Just be careful. It doesn't take but a little foolishness to do something you regret."

"I'm a dunce for sure, Dad," Nellie Mae said slowly. "But I don't understand where that line is."

He sighed and pondered her question while Mother sat silent at the table, shaking her head. Her parents exchanged a glance and smiled.

"Just remember," Dad continued. "You always honor your good name. In doing that, you'll honor God, your family and yourself all in one."

Nellie relaxed. She wished she could lean over and kiss his cheek, but her father was uncomfortable with physical displays of affection. It just wasn't his way, as loving a father as he had always been.

"Now, git, girl, and put a pair of Manny's overalls on so we can hit that swimming hole before those boys do permanent damage to each other."

"Yes sir!" She jumped up. She turned to follow her father out of the room, but the look on her mother's face stopped her. She knew that expression. She knew what she was about to say. Nellie's happiness turned sour in her stomach.

"What is it?" she asked.

"Nellie Mae, we heard from your aunt this afternoon. Uncle Mort is in the hospital."

"I'm so sorry to hear that. Hope he's back to his old self directly." Nellie Mae tried to pretend the news had nothing to do with her. She even attempted to leave the room before her mother could say another word, because Nellie knew what the word would be. But when she heard her mother speak again, she stopped.

"Your aunt is plumb tuckered trying to look in on him and take care of little Harvey at the same time. You understand. The hospital is a good bit away from her home and she needs help taking care of him."

Nellie Mae sighed inwardly. "Aunt Nellie? All the way in Indiana?"

Mother shrugged as if it weren't all that far. "I told her I'd send you out for a few weeks, maybe a month or two until Uncle Mort is back on his feet."

Months? It hit her like a punch in the gut. Mother was sending her away. Nellie wondered if she was being punished for earlier. A rush of guilt came over her so strong she felt dizzy in its wake.

"We're family, Nellie Mae," Mother said more firmly, reading Nellie's reticence. "Family takes care of each other."

Nellie bit her tongue to keep from reminding her mother that mothers were supposed to take care of their children. "What about school? I'm set to graduate in a couple years if I can keep at it."

"Would you value school higher than your poor unfortunate aunt and uncle?" Mother answered. "School will still be there when you get back."

Her father peeked back into the room. His soft voice cushioned the overwhelming dread that overtook her. "You're a smart girl, and you've done so well in school, honey. You passed me up in education long ago. I'm so proud when I sit in the audience and watch you play your bass violin or sing in the concerts. But everything has to have a priority in life. If it's important, you'll finish when the time is right."

Nellie was out of arguments. Her face went hot and her eyes stung with tears, but she knew by the grim set of her mother's jaw her mind was made up. Nellie would go to Indiana.

And it will be the end of the world, she fumed inwardly.

Three

Beech Grove, Indiana, 1941

"Doesn't get much better," Johnny sighed, hating to interrupt the sound of the creek water trickling by, but realizing the words needed to be said. He stuck his fishing pole in the mud and reached over to scratch the ear of his dog, Lucky.

"That's for sure," his cousin, Peter, affirmed.

Lick Creek continued its quiet dripping and rolling along as Johnny watched minnows dart around the bait in the water. He loved it here. He loved the small town of Beech Grove, the only home he remembered. Still, he'd be a fool not to admit there was something missing.

"Suppose we gotta make something of ourselves, huh?" He brought up the subject with Peter. Though they were cousins, they'd grown up like best pals. Brothers even, since Johnny only had a pair of sisters. There wasn't a thing in the world he couldn't say to Peter, and he knew his cousin felt the same.

"Suppose so," Peter agreed, his cheek pressed up against his fist as he watched the water. "But you have a job, anyway."

Johnny raised an eyebrow and caught his cousin's smirk. "A job my pop got for me. Doesn't pay room and board even."

"You have a car." Peter nodded toward the black Ford Sedan sitting a ways back in the field next to the creek.

"I sure do." Johnny couldn't resist a proud peak at his pride and joy. He'd bought it after only a year of working at the railroad as a press operator. The car wasn't new, but it ran great and shined up nicely. He'd had Peter snap a few photographs of him with it the day he brought it home.

"Maybe you oughta pick out a pretty girl to go with your car. Then you'll be set." Peter laughed while Johnny rolled his eyes, fighting the grin that wanted to appear. There were a few pretty girls in Beech Grove. But none that made him want to swallow his shyness and talk to them. He figured he'd know the girl for him if ever there was one worth the risk.

But finding a girl wasn't on his mind today. Johnny decided there was no better person than his best friend to tell his secret. "I'm thinking about volunteering."

Peter was silent for a long time. "Yeah. Suppose I am too."

"Marines?"

"What else?"

Johnny could read his own thoughts in his cousin's eyes. They were both able-bodied young men and there was a terror trying to take over the world. They could lie to themselves all they wanted and pretend life didn't exist outside the bubble of predictable little Beech Grove, Indiana, but as the war raged around the world, the bubble continued to get smaller. Thinner.

"There's talk America will get involved."

"It's inevitable," Peter agreed. "We go to our jobs and come home and eat our ma's meatloaf and potatoes. We go to church and listen to our tunes on the radio and across the ocean folks are getting killed for no other reason than the blood running through their veins. And it isn't just in Germany anymore. Seems like everywhere else is falling apart, too. We declare war on you, and you declare war on them … like the whole world is going crazy."

"America can't stay neutral much longer. And if we don't volunteer now, we'll get drafted anyway. Might as well go early and have some say in where we end up."

Peter exhaled and stared at the stream for a long moment. He didn't speak but Johnny could almost hear his thoughts. *How will it end? Is this THE end? Or is it just our end, fighting and dying to keep our countrymen free from evil agendas?*

"Johnny, you wanna go to church with me?" Peter asked suddenly.

Johnny almost laughed at him. "I go to church same as you."

"Not that church," Peter said slowly. "There's this little Baptist church I've been thinking about visiting. They're having revival meetings this week. But I'd rather not go alone."

Johnny didn't know what Peter thought he was going to find at that church that was different from anywhere else, but he shrugged. "Sure, Pete."

"Good. Sunday then."

"And then Monday we join up," Johnny said.

"Monday it is."

Nellie Mae stared out the window at the flat landscape. She missed the hills of Missouri. She pouted and turned away from the depressing view through the cloudy train window. She rummaged through her purse for her lipstick and discreetly applied it. Her lips felt dry and cracked from the dust coming through the open window. She shifted on the velvet seat, wishing Dad had been free to bring her in the car. His gas station and mechanic's garage were busy these days. Mother had prayed for God to provide a way for Nellie Mae to get to Indiana, and that very night a church member had asked if they could use a train ticket from St. Louis to Indianapolis. Nellie

Mae had wanted to ask the Lord if he might not be so quick to answer next time. At least give her a moment to breathe. But as it was, she was sent off on her "adventure," as Mother called it, only two days after the idea was first mentioned.

She picked up a newspaper lying on the seat next to her, abandoned by a previous passenger. The headlines on the front page were dismal. The whole world was going to war.

"We won't be far behind, I guess," she murmured. Concern for her brother in the army deepened. She prayed he'd make it home. So many people dying. So many people's lives ruined for the warped vision of a madman. Where was God in all of this? Was he going to stand by and let his chosen people be annihilated?

She pushed the paper away, thinking of Senator Truman, and his predictions of what war would do to the still recovering economy. And yet he believed it was an endeavor that would have to be taken. The United States couldn't call themselves the "Land of Liberty" if they allowed oppression. Sooner or later the tyrants would come knocking down their door, just as they had other countries.

Nellie was glad she didn't have to make those decisions. Just thinking about it made her head spin. She tried to focus on the mission ahead of her. Her mother's sister, her own namesake, Aunt Nellie, would be waiting for her in Union Station in Indianapolis, so she was not to dawdle getting off.

Nellie Mae wished all over the place she hadn't been named after the woman. As the story went, her father had taken one look at her and said "Well, hello, Nellie Mae!" because she apparently resembled her aunt. With her mother in such a bad way after her birth, no one had bothered to think of a better name.

She hated her name. Why in the world couldn't she be a Linda or a Teresa – something beautiful and refined? Why did she have to have the most hillbilly name there could possibly be?

Well, after all, she *was* a hillbilly, her mother would remind her.

She could buy as many pairs of heels as she wanted. She could attempt to copy the latest fashions when she made her dresses. Not even curling her hair just like Linda Darnell would make her fit in. She belonged in the hills with the rest of her kin and their missing teeth.

Thinking of kin, she remembered the matter of Aunt Nellie. She considered her aunt as the train pulled closer to the station in Indianapolis. Aunt Nellie had been married twice. After the first husband up and bought the farm, she claimed she didn't have any way to support her three small children, so she left them at the orphanage.

A couple years later she married again and had another baby. Her husband's health was tenuous, and she seemed desperate for help with her son. Nellie Mae secretly wondered why the woman didn't just send him along to the orphanage with his siblings. She didn't exactly appreciate being thrown into the middle of it all.

She shook her head, trying to snap herself out of her funk. She was doing her Christian duty, as her mother would say. Nothing was more important than giving aid to her fellow man. Not even finishing high school.

She *would* finish high school. Even if her only option was a one-room schoolhouse in the hills of Missouri. Even if the only teacher was two bricks short of a load. She'd have that diploma and be better for it. Maybe she'd even go to college.

That would show the lot of them that she was worth more than cleaning house and minding babies.

Union Station came into view, reminding her that she couldn't even stand up to her mother long enough to avoid another assignment two states away.

Four

Johnny watched sparks fly from behind his face shield as the drill press lowered to create a hole through thick sheet metal. He nodded, satisfied that he'd set the drill in place correctly. He stopped it and took off the shield to mop his face with his handkerchief. The August humidity was stifling enough without the heat generated by the press.

"Hagaman, run over to Arrival C. There are a few boxes coming in with the train that I need down here."

"Yes, sir," Johnny answered. He liked Mr. B. okay. For a boss, anyway. He didn't talk much and wore a persistent frown, but he was fair. Johnny preferred the company of talkers. The less he had to think of to say, the better.

He stood at the round-about waiting for the locomotive, which he could hear huffing and puffing its way into the station. As he waited, he pushed his hat high on his head and folded his arms across his chest. He liked the idea of a train full of strangers pulling into the city. Who knew who was on that train? Maybe a movie star. Maybe a president. Maybe a bank robber he'd have to chase and take down all on his own. He couldn't help his grin.

Turned out there was a bad guy on board, but the kind that was a dime a dozen and perfectly legal. He knew it the moment he saw a white man hollering after a black man who stumbled on the exit steps. Apparently the first man believed the second had made him drop his suitcase and spill the contents. The white man called out derogatory names that sounded like sandpaper in Johnny's ears.

"Who do you think you are – riding on this train? Get your own train! Why, if any of my things are damaged … do you know who I am?"

Johnny's fists curled into balls as the darker man tried to pick up his own belongings that had fallen when he stumbled.

I should say something. No, I should just give that suit a taste of my knuckles.

Even as the idea flashed across his mind, he knew he couldn't. He needed this job, and Mr. B. wouldn't have any mercy on him, being an honored member of the KKK. Johnny had seen the picture on his office wall enough times. Mr. B. decked out in that white robe, parading down Meridian Street like he'd done something wonderful for the world by judging folks. By Johnny's estimation, anyway.

Johnny's fists relaxed and he sighed in frustration. He was a coward. He hated feeling small and weak. Sure, he hoped to be on his way to boot camp soon, but for all he knew they'd turn him out for being colorblind. He knew others like him had been sent home. And he was as colorblind as a person could be. It had taken him a few years of his childhood to figure out why everyone else seemed to know things he didn't know. See things he didn't see. He was flabbergasted when he realized that there was a rainbow full of colors in the world his eyes had no ability to grasp. He only saw one color that wasn't drab and gray.

That very flash of color caught his eyes. Suddenly all thoughts halted as he stared at the face hesitating at the exit steps of the train. She wasn't tall. She was a tiny thing by all respects. Eighteen, maybe? Her hair was light brown and feathery, the top part tied back in a loose bow while the rest hung in waves around her shoulders. Every feature of her face was flawless, like a movie star's, from her perfectly shaped nose to her creamy white skin to her shining eyes.

There weren't too many times in Johnny's life he'd wished he could see the colors others saw. But suddenly, he was hungry to see her – the color of her lips, her eyes, her cheeks – see her the way everyone else could. All he could see was the color of the dress that flowed around her knees and cinched in at her waist.

Yellow.

The white businessman who'd been raging at the black man turned and saw her the same moment Johnny did. His face immediately broke out in a smile.

The girl spoke. "Why, my goodness' sakes, I'm so glad you weren't hurt!" Yellow Dress's voice matched her looks. It had a pretty southern lilt, like bells tinkling.

The businessman chuckled. "I'm just fine, little miss," he began, but Yellow Dress walked right past him as if he didn't exist. She leaned down to help the black man retrieve his belongings.

"Oh, you don't have to do that," the man said in embarrassment, even as the white man's face turned purple with embarrassment and anger. Johnny knew in a heartbeat if that man laid a finger on Miss Yellow Dress, he'd send him to kingdom come.

She didn't seem too worried. She stood up and waved goodbye to her new friend with – hands down – the prettiest smile Johnny had ever seen. Without even a glance in the white man's direction, she picked up her bag and marched off in the direction of the terminal.

Johnny's mouth was dry as a bone. *This* was the girl that was worth the risk. He scrambled for something to say. He couldn't let her get away without at least finding out her name. He took the tiniest step toward her, reaching out his hand and trying to make his voice work.

"Hey, you! Boy! Help me with these trunks. What are you, blind?" The businessman, damp with sweat, called to Johnny, impatiently motioning him over. In the second it took for Johnny to look away, Yellow Dress disappeared into the terminal. He sighed with disappointment. Who knew if he'd ever see her again?

It was all Johnny could do not to throw the man's suitcase on the train tracks and give the narrow-minded man the punch in the face he'd been asking for.

Nellie tried to forget the man's intolerable words and actions as she stood in the great hall waiting for Aunt Nellie. She couldn't stand bigotry. And there was plenty of it to go around in Missouri. She closed her eyes and remembered one of the times the KKK showed up at her house to intimidate her father. She'd stuck her fingers in her ears and sang hymns until her father came back inside the house.

"It's alright, Nellie Mae. They're gone. Jesus kept you safe as he always does, now, didn't he?"

"Why do you make them mad, Daddy?" she cried, throwing her arms around his neck.

"Because somebody has to tell them what they're doing is wrong. We have a responsibility to fight the hate in Jesus' name."

Fight the hate they did. And they moved time and time again in the sixteen years she'd been alive. Always trying to stay ahead of the mob of haters.

Nellie opened her eyes and forced herself to take a deep breath. A man stood before her, staring at her like she had grown horns and a third eye.

"Are you Nellie Mae's niece? Traveling by yourself?"

"Yes, sir. Nellie Mae Thomas. My dad couldn't bring me in the car."

The man frowned as if he thought her dad was irresponsible for letting her come on her own, but he didn't comment. If he had, she would have argued. Her dad would die before he'd put any of his kids in harm's way. And nobody better say any differently.

"I'm Mr. Clarkson, at your service. Nellie asked me to bring you by the hospital."

"That'd be fine, Mr. Clarkson," Nellie said, forcing a cheerful smile. Mr. Clarkson must have been friendly after all, because his face lit up after that.

Five

Whatever Nellie had been expecting, seeing Uncle Mort lying in the hospital bed as pale as his sheets made her ashamed for thinking ill of his family. Her Aunt Nellie hovered near the bed, anxiously fussing. Nellie felt a stab of pity. Her aunt had already buried one husband.

Her sympathy lightened up quite a bit when her aunt sat her down and gave her the list of chores. She endured about ten minutes of lecturing before she wondered if it would be impolite to throw herself out the seven-story window.

"And if you have a few extra minutes after Harvey goes to bed, I'd like you to clean out the pantry and give it a coat of whitewash."

Nellie gave her bravest smile, praying there was nothing else. Her aunt patted her on the knee and gave her a prim smile. "I don't mind that you didn't bring any flowers, dear. No sense wasting your money."

Nellie choked back a laugh of disbelief. She nearly asked Aunt Nellie where she thought her sister had come up with the nine dollars her train ticket cost, but she managed to bite her tongue just in time.

An hour later she held a firm grip of two-year-old Harvey's hand as she walked him home from the Clarksons' to her aunt's house two doors down. She eyed it. Compared to some of the crude dwellings she'd shared with her family in Missouri, the solemn, two story, white paneled house with sturdy brick porch was fairly luxurious. But to read Aunt Nellie's letters one would have believed she was in the next palace over from the King of Siam. She clutched the long list of chores she'd been given, crunching the paper just a bit.

"Hmm," she said, peering down at her charge who eyed her with the same incredulity. "We've definitely got some work to do, don't we now?"

She marched him inside. Her first order of the day was to get the boy's supper on the table. She found some cheese and bread and butter in the icebox and paired them with apples she pulled off the tree in the backyard. As she diced her little cousin's supper on his plate, she sang her dad's favorite song.

When it's springtime in the Rockies
I'll be coming back to you
Little sweetheart of the mountains
With your bonnie eyes of blue
Once again I'll say I love you
While the birds sing all the way
When it's springtime in the Rockies,
In the Rockies far away.

Harvey watched her with curious eyes as he sucked his thumb and kicked his feet against his high chair.

"Tough crowd." She heaved an exaggerated sigh, which made him smile.

When he was done an hour later, he'd managed to take about three good bites and the butter from the bread had found its way to the floor, the walls, his clothes and his hair. She pulled him out of his chair.

"Have it your way, Harvey. We'll just have to throw you in the bath."

Apparently, her words unleashed Harvey's long-held anxieties concerning bathing, because he let out a holler that made her ears ring and lasted until he was tucked into bed twenty minutes later. She said his prayers for him while he wailed and kissed him on the head. When she stood up, his wailing died down and his thumb found its way back to his mouth.

"Now, Harvey, tomorrow we will tackle the whole length of chores your mama has decided we're going to do. I shall do my best not to complain if you promise to cooperate."

He stared at her with big gray eyes and made no promises at all.

When she got downstairs, she took one look at the pile of dishes and the layer of dust and the basket of clothes needing washing, ironing and mending. She sighed and slumped into a chair.

"If I'd wanted this for my life I'd be married and a mother by now." She huffed. "If I can't avoid it either way, it might as well be my own mess I'm cleaning up!"

She waved her hand at the disorder as if that might make it magically disappear and stepped out onto the front porch instead to avoid looking at it. It was still light out and the summer breeze was warm. She breathed deeply and leaned over the high brick porch, listening to cicadas singing in the trees and frogs croaking in some nearby pond or creek. If she closed her eyes, she almost had enough imagination to pretend she was back home. Until an automobile whizzed by.

She opened her eyes and watched the black sedan pull into the driveway across the street. She wondered about the neighbors. The Clarksons were nice, but what of the others? She was anxious to meet them all. Maybe there would be a girl her own age to help pass the time. If not, she'd be lonely indeed.

"Good morning, Johnny." His mother looked up as he came into the kitchen. He nodded to her. His younger sister, eighteen-year-old Nancy, sat at the table, engrossed in a book. He flipped her pages and grinned when she gave him a disgruntled glare.

"It *is* a good morning. Saturday. No work."

"Don't get too comfortable," his mother replied, calmly turning the eggs in the frying pan. "Miss Ada across the street telephoned and asked for you to come over and mend a fence."

"Aw, why can't Pop do it?" Johnny slouched in a chair and waited for his breakfast.

"He's working today." She shot him a disapproving glance as she placed the heaping plate before him.

"Shucks." Johnny dug into his breakfast, glad at the volume of it. Maybe the recession was lifting after all.

"You could always get Peter to help." Nancy put down her book long enough to eat her breakfast.

"I just might," Johnny said and made a face at her.

Peter came along right after breakfast, wanting Johnny to go fishing, so Johnny enlisted his help for the fence. Peter easily agreed, not given to half-heartedness or selfishness.

Johnny loaded up his toolbox before they crossed the road to Ada Pritchell's Craftsman Bungalow, standing neatly in a row with all the other nearly identical houses on Emerson Street. She greeted them with excitement, probably happier to have company than to get the fence repaired. She insisted they have cookies and lemonade in the parlor before they started, even though Johnny tried to explain he'd just eaten a huge breakfast. Ada waved off his protest and began to gossip as if she was a boiler nearly set to explode if the pressure wasn't released.

"I'm not one to put a bee in anyone's bonnet, but I have the word

36

on the new sitter at the Finch place."

Johnny stuffed a couple cookies in his mouth as he eyed the house next door. He'd never paid much mind to Mort and Nellie Finch. When he did, he found their lives confusing. They seemed to have quite a few more children when holidays came around. Not to mention the children always seemed happier leaving than coming.

"She's a pretty little thing," Miss Ada said. Johnny and Peter exchanged glances.

"Who?" Peter asked, taking another cookie.

"Why, the little girl who came to look after Harvey. I'm sure it's a relief for Mrs. Finch to know her baby's safe while she's away at the hospital. But, my goodness, she must be worried about her poor husband. I sure do hope she won't have to bury another one and send Harvey on to the orphanage as well."

Johnny inwardly sighed as Pete squirmed. "What did you need us to do, Miss Ada?" he asked.

Ada sniffed. "I'll show you the fence in need of repair."

The fence was in bad shape. A recent windstorm must have blown it down. New pieces of wood were stacked beside it. With a sinking feeling, Johnny realized this could be an all-day affair. He watched as Pete got right to work tearing down the old fence.

"Heard the Marines are really looking for recruits. You might get in after all, Johnny," Peter said as he worked.

"Don't know. This war'll run out of gas sooner or later."

"I hate to say it, but I think it's just getting started." Pete set his hat on the fence pole and started prying out old nails with the hammer. Johnny watched him until movement in his peripheral vision caught his attention. He glanced at the next yard where two-year-old Harvey Finch came tearing out of the back door like a banshee. Johnny was unprepared for his shock when the young woman followed the toddler out, in the process of tying her hair back in a handkerchief.

"Now you come right back here and let me wipe those crumbs off your face," she said loudly in that familiar, tinkling voice.

There was no way he'd have ever forgotten the sound. "Yellow Dress," he whispered.

"Yellow Dress?" Pete raised an eyebrow. He looked over at the next backyard and chuckled.

"I don't see a yellow dress, Johnny. I see a pair of men's coveralls." Pete stopped working to watch her for a moment. He whistled softly. "Would you get a load of that? There's a honey you don't see every day."

Johnny tore his eyes away from her face and busied himself with the nails. "What do you mean?"

Peter smirked at him. "You know exactly what I mean. She's in old coveralls and she still looks like she stepped off a movie screen. That's what I like to refer to as a *looker*."

Johnny didn't answer. He grabbed the hammer from Peter's hand.

"You know her?" Peter asked.

"No." Johnny glanced at the girl again without meaning to do so. Yellow Dress was wiping out an old washtub, presumably to get laundry started. She was a busy little bee for sure. No stranger to the tasks of homemaking.

Peter laughed. "Let me guess. You've seen her before but you didn't have the guts to talk to her."

Johnny glared at his cousin but didn't answer.

Peter shrugged. "Fine. Long as she's up for grabs, think I'll say hello."

Johnny stood awkwardly. "Don't."

Peter folded his arms across his chest and eyed Johnny with challenge in his expression. Johnny panicked. He couldn't let Pete get to her first. Pete was a smooth talker. There was no way she'd ever notice Johnny if he didn't introduce himself first. But talk to a girl? His heart raced just at the thought.

"What's the matter? Too scared?"

Johnny's pride surged ahead of his fear. "Nah. Get out of the way, knucklehead."

"Show me how it's done." Peter swooped his arm in her direction.

Knowing full well his cousin had been playing him, but not willing to take a chance, Johnny took a step forward toward the fence, his heart nearly beating out of his chest.

Six

Nellie Mae kept one eye on Harvey as he raced around the garden pretending to be a bird. She scrubbed the curtains she'd found coated with a layer of dust. She rubbed the cloth severely against the scrub board, stopping only to roll up her sleeves when they fell.

Aunt Nellie had an electric washing machine in the house, but Nellie Mae had never used one before. The thought of it made her nervous. She didn't want to flood the house with soap bubbles or something. She'd stick to what she knew.

She whistled as she scrubbed, glad for her brother's coveralls she'd sneaked into her suitcase. She had always found her brothers' clothes to be quite useful for activities such as swimming to picking apples. Manny'd surely never miss this old pair, covered in patches and frayed at the hems.

"Nonny!" Harvey suddenly yelled and went flying toward the fence. She gasped as she realized two young men were standing at the fence staring right at her.

"Hey, Harv." The taller one leaned over the fence and gave the boy's hair a ruffle. Harvey soared away as quickly as he'd come.

Nellie got her wits about her and stood up, brushing off

imaginary dirt from her clothes and cringing at the sight she must be. She worked up a smile, walking toward the one who had spoken to Harvey. No one in Willow Springs would ever think twice seeing her in coveralls doing laundry, but these were city folk. They probably expected her to be missing a few teeth.

"Morning, gents. Sorry you caught me in my work clothes." She smiled. Both of the faces in front of her smiled back. They must be friendly folk. Both were tall and handsome, but the taller one with the ears that stuck out from the sides of his head caught her eye. He had a lazy smile with eyes that seemed half-closed as he watched her.

He didn't say anything, so she wiped her hands on her pant legs and held out her right. "Nellie Mae Thomas. I'm up from Missouri visiting my aunt."

There was a long pause as the tall fellow stared at her. Finally, he put his hand in hers for a quick shake. The man must have been made of electricity, for she was sure she felt a buzz as his skin touched hers in the brief gesture.

"Johnny," he said so quietly she had to strain to hear him. "Johnny Hagaman."

"Well, Johnny Hagaman, what's cooking? Do you mend fences for a living? And who's your friend?"

The other young man chuckled and held out his hand to shake. Just a little too firm for her liking. "Peter Hagaman. Nice to meet you, Miss Thomas."

"Oh, please, call me Nellie. Are you brothers?" She looked from one to the other, noticing the resemblance.

"Cousins," Peter said when Johnny didn't answer. "Might as well be brothers, though. Johnny lives directly across the street from you and I live three doors down. And no, we don't usually mend fences. Just being neighborly."

"Where do you work, Mr. Johnny Hagaman?" Nellie turned her

attention back to the tall, quiet one – the one who intrigued her.

It took him a moment to answer. "The railroad."

"New York Central? I was just there yesterday. What a fancy place that Union Station is! Nothing like it where I'm from."

There was a moment of silence before Peter gave Johnny a look of exasperation. Since it seemed Johnny was determined not to speak, Pete gave her an apologetic smile. "What part of Missouri are you from?"

"You probably already gather I'm from the sticks," she joked. "All around, but mostly Mountain View and Willow Springs."

"And you're visiting your aunt?" Peter continued politely when Johnny said nothing.

"My uncle, bless his heart, is laid up at the hospital. Aunt Nellie asked if I'd come for a few weeks and help out with Harvey at the house. Mother sent me."

Johnny thought he heard some sort of undertone in the last three words she spoke. He wondered if her relationship with her mother might be strained. He also wondered what it was like to grow up in the sticks. He had a feeling he'd like it. He wondered a hundred other things about Nellie Mae Thomas in the space of the few seconds of silence that passed after she spoke. Peter cleared his throat and jabbed him in the ribs with his elbow.

Johnny swallowed hard, not sure he was capable of asking this angel out. What if she turned him down flat?

But he knew somehow he'd have to ask her. He couldn't go on from this point if he didn't. It was the very definition of being stuck between a rock and a hard place.

"Uh, Miss Thomas – I mean, Nellie," he began, his voice barely more than a whisper. Why'd he have to be such a coward? He should speak up and be a man about it. Nellie Mae raised an eyebrow, waiting with her hands perched on her hips not quite hidden beneath her boyish overalls.

She leaned toward him. "I'm afraid you'll have to speak up a bit, Mr. Hagaman. I must be as deaf as a post!"

He desperately searched for the right words. "Miss Thomas … would you care to … I mean, uh …"

Peter kicked him lightly in the shin as if to knock the words out of him. Nellie Mae stared at him, her eyes narrowing like she was losing her patience. He had to say something. Now.

"Would you care to … tell me how old you are?"

"Well, sure, I guess I'd care to." Nellie laughed heartily. "I'm sixteen if I'm a day. How old are you, Johnny Hagaman?"

"Twenty," Johnny answered, glad for a question that was easily answered in one word. He was surprised by her age. "I thought you might be older."

Nellie shrugged. "Nope. Been on the good earth for sixteen years just this past July."

"You do seem older," Peter said. "You must be mature."

Nellie laughed again. Johnny was sure it was the nicest sound he'd ever heard. "First time I was ever accused of being mature!"

Another pause followed, as Peter and Nellie stared at Johnny expectantly.

Nellie finally broke the silence. "Well, I better get back to work. Aunt's got quite a list for me and that's for sure."

She gave them a smile that spread across her face like the sun rising in the morning. Johnny watched her walk away; his tongue hopelessly tied.

Peter sighed as he got back to work. "Why in the world are you letting her go?"

Johnny didn't answer. He didn't have an answer aside from the way his stomach turned inside him. He watched Nellie set to work scrubbing. She called cheerfully to the toddler who was busy tasting a bug and eating a little dirt on the side. Harvey's luncheon didn't seem to concern Nellie Mae. She just smiled at his face full of dirt and took a handkerchief out of her pocket to wipe him off now and then.

For all his ogling, she surprised him by actually returning to the fence later on that afternoon. "Nice to meet you, boys. I'm heading in. Just wondering if you knew where my aunt's other kids are. I heard they stay at the orphanage, but I didn't believe it till I got here and found them missing."

Peter shrugged and looked at Johnny. Johnny worked up his courage. "They come by on the holidays. There's a boy and a girl. I forget his name but the girl is Lola."

"Strange." Nellie backed away from the fence, watching Johnny with something akin to curiosity.

He stood to his full height and tried to make his voice work. "Miss Thomas, seeing as how you're new to the area, would you care to have someone show you around?"

"Someone being ...?" Her voice trailed off and she waited.

He cleared his throat, sure she was about to reject his offer. She'd most likely scoff at him for even suggesting it. "Well ... I could."

His heart felt like it stopped as he waited the split second it took her to answer. She stared at him for a long time, and he wanted more than anything to turn and run away before she had a chance to tell him to go pound sand.

"You're a Christian, aren't you, Johnny? I wouldn't ever go with a boy who wasn't."

He chuckled. "Well, sure. I go to church same as everyone else."

She still looked troubled, but she finally answered him. "That sounds right nice. I'll check with the Clarksons and see if they can keep Harvey, but assuming they can, why don't you pick me up at six? I'll even wear a dress." She gestured to her overalls and chuckled.

Peter laughed out loud as Johnny watched her leave, her curly hair bouncing as it tried to work free of the 'kerchief. Johnny couldn't take his eyes off her.

"Johnny, I didn't think I'd ever say this, but I do believe you got yourself a date."

What in the world had she said? Pick me up at six? What kind of girl spoke so forwardly to a man? Her mother would up and have a heart attack if she had heard Nellie's words. Nothing good came from easy girls who asked complete strangers out on dates.

"I've never gone with a boy in the city," she told Harvey. "What in the world am I going to do? He's so handsome. He was just being polite and I all but threw myself at him. Goodness, he's four years older than me!"

Harvey didn't seem to care much about her predicament. He started whining for lunch.

"I don't know how you could be hungry after the worms and dirt you just ate," she said, moving to make him something.

She diced up some cheese and bread as she went on. "I'm not exactly keen on repeating what happened with James William, if I'm being honest with you, Harv."

She determined she'd just have to make the best of it. In fact, she was happy she'd see the tall, silent stranger again. There was something about him. She could feel it in her bones, as her mother would say.

Her bones were rarely wrong. If you didn't count James William, that is.

"Well, I suppose I better get you down for a nap and see about the Clarksons keeping you tonight."

Harvey munched on his cheese and stared at her tolerantly. If only everyone's lives could be as uncomplicated as his: playing in the garden, eating lunch and taking a nap.

Seven

Johnny watched out of the window as Nellie marched Harvey to the Clarksons' that evening. He didn't know what color dress she was wearing, but he imagined it was a pretty one if it matched the rest of her.

"Guess this is really happening," he said to himself. He wasn't as nervous now that he had found another couple to join them. Peter was busy, so Johnny had almost backed out of the date. He didn't think he could be alone with Nellie and come up with a single thing to say. He'd called up a friend from work and asked if he was busy that night. He didn't know Frank all that well, but he was talkative and that's all Johnny cared about.

"That's her? She's too pretty for you." Nancy leaned on the windowsill next to him and smirked at him.

He nudged her until she lost her balance and had to catch herself from falling. She righted herself and crossed her arms over her chest. "Bet she's pretty dumb if she's that pretty."

"She's smart and pretty."

"Doesn't matter either way. When she finds out what a dud you are, it'll be all over."

Don't I know it. Johnny stood up. "I'm off. Wish me luck."

"Break a leg." Nancy raised an eyebrow.

Johnny called a goodbye to his parents and forced one foot in front of the other. All the way down the porch steps to the curb. He made it across the street without breathing and paused at her front door for a long, deep breath.

"Be charming," he muttered to himself. "Be Pete. Do not, under any circumstances, be Johnny Hagaman tonight."

He reached his fist to knock, but before he could she opened the door. He stared at her smiling face, speechless. She was a vision.

"Hello, Johnny. Come on in while I find my wrap."

He stood awkwardly in the doorway while she went to the closet. She wore a flowy skirt and a white, ruffled shirt. Her hair was curled and combed around her face like Greta Garbo's, and her cheeks and lips were stained as red as cherries.

When she turned back to him her eyes sparkled like diamonds. He didn't know what on earth he'd ever done to gain the attention of a girl like Nellie Mae Thomas, but he wanted to get down on his knees and thank his lucky stars right then and there.

"What are you thinking?" She fussed with her hair like she was self-conscious, which made no sense to him. "I know I'm a mess compared to these city girls."

He couldn't help a chuckle of disbelief. "I've never gone with a doll as pretty as you." *Or any doll, for that matter.*

He wanted to catch the words in the air and reign them back, but he knew he couldn't. So he stood there and stuffed his hands in his pockets like an oaf.

She raised an eyebrow with a secretive smile. "I haven't gone with any city boys, either."

He found that hard to believe. She smiled at the question that apparently hung in his expression as she closed the door firmly. "My … I was raised by a minister. Mother and Dad always go on about being careful and such." She swung her purse on her arm and headed for his car, parked on the street in front of his house.

"How did you know that was my car?" he asked as he opened the passenger side door for her.

She stepped back to admire the sleek lines of the black sedan. "I saw you with it before. Nice! Nicer than most of the cars that come through my dad's garage." She ran a small hand along the hood. He was a little jealous of the vehicle if he was being honest. "Where'd you get it?"

"I bought it from the used car dealership after I got my job at New York Central." He didn't mention the details, like the fact that he'd thought he heard the car calling his name from across the lot.

"Best way to go," she said with a nod of approval. "My dad says it's always better to buy a used car in good condition than a new car. You never know if you'll end up with a lemon."

"Spoken by someone who knows her cars," he said before he closed her door and ran around to the driver's seat.

"Like I said, Dad opened a garage." She sounded sheepish. "I guess I've picked up a thing or two. Or maybe I'm just blowing hot air and I haven't a clue what I'm talking about."

"Sounded good to me," he said with a shrug as he started the car. "And I'm good with machinery."

She smiled at him like she was sizing him up. "I don't doubt it a bit."

They rode in silence until he turned down the street and headed for Frank's house.

"I hope you don't mind; I asked a friend and his girl to join us." Johnny cringed, hoping she wouldn't be mad.

She looked surprised for a moment, but she nodded. "Sounds fun. What's the plan, Stan?"

He sneaked a look at her and breathed in her musky scent. Was it possible to be intoxicated by perfume?

"Um ... I was thinking of trying the barbecue place on Main

Street." He glanced at her again. "Do you like barbecue?"

"Do you have to ask?" She laughed. "I *am* from Missouri." She touched his arm in her excitement, which sent a shock to his system. "Then what?"

"I thought we could drive around. See the sights."

She nodded and folded her hands in her lap. He eyed them. Boy, would he ever like to hold her hand. He didn't know if he'd ever wanted to hold a girl's hand so bad. He wondered if he wanted to bad enough that he'd actually do something about it.

Probably not. Touching this angel would probably stop his heart.

Nellie tried to control the fluttering of her heart. There were so many times when she had chafed under the discipline of her parents, but right now she could see why they'd been so concerned about her dating.

As much as she liked Johnny and wanted to get to know him better, there was a part of her that wanted to open the car door at the next stop sign and run home. He was going to see right through her and know she was a phony. She folded her hands tightly in her lap and tried to swallow back her uneasiness.

Johnny looked like he was about to pass out. His ears were as red as a beet and he was breathing fast. He kept opening his mouth like he was going to say something, but then he'd close it again. She wondered if she should talk, but she didn't want to interrupt if he had something he was trying to say. My, but this one was shy!

"So you mentioned your father is a minister?" Johnny finally asked, breaking the long silence with his soft voice.

She gulped. She had hoped he hadn't caught that. She didn't want to admit the truth for the life of her. She considered lying, but she knew she couldn't bring herself to do it. "Well, no, not exactly. As I said, my dad owns a garage."

Johnny didn't say anything else, but she could tell he was waiting for an explanation. She wondered how she could change the subject without being completely obvious.

Finally, she blurted out the truth. "My mother is the preacher." She waited for his laugh or worse – his ridicule.

"Huh," was his reply.

"We're Church of God folk," she explained, emboldened when he didn't curl up his lip in disgust. "You know, the Holiness movement? Our church considers the husband and the wife to be the preaching unit, but it's my mother who has the gift for speaking the Word of God. Most of our preachers are men. My mother is one of the exceptions."

Johnny nodded. "Huh," he said again. He sounded cheerful enough.

"But she never lets anyone call it preaching. She would say she *speaks* from time to time." Nellie Mae smiled. Maybe it was being so far away, or maybe it was his easy acceptance of her admission, but she thought of her mother and didn't cringe. "They have to get her a packing crate to stand on so people can see her."

He was quiet for a long moment, which made her wonder if she'd shared too much.

"I bet it would be hard to be a preacher's kid."

Nellie looked at him with a bit of wonder. She couldn't remember anyone ever acknowledging the difficulty of her position. Was someone in this great wide world actually trying to understand where she'd come from?

"Yeah, it sure is hard," she said softly, staring at him. "Everyone always expects you to be down-right perfect when you don't have a perfect bone in your body. I mean, sometimes before revivals my mother gets up at two in the morning and prays for hours. I can't even stand getting up at six to milk the cow. How does she end up so perfect and her daughter such a mess?"

Johnny watched the road and didn't say a word. Nellie wondered what he was thinking. Embarrassed, she tried to fill up the silence.

"I have two older sisters, one married, one engaged, plus an older brother headed out with the army, and two younger brothers. What about you?"

"Two sisters. I'm the eldest," Johnny replied.

"Are they married?"

"No." He looked surprised at her question. "Rena works at the grocery and Nancy's still in high school."

Nellie didn't mention that her own mother had been married at the age of fourteen. "Well, that's nice. You lived here all your life?"

"Nope. I was born in Virginia."

"How in the world did you end up here?"

"My father is a bit of a restless soul. He heard of opportunities in Indiana, so he and his brother came out here to work for the railroad."

Nellie heard the inevitable lull in the conversation and struggled to come up with something else to say. She envied his apparent comfort with shutting up and staring straight ahead. It must be nice not to feel responsible to lead the conversation.

"What do you think of this awful war going on in Europe?"

She saw his eyes brighten at her question. "I think I'll be heading out soon. Peter, too. We're joining up next week."

Nellie sighed and looked out the window. She supposed there was no use getting her hopes up about a future with Johnny. He'd be lost to the war like James William. "Fixing to join the army, then?"

"Marines."

She shot him a look of disbelief. She didn't know all the ins and outs of the military, but she was pretty sure the Marines were an elite group. The bravest of the brave. She felt a stab of pride to be sitting next to him.

"You think you'll make it?" she asked.

He shrugged, but his eyes betrayed him. He was intently focused. His jaw clenched in determination. He'd make it or die trying, she figured.

She couldn't help but admire his courage. She could use a little more courage herself.

Nellie thought the rest of the evening went pretty well. The other couple took some of the pressure of conversation off of Nellie's shoulders, so she appreciated that Johnny had thought to invite them. They were a fun couple and at ease with each other, so they spent a good part of the time laughing. After they'd eaten and Nellie received the grand tour of downtown Beech Grove, Johnny dropped Frank and Harriet off at his house and drove back to Emerson Drive in silence.

Nellie began to worry as the car came to a stop in front of his house. She hoped he wouldn't try to kiss her goodnight. She'd be positively mortified.

And thrilled.

But mostly mortified.

He stopped the engine but made no move to get out of the car. She stole a look at his long face and those half-closed eyes shining in the lights of a passing car and she decided maybe it would be more of a thrill. Even if Mother's voice of reproof was in her head the whole time.

Go ahead, Johnny Hagaman. Mother's a blessed sight removed from here. Show me what you're made of. She secretly dared him. And immediately chastised herself for her dangerous thoughts.

Go ahead, you idiot. Show her what you're made of! Johnny

heard the voice inside his head, which sounded a lot like his younger sister's. He reminded the voice it was only the first date and tried to steer his thoughts to a safer path.

"So you're a church-goer, then?" he asked.

She smiled. "I am. Or at least I 'better be if I want to see next Tuesday,' as my mother likes to say."

He nodded as she studied him inquisitively.

"You're a God-fearing man, right, Johnny?" she asked after a moment's hesitation.

He shrugged, thinking they'd already covered the subject. He repeated his words. "We go to church same as everyone else."

He knew the tone of his voice told her more than his words had. She looked down at her hands folded in her lap, obviously troubled by his answer.

"It's not that I don't know God," he said slowly, forgetting his shyness for a moment because he wanted her to understand him. "But sometimes I wonder if there's more to God than what my church says. Seems a little empty to me."

He wanted to shrink through the car floor and melt into the street. He couldn't believe he'd spoken so forwardly. She was going to think he was a fool.

But she nodded. "I kind of know what you mean." Her voice was soft. "I try so hard to know God. And sometimes... I think I almost do. But then I mess up again and I feel like he's pushing me away."

Both of them lapsed into contemplative silence.

Johnny was going to pull into her driveway but she waved him off.

"Just walk me to my door," she said cheerfully.

After he opened her car door, he shoved his hands in his pockets and followed her across the street. He surveyed the dark house. "How long you going to be living here by yourself?"

She shrugged. "Beats me. I sent Dad and Mother a letter telling them no one's around, but I've yet to hear back."

"Well, if you need anything or you get scared, you know where to find me." Johnny smiled.

She returned his smile and watched him thoughtfully. "You have a nice smile," she said. "You should smile more."

He didn't know what to say in response to her observation, and the thought of kissing her was suddenly overwhelming, so he took a step back and didn't say a word. She seemed embarrassed, but he had no idea how to explain, so he didn't.

"Well, I best get Harvey." She stuck out her hand for him to shake. He took it gladly, lingering just a moment longer than was required for a decent handshake.

"Goodnight, Johnny."

He walked home. When he got inside, he watched her head down the sidewalk to the Clarksons' to get Harvey. It occurred to him just how far out of his league a beauty like Nellie Mae really was.

And yet she'd said yes. That did beat all.

Eight

"Talk about out of my league," Nellie muttered to herself as she glanced out the window at the Hagaman house.

Johnny hadn't so much as spoken to her in a few days. Nellie's heart did a little dance when she saw his tall form hopping into his car. Probably headed off to work.

She'd tried to make opportunities. She'd taken Harvey out on the front lawn every evening to eat their supper together. She'd laughed out loud at Peter's jokes when he stopped over to say hello nearly every day. She'd introduced herself to Johnny's sister Nancy. But there had not been a single word from Johnny himself.

She shouldn't be so surprised. After all, he was a motivated young man with an important job and an exciting future as a marine. What was she thinking – hoping that he'd find a sixteen-year-old hillbilly with a gap between her two front teeth alluring enough to hold his interest past one date? Especially one who talked as much as she did!

She sighed and turned away from the window. Her reflection caught on the glass pane of the china cabinet. She lingered, fluffing her curled brown hair and biting her lip in critical awareness.

"He's too good for you, Nellie Mae Thomas," she told herself.

"Accept it and move on."

As she went on with the day's work, she continued to seethe. It was going to be one of those days when she felt tired even before she got going, but she had to push through and get everything done just the same.

She heard a car honk in the driveway and pushed back the curtains to see who it was. A man she didn't know was helping a girl about her age from the front seat. The girl looked familiar. She came to the steps of the porch alone as the man drove away.

Nellie Mae opened the door and waited with an expectant smile. "Hello, there," she called as the girl came up the steps. "How can I help you?"

The girl gave her a polite smile that didn't quite reach her eyes. My, she was a pretty one, though. Nellie envied her dark, silky curls and brown eyes.

"Hello, Nellie Mae. I'm your cousin, Lola. I heard my mother's new husband was sick and I came to see if I could help."

"Well, aren't you just the sweetest thing?" Nellie stood back and ushered her cousin in, feeling somewhat awkward as she did. What did one say to one's cousin – flesh and blood – who had been turned out from her own home? Was Lola bitter about living in an orphanage while her mother kept house in the next city over?

The thought of it was a harbinger for dark thoughts of her own mother, this girl's mother's sister. Nellie had heard the story of her own birth many times – how her mother couldn't take care of her because of her grief. She supposed she should have been sympathetic to the great loss her mother had suffered before she came along, but if she was being honest, the story only made her feel slighted. Cheated out of the beginning she should have had. She could understand how Lola might easily get swallowed up by bitterness, too.

Morbid curiosity almost convinced her to ask, but she bit her

57

tongue instead.

She didn't know whether to give the girl instructions or let her take the lead. She stood and watched Lola primly pick up her worn leather suitcase and proceed to the back room Aunt Nellie used mostly for storage.

Lola didn't make a reappearance until suppertime, so Nellie fried some chicken and boiled potatoes to mash. As she worked, she sang *Barbara Allen* to Harvey while he played with blocks on the kitchen floor. The song never failed to move her, but maybe her present tears were because she was missing home. She thought of Dad, sitting in the front yard on an old kitchen chair, blowing a mournful tune on his harmonica. Though never a word was uttered, the sound of his melody floated into the breeze and seemed transformed into a million different feelings, melding into the atmosphere and flowing right through her. When he stopped playing, he'd stare off into the brush where the Mark Twain National Forest began. She always wondered what he was thinking. Was he checking for KKK spies? Trying to keep their family safe in a world gone mad?

When Nellie Mae had the plates dished up, Lola reappeared. Nellie saw her cousin had donned a pretty yellow sundress that complimented her dark hair and eyes. She wore a matching bow in her hair. Nellie felt another stab of envy.

Lola gave her an indecipherable smile. "I find the clothes we have in the orphanage a little unimaginative. When I'm away I prefer to dress with more color."

"Well, sure you do," Nellie Mae managed as she passed her a plate. She cringed at the sound of her southern accent. Lola's refined mid-western intonation made Nellie sound next door to a perfect hill-jack.

"I don't suppose you've seen John out," Lola said after they filled their plates, and Nellie had prayed over the food.

Nellie nearly dropped the spoon she held out to feed Harvey his potatoes. "Who now?"

"John. John Hagaman across the street." Lola seemed impatient. "Two sisters? Loves animals and cars, works as a drill press operator at the railroad?"

Nellie lifted her chin. "Well, of course I know who Johnny is. I just didn't realize *you* knew him." Meanwhile, Nellie had no intention of revealing how hurt she was that Lola had managed to get so much information from Johnny about himself.

Lola seemed to be smirking, which caused hot indignation to burn in Nellie's chest. "It's to be expected, Nellie Mae, since I live here and you're just visiting."

Lola said the words with a polite smile. Nellie felt awful for thinking the worst of her, but she was sure her cousin meant to rub it in. She bit her tongue again lest she spat off some retort about Lola living in an orphanage most of her life.

After dinner Nellie Mae washed the dishes. Lola cleaned Harvey up and took him out the front door. Before Nellie could dry all the silverware, that infernal Johnny Hagaman had sauntered across the street, hands buried in his pocket and lopsided grin stretching from one extended ear to the other. Peter followed him as they both came up to greet Lola, who suddenly seemed a whole lot less reserved than she had been with Nellie.

"Well of all the nerve," Nellie said under her breath. After a quick application of the reddest lipstick she owned, she stormed out the front door and purposefully walked right up to Peter Hagaman, ignoring Johnny completely.

"Why, Peter Hagaman, how nice to see you again!" She looped her arm through his. He smiled, though his face turned red as he glanced at Johnny. "How have you been, Peter?"

Lola raised an eyebrow as she set Harvey down to take off on his own down the sidewalk. "Peter, John, I'd like you to meet my cousin from Missouri. Nellie Mae. She was named after my mother."

Nellie smiled at her cousin. "Thank you, honey, but we already met. Didn't we, boys?"

They stammered, not managing to get out any coherent words. Nellie was undeterred. "Now, Peter, didn't you tell me you were joining up with the army this coming week?"

"M... Marines," he said. He cleared his throat. "Johnny too."

"Y'all are so brave," she said with a dreamy sigh, slightly leaning against Peter, just until she saw Johnny narrow his eyes. "I'm so grateful for heroes like you."

"Well, we aren't heroes yet," Peter said with an awkward laugh. "We'll wait and see."

Later, as Nellie Mae sat in front of her aunt's vanity mirror and brushed her hair, she swallowed back the sick feeling that kept rising up from her stomach. What had she done? Mother would be ashamed at her display – flirting with Peter just to irk Johnny and Lola. And why had she done it? Jealousy, pure and simple. She was jealous of her poor cousin who lived in an orphanage with a parent yet alive and kicking.

Nellie was disgusted with herself. Surely Johnny deserved better than her.

"I'm awful sorry, Lord," she whispered a prayer. "Please forgive me and help me to love the way I should. Show me how to make amends. Sometimes my temper just gets the best of me, and I run off my mouth without thinking it through."

She felt marginally better, but as she glanced outside and saw the lights in Johnny's house, her stomach turned sour again.

Johnny saw Nellie out in the front raking up sticks Saturday night. She was alone. He tried to work up the nerve to go over and say hello, which took him a good twenty minutes.

"Why, Johnny!" She seemed surprised to see him. But she didn't seem near as cold as she had when Lola had been there, so maybe she hadn't been mad at him. He hoped.

"Fine night, isn't it?" He kicked at the dirt and glanced at her. Her brilliant smile dazzled him so he couldn't think straight to come up with anything else to say.

She looked like she was going to say something, but then she stopped and returned to her raking. He tried to make his tongue work. Honestly, he tried. How he wanted to tell her everything going on inside his head. He wanted to tell her she was lovelier than an angel. That her voice sounded like music when she talked and her eyes sparkled like diamonds. He wanted to say her lips looked like they must taste like strawberries for all their sweetness.

But he couldn't speak a word. And she didn't understand why. He could see the hopeful light in her eyes dull as she bent to pick up an armful of twigs to throw in the pile.

"Why did you come over here if you didn't have anything to say?" she asked quietly. Her words had a sharp edge, as if she was tired or frustrated. He cleared his throat and shuffled his feet. Boy, but this girl could turn a mood on a dime. He'd thought his mother and sisters had mood swings, but Nellie had the astounding talent of going from sunny to stormy in a second. Just like a little kitten, mewing and playing one moment, turned on him the next and hissed and scratched his hands to pieces.

Just as he liked kittens, he liked her spunk.

"You going to church tomorrow?" she said the words in what sounded like an accusing tone. Did she figure he probably wasn't, and she was going to make him sorry?

"As a matter 'a fact, Peter and I are visiting First Baptist over on

Churchman Street," he said.

"Baptist, huh." Nellie Mae didn't seem exactly impressed. She picked up a particularly large stick, making him realize he should probably be helping instead of standing there like a dolt.

"You don't think it's a good idea?"

"I'm not here to tell you what to do," she said with a shrug. "It's just … Baptists and all."

"Something wrong with Baptists?"

"Oh, they're just fine for conversation and socializing, but sometimes that's all they're good for," she explained. "You want to find yourself a church that will teach the good Word, no matter how hard it is to hear it."

Johnny had no idea what to make of her statement. He watched her curiously as she wiped her hands clean on her apron. She sighed deeply and glanced at the sky. "Don't you mind me, Johnny. I'm just in a mood. You go ahead to church wherever you want, and afterward you come tell me I was full of bologna."

He smiled, wishing he could smooth back the lock of hair that had worked itself free of her bow as she worked. He imagined how she'd look up at him in gratefulness, and they'd stare into each other's eyes…

"Look, Johnny, I'll tell you how it is. You gotta trust the Bible. Nothing else, no one else. We all get God's message wrong sometimes. But his Word never lies. Trust it, and you'll be just fine, no matter what pew you're sitting in."

He didn't answer, but her words affected him. He gave a small nod.

"Come tell me about it tomorrow?" she asked. He nodded again and stuffed his hands deeper into his pockets as he turned and walked home.

Nine

As soon as Johnny crossed the threshold of the little church, he was in a different world. He'd passed by the church so many times over the ages and never once considering going inside, but here Pete and he were, standing in the back of the small sanctuary. Everyone turned around and smiled at them, which made him feel uncomfortable and welcomed at the same time.

He slunk into the back row and hunched over, hoping to go unnoticed. Peter shook a man's hand and exchange pleasantries before he sat down beside him.

Fortunately for Johnny, the piano player was already staunchly banging out the opening hymn. The song leader was headed for the pulpit, so the hungry eyes of the friendlies all around gave up their pursuit of new blood in favor of worship.

His thoughts turned to Nellie before he could stop them. That seemed to be happening often lately. He knew Nellie was a religious sort of girl. A preacher's daughter, though Johnny had to admit it was a little strange that her mother was the preacher. He liked it, though, the more he thought about it. Nellie was unconventional. She didn't fit into the mold. He liked things that stood out. He had a feeling he'd like her mother.

He thought back to yesterday and the talk he'd had with Nellie Mae. Why had she seemed so distrustful of these folks? They looked friendly enough. And why had he come anyway? Surely Nellie knew more about church than Johnny did.

But then again, he did know. He knew about that hollowness down deep in his soul that wouldn't be satisfied by diversions, pastimes or notions of career or adventure. There was that place inside him that desperately wanted something better, something more real and less earthly. Something that would make his existence make sense. He knew some folks had a peace about them, and they usually claimed they had found it at church. Wasn't it worth checking out before he headed off to war to have his life stolen away before it had hardly begun?

If he was going to die, he should try to find religion. At least more religion than he'd ever found sitting in the back row of his family's church, singing the same dull songs no one gave a thought about, paying tithes and enduring sermons with no substance. Was church more than fulfilling a duty to be present? He had to believe there was more. He knew Peter was searching as much as he was. They'd had long discussions about it over fishing poles.

The preacher stepped up to the pulpit, and Johnny's whole life changed.

"I know there are likely young men in this room tonight about to join up or be drafted into this terrible war. You're headed for that battlefield. Did you come here tonight because you're missing something? Because you know the weight of your sin but you don't know what to do about it? Have you tried the pleasures of this world only to find out they can't satisfy the need of your soul? Are you afraid of looking death in the face, uncertain of what lies behind that curtain?"

Johnny's eyes nearly bored a hole in the checkered linoleum beneath his feet. Was the preacher talking straight to him? How could he know what Johnny was thinking? His face went hot. Everyone in the room must be staring at him.

"God knows your need. You can't do this on your own, but he can. His power far exceeds yours. His love is deeper than your parents' or your friends' or your sweetheart's could ever be. The Bible says in John: *For God so loved the world that he gave his only begotten son, that whoever believes in him shall not perish but have everlasting life.*

"That offer is available to you today. Maybe you are a good man, a churchgoing man, even. Maybe you haven't done all the things your friends have done. Maybe you've been pretty good. But even our best can't be good enough for the holiness of God. You must have Christ's forgiveness on your behalf, because of the blood he shed for you, the life he gave. It is the only way to peace. It's the only way to escape the just punishment of hell. Jesus says *I am the way, the truth and the life. No one comes to the Father but by me.* You can't find peace on your own."

Johnny gulped back the knot that had risen up in his throat. Peter shifted beside him. Was he feeling it too? That uncomfortable panic in his chest that told him to either get up and run out of the building as fast as he could – or give in and find this forgiveness Jesus offered? He didn't know which one he wanted more.

In the end, the need for peace won. He wanted assurance. He knew he was prone to wander after pleasure. He knew how easily he could follow the crowd and do whatever anyone else did. He'd been told all his life to be good so God would accept him. Follow the rules. Be polite. Look smart. Do his work.

These ideas were new. What if this preacher was right, and everyone else he'd ever listened to was wrong? What if Jesus was being honest when he said there was no other way? If it said so in the Bible, shouldn't Johnny believe it?

He was confused. Angry, even, that Jesus being the only way

had been right there in the Bible all along and no one, not his church, not his parents, no one in the world had ever told him so before. He was strolling right along on his way to hell and no one had ever bothered to tell him the truth.

But Nellie had, hadn't she? She'd told him to trust what the Bible said.

He fingered the Bible sitting on the pew next to him. Since no one else occupied the pew, it must be there for someone like him. Someone like him who'd never cracked open a Bible in all his years, thinking it was the minister's job to tell him what it said.

"Sinner, as we sing our final song, I invite you to come forward. Be saved. Invite Jesus into your heart so you can take him to the darkest corners of this earth and still have peace. Assurance. Take his light into the darkness. Come and be saved."

Johnny heard the platform creak as the pastor stepped down into the center aisle. The song leader returned to the pulpit and the piano began to play. The crowd sang reverently.

Softly and tenderly Jesus is calling
Calling for you and for me
See, on the portals he's waiting and watching
Watching for you and for me.

Come home, come
Ye who are weary come home!
Earnestly, tenderly, Jesus is calling
Calling, O sinner, come home.

Johnny wasn't one for dramatic scenes. He loathed being the center of attention and nearly every part of his being resisted walking that aisle in front of those strangers and asking for salvation. But a voice spoke to him, silently within, though at first, he thought everyone in the room had heard it. It was a voice he'd never heard before.

Come.

He stood in his place, his face hot with fear as he sensed a presence near him. He was afraid to look up. Afraid there would be some specter standing there to drag his soul away. But the presence was peaceful. He felt like whoever was there understood him, and precious few had ever cared to understand quiet, stoic Johnny Hagaman.

Lord, if you're there, I'm asking for peace. I want to be brave and not afraid to die. I never realized you're a person I can know. I don't have this all figured out, but I'm here if you want to show me. Help me, Jesus. Don't let me go, even if I fight you.

Without warning, an invisible force passed through him, so strong he gasped out loud. Suddenly, a burden he hadn't realized he'd been carrying was lifted. He stared around the room in surprise, knowing peace for the first time. Freedom. Nothing else mattered. He was safe in Jesus.

"Thank you," he whispered. Peter looked at him, and Johnny knew he wasn't the only one. They both smiled.

Ten

Nellie Mae glanced out the window and her heart filled with joy. "Dad!"

Her father was standing next to his car in the driveway. He must have driven all night to get there.

"Glory be!" she said as she grabbed Harvey from his playpen and ran outside, reverting to old habits and forgoing shoes.

Aunt Nellie was with Dad, and they stood in front of the house talking. Nellie practically tossed Harvey in his mother's arms before she ran to hug her father.

"There's my beautiful girl," he said with a chuckle. "How are you, daughter?"

"I'm good, Dad," she said, tears stinging her eyes. She hugged him again, breathing in his familiar scent. The scent of home.

"Are you a little homesick, then?" he asked as she got a hold of herself and stepped back.

"Guess I am," she admitted, wiping her tears away.

Aunt Nellie sniffed indignantly at their reunion. "Has Harvey been fed?"

"No, he just woke up," Nellie said. Her aunt glanced at her disapprovingly, as if the hour of seven was far too late in the day for her son to be unfed. Her aunt took her son promptly inside.

Nellie Mae turned to her father. "How's Uncle Mort?"

Dad sighed. "He's doing a little better, but he still has a long road ahead. His heart isn't as strong as the doctors would like. Nellie will probably need you a couple more weeks."

"But I've already been here a month," she said, disheartened at the thought of school starting without her.

"I know, Nellie Mae, I know. Sometimes the Lord calls us to places we didn't expect and we have to rearrange our schedules for him. But he always has a good reason."

"The Lord, or Mother?" Nellie said before she thought better of it.

Her father considered her. "How do you know the Lord can't use your mother to call you to a certain place at a certain time? You don't think he wanted you here in Beech Grove for a reason?"

Johnny's face appeared in her mind immediately. She'd come here to meet Johnny. She didn't know why, but she was sure of it, as sure as she was standing right there on the driveway next to her father. God had wanted her to come and meet Johnny.

But why? His strange, quiet way had prevented them from having any decent conversation. She didn't even know if he knew she was there half the time. And he'd be enlisted by the end of the week anyway. Odds weren't in his favor for returning after the war. Why did God want her to meet him if they were just going to go their separate ways?

"Hello, there, Nellie Mae. Mr. Thomas."

As if reading her thoughts, Johnny walked toward them. As usual, his hands were buried in his pockets. He pulled one out so he could shake her father's hand. "At least I assume you're Nellie's father?"

Dad smiled. "Ollie Thomas. And you are?"

Nellie spoke up on Johnny's behalf. "This is Johnny Hagaman,

Dad. He lives across the street with his family."

"Hello, Johnny Hagaman." Dad grinned even wider. "You two been spending a lot of time together?"

Nellie wasn't sure how to answer that question, but Johnny spoke first. "I actually came over to tell Nellie Mae some good news."

Nellie had a feeling she knew the news and she wasn't so sure it was good. "You enlisted?"

Johnny seemed surprised by her response. "No, not till tomorrow or the day after. But you asked me to come tell you how church went."

She glanced at her father, who was smiling at her. She turned back to Johnny. "So how did church go, then?"

Johnny actually smiled. She saw something different in his smile. Something past his shyness and the hard outer shell he used to keep people out. She saw the real Johnny, and it stole her breath away. She'd never been more drawn to a person in her life. The ache of bittersweet feeling threatened to overwhelm her. It grew as a lump in her throat she couldn't swallow back. Here he was, finally being real, and he was going to up and leave forever.

"I always thought I was okay. But it turns out I never asked Jesus to save me like the Bible says. I asked him last night. And he did. I know it." He sheepishly kicked at the dirt as he quietly shared the news.

Nellie's father gave a joyful laugh. "Saints alive! Ain't that the best news we could have heard today, Nellie Mae?"

She felt a well of joy rush up within her. She couldn't contain it, and before she knew it, she was launching herself into Johnny's arms. She hugged him tight as tears rolled down her cheeks. Her heart hadn't felt quite so full in a long time.

She caught both men off guard with her reaction. She hadn't meant to do it, but once she was holding him it was hard to let go.

He smelled like everything she imagined a man should – cut grass and Old Spice – and her heart skipped several beats when he actually put his arms around her and hugged her back.

With her father and half the neighborhood looking on, she knew it wasn't proper to linger. She unwillingly pulled back and straightened her dress, clearing her throat. "I'm just so happy for you, Johnny. It's wonderful."

"A very good time to decide to follow the Lord," Nellie's father said, his eyes merry as he looked at her and then at Johnny. "With the war and all, I mean."

"Yes, sir. I have peace now. If I'm to die in battle." Johnny nodded his agreement.

Nellie felt melancholy at his words. She was a little envious of this peace, if she was being honest. How come she'd done everything right and asked Jesus to save her so many times she'd lost count, and she still wasn't sure about anything? Why couldn't she manage to keep up her good behavior for any length of time? What had that Baptist pastor said that had given Johnny such assurance?

Wouldn't it be something to have the matter settled for sure?

"I'm going to head in and visit with your aunt," Dad said, squeezing her hand before he slipped away. She turned and faced the man she might be about to lose as quickly as she'd found.

They stood in silence. He watched her, his gaze inquisitive and gentle. She dared to look him full in the face.

"I'm so happy for you, Johnny, really," she said again, her voice hushed in the still morning air.

He took a small step closer and reached to brush her hand with a finger. "Thanks for inspiring me."

She shrugged. "What did I do?"

"I never gave much thought to my need for God before I met you. At least not enough to do something about it."

71

"What did I say?" She tried to remember their conversation.

"It wasn't what you said. It was the fact that I could tell you had something I didn't."

She stared at her feet, which she suddenly realized were bare. But she knew he didn't care about her feet, so she put it from her mind. *If that's the truth, why am I jealous of what you found, Johnny?*

"There's a roller derby in the city tonight."

She met his eyes again. He was grinning again, and it made him look boyish. Like a boy she might befriend at high school. He was hardly more than a boy, after all, his life just getting started.

"And?" She smiled, suddenly in the mood to tease.

His cheeks turned red. "And I'd like to take you … if you were of a mind."

She twisted her mouth and put her hands on her hips as she considered the proposition. He looked miserable while he waited, fingering his hat in his hands.

She laughed. "Of course. I'd love to go."

It was a night Nellie Mae would always remember, no matter what memories she lost along the way. Exhilaration made her almost float into the arena on his arm, the cool air gently whisking her hair back. He guided her like he'd been there a hundred times before. She was breathless when he leaned close to explain what was happening. She wanted to giggle when his breath tickled her ear. As the race started and the athletes pushed and fell in their efforts to get over the finish line, Nellie's competitive spirit kicked in. She stood to her feet several times, yelling at the bullies and cheering on the underdogs.

Once, she looked back and caught him staring at her. She'd never forget that look on Johnny's face. It almost made her believe he cared about her the way she cared for him.

When the race was over and the crowd was pressed together trying to get out the single door, she felt his fingers thread through hers. "Don't want to lose you in the mob," he said next to her ear.

She stared at their joined hands while they walked. His long fingers covered her short ones protectively. She wondered what her mother would think of her now. She'd held hands with boys before, but she'd never had the feeling she had now – this tornado of breathlessness and anticipation for something she couldn't even put her finger on.

Now she understood why it worried her mother. But it only made her hold him more tightly.

Eleven

"How long you figure we been standing in this line?" Peter asked, reaching into his shirt pocket for his handkerchief. He mopped the sweat from his face. The August sun mocked the men waiting outside the Fort Harrison Enlistment Center. Didn't it know they were trying to become heroes? Save the world? Maybe even give their lives?

"Couple hours, anyway." Johnny shifted his stance and read a flyer on the bulletin board outside the offices. "Everyone wants to be a marine, I guess."

"No kidding," Peter huffed. "Why would we want to be anything else?"

Johnny grunted his agreement.

"What are you reading?" Peter glanced at the hazy sky, his eyes squinting.

"Reasons for rejection." Johnny had an uneasy feeling in his stomach. That feeling he got that told him he was barking up the wrong tree, no matter how much he wanted something. It wasn't going to happen. He was wasting his time. "Says you can't be a marine if you have vision problems."

"You see fine," Peter said with a shrug. "You don't even wear glasses. Plenty of guys here do."

Johnny looked at Peter. "You know full well I can't see colors." He said the words in a low voice so the others around them wouldn't overhear.

"Well, sure, but why would that keep you out of the marines? I can't think why it'd be that important."

"Spoken by someone who's never had to wonder whether he's looking at red or green or blue," Johnny mumbled. He fidgeted uneasily. Was the line moving faster now?

Eventually they got inside and to the front desk. A staff sergeant handed them applications with instructions to sit down and fill them out, which they did. A man in a white coat came out and asked them to come in the back. They entered a large, noisy room filled with young men standing around in their underclothes. Some were on scales, staring intently at their total as if they could will themselves a few extra pounds. Some were having height measured; some were seated as doctors checked their vitals and asked questions, making notes in their files.

Johnny and Peter were told to undress and follow the man to the scales. A half-hour later, John's brain was spinning from all the questions and directions. Sometimes he didn't even know how to answer. A man couldn't very well take his mother along to recruitment, but she was the only one who'd know the answer, and he told the doctor as much.

"Okay, son, I'm going to give you a vision test."

Johnny swallowed hard. He glanced across the aisle at Peter, who was waiting for his doctor to finish writing something. He smiled and nodded his support.

"You have any vision trouble?" The doctor held out a card for Johnny to hold.

"Nope." But Johnny's confidence fell when he looked at the card and saw the telltale shades of gray.

"Point to the red dot." The doctor didn't look up from his paperwork.

John squinted. Cocked his head. Which one of those gray dots did the rest of the world seem to recognize as some mysterious color John had never seen before? Sometimes he could tell between the different shades of gray, but this time, the dots were too similar. Wouldn't the red one be first, though? It seemed like it usually was.

He pointed to the first circle. The doctor stopped writing and frowned at him. "How about the green?"

Had he got the first one right? He sighed and stared hard at the chart. He pointed to the second dot.

"Son, you're colorblind."

Johnny shrugged.

"I'm sorry to have to tell you the Marines cannot take colorblind men. It's too much of a risk. What if some split-second decision that could save the lives of your men depended on your ability to see a certain color?"

Johnny wanted to argue, but he kept his mouth shut. He felt useless and fragile for being turned down. And more than a little foolish for trying it in the first place. He should have known the Marines were too good for him. He went to get dressed with a heavy feeling in his chest.

The doctor followed him. "Try the army. I hear they look for colorblind men sometimes, because you're good at finding camouflage. You may have a place yet."

Johnny nodded his thanks and stood by the wall waiting for Peter. When his cousin joined him, he was grinning.

"I'm in," Peter said as he pulled on his trousers. "How'd the vision test go?"

"I'm out." Johnny shrugged and pushed his hands into his pockets. "Congrats."

"Thanks." Peter sighed and shook his head as he buttoned up his shirt. "I'm sorry, Johnny. I'd hoped we'd go together."

Johnny nodded. "Doc said the army needs colorblind soldiers sometimes, so I'll try there next."

Back at home, he could tell his mother was relieved to hear he had been turned away, but he saw disappointment in his father's eyes.

"Well, you tried, son." His father took a bite of green beans that had come from the victory garden behind the house. Johnny saw the hard stance of his father's jaw. He was a restless sort of man that wished for youth again just so he might go off to war himself. Adventure. Danger. Everything a man wanted that couldn't be found in Indiana. Or America, for that matter.

"I'm going to try the army tomorrow."

"Won't they just turn you away, too?" His mother turned around, an edge of worry in her voice.

"The boy's colorblind, not an invalid," his father said sharply. He saw his mother's eyes narrow.

"I know he's not an invalid, Henry. I only meant to suggest they might feel the same way about the colorblindness."

All eyes turned back to Johnny.

"Well, big brother, what's the verdict?" Nancy finally asked. She made a face at her green beans and liver. They were all tired of wartime food, but organ meat was cheaper and more readily available. The good cuts often went to the soldiers who needed health and strength.

"I think they'll take me." Johnny had no actual confidence they would.

But they had to. He had no intention of whiling away the war sitting at a drill press while all the other men his age were out fighting. He wanted to be on the front lines. He wanted to wear the uniform and see the girls swoon. He wanted to walk in the parade and have everyone cheer for him. He wanted to do something that mattered. Maybe he had something to prove; maybe he was just as restless as his father, but he didn't want to take the safe road. He would find a way to make his existence matter, if it was the last thing he did.

Besides, wasn't that his goal now, as a Christian? Wouldn't God want him in some honorable work? What was more honorable than fighting tyranny and oppression? And wouldn't he be fighting alongside men who were ready to hear the truth about Christ, since they were daily facing the very real possibility of death?

He retreated to his bedroom and spent some time reading the Bible he'd bought. He'd started at the beginning with Genesis, blown away by the details of creation and the flood he'd never noticed before. He hadn't ever cared how the world got started until now.

"God, I know you made this whole world and you made me. I'm yours. I'll go wherever it is you want to send me. I'll do whatever task you have for me. I'm far from perfect, but you can trust me to do something strong and brave for you. Use me. I'll get the job done."

Wednesday was hotter than ever, and the line at Fort Benjamin Harrison was long and slow. Much longer than the line at the Marines' office. This time Johnny didn't have Peter to wait with him and shoot the breeze.

When he finally got inside, the procedure was nearly the same as it had been for the Marines, only this time there were more doctors and young men standing around the big room. It made Johnny sick thinking it might all go the same way it did with the Marines doc. When the doctor pulled up the vision test card and asked Johnny the same question the Marine doctor had asked,

Johnny took a deep breath and stared hard at the shades of gray. He tried to remember which one had been red, hoping it was the same card. He squinted. The gray color others designated red was usually just a little bit bolder than the other grays. Should he go with the darkest one? He knew it wasn't the one he'd picked last time, so that ruled out the middle.

"That one," he said, pointing to the dark gray. The doctor didn't comment. He set down the card and started writing something on the medical form. Without comment, he handed John a card and directed him back to the front desk. Johnny was stunned as he made his way through the line and came to stand in front of a bulky, stern-looking man in a sharply pressed uniform.

"Okay, Mr. Hagaman. What field are you interested in? Infantry?"

Johnny shrugged, his only thought being relief that he'd passed the color test.

The man handed Johnny a flyer explaining the different branches of service. He knew he didn't want the navy. His boss wanted him to join the navy as a machinist so he'd be better at his job when he came back, but Johnny couldn't imagine being a noncombatant. It wasn't an option. He also didn't see himself being a pilot. He wanted to be free, crawling along the trenches beside his fellows. A picture of a man dropping out of a plane caught his eye.

"Paratrooper," he said before he had a chance to second guess himself. "I want to be a paratrooper."

"Son, you realize the Paratroops are about the nearest thing to a suicide mission we have." The sergeant looked up from his paperwork.

"I know." Johnny tossed back the brochure. "That's what I want."

"For glory or for money?" The man smiled and marked the appropriate boxes.

"Both, I suppose." Johnny shrugged, trying to hide his grin.

"Screaming Eagles it is, then," the man said, nodding his approval. He pulled an envelope from his desk drawer and handed it over. Johnny opened it and saw a train ticket to Toccoa, Georgia.

"Your train leaves Sunday morning. You'll receive further instructions when you get there. I suggest you spend the rest of this week putting your affairs in order."

Johnny turned toward the door flooded with bright sunshine, his eyes wide and his heart beating fast. It was surreal to think he'd just signed up for something that could very well kill him. A rush of adrenaline flooded his system.

He sat in his car for a long time, trying to comprehend what he'd just done. As determination conquered disbelief, he turned the key and started the motor. He'd do this. He'd be the best paratrooper there ever was. He'd soar the skies and kill the enemy and set his country free again, and then he'd live to come home and tell the story. He'd beat the odds and marry Nellie Mae Thomas.

He looked around, shocked that he'd had the thought. It was bold. Too bold, maybe. But he liked the thought of spending his life with her. He grinned as he sped out of the parking lot.

As he pulled into the driveway a few minutes later, movement from across the street caught his attention. He saw Nellie Mae standing in the middle of the neighbors' living room. Her face was lit up with a smile as she talked to her father and her aunt. The sight of her made him breathless.

"Kitten," he said under his breath, trying out his secret pet name for her. Even from all the way across the street she radiated vibrancy and warmth. The picture she made would carry him to the darkest, coldest place the war could take him, and he'd still be just fine. What was it about her that he couldn't get over? No doubt she was beautiful – anyone would say so. A rare beauty. But there was something harder to explain beneath the surface. It was the way she made everyone around her feel like they were her favorite person. It was the way her smile lit up a room. It was the way her spunky spirit and teasing lilt made his stomach do flip-flops inside him.

She'd gotten to him when she flirted with Peter. He wondered if she'd known what she was doing. He wanted to be jealous, but he knew he had no right. Did she like him as much as he liked her? Probably not. It was probably all a game to her. But since he was heading off to war to die, anyway, he felt a surge of unusual boldness. He'd ask her. He'd find out. He'd declare his intentions. Because after Sunday, he might never see her again.

But when he sat in his car and tried to practice what he'd say, the words wouldn't come.

"I'll write her a letter." He jumped out of his car and slammed the door shut. He ran up to his room so fast he didn't think anyone inside even saw him come in. He pulled out paper and pencil from his desk and chewed on the end of it until he figured out what he was going to say. Then he began in deliberate handwriting to tell her what was on his mind.

Dear Nellie,

I hardly know how to start this letter, but here goes. You stole something from me last time I was with you, and you made me miserable. See, you've stolen my heart.

John stopped and stared critically at his composition. He was pretty sure girls liked flowery words like that, but would she laugh at him?

He shrugged. Who knew if he'd get the courage to give it to her anyway? He might as well be honest.

Perhaps I didn't show it when I was with you, but you mean more to me than any other girl in the world. I didn't show you my feelings because I was afraid you didn't feel the same way.

I need to see you. I keep thinking about you. Every time I go somewhere, instead of enjoying myself I think about how happy I'd be if you were with me. I even dream about you.

As you know, I've joined the army. But please let me see you before I go. I know you're probably tired of me hanging around, but it would make my day to find out you missed me even one-tenth of how much I miss you. If you don't want to see me, maybe you'd write to me instead?

I guess I'm trying to say I care for you. I don't exactly know how to put it in words, but I hope you understand, and I hope you care about me, too.

Sincerely,
Johnny

He stared uncertainly at the "sincerely." Cordially? No. Love? No. He wanted it to say something more than either of those words. He felt a surge of daring curiosity to see it written on the page – the feeling that he truly felt about her at that moment. He erased the closing and signature and rewrote it.

All my love,
Johnny

He surveyed the letter critically, worried that his writing wasn't as neat as it could be. But the thought of rewriting the whole thing was exhausting, so he added a postscript at the bottom of the page.

P.S. I sure hope you can read my writing.

There. He nodded to himself in satisfaction. It was as good as it was going to get. He knew he was a passable writer. He'd much rather write than speak, that was for sure.

On the way to work the next morning, he dropped the envelope in her mailbox. He stared at the box in an exhilarated panic before he walked back across the street. The feeling was almost like the one he'd had walking out of the recruitment center, knowing he was off to war.

No going back now.

Twelve

Nellie couldn't believe her eyes when she saw the letter in the mailbox that morning. She shifted Harvey on her hip and stared at her name in the clear, deliberate handwriting. Somehow, she just knew it was Johnny's.

She hurried inside and put Harvey in his high chair so she could open the envelope. Her fingers trembled as she held the paper in her hand and saw the neat, even writing. The calming sight of the organization helped her feel at ease to read it. If it had been a messy scrawl, she was sure it would have made her too nervous to even start the first line.

She read through the letter quickly, her eyes darting ahead to the next line and the next before she'd finished the last, hungry to see what else he would say. A delicious sort of warmth spread over her. She laughed at his postscript.

"Your handwriting is a far cry better than mine," she said to herself of his meticulous script.

"What did you say?" Lola came into the kitchen, wrapping a robe around herself. She went to the refrigerator.

"Nothing." Nellie folded the note and tucked it back into the envelope. She set it face down on the table and reached for Harvey's bowl to feed him.

"Who's the letter from?" Lola abandoned the orange juice on the counter and stared curiously at the table where the letter rested. "Peter?"

Nellie tried to hide her smile. "No."

Lola's eyes narrowed. "Johnny?"

Nellie shrugged. "Suppose it's possible."

Lola looked angry for a moment, but she shrugged and a cold expression hardened her face. She finished pouring her juice. "I don't see the two of you going anywhere," she said, taking a sip. "He's so awful quiet and you talk people's ears off. You'd drive each other mad."

Nellie felt the sting of her cousin's words, knowing there was truth to them. At least she was afraid there was. She bit her tongue to keep from speaking the response that came to her lips, which was anything but charitable.

"What did he say?" Lola shrugged as if it didn't matter to her. She was only trying to make conversation.

"He's enlisting. He wants to see me before he leaves."

Lola sniffed, but she didn't reply. Silence hung heavy between them. Nellie was suddenly sad – even to despairing. Why did the world have to have this crazy war? Why did young men just beginning their lives have to march off to distant lands to be hunted, shot down and blown up? Was this any way to solve problems?

Love makes the difference. She remembered her mother's mantra. Surely there was no love in war. No point.

"I hate war." She leaned back in her seat and stared at the letter on the table.

"Me too." Lola stared out the window, and neither girl said another word.

MY GOOD NAME

Nellie sat down at the desk in her room to try to form a response to Johnny. She stared out the window as her pen hung idle in midair and the empty page mocked her intention. She sighed. She'd much rather have a conversation face to face than try to form her thoughts on paper. But she'd do things his way.

Dear Johnny,

I received your letter this morning. It surprised me! I hadn't thought you cared that much. We are so different. Not to mention you're always so quiet around me. I figured you thought I was a dimwit for sure.

Sure, I'd like to see you. I had a good time at the Derby. Those girls went so fast and I nearly had a heart attack every time they pushed each other into the barrier. Sorry I got so worked up. You probably thought I was a dolt if you didn't know it already.

I guess I'll see you soon. Dad says he'll come get me in another week or so, so I might even get to see you off on the train when you head out. Wouldn't that be something?

Love,
Nellie Mae

She scrunched her face in disgust at her messy writing, but he might as well know it about her. She shoved the letter in the envelope and went downstairs. Lola had Harvey in the backyard, which was good for Nellie. She didn't want Lola to see the letter. She quickly stole across the street to the mailbox in front of Johnny's house.

"Dear Lord, I pray you won't let anyone see me," she said under her breath.

She meant to quickly leave, but the mail had been delivered and the box was full. She tried to shove her letter on the top, but in the process, she knocked out an envelope, which appeared to be some official document from the bank. She leaned over to pick it up, but the wind caught it and blew it a few feet down the sidewalk.

"Dad gum it!" She chased after the envelope, leaning over to get it but foiled again and again by the teasing of the breeze. She reached out one last time, determined to grab it, but it slipped through her fingers and landed in a small puddle from a recent rain. When she picked it up and shook it off, it was wrinkled and muddy.

She marched back to the mailbox and shoved it inside, hastily checking her surroundings to see if anyone had seen her. Nancy Hagaman was standing on the porch watching Nellie.

"You trying to steal our mail?" Nancy put her hands on her hips and tried to look severe.

"Why ever would I do a thing like that?" Nellie Mae said, flustered at being caught.

"I take it you're trying to leave a note for my brother?" Nancy motioned to the mailbox. Nellie looked and saw her note had fallen out and was lying in the flowerbed underneath.

Nellie sighed and stared at it. She didn't want to leave it with anyone else. What if it never got to him?

"I won't lose it." Nancy came down the path and held out her hand. "And I won't open it, either."

Nellie Mae unwillingly handed Nancy the letter. She prayed she'd sealed it well enough to deter anyone from opening it.

"Thanks," she said before she turned on her heel in the direction of her aunt's house.

"Sure," Nancy said. Nellie could feel the girl's eyes on her until she was back inside her house.

Nancy must have been about the same age as Nellie, but she

made Nellie feel like a silly little girl. She wondered if she had done something to cause a rift between them.

She tried to shake off her agitation and threw her energy into mopping floors and shining silverware. Nothing like Aunt Nellie's list of chores to take your mind off your troubles.

She rolled her eyes.

Thirteen

Wednesday, August 12, 1942, Johnny sat up straight in his bed. Butterflies were flapping all over his insides. It was so distracting he could hardly get his breakfast down.

His mother fussed and flitted around the kitchen. His sisters sat up straighter than usual, staring at him like they were memorizing what he looked like. As if they thought this might be the last time they ever saw him.

And it well could be, he reminded himself.

His father had stayed home from work long enough to see him off. He sat at the table and read his newspaper like every other morning, shaking it every so often, his leg crossed over his knee. Henry Hagaman wasn't worried about his only son leaving to join the suicide mission known as the Screaming Eagles. Any time he spoke of it, he only sounded jealous he couldn't tag along.

Inevitably, Johnny's thoughts drifted to an angel face with curly blonde hair and a mischievous grin. Would Nellie Mae meet him at the station? She'd said in her letter she might. He prayed she would. He didn't want to leave without seeing her one more time.

If she showed up, would he have the courage to kiss her goodbye? He'd seen the scene before, plenty of times. Young men lined up on the train platform with their girls reaching up to kiss them. No one would fault Johnny for trying it. It was the perfect opportunity. Worth heading off to war in the first place.

"Johnny?" His mother's voice brought him back to the kitchen.

He shook off his daydream. "Yeah, Mom?"

"Do eat up. You don't know when they'll feed you again." She heaped another helping of eggs onto the mound he already had. His mother was convinced the army tried to starve its men to make them tougher. Johnny wasn't so sure that was true.

"You make sure you wash behind your ears," she went on in a feeble voice. She sounded older. Tired. Reciting all the generic mother-to-son advice she could think of before he'd be out of her sight for good. "Go to bed early and get as many greens as you can."

"In the army, you do as you're told," Henry said sternly from behind his paper. "You just do what they say, John."

"Don't worry, Mom," Johnny said to his mother without acknowledging his father's words. "I'll be alright." He scooped up a big bite of eggs and shoved them in his mouth to make her feel better.

He'd meant the words to be comforting, but now they sat on the still of the air, foreboding, ringing in their ears. There was no way he could promise he'd be alright. That she didn't have to worry. Of course she did. She had every right. Her only son had signed up for a course likely to end in death.

Henry lowered his newspaper, his tone softer as he spoke. "John has a good head on his shoulders. He can take care of himself."

It was the truth. Johnny had always been good at looking out for himself. He'd come back. He'd survive. He'd do it for his mother.

For Nellie Mae.

They drove to the train station in Johnny's car. His father drove, commenting on the mundane. Would it rain later? Why did Bob Lasseter have a closed sign on the barber shop door? No one responded to his questions, but somehow the benign rambling comforted him. If they didn't draw attention to the obvious danger of what Johnny was doing, it couldn't hurt them.

Or so they hoped.

At the train station, his mother said goodbye several times, her voice thick as she kept up the motherly advice to keep from bursting into tears. He teased his sisters to ease the awkward silence and shook his father's hand.

"Go with God, son," Henry said with a proud smile. For a moment, Johnny thought maybe there was a sheen of unshed tears in his father's eyes.

"Thanks, Dad."

And then he saw her out of the corner of his eye. Her yellow dress lit up the throng of black and gray, putting them all to shame. Her face radiated even brighter light. He was drawn to her like the moths gathered at the porchlight in the night.

"Pardon me," he said to his family. "A friend is here to say goodbye." He picked up his suitcase and walked quickly to the other side of the platform to meet her.

Lola stood next to Nellie Mae, whispering something in her ear. He momentarily wished Nellie had come alone, but he wasn't going to complain. At least she was here. He'd wanted more than anything for her to show up. He cleared his throat and tried to overcome the wave of shyness and emotion that came over him at the sight of her.

"Thanks for coming, Lola." He nodded to Nellie's cousin, trying to get that goodbye out of the way quickly so he could focus on Nellie. "I'll see you later."

"You be careful, John. Come back to us," Lola said, reaching for his hand.

He squeezed it. "I will." His eyes returned to feasting on the sight of Nellie Mae. She stepped closer to him and slipped her small hand into his.

"Thanks for your service. It'll be nice to think of you out there, looking after us even while we sleep. I'll pray for you."

He smiled and scrambled for something even half as nice to say in return. Nothing would come to mind. Her face began to fall as if she was giving up hope. As he opened his mouth to speak, a shadow fell over them and someone pushed past him.

"Well, if it isn't Nellie Mae Thomas, prettiest girl in the whole state of Missouri." A man with a southern accent grabbed her hands and shook them as he chuckled.

"Well, I'll be," she said, breathless with surprise. "James William? I hadn't heard from you in so long I figured you were dead!"

He laughed and embraced her, a sight that made Johnny want to give him a good licking. His fists clenched.

Nellie Mae laughed. "I'll be, I never imagined I'd run into you all the way in Indianapolis, of all places. What brought you out of Mississippi?"

"Oh, the army," the man said in dismissal. Johnny didn't like him. Not a single bit. Never mind him hugging Nellie Mae like she was his possession – there was a look in his eye that told Johnny the man would do anything it took to be in charge.

"Well, of course," Nellie Mae said. She seemed flustered. Did she notice the same about the man? He didn't think so. She was probably just self-conscious. She put a hand on his arm, which caused a visceral reaction in Johnny's insides.

"There's not a cowardly bone in your body, James William," Nellie Mae went on. "You'll probably be a general before the war's over."

"Ah, now, Nellie Mae," James William said in obviously false self-deprecation. Johnny seethed inwardly at the pompous soldier.

"Where are my manners?" Nellie Mae said, her hand fluttering at her collarbone. "This is my cousin, Lola, and my friend, Johnny

Hagaman. Johnny's off to be a paratrooper."

Johnny shook James William's hand as firmly as he could without drawing attention to himself. He saw the challenge in the other soldier's eyes.

Nellie went on, unaware of the animosity that simmered between the two men. "Johnny, this is James William Liman. We go back a ways. Had some good times last summer, didn't we, Jamie?"

"Sure did," James William said in a low voice, still staring threateningly at Johnny. His grip was firm on Johnny's hand, but the other was latched to Nellie's shoulder. "Good to meet you, Hagaman." He looked back at Nellie with a smirk. "You probably don't know her well enough to realize it, but you better keep your eye on this one. She likes to play games."

Johnny wasn't sure if Liman had meant the words lightheartedly, but no one laughed. Nellie's face turned red and her eyes darted to the ground. It was all Johnny could do to keep from punching his lights out.

Liman gave Nellie another possessive embrace and moved on toward his train. Johnny was still fuming as he tried to focus on the two girls in front of him rather than Liman. He couldn't think of a thing to say. He had none of Liman's arrogance that showed like confidence. But Johnny could do one thing, and he wasn't about to talk himself out of it now.

He bolstered every bit of nerve he possessed – which admittedly was not a whole lot – and grabbed Nellie's shoulders. He pulled her close and leaned over. As he pressed his mouth against her cheek, as close to her lips as he dared, a thrill coursed through him like lightning.

It only lasted a second, but it was enough to send his spirit soaring. He would remember the smell of her perfume and the way her breath tickled his ear. He'd take it with him, wherever in the world he was destined to go.

"Goodbye, Johnny," she said in a delicate, breathless voice. He slid his hand down her arm and gripped hers. It was so small and cold to the touch.

"Goodbye, Nellie Mae." He picked up his suitcase and gave a nod to Lola, who he'd honestly forgotten was standing there next to Nellie Mae. He walked away from them, clutching the handle of his bag until his knuckles were white and his joints ached. As he handed the attendant his ticket and stepped on board, he felt like he was floating six inches off the ground. He sat in an empty seat and surveyed the platform until his eyes found her. She smiled and waved.

He waved back, watching her until the whistle blew and the train lurched forward. He remembered his family and turned to wave to them as well.

All the familiar faces eventually faded from view, and from that moment on, his life was never the same again.

Fourteen

Nellie Mae watched the train until it disappeared from sight. She felt like she'd lost something she didn't yet have. What a silly thought! Johnny had made her no promises, yet his train sped away as if it were running off with a part of her heart.

You've stolen something from me, he'd said in his letter.

Perhaps she wasn't the only one stealing things.

She glanced at her cousin, ashamed of the satisfaction she felt in seeing Lola's disappointment. She was sure Lola had been hoping for the goodbye kiss Johnny had given to Nellie Mae instead. Nellie felt worse when Lola's eyes dropped to the ground. For a moment she looked like the daughter-yet-orphan she was. Maybe she hadn't really expected anything to work out in her favor, because things never did.

Nellie cleared her throat. "I'm sorry, Lola," she said quickly as they walked. Lola glanced at her, then shrugged. If only in that moment, the two found an understanding that was almost a comradery, but not quite.

"It's no surprise, Nellie Mae," Lola replied. "You're so bright, everyone around you is in shadows. He's no fool."

"Oh, go on!" Nellie Mae clucked and waved her off. "I'm just louder. He can't help but notice my big mouth."

Lola gave a soft laugh that wasn't quite happy, but she didn't say anything else.

It was true, though. There was no denying it. What would Nellie give to be as modest as Lola for just ten minutes? She hadn't a demure bone in her body.

Lola returned to the orphanage the next day, making Nellie Mae wonder if Johnny had been the sole reason for her cousin's visit. The day after, Aunt Nellie and Uncle Mort pulled into the driveway at lunchtime. Mort was weak and took to his bed almost immediately, but within a week he was ready to go back to work.

"We're grateful for your help," Aunt Nellie said at the breakfast table as Nellie waited for her father to arrive. Nellie was surprised by her aunt's words. Maybe she didn't have her aunt figured out after all. It endeared her to the woman in a way she'd never felt before.

"You're welcome," Nellie Mae answered softly. She wiped Harvey's face and set him free with a kiss on the head.

As she cleaned up the breakfast dishes, her heart started to race with anticipation. Any moment her father would pull his car into that driveway and Nellie Mae would be free. She'd be home in time for school, and she wouldn't be too far behind the other students her age. She'd finish on time. Maybe she'd even go to college. That would set her apart from her family and friends for sure.

Her first two years of high school had been memorable. It had been a pleasure to escape to the two-story brick building on Fourth Street every day. No one there told her education was second to wiping the noses of other people's children or cleaning house for some ailing farmwife. In school, she was expected to earn a diploma. Nellie loved the competitive atmosphere and the potential to rise to the top with her marks and activities. She loved learning lines for plays and playing her bass violin in the orchestra. She loved singing in the chorus and performing for P.E. exhibitions. She felt like she had been made for the school environment. She flourished there. She was herself there. She could be with her friends and be the person she couldn't be at home within her mother's hearing range.

Nellie was ashamed of her thoughts. She didn't really mind helping folks down on their luck. She did want to be a servant like Jesus, who had bent down and washed his disciples' filthy feet. But Nellie also wanted to learn. To excel. To do something just for her. Was that so selfish?

Nellie packed her things into the worn leather suitcase her mother had loaned her for the trip. It was an ugly thing for sure, with silky pink fabric draping down on every side like the inside of a funeral casket.

She supposed even as she had packed her things, she'd known it was too good to be true. Her uncle started a coughing fit in the other room, and before Nellie knew it, her aunt was on the phone, her voice high and anxious. Nellie went to soothe Harvey, who had started fussing.

"We're going back to the hospital, Nellie Mae," her aunt said as she entered the room, gathering her purse and gloves and Uncle Mort's bag.

Nellie Mae nodded, swallowing back her childish protest and tears. *This is God's will for you in Christ Jesus,* her mother would chide her from the Good Book if she was there. Nellie would just have to grin and bear it and do her duty *as unto the Lord, and not unto men.*

But she didn't have to like it.

97

MY GOOD NAME

Another thirteen months would pass before Nellie Mae got to go home for good.

Fifteen

What in the world had Johnny gotten himself into?

He stood in a line of other young men. They were all quiet, overwhelmed at the events of the day. As soon as the train had pulled into the station, the recruits who were just celebrated as heroes, sent off with cheering, had suddenly become children again. They were told what to wear, what to own, how to dress, what to eat and when. Johnny's hair had been unceremoniously buzzed off in seconds. He'd been sent down the line to collect his uniform, identification tags and papers. They were shown to cookie cutter buildings with rows and rows of basic cots. He was told where to put his belongings and which cot he would use during training.

He didn't say much to anyone. To be fair, no one was saying much. Everyone seemed a little shell-shocked. He saw the telltale look of yearning in everyone else's expression. They all wanted to go home. Already.

Johnny thought of the comfort of his home and the stability and respect he had earning an income. There he was an adult who contributed to society. Here he was treated like a naughty school boy. He supposed that was what it took to make soldiers out of them. But should he survive this war, would he recognize himself when he finally went home?

He did love his country, and that made the journey worth it. He was surprised by murmurings among the recruits, mumbling against the government and United States leaders. He hadn't realized so many people were unhappy with their great and free nation. Would they rather live in Germany under the control of Hitler, with his goal of world domination and the destruction of everyone he deemed unsuitable?

Johnny stared around him at the table in the mess hall and felt alone. Surrounded by men he didn't understand or relate to in any way. They would parachute into battle together. He'd have to depend on them. Maybe die with them. But he wasn't like them. He was dressed identically, he ate the same meals and slept on the same type of cot, but he was different.

Long after the lights were turned off and they'd been told to get their rest or they'd regret it, Johnny lay awake.

He worried over his fate. How would he get to know the other fellows? How would he go about sharing his faith? Would he survive the training? Would they find out about his colorblindness? Would he be humiliated and sent home?

He thought of home. His father coming home from a long day at work, his mother cooking at the stove or sweeping the front porch. He thought of his younger sister walking to school, blowing bubbles with her gum and twirling her hair as she greeted friends.

He thought of Nellie Mae. Had she gone home to Missouri? Would she go off to high school and forget all about the awkward soldier who had kissed her cheek when he said goodbye? He had no doubt she'd have a string of young men following her around by the end of the first week of school.

There was no way she'd remember him. And he definitely couldn't expect her to wait for him. His life had changed, and his future was unclear. It could be years before he left the service, if he even survived the journey in front of him.

He finally fell into a fitful sleep in the early hours of the morning.

Johnny woke when it was still dark. He couldn't sleep, so he got up and dressed. He made his bed like his mother had taught him and reached for his boots. The room was a peaceful sea of sleeping men. Some snored, creating a rhythm that almost made Johnny feel comradery with these strangers.

He glanced at his watch, wondering what time they would get up. The drill sergeant didn't give them much information about what they were doing next. Instead, he yelled at them and called them worthless pansies who needed a wake-up call to be real men. He said the 101st was no place for sissies, so they needed to check their lady undergarments at the door.

Johnny didn't like him much. He supposed the tough act was meant to make them respect their instructor, but it had the opposite effect on Johnny. He could esteem a man who led by example. Someone not afraid to get into the thick of it with his men. That was the kind of leader Johnny would be, should he ever be given the chance.

Colonel Sink seemed a decent enough fellow, but Johnny noticed he didn't relate much to the men of Johnny's station. He rode in his limousine and smoked cigars in his office from what Johnny heard. Major General Lee was even more of a mystery. It was rumored he was having health issues.

The bugle began revelry at exactly 4:30 a.m. The men began to stir, groaning in protest. A few rose quickly, but more pulled their blankets over their head and went back to sleep.

The door opened, banging against the wall. Lieutenant Winens, whom everyone just called *LT*, stepped into the barracks with his hands on his hips and a severe frown of disapproval on his face. He stomped between the rows of bed, yanking blankets from men's sleeping forms and kicking bodies out of bed. Johnny didn't know what to do, so he stood at attention beside his bed.

"When you hear the bugle call, you get your sorry butts out of bed and dress. You make your bed without a single wrinkle and you scrub these barracks from top to bottom. Then, and only then, do you stand in place and wait for inspection."

Winens looked straight at Johnny. "Well, looky here. A brown-noser on the first morning. What's your name, Private?"

"John Hagaman, SIR!" Johnny shouted, staring straight ahead like they'd done a thousand times the day before. They'd learned quickly things didn't go well if they didn't. Johnny's arms were still sore from the pushups he'd been forced to do when he forgot.

"Mr. Hagaman, did you get up early and fancy yourself just for me?" LT leaned into Johnny's face.

Johnny fought the urge to take a few steps back. "Sir! No, sir! I woke up and didn't know what else to do!"

LT barked a laugh. He continued down the line, shaming every man who hadn't managed to get up yet and humiliating every man who had. Two men who were still asleep were sent out to "beat their faces," or do pushups, on the lawn outside in full view of the entire camp.

"This isn't Bible camp, folks. You're here to be soldiers, not Bunker Bunnies. I'm going to make sure of it. So instead of opening exercises and breakfast, you're all going to run up the Currahee Mountain. Strip down to your shorts and shirts, gents. It's time to make men out of you."

LT obviously didn't mind if the men liked him or not. He was determined, and he got his job done. By the end of the first week, having run the three miles up and three miles down Currahee Mountain several times along with countless other training courses and calisthenics, the bewildered, soft young men became noticeably stronger and more agile. Johnny wouldn't have thought it was possible to do thirty pushups without being winded, but he could. And a tiny bit of respect took root within. Maybe LT's way was good. Maybe it was a kindness to make them strong. Johnny hadn't known how much he wanted to be strong until he realized he could be.

He continued to keep to himself. He did what was asked of him, ate his dinner in silence, and listened as the other men around him laughed and carried on. He spent his free time on his cot writing letters. Truth be told, he didn't write much he actually planned on sending. Most of them were addressed to Nellie Mae, and he didn't have her address in Missouri.

In his letters, he didn't speak much about what was happening at the camp. He told her how beautiful she was, how she lit up the room when she walked into it. He wrote about how it would feel to take her riding in his car. He wrote about what it would be like to kiss her on a moonlit night. It was sappy drivel and he knew it. Most of the letters ended up in pieces, thrown over the top of Currahee.

"I miss you, Nellie Mae," he'd whisper when he was sure no one else could hear him. Then he'd run back down the mountain, leaving his feelings there to flutter in the breeze and amuse the wildlife.

"Hey, Johnny," a voice spoke behind him at the breakfast line one cool September morning. The sun was high in the sky. They'd been up for hours following crazy, nonsensical orders out in the field. Stand in the field without moving a muscle for sixteen minutes. Run as fast as they could to the other end while screaming their heads off. Do ten summersaults and run to the far flag and back with a thirty-pound pack in their arms.

Johnny didn't like doing things when he didn't know why. His mind resisted orders that didn't make sense. But he could appreciate why soldiers needed to follow orders no matter what.

"Hey, Ken," Johnny answered.

Kenneth Day was in Johnny's squad and slept six beds down from him. He was a friendly guy who always smiled no matter how hard things got. For some reason, he'd taken a liking to Johnny and followed him around, even though Johnny hadn't spoken more than a greeting to him.

"How you holding up?" Ken loaded his plate with biscuits, fried eggs and bacon. John's plate was piled high as well. The army fed them well for all the work they did in return.

"Pretty well," Johnny said. He took a cup of orange juice and went to find a seat in the back corner. He liked sitting where he could observe without interacting. Ken followed and sat next to him. Johnny closed his eyes and said a silent prayer of thanks for his food.

"You a God-fearing man, then?" Ken asked as he dug into his meal.

"Yep." Johnny ate a biscuit in two bites. The food wasn't much for taste, but he appreciated the volume.

"Me, too. Raised Methodist. Haven't seen much need for it, though, you know? God seems pretty far away in this war. You think he's given up on us?" Ken still wore an easy smile.

John stopped eating and dared to look the other man in the eye. "No, I don't think he has."

"I hope you're right." Ken turned his full attention to his food.

Johnny considered the conversation. Did he believe God was at work even in this war? Was it possible God had left them? The world was full of evil. Johnny had never imagined the scale of it until he became a part of the struggle.

He considered his desire to join the Screaming Eagles to share his faith with men who stared death in the face. So far, one conversation with Ken was as far as he'd gotten speaking to anyone about God. Some of the boys went to chapel on Sunday morning, but no one discussed spiritual things. Johnny had almost forgotten the things he'd decided so clearly in that church not long before.

It was easy to forget in this place.

Sixteen

Nellie Mae stared longingly at the high school building. She knew plenty of kids her age dreaded entering those double doors, but she'd give up pretty much anything to be able to join everyone headed up that cement path.

Instead, she continued walking past, headed for Odgen's Grocery, which had sat on the same corner for as long as anyone could remember.

Her parents and brothers had welcomed her home with open arms, though her sister had immediately been sent down to Arkansas to help with a pastor's family who had gone there to start a church. They had nine children and were dealing with a lingering illness. Nellie Mae felt a pang of pity for her sister when she heard.

Nellie had come home just after the New Year, finally set free from her aunt's household. She had planned on going straight to school to register for the rest of the year. She should have gone there first, because the moment she had entered the house – a different house than the one she had left the summer before, this time even further from town – her mother announced that she had another job for Nellie.

Nellie Mae had reached her fill of ministering, but she knew she couldn't question her mother. There was no point in it, because the outcome would be the same.

At least her new job wasn't more than an hour's walk. Nellie Mae could come home in the evenings. But there would be no school. Instead, she would monitor five young children and clean house for a church member who had lost her husband and was attempting to run their farm in his place.

"They have next to nothing," Mother said, pressing a five-dollar bill into Nellie's hand. "Get something for the children to eat on the way."

Nellie didn't ask where the five dollars came from. Her mother had a way of praying things into existence. Nellie wouldn't be surprised if the money had just appeared on the kitchen counter that morning.

She bought some staple foods at Ogden's, keeping in mind the woman probably had chickens, a milk cow and canned fruits and vegetables from last year's garden.

"Shouldn't you be in school, Nellie Mae?" Mr. Ogden smiled as he rang up her purchases.

"The Lord's work comes first, Mr. Ogden," Nellie said brightly. He would never suspect she would have chosen school if the decision had been hers. No matter the awful thoughts she kept to herself, she would honor her good name. For her father's sake. "There'll be plenty of time for school another day."

"Smart thing like you should be in school," he huffed. She smiled her appreciation as she gathered up the bag and her purse. At least someone understood.

"I fully intend to finish school. Just as soon as folks stop needing a hand."

He chuckled and patted her arm. "I hope that day comes soon."

"Thank you," she said, and she meant it with all her heart.

She continued through town, lost in thought. She adjusted the bag under her arm as she passed the soda fountain and theater. She turned the corner and saw the boarded-up office that used to be Dr. Davis's clinic. A shudder passed through her at the sight.

Dr. Davis had seen to her childhood diseases and her brothers' broken bones, of which there had been many. He'd been a kindly man, not young and not elderly, with merry and intelligent bright eyes hidden behind spectacles and a no-nonsense voice.

When Nellie Mae was eleven, not even a week after she'd been seen in the office for a case of bronchitis, a local man had gotten it into his addled head to rob the doctor so he'd have money to marry his sweetheart. Things had escalated, and the good doctor had been murdered.

The event had scarred her, though she definitely wasn't the only one. It had affected many of her friends and their families. The funeral, held in the high school, had been devastatingly sad. Not only had the town lost a beloved physician, but they had lost confidence in their safety. Their small-town existence, where crime was a concept only understood when reading big-city newspapers, came crashing down. Suddenly mothers didn't let little ones roam. Kids were afraid to venture into the woods. Especially the woods out by North Folk River where the doctor had been killed.

Nellie Mae had gone there once, on a dare, and vowed she'd never return. Even in the middle of summer the air had held a chill. She was sure she saw red splotches on the rocks by the river. Her brothers told her it was the good doctor's blood refusing to wash away. Nellie Mae had shuddered with fear almost as bad as when the boys talked about the spook lights people saw out on the road called the Devil's Promenade.

Nellie Mae's mother had made light of her worries. At the age of twelve, Nellie trying to explain to her mother why she didn't want to cut through the woods only resulted in humiliation.

"Do you not trust that God can protect his child? We cannot be afraid to leave our house just because evil lives in this world. This is a way Satan keeps God's people in bondage. Go right now and don't give it another thought."

Nellie knew her mother was right. Bad things could happen anywhere in the world. Good people could go to work one morning and end up dead in a river by the end of the day. Young men full of vigor and promise could head off to war and never return.

Nellie thought of Johnny. His shy smile, his ears sticking out in their endearing way, his hair slicked back. The way he smiled only at her. The way he kissed *her*, not her cousin.

For all she knew, he could be lying dead in some foxhole by now. Shot by a German soldier who gave him no further thought. She felt tears sting her eyes.

She arrived at the Tharp farm and was greeted by a gaggle of little ones coming to help her. She knelt and handed out food items that they each might take inside to their mother.

"Oh, thank heavens you're here, Nellie Mae," Mrs. Tharp said from the kitchen door. Her shoulders seemed to relax some. "I'm beside myself trying to keep it all together."

Nellie Mae could see the woman was having a hard time fighting off the tears. Her children whimpered and hung on her skirts while Nellie came quickly to her side and grabbed her hand. Nellie's heart went soft. This woman and her children needed Nellie far more than Nellie needed to be in school, flirting with boys and competing for the highest marks. Her mother was right, yet again. Knowing it made Nellie ache with guilt.

"Your mama saved my life," Mrs. Tharp continued as she wiped her eyes and kissed her baby's head. "Mary Ellen had the croup something awful. Your mama prayed over her and held her hand on her forehead. She just sat there, for over an hour, praying. Mary woke up the next morning completely well, as if she'd never been sick. If I wasn't a believer before that, praise the Lord, I am now! And if it weren't for Beulah Thomas, I'd have had to send my babies away to relatives. I'd have died for sure."

It wasn't the first time Nellie Mae had heard stories of her mother healing folks through her praying. More reason to feel worthless in comparison. She shook off the bitterness. "It's no trouble at all, Mrs. Tharp. I'm awfully glad to help however I can."

While Mrs. Tharp took to the field to plant the spring crop, Nellie Mae swept and cooked and wiped noses and washed laundry over a big steel tub on a fire in the backyard. In the afternoon she read Bible stories to the children, and then she told her own tales, delighting them with her imaginative characters she based on people she knew. When she headed home after supper, they cried and hung on her skirts.

She tried to make the most of her free evenings. Sometimes she stopped at Shorty's or Ferguson's, where the high school crowd gathered. She would sit with Henry and Bill and laugh until her sides ached.

One night near the end of the school year, Nellie Mae stood at Ferguson's counter waiting for her soda. A girl came up and stood next to her. She was shorter than Nellie, which was saying something, because even in the highest heels she could find, Nellie was still one of the shortest girls in her class. This girl's face was sweetly rounded and dark curls fell over her forehead in an easy way Nellie envied. She could never get her hair to look effortless and beautiful at the same time.

"Hello," the girl said with a sweet smile. Nellie noticed just the hint of mischief tucked away behind her expression and liked her immediately. "I'm Martha."

"Hi, Martha." Nellie turned toward her. "I'm Nellie Mae."

"You seemed pretty lost in thought there," Martha said as she reached across the counter to take her order.

"Oh, I was just thinking there's a new girl so pretty I'll have to hide all my boyfriends so they don't forget all about me." Nellie laughed as the waiter handed her the soda.

Martha laughed, too, like laughing was as second nature to her as breathing. "I was thinking the same thing about you."

"Where are you from?" Nellie Mae asked her new friend as she smiled brightly at the young man behind the counter when he held out her change. The boy turned red.

Martha didn't miss it. She smiled as she answered. "We just moved from Texas. You sure have a way, don't you?"

Nellie Mae glanced at the apron-clad young man with the red face and scoffed. "Oh, Pshaw. It's just warm in here. Come sit with us?"

Martha nodded and Nellie Mae brought her back to the table with Bill and Henry. They had a jolly time getting to know each other. After what only felt like a few minutes, Mr. Ferguson was telling them the store was closing.

After that night, Nellie and Martha were inseparable. Martha became the kind of best friend Nellie had always dreamed of having. They spent the summer perpetually together, especially when Mrs. Tharp finished the planting and didn't need her as much. Martha's family lived close to town. Nellie spent many nights there since it was closer to the Tharp farm. On the weekends Martha walked out to Nellie's house. On hot summer nights they would take the kitchen chairs out to the front yard and listen to Nellie Mae's father sing and play his harmonica. Sometimes Mother would even join in on her guitar if Dad was in the mood to play hymns. One time, they got so caught up in the music, they didn't notice the temperature suddenly drop and the trees start tossing in the wind. A bolt of lightning caught one of the metal chair frames and sent sparks into the air, making them all hum with electricity.

After a moment of surprised silence, Dad laughed. "Guess we better take this concert inside."

When the days were cooler and the sign for registration went up in the high school yard, Nellie Mae and Martha were the first to sign up for classes. They made sure all their classes were together. Nellie was sure it was going to be the best year of school she'd ever had. Never mind she was a year behind everyone else her age.

Only one thing could have made it better. If a certain soldier's face suddenly appeared, or at least if she had recognized his neat script on a letter handed over to her at the post office.

Which, to her delight, finally happened.

Seventeen

Dear Nellie.

John stared at the words on the otherwise blank sheet of paper. What should he write? Should he even dare to actually write her a serious letter? And send it?

He'd written to his sister Rena, asking her to get Nellie's address in Missouri. His mother might disapprove of him writing her, and Nancy would tease, so he counted on Rena's ability to keep a secret. It seemed like forever before he got a reply, but finally she wrote back and gave him the address.

Now if he could just figure out what to say.

He glanced around at the other men in the barracks. He had tried some of the nightly activities. The camp recreation center, called the Post Exchange, had basketball. Sometimes a baseball game was organized in the field behind the barracks. There was pool, ping pong and beer in the mess hall. But Johnny preferred the quiet of his bunk. The scattered presence of a few others suggested only a few agreed with him. They were a good bunch to be around, for everyone sat in their bunks reading or writing letters. They had an unspoken rule that the room be as quiet as a library. No need to socialize.

His eyes nearly crossed as he focused on the blank paper. What to tell her? Did she want to know that they might be headed to Fort Benning soon? He wasn't sure about anything. The army didn't tell them much. He wondered how long it would take for them to be ready for war. It was a little surreal to consider jumping out of airplanes and getting shot at. Or shooting at someone.

He scratched his head, wondering again what to tell Nellie Mae. He couldn't tell her he was terrified of the idea of fighting. He wanted her to think he was as brave as Captain Wilson, Lieutenant Winens or Sergeant Grovenburg. He could tell her about them, but it didn't feel proper to speak of other men to a young preacher's daughter. They were good men, and he respected them, but their language and drinking and smoking would be a jolt for Nellie Mae to hear about.

He could tell her what he did all day. About weapons instruction at the shooting range, watching training films, calisthenics, hikes up Currahee Mountain, obstacle courses. But would she care about his life? They had no understanding between them.

Maybe it would be better to talk about the future. But was there even a future to talk about? She might expect him to be killed in the war. Not to mention, if he did happen to make it home, they lived five hundred miles from each other. Why in the world should Nellie Mae Thomas even give him a second thought?

He finally decided he would just tell her more about himself. His past. Who he was. His eyes caught on the dime novel the man across the aisle was reading. He would tell her his story, but in fictional form. Wouldn't that be interesting? Clever? She probably thought of him as a dunce since he rarely spoke a word. This would prove he was intelligent.

He began to write so fast his wrist ached and his fingers tingled.

I won't put any date on this letter because I probably won't finish it for days. Busy, you know. I've just gotta say so many things to you that are very important to me and I don't know how in the world to start. I'm so very much afraid that I won't be able to make you understand what I want to say. I hardly know myself.

I remember once writing a biography or an autobiography (I don't know the correct word) of my life. Perhaps if I told you a story it might help for me to explain myself.

The story is about a fellow named Joe. Joe isn't really his name, but since every story you read these days has a "Joe" in it, I may as well put a Joe in mine.

Joe is an average American youth. You know him pretty well. I bet you'll recognize who he is before too long.

Back before training for war, Joe worked in a factory. He hated it. His brain overflowed with dreams of travel and adventure. He'd spend his monotonous hours at the factory daydreaming. If you looked in on him as he was working at his machine, you'd be sure he was intent on his task.

Well, Joe was working one day on the humming machine as it cut down through the hard metal, but his mind was far, far away. A few times an expensive piece of metal was ruined all because of Joe's daydreams. (In spite of this, Joe was still considered a valuable man by his employer.)

During this time two things happened to affect his destiny. One of them was a girl. I think I'll call this girl Kit. She reminds me of a kitten – purring sweetly one moment and a second later ready to fight.

Joe and Kit met on a nearly-blind date one winter night. I should remember just when it was, but I don't. They saw each other a few times. I think Joe knew Kit for about a month before the other important thing came into his life. The greatest thing that ever happened or ever would.

Joe slipped away from it all one Sunday evening and went to church. That very night Joe was born again. He accepted Jesus as Savior from his sins. Of course, from that time on, he was a new man. He loved the Lord and wanted to work for him. He spent his spare time reading the Bible and praying that God would lead him into Christian work. God never did call Joe that way. Of course, Joe didn't blame God because he knew God's ways are best.

Johnny stopped and looked back over the pages he'd written. The other guys were coming in for the night, so he tucked the letter into an envelope and hid it at the bottom of his trunk. He'd send it to Rena and add more as time went on.

The next morning after breakfast they hiked to the thirty-four-foot training tower on the edge of the property. The structure loomed over them, taunting them with its very real power to end their lives.

Johnny's heart seemed to jump into his throat as he thought about what could happen if that harness broke. The drop was enough to kill a man. But he looked around at the other white faces and determined he wouldn't be the wimp that refused to do what he was told. He'd swallow the terror and be the first man up the ladder.

LT nodded when he asked to go first. He shimmied up the ladder as quickly as he could so he didn't second-guess his choice. The instructor at the top secured him in the harness as he made a few jokes about "never knowing if those straps are going to give out." Johnny tried to ignore him and glanced at the sawdust pit far below him. He decided to look out instead. Then he closed his eyes and jumped.

The sensation of free-falling should have scared him. He'd heard of men who blacked out the first time. But he only felt a delicious rush of adrenaline. In fact, he was suddenly sure he hadn't really been alive before this day. Or he was just waking up from a sleepy dream, and life was about to start. He laughed aloud as the lines played out and a cable eased him down the rest of the way. He was supposed to follow the techniques they'd learned to come out of a real jump. He should have rolled over to ease the impact, but he forgot in his elation and landed unceremoniously in a jumbled heap of limbs. Everyone laughed at him.

"You're a showoff, Hagaman," LT said with a smirk, his arms folded across his chest.

"No, sir," Johnny answered. "Do we get to go again?"

LT raised an eyebrow. "You just wait for C stage."

"What's C stage?" Johnny dusted himself off when he was free of the harness and climbed out of the pit. Another man jumped off the tower, screaming like a little girl.

"250-foot drop."

Maybe it should have worried Johnny, but he only felt a thrill at the thought.

The next man held on to a post at the top of the tower and refused to jump. LT cursed. "What did these boys think was going to happen when they signed up for paratroops? The whole idea is to jump out of a plane."

Johnny smiled. "I guess for some the idea and the actual doing are two different things."

LT glanced at him. "For some," he repeated. He looked back up at the tower. "So why are you here, Johnny? Were you drafted?"

Johnny shook his head. "I love my country. I signed up."

LT shook his head. "Ain't too many boys that feel that way."

Johnny nodded in agreement.

"You planning to move up the ladder?" LT asked. "You're quiet, but fearless. I get the feeling you'd earn promotions if you went after them. You'd have to learn to be a leader, though."

Johnny considered it. He hadn't contemplated leadership. But when he did, he liked the idea of a group of men following him and learning from him. He liked the idea of making decisions for the group and being an example. Maybe God could use that.

He shrugged. "Maybe."

The third jumper came flying into the sawdust, missing the entry and howling in pain. He rolled on the ground and held his leg, crying out.

"Go get him up." LT nudged Johnny in the ribs.

Johnny eyed him for a moment, then nodded. "Yes, sir." He jogged to the pit and leaned over the side. "Come on, Hawkins. Grab my hand. No use laying there and yelling."

"My leg's broke!" Hawkins managed.

"Can you move it?" Johnny glanced at LT, who made no move to intervene. Hawkins was rolling around, so Johnny doubted it was a serious injury.

"It hurts!" Hawkins yelled again.

"What are you going to do when you're rolling around on the ground after jumping out of a plane into enemy territory? Gonna cry for your mama then?"

It seemed harsh, but it did the trick. Hawkins stopped bawling and narrowed his eyes.

Johnny showed him no sympathy. Sympathy would get a soldier killed. "If you aren't dead, get on your feet and get out of the way."

The man quickly crawled to the side of the pit and let Johnny help him out.

Johnny stood back and watched the next jumper. He heard LT speak behind him.

"Nice work, Hagaman."

"Thank you, sir."

"Hey, Hagaman," LT said. Johnny looked at him. LT smiled. "Why don't you get back up there and have another go?"

Johnny smiled.

Eighteen

Nellie Mae saw her father standing outside the garage as she approached. He was wiping a tool with a dirty rag, listening to another man, who was a bit shorter and sharply dressed. He looked to be around the same age as Dad.

The other man pushed his spectacles up on his nose and shook his head. "It's a crazy time to be in politics," the man said, his hands on his hips. "I don't feel nearly prepared for Washington. There is so much dishonesty and greed. I've been trying to shed light on it. Do something about it. But few and far between are the men who see it as a problem."

Dad nodded. "I know what you mean. But I'm encouraged to hear you say you don't feel equipped for the job. I'd say that's a good thing." Dad set down his tool and rag and glanced over at Nellie Mae, smiling. "You go into the vice-presidency with humility, no telling what the Lord can do through you."

"I'm under so much pressure to please everyone. What if something happens to President Roosevelt? I wouldn't be a good president. I'd have no idea what I was doing," the man said.

"Do any of us?" Dad gave a short laugh. "You're just man enough to admit the truth."

The man didn't answer. He stared at his car, which Dad had

evidently been working on.

"What would you do about the war?" Dad asked, eyeing him.

The man sighed and looked back at Dad "I know plenty of folks don't want us involved. But we're facing a bunch of thugs over there, and the only theory a thug understands is a gun and a bayonet."

"For sure and for certain," Dad said with a nod. He glanced back at Nellie Mae and motioned her forward. "Come, Nellie Mae. Meet our very own Senator Truman."

Nellie was shocked. She smoothed back her hair and hurried forward. "I'll be! Mr. Harry Truman, in our garage?"

"*Senator* Truman," Dad admonished softly, but Truman only smiled at her.

"Senator," Nellie said and extended her hand. "I'm so glad to meet you."

The senator shook her hand. His expression was kind. "I have a daughter about the same age as you," he said. "I bet you make your parents proud."

Nellie Mae put an arm around her father. He squeezed her shoulders. "I'm sure I don't make them as proud as they make me."

Senator Truman chuckled.

"What brings you to humble ole Willow Springs?" Nellie asked, gesturing to their small town.

"My car broke down. Fortunately for me, it turns out."

"How's it fortunate that your car broke down?" Nellie asked in confusion.

"Because I got to meet your daddy. He happened along and helped me tow it to his garage. He fixed it, but now I find I don't want to leave."

"I'm sure you have somewhere important you need to be," Dad said with a chuckle.

"Sure. But sometimes God redirects us to other important

meetings, doesn't he? You've given me good, sound advice. And I need it. So many decisions to make."

"We all need good advice sometimes," Dad said as Nellie Mae leaned against her father.

"Ain't my advice," he added. "We have all the wisdom we could ever need in the Good Book. All I'm doing is reminding you."

The Senator smiled and nodded. Nellie bade them goodbye before she made her way across town. She stopped by the post office to collect the week's mail at her mother's request, thinking about her father's words as she walked. She had her doubts, if she was being completely honest. The Bible sure didn't say anything about what to do if your parents are too good for you. It didn't tell her how to pick herself up out of the gutter when she fell into her melancholy times. It had no advice – at least that she had ever found – for someone struggling with fatigue so strong it made her want to lay down and quit trying so hard to survive some days. And what about when a soldier she couldn't stop thinking about went off to war? What did the Bible say to do with those feelings of despair, knowing he probably wouldn't be coming back to her?

No, sometimes life dealt you puzzlers without easy fixes. To her parents, the answers were black and white. If you struggled in your life, you didn't have enough faith. You didn't trust God. You weren't saved, but still dead in your sins. If you weren't moving on toward perfection at a pretty steady pace, something was wrong with your soul.

Something must be very, very wrong with Nellie's soul.

She tried to shake off her dark thoughts as she stepped inside the post office. The postman greeted her with a welcoming smile as she reached up to grab her family's mail from their box.

"Something special came for you," Mr. Arden said, pulling a letter from the top of his pile. "Something in care of Miss Rena Hagaman of Indianapolis."

"Why, of all the places," she said breathlessly, embarrassed, but incredibly curious as she took the letter and set it on top of her pile. "Whatever could this be about?"

The postman's eyes twinkled as if he knew exactly what, but he didn't comment further as he continued to sort the mail.

"I suppose the rest of the town has a pretty good idea, as well," she said under her breath as she stepped back into the street.

She didn't know quite what to make of the letter he'd sent her through his sister. He'd evidently been working on it a while, sending pieces here and there. It was his story in fictional form, as a man called Joe.

Kit. He'd called her Kit, short for a temperamental kitten. She wasn't sure exactly how to take it. She had half a mind to write him back a scathing letter, but she realized that would only prove him right. Anyway, she knew it was an accurate description. She just didn't like so much hearing it from him.

Yet she was also warmed at the thought he'd given her a pet name.

She stuffed the letter back in the envelope and set it in the top drawer of her nightstand. She didn't want to think about a soldier, next thing to dead, heading into the midnight of a world war. It would hurt too much to lose him if she paid him mind. Wasn't that what all the girls were saying? *Don't give your heart to a soldier. Dance with them, flirt with them, write them letters to keep up their spirits, but don't ever fall in love with them, or you'll regret it.*

The trouble was, Nellie was pretty sure she'd already fallen for him.

"Nellie Mae, thank goodness you're home." Mother was standing on the front porch when Nellie hiked in from the main road an hour later. Her mother was dressed in her Sunday best. Was there a service tonight?

"Elder Smith called an emergency camp meeting out at Tabernacle." Mother ushered her in. "I need you to fix my hair. Elder says the Lord has called on me to bear witness tonight."

Nellie Mae followed her mother into the bedroom where Beulah sat down in front of the round mirror on her dressing table and handed Nellie the brush. "The Lord didn't bother to check with me first," Mother said under her breath. Nellie knew it was her mother's way to get anxious before she spoke.

"You'll do just fine," she assured her mother. "You always do."

"Well, that's because the Lord always shows up." Beulah sighed as if she were trying to release some of her nervous energy. Nellie pulled the brush through her mother's thick hair.

"Ow! For heaven's sake, Nellie Mae, take a little care."

Nellie Mae worked in silence for the next twenty minutes while her mother practiced her speech and gave instructions on her hair. When she was done, she sat on the bed and listened to her mother lecture while she dressed.

"You've been wearing too much rouge and lipstick, Nellie Mae. God didn't make you a clown. And those ridiculous heels! You're going to break your neck …"

Nellie Mae stared out the window and sighed.

"And I don't ever want to hear tell of you setting foot outside this house without a girdle on. It's downright indecent, the way girls prance around these days."

Nellie stared at the worn rug and chewed on a ragged fingernail.

"And sit properly, for goodness' sake, Nellie. Don't cross your legs. You look like a hillbilly."

"I am a hillbilly." Nellie Mae couldn't resist. Her mother didn't seem to hear her anyway.

"… always keep your elbows off the table and don't laugh loudly."

Nellie Mae frowned. Did she laugh too loudly? She stopped chewing on the nail, worried that she'd ruin her fresh manicure and clear polish. Everything about her was scrubbed and polished and neat, but it was the opposite of how she felt inside. Within she was wild, like an angry painting without any pictures, just jagged, bold brushes of color. Red, black, yellow, blue. Thrown onto the canvas of her mind in raging splotches.

She cleared her throat, worried that her mother might read her mind and see the untidy cavern it was.

"For crying in the night, child, go iron my dress, will you?" Her mother held the clothing out, and apparently had been for a while as Nellie was lost in thought. "Time's a wasting!"

Nellie Mae took the dress and went to the laundry room in the lean-to off the kitchen to iron it. "Mama," she called in a sudden fit of boldness. "Can I spend the night at Martha's?"

"What about camp meeting?"

"Please?" Nellie Mae watched her mother fly around the kitchen, putting together a cold supper as she was clad only in her slip and nylons. Her mother met her gaze, and Nellie saw her relent.

"Go on ahead to Martha's. Goodness knows you work hard. I'll finish the dress now."

Nellie Mae was shocked by the uncharacteristic response. She wouldn't have seen it coming in a hundred years. But she didn't question. She handed her mother the dress and ran out the back door before Mother could change her mind.

Nineteen

Being confident of this very thing, that he which hath begun a good work in you will perform it until the day of Jesus Christ.

Johnny hadn't been able to get the verse out of his mind all day. They'd left the station in Toccoa that morning, and rumor was the train was headed for Fort Benning. There'd been talk of making the men walk a good part of the way. Johnny didn't know if he was happy about it when they didn't. It would have been something to say he'd walked a hundred miles. Johnny liked saying he'd done something most had not.

It was November, and there was a chill in the air, even being further south than Johnny had ever been. They couldn't see much in the dark, but Johnny had the impression that Fort Benning was huge in comparison to Camp Toccoa. Foreboding struck him with such a force he felt dizzy. He hauled his trunk off the back of the truck that had brought them into camp and tried to look around in the dim light. Rows and rows of no-nonsense white army barracks stretched in perfect cohesion as far as the dim light would allow his eyes to see. This place was not for beginners. This was a place where men learned to survive. Where they were taught to jump from airplanes and defend themselves. Where they were taught to kill without hesitation. From this place, there was nowhere to go but straight into the howling storm of the war that ravaged the earth.

His heart felt like it skipped a beat at the thought. He hoped no one knew he was afraid. He wanted to be brave. He wanted to be the hero who kept his country safe. Who kept his parents and sisters protected. Who defended the life of Nellie Mae Thomas.

He took a deep breath and let it out, resolved to stand his ground. What was his life, anyway? He hadn't done much with the twenty-one years he'd already used up. It was time to make something of himself.

John Hagaman was going to step up and prove he was worth the skin God gave him. If he died in this war, at least he'd be giving his life to a cause that meant something. He'd die ridding the world of the evil spread by the likes of men like Adolf Hitler.

"Is it okay to be scared?" Ken Day whispered behind him as he heaved his own trunk.

Johnny shrugged. "Think of it this way: we don't have time to be scared, because we're determined to rid the world of a bully."

Ken didn't say anything, but John thought his friend stood up a little straighter.

"Well said, Hagaman." Sergeant Grovenburg was the newly appointed leader of Johnny's squad of eight men. He gave Johnny a short nod. "You'll get far with that attitude."

Grovenburg was called over to speak to the lieutenant about barracks assignments while Johnny considered his words. He wasn't sure how he felt about that.

They weren't allowed much time to acclimate to life on the vast military base. The first two weeks they spent long mornings doing the usual calisthenics and running. They sang songs that would make Johnny's mother blush. They started hand-to-hand combat training in the judo pit the second week, which Johnny liked. He was good at it, and the accolades he received bolstered his confidence.

"You might come out of that shell after all," Lieutenant Winens mused. "We'll see how you do tower week."

They were taught to pack their parachutes … with the knowledge that they would be using the parachute they packed on their own. This made everyone take it a little more seriously than they'd taken packing their trunks to move out.

"Your packing will either save your life or kill you," Dick Turner yelled from the front of the room as they all wrestled with the huge, unruly messes of fabric and string. "You gotta be careful. Like porcupines making love."

Johnny's cheeks must have gone red because he got a good ribbing from a few of the other guys, but he packed his parachute with more precision than he'd ever done anything in his life. No daydreaming this time. The stakes were more than a ruined piece of metal now.

They did a few exercises with parachutes and practiced climbing the tower. Getting up there was really the hardest part. Johnny thought it was fun. At the end of the third week, he woke up one morning to realize it was time. He opened his eyes at dawn and stared at the ceiling for a good hour thinking about it. After breakfast, which he wasn't sure he was going to keep down, he'd be strapped to the shock harness.

Since his name started with *H,* he was halfway down the list of men. He was eternally grateful for his father not giving him an *A* name, but he wouldn't have minded a *B* or a *C.* He had to watch man after man crying like a baby two hundred feet in the air, staring down at the ground.

The harness was applied as the men lay face down on a mattress thrown on the ground. Two rubber shock cords were hooked to the harness. As the unfortunate fellow watched in horror, he was hoisted all the way to the top of the tower. The first guys who came off said the mattress at the bottom looked like a postage stamp from way up there.

When the signal from the jump instructor was given by megaphone, the man had to pull the rip cord on his chest and free fall until the parachute caught the wind. It felt like falling to an imminent death, but the soldier still had to have the presence of mind to put his arms out to both sides, bring them back together and pass the cord from the right to the left hand.

Most of the first ten men dropped the cord completely or forgot to do anything except scream in holy terror. They earned themselves the privilege of getting back in line to do it again. Johnny was determined not to be one of them.

"Here," Ken surreptitiously passed Johnny a silver flask from inside his jacket pocket. "It'll help."

"Nah, I want to be clear-headed," Johnny said, though he stared at the flask, tempted for the first time in his life to take a drink. He'd never had an interest before. His father had the occasional drink, but he never offered Johnny any, and Johnny never asked.

Ken laughed. "It won't affect your thinking unless you drink too much. Just take a sip."

Johnny hesitated. It was a big decision. Almost like something he couldn't take back. He knew some preachers said drinking alcohol was a sin. But didn't Jesus drink wine? He eyed the tiny dot far up in the sky he knew was a whimpering paratrooper helplessly dangling, about to be released at any moment.

In one quick motion he took the flask and drank down a big gulp. He swallowed before he registered the acrid taste or felt the heat radiating on the back of his throat. He sputtered, coughing. Winens turned around and stared at him. He managed to salute and look back up at the tower, swallowing back any more coughing by sheer will.

"Good man," Ken said with a chuckle, slapping him on the back. "Feel better now, don't you?"

Johnny shrugged. Beyond the fire trailing down his esophagus, he supposed he felt slightly less anxious than he had a moment before.

He took another quick swig before he handed back the flask. Ken also took a long draw before he slipped it back in his jacket.

"At least no one will call us cowards," Ken said as they moved forward in line.

All in all, the moments leading up to the shock harness were worse than the experience itself. When the harness was being hoisted up, there was a moment of panic as he stared, trying to comprehend just how far down the ground was. He would die if that harness failed. He was putting a whole lot of faith in a bit of fabric and rubber.

But he wasn't. Not really. His faith was in Jesus Christ. If the harness didn't hold, it would be the will of God. He would be free from a war-ravaged life of uncertainty.

He squinted and tried to make out the individual ants on the ground he supposed were his fellow soldiers. The alcohol in his stomach threatened to make a second journey along his throat. He may go to heaven, but first he'd face the matter of smashing into the ground.

When he was given the signal, he released the rip cord before he could second-guess it. He immediately went into a free fall and bit back his scream. He wouldn't be one of those guys crying for their mamas. The ground raced toward him, and for a moment his mind blanked and he forgot what to do. But the thought of having to do it again got him focused. He passed the cord from his right hand to his left, hoping that was right. The cords caught and jerked him after twenty feet or so, and he managed to hold on. All the while he stared down at that little bit of white on the ground he knew was the mattress. He wondered how it would feel to die landing on a mattress.

Then he laughed. He whooped and threw his fist in the air to scattered cheers below. He'd done it. He'd mastered the tower.

Now it was time to master the plane.

Twenty

Johnny wasn't as nervous jumping from the C-47. He wasn't sure why, except that jumping out the airplane somehow seemed more natural than jumping with a flimsy harness from a 250-foot tower. Even so, his stomach churned the first time they approached the drop zone and every time after

When the instructor gave the signal, they stood up single file in the center walkway of the plane. They hooked up to the static line hanging from the ceiling and waited, everyone holding their breath with eyes glued to the instructor.

It seemed like forever. Finally, the instructor told them to double check the pack of the man in front of them. Then they waited again.

In a sudden and shocking turn of events, the instructor suddenly slapped the rear of the first man, which happened to be Ken, to signal him to jump. He only gave a split second of hesitation before he gave a whoop and tossed his body out of the open hatch. The wind immediately caught him up and carried him away before the next man jumped, and the next, and the next, and before Johnny knew it, he was standing in the doorway. Then his feet were standing on nothing and he was floating.

It didn't feel like falling as he had come to expect. He didn't go straight down. The wind gave him wings and for a few moments he knew the sensation of flying like a bird. He laughed, but the sound caught in his throat. After a few seconds he felt the parachute open, and the tell-tale jerk assured him everything was in working order.

He enjoyed the flight. He scanned the ground and wondered where he would land. The instructor had said there were landing zones for each of the three battalions, and his was expected to land in the red zone. So, there would be red smoke where the 1st battalion was supposed to be. He could probably spot the white, but blue and red would be hard to distinguish.

He spent the rest of the jump looking for smoke. When he finally saw it, he panicked. He couldn't tell the difference. He tried to look around and see if there were familiar faces nearby, but he couldn't tell.

What do I do? If I don't land in the right zone, they'll know I'm colorblind. They'll send me home.

His heart started thumping hard in his chest. Suddenly, he saw a tree, and a rather unfortunate soul yelling as he launched right into the top of it. No one would ask questions if they were trying to extract him from a tree, would they? They'd think it was an accident.

Johnny tested the straps, wondering how much control he really had over the steering. He decided to go for it. He memorized the placement and look of the wisps of smoke rising lazily in the air. He'd ask Ken later which was which. And he wouldn't forget when the next time rolled around.

He braced for the landing, but nothing could have prepared him for the jarring sensation of breaking through the tree line. He grabbed for a branch near the top, but it slipped through his fingers. He ended up dangling from the line of his parachute. He tried wiggling out, but he was too far away from any of the sturdy branches. He was stuck until someone came to rescue him.

He imagined there would be some teasing involved for his haphazard landing. But it was better than being sent home in shame. That wasn't going to happen as long as he could help it.

They had four more jumps the next week. By the time the night jump came, they had all grown used to the process and most of the men had started showing off. They purposefully jumped out head first or backward to receive a harder jolt when the parachute opened. They bet on who could be the most daring. They teased the few who remained tentative about jumping.

There were quite a few men on crutches with their legs in casts. Johnny usually saw two or three on the way to meals or assemblies. He managed to avoid major injury and indeed started to believe he was just plain immune to getting hurt. He was going to survive this whole thing. It didn't matter how many Jerry bullets aimed his way. He wouldn't die. He couldn't.

After the night jump, which proved to be the single most exhilarating experience of Johnny's young life, the men in his battalion were awarded their jump wings, save the ones disqualified for not completing the task. Johnny wore his silver pin with pride and bloused up his trousers around his boots to show he was among the elite. He felt himself starting to look down on the regular army soldiers. Paratroopers were the best. They would be the reason the Germans were defeated and the world was set free.

Gone were thoughts of Johnny telling his fellow soldiers about the experience he'd had in church only a few months back. Who wanted to think about spiritual things now? They were going to live forever.

As spring woke the world around them and warmed the days, they finished jump training and were moved to Tennessee to begin simulated combat training. Johnny thought it was fun. Wasn't war just a game when it all came down? Weren't they all just pawns, moved about the grand playing board in a strategy to win?

Just as he began to assimilate himself into the life of a soldier, throwing off all remnants of his former self, Johnny received an unexpected letter from his mother.

Come home, Johnny. Your aunt has been killed.

Twenty-One

Nellie's work with the farm assignment ended abruptly at Christmas when the good widow decided to take her children and go east to live with family. Nellie was relieved to be free, but she chafed that school was too far gone for her to join and be able to finish. What would she do until fall when school started again?

Another revival was in full swing at church. Mother was there every night and plenty of the days as well. She stayed late, praying for sick and laying hands on them. Her testimonies shook the simple building like she was calling down holy fire.

Nellie Mae stood in the back of the room with her arms across her chest, trying not to let the tears sting her eyes. She could give in and feel the same spirit everyone else felt. But she'd tried and failed so many times to summon up that spirit on her own. It was exhausting. Why did God seem to approve of her mother but not Nellie? What had she done wrong? She'd gone to church her entire life. She read her Bible every day, prayed with all her strength for the people she loved. She attended meetings and expected God to move. But it never seemed to work for her the way it worked for her parents and sisters. Even her brothers, with all their immaturity.

God must love everyone else more than her. She didn't blame

him, considering her nature. But if he'd known she was going to be so contrary, why'd he bother to put her on the earth in the first place? Why didn't he take her the same way he took Marjorie, the baby born dead just a year ahead of her? If Nellie had died before she'd lived, she wouldn't have shamed her father's good name. The name he gave to her.

Why was I born into THIS family and not another? Her thoughts continued. *Perhaps one with a name that I could live up to instead of one to which I would always fall short?*

The men's quartet stood up to sing a song. People held their hands in the air and smiled as if the words were happy, but they sat on Nellie's spirit like a dead weight, accusing her.

> *I saw the light, I saw the light!*
> *No more darkness, no more night.*
> *Now I'm so happy, no sorrow in sight,*
> *Praise the Lord, I saw the light!*

Happy? No sorrow in sight? Wasn't a war raging? What right did they have to claim no sorrow, just because it was hidden behind a veil of ocean? Couldn't they feel its sting in the rationing? In the fact that every young, strong male was disappearing into that void?

Nellie must not see the light they were singing about. It only looked dark from her vantage point. She only saw the night.

She slipped out of the room as it filled with a spiritual energy she couldn't share. Outside, the stillness and cold immediately invited her to be at peace. Her breath billowed puffs of steam. The stars shone clear in the crystalline atmosphere of the winter night.

Here, she sensed God. It was harder for her to find him in the overcrowded, stifling room where her mother proclaimed and all spoke their *amens* and *hallelujahs* of assent. But Nellie could feel him in the stillness. It was why she believed, even though she didn't see. She closed her eyes and breathed deeply.

And he walks with me, and he talks with me
And he tells me I am his own
And the joy we share as we tarry there
None other has ever known.

The lyrics of the hymn seemed to gently rush around her in the breeze. She walked a way down the road, pulling her coat tightly around her and tying her scarf under her chin.

"Dear Lord Jesus," she whispered. "I'm a mess inside. Just a jumble of thoughts and feelings. I don't know what I should do or where I should go. I only know I'd rather Mother didn't get to decide this time. Can you help me? Can you show me your peace?"

She took another deep breath of icy air. The silence surrounded her like a blanket of warmth despite the chill. She sighed in relief.

Until the church doors opened and all the happy bodies tumbled out. At the sight of her parents and siblings, she felt that squeeze around her heart again.

Late that night when Nellie thought Emma Jane was fast asleep, her sister nudged her. "Why did you leave church tonight, Nellie Mae?"

Nellie sighed. Why indeed? Mother had already grilled her on the subject. Didn't Nellie realize her actions were reflected on everyone else in the family? How could the congregation trust their elders if their own children were unruly?

Nellie had said nothing out loud. *I'm just not like you. I don't think I find God as easily in a crowded room with a lot of noise. I like to walk and pray on my own. It's easier to focus.*

"You don't get to come to God the way you want, Nellie." Her mother's voice was forceful. "Hebrews 10:25: 'Not forsaking the assembling of ourselves together, as the manner of some is; but exhorting one another: and so much the more, as ye see the day approaching.'"

"The Bible also says for women to learn in silence and not to teach or usurp authority over a man."

There. Nellie had said it. She cringed for the swift punishment for talking back. For about five seconds, she actually left her mother speechless.

"Nellie Mae, don't go and use the Good Book for your own ends to disrespect your mother." Dad spoke from the kitchen table in the next room. His tone was firm, but she knew he'd been trying to spare her Mother's reaction.

Nellie lowered her head. "I'm sorry. I don't mean disrespect, really. I guess I'm just asking what that verse means and why it doesn't apply," she said in a penitent tone. She almost added *to you, Mother*, but she was afraid to be that direct. She was already skating on thin ice.

She waited, staring at her hands fidgeting in her lap.

Her mother cleared her throat, and when she spoke her tone had the faintest hint of defensiveness. "The Bible is meant to be understood as a whole, not in parts. And it is also meant to be understood through the context of the early church. What it meant to them."

Her mother's answer, as usual, made sense, but she wasn't sure her question had really been answered.

"Nellie Mae, we are a congregation that believes God can call anyone to stand up and proclaim his word, just as he did in the Bible with men and women of faith. You know that. The passage you are referring to addresses specific problems in a church where women without knowledge were attempting to take control. That's not how our church works."

Nellie gave a slight nod, staring hard at her fingers in her lap.

Her father came to the door and leaned against the doorjamb, considering his wife with a gentle gaze. "Sometimes God calls women to preach. Your mother has felt that burden since she was a little girl. I fully support her allowing God to work through her, and the two of us are one in the eyes of heaven. We've discussed this before. Why are you doubting?"

Nellie Mae only shrugged.

"It's been no secret you've been unhappy here," her mother said in measured tones. "I know of a family in Mississippi who needs help –"

"No!" Nellie Mae sat up quickly. "Please don't send me off again! I just couldn't bear it."

Her mother's face went red. Nellie could tell she was angry, but so was Nellie, and she was tired of concealing her emotions to defer to her mother's.

"There is no greater calling than servanthood," her mother began, but her voice faltered.

"What is it you want?" Dad spoke suddenly to Nellie.

Nellie thought about the question. She had no solid answer. Did she want to marry Johnny and move to Indiana? She wasn't sure, and she wasn't sure it mattered at this point whether she wanted it or not, since he might not come back and surely wouldn't for a few years. Did she want to go to school? Yes, but she couldn't. Not for a few months. So what did she want to do in the meantime?

She had no earthly idea.

Nellie felt Emma Jane reach for her hand. "I'm not getting married till fall. I think you and I should go to Indianapolis and work at the war plant."

"The RCA plant?" Nellie was surprised. "You really want to do that? Don't you have a wedding to plan?"

"Edward doesn't come home on leave until May. We've got a

few months to give our service to our country. Our men can cross the ocean and fight evil over there, so why can't we give our summer to help fight it here?"

Nellie Mae squeezed her sister's hand. "Let's do it."

Twenty-Two

Emma Jane's suggestion turned out to be the best idea Nellie thought she'd ever had. And to their surprise, Mother agreed, thought maybe Mother was just tired of dealing with them. Regardless of the reason, the result was the same. Dad drove them in the car to Indianapolis where he left them in the care of a boardinghouse owner who specialized in overseeing girls working for the war effort.

Mrs. Miner showed them around the house as she recited a long list of rules. There would be no breaking curfew of ten p.m. No male visitors were allowed except in the parlor and with permission, and Mrs. Miner would attend all such meetings. They were not to have food in the bedrooms as it encouraged mice. Their skirts must not be shorter than the knee, they must not wear gaudy makeup, and they must never drink alcohol. No noise or lights after curfew.

Despite the abundance of rules, they liked their hostess. She showed the girls to a pleasant dormer room. Two other girls who worked at the war plant lived in the mirror room across the hall.

They all got along fine, and Nellie even felt a twinge of happiness.

For the first time in her life, Nellie felt free. She wasn't, though. Not really. In some ways, her time would be more restricted now than ever before. But the burden of her mother's expectations was gone. Her work would be of her own choosing, not forced upon her.

It wasn't hard to secure jobs at the plant. The man who oversaw the girls, Mr. Smith, seemed happy with them. He sent Emma Jane straight to the floor to begin working in the factory. Nellie Mae was kept in the office to assist with paperwork. She figured it was because she knew shorthand and had typing and math skills, having taken her school classes a little more seriously than Emma had. Those abilities came in handy in an office setting. She didn't think she was all that good, but as long as Mr. Smith was satisfied, she'd do the best she could.

"Nellie Mae, you know he thinks you're pretty," Emma Jane whispered that night after lights were out and they were in bed. Nellie had been saying she had no idea what on earth that man was thinking making her his secretary.

She knew her sister was just trying to make her feel better. Nellie knew she was plain. Not quite homely, but not at all pretty. It was nice of Emma Jane to try to spare her feelings, but it wasn't the truth.

"I look like a goat," Nellie Mae huffed. "And we both know it."

Emma Jane sighed loudly. So loudly Nellie was afraid their hostess might overhear. "Nellie, you're such a dunce. You just say things like that to get attention."

"Say what?" Nellie had no idea what she meant.

"That you're ugly as a goat. As if you really have no idea you're the most beautiful girl to walk into any room. Like you don't know the effect you have on any given male in speaking distance. Surely you're just playing humble to get attention."

Nellie was incensed. "I am doing nothing of the sort, and you stop teasing me about my looks!"

Emma Jane gave up with another disgusted sigh and stopped talking. She was asleep within a minute. Nellie Mae stared at the ceiling and let the blackness overwhelm her soul.

You're not good enough. You're disgusting. How could you ever make anyone look at you, you toad?

She wiped away a tear in the corner of her eye and tried to push back the evil thoughts. She tried to remember all the nice people she'd met that day. She tried to be thankful they were on their own in the big city of Indianapolis. But her mind only wanted to ruminate.

She was ugly.

She was a burden.

She'd never amount to anything.

After work on Friday, Emma tried to convince Nellie to go to the local dance hall instead of going back to the boardinghouse for dinner.

"Emma! You know mother wouldn't approve of dancing," Nellie reminded her sister, surprised she'd even suggest it.

"Mother's not here," Emma Jane replied with a wink. As Nellie shook her head in dismay, Emma laughed. "Oh, come on, don't be a fuddy duddy. We won't dance, of course. But it's our duty to help cheer up the soldiers on leave, isn't it?"

So Nellie applied her brightest red lipstick and fluffed her curls the best she could. She wore a bow in the center of the back of her head, but Emma wore hers to the side, since she was engaged to be married. Nellie saw it and felt a momentary stab of envy. She wanted to belong to somebody. Maybe then she'd feel worthy. She wouldn't just be a waste of skin.

Nellie was only at the dance hall fifteen minutes before she knew her sister was right to insist they come. It was a happy atmosphere.

Not an easy, calm happy, but an urgent happy, as if everyone in the building were determined to have the best night of their life, since it well could be their last.

Emma Jane bought burgers and sodas while Nellie scanned the crowd. A couple soldiers approached before she'd gotten her scarf off.

"Wanna dance, sugar?" The first one held out a hand. Nellie's face flushed hot, but she flashed him her brightest smile.

"Sorry, soldier, I don't dance."

He was disappointed, but he stayed to talk to them for a few minutes. While he was telling the story of how he'd joined up, Nellie's eyes fell on a familiar face. She gasped in surprise.

"What is it, doll?" the soldier asked with a smile.

She shook her head. "Excuse me, will you?" She patted his arm and thanked him for the conversation.

She stared across the room to the very outer edge, shaking her head in disbelief. How could he be here? He was supposed to be on the other side of the world. And yet she'd know that soulful pair of eyes anywhere. Solemn, but with a hint of teasing. Bearing the weight of the world. There was no mistake – it was Johnny.

She started to approach him when a hand caught her arm from behind. She whirled around and saw Lola.

"Oh, hello," she said, glancing back toward Johnny to make sure he hadn't been a daydream. She didn't think he'd spotted her yet. If he had, he didn't want her to know. Maybe he didn't care that she was there. Maybe he had his eyes on someone else. After all, she hadn't seen him in months. He could be a different person by now.

She looked back at Lola. "What are you doing here, of all places?" she said with a forced laugh. But Lola didn't smile. Her eyes traveled to where Johnny stood before she looked back at Nellie in desperation.

"Let me," Lola pleaded, nodding toward Johnny. "Just let me

have a chance first."

Nellie Mae started to argue. Then she remembered that for every opportunity she'd had in life, Lola had missed one. Nellie had parents who cared very much what happened to her. Lola had a bed in an orphanage. It was time for Lola to have a chance, and both the girls knew it.

"Go," Nellie said with a nod. She even managed a smile. "Good luck."

Lola hurried across the room. Nellie didn't miss the way Johnny's eyes lit up when he saw her. He took off his paratrooper cap as he greeted her. She hugged him, and he led her to the dance floor.

"Isn't that Johnny?" Emma Jane said as she brought the baskets of food and the drinks to their table. "Of all the people I expected to see here tonight – he wasn't one of them." Emma glared at Nellie Mae. "Why in the world aren't you with him?"

Nellie Mae shrugged and sank into her seat, crossing her legs and taking a casual sip from the straw of her soda. Her lips left dark red prints on the white straw. "I'm sure he isn't interested."

"Nellie Mae Thomas, you stop that right now!" Emma Jane stamped her foot for dramatic effect. "I'm so tired of hearing it. You're a beautiful girl with a lot to offer any young man. Besides, you have to at least have an inkling that half the men in this room are staring at you. Including Johnny!"

Nellie Mae rolled her eyes. "You have quite an imagination, that's for sure."

Emma looked back at Johnny and Lola. "Isn't that our cousin? She's dancing with him, Nellie." Emma Jane sat down and took a bite of her burger. "I hardly think he'd choose to talk to her over you."

Nellie Mae looked at her sister in surprise, but she saw the humor in her eyes. She chuckled. "Shame on you, Emma Jane."

"Seems to me Johnny's eyes are straying this way. Don't you think?"

"You're plain awful." Nellie kicked her sister under the table. "Now stop it."

"Here he comes!"

Nellie looked up from Emma Jane's triumphant smile to see Johnny walking toward them. Lola trailed behind with a sour expression.

"Well, look what the cat dragged in." Nellie Mae tried to be aloof, and earned a glare from her sister.

Emma Jane stood and took Lola's arm. "Why, if it isn't my dear little cousin. It's been too long! Sit down and tell me all your news. Nellie, now move, and let Lola sit there."

Nellie Mae knew exactly what her sister was doing. She hesitantly stood up and offered Lola her seat, which left her standing next to Johnny. An electric thrill filled her and made her heart beat faster. He took her hand and gestured to the dance floor.

"Sorry, Johnny. I can't dance with you."

"Why not?" He looked wounded.

"It's not you," she said with a laugh. "I just don't dance."

He smiled and nodded as he led her to a bench instead.

"Something's different about you," she said, watching his face thoughtfully. She saw an added measure of confidence and assumed the army had instilled it in him, but she saw something else, too. Grief? "I can't put my finger on it."

He shrugged. "I'm stronger, I guess." He grinned and flexed his solid shoulder muscles so she could feel them. He wasn't kidding.

"That's not it." She smiled at him. He was taller and thicker, though it wasn't saying much considering how thin he'd been when she'd met him. It was all written in his eyes.

"You seem more alive," she finally said. It occurred to her the words might sound silly, but he nodded in agreement.

146

"I've jumped out of planes at twelve hundred feet, Kit," he said in a quiet voice only meant for her. She felt her cheeks warm at the sound of the nickname. "There's nothing on God's green earth that can make you feel more alive than that."

"I think I'll take your word for it," she said with a laugh.

"Aw, you could do it," he disagreed. "You're spunky. I bet you would if I dared you."

She playfully narrowed her eyes and pinched his arm, realizing there wasn't much skin to grab hold of with all the muscle. He didn't even flinch. She laughed. "And then I'd kill you."

"Nah, you like me too much."

"Why, Johnny Hagaman, you're a downright flirt these days!"

He smirked. She saw it again. The briefest glimpse of sadness behind his smiling eyes. She realized he hadn't told her why he was home. She was afraid to ask.

"What are you doing back in Indianapolis?" he asked. "I didn't expect to see you. Only hoped."

She sighed. "I didn't want Mother to find me another job before school started. I'm determined I'm going to finish high school, and she seems determined I don't. So, when Emma Jane suggested we come up and get jobs at the RCA building for a couple months, I jumped at the chance. We're doing something good, anyway, for the war effort."

"Why wouldn't your mother want you to finish high school?" Johnny glanced around the dark hallway where couples stood close together, talking softly.

She shrugged. She didn't want to talk about Mother. "Johnny, what's wrong? Why'd you have to come home?"

His gaze went to the floor and his jaw flexed. "My aunt died."

"Do you mean Peter's mother?"

He nodded.

"Oh, Johnny, I'm so sorry," she said quietly. "What happened?"

He mashed his lips together and stared at the floor for a long moment. "She was murdered."

Twenty-Three

Tears blurred Nellie's vision. She scooted closer and slipped her arm around him. "Oh, Johnny."

"She went into the city for a few things. She was walking home from the station and a guy in a truck offered her a ride. She wouldn't have thought it odd; it happens all the time in Beech Grove." He raised his gaze and stared out the open door. "She had parcels and she was happy to accept. But once he got her loaded up and started down the road, he sped up and passed up her street. Who knows what happened inside the truck, either she tried to escape or he pushed her out, but she was thrown from the truck and smashed her head on the road. She was dead before anyone could get to her."

Nellie swallowed hard. "I can't even imagine being thrown from a car like that. The poor woman."

"I can't even believe it's real. She was the sweetest lady you could ever meet. She was like a second mother ... I spent so much time over there growing up." Johnny's voice was gravelly. "When I think about some lousy drunk doing that to *my* mother ..." He stopped talking and his gaze returned to the floor.

Nellie didn't know what to say and she wasn't sure her voice would work, so she just kept rubbing circles on his back with her fingers.

"Funeral was yesterday. It's a somber place at home. Peter came home from the Marines. He's just ..."

As his voice trailed off, Nellie nodded. "Heartbroken."

"Yeah."

They were quiet for a long time. Nellie half-listened to the conversations all around her. Boys confessing their undying love, maybe even to girls they'd only met that night. She would have laughed if the mood had called for it. Conversation sure wasn't Johnny's strong point.

But looking at him now, she understood. She needed to take his mind off his pain. "Look at you," she said, suddenly awed by his accomplishments in such a short time. She brushed her fingers against the silver jump wings pinned to his crisply ironed shirt. "I don't know why you want to sit with little 'ole me. You're a hero."

He breathed a short laugh and sat up. "No place I'd rather be." His arm went around her shoulders. "How's Missouri?"

Nellie brightened. "Oh! Dad met Harry Truman. They were having quite the conversation when I happened upon them."

"Harry Truman, the senator? He's a big deal. Some say he might run with Roosevelt for the presidency."

"I don't know about all that," she said, thinking more about his fingers wrapped around her shoulder than politics.

"Is your mother well?" Johnny's question was polite. Like he was playing along, trying to get their thoughts on things other than funerals and grieving.

Nellie tried not to let her voice falter as she answered. "She started preaching regular in church. I want to be proud of her, I do, but sometimes I'm just embarrassed."

She didn't mean to say the words aloud. She expected Johnny might admonish her for her uncharitable words, but he didn't. He only nodded. "I can imagine." He was thoughtful as he stared down the dimly lit hallway. "I think you always hanker for your mother's attention, but you feel like she's distracted by her ministry."

She stared at him in surprise. "Exactly. Yes. I'm a work horse to be hired out, not a daughter to be loved."

He nodded. "I can see how that might be hard. But I can also see her position. Maybe there's a reason she isn't able to be the mother you want. Maybe it doesn't have anything to do with you, but she doesn't know how to explain it."

"Well, if that doesn't beat all," Nellie said, unsure whether to be insulted or to kiss him right then and there. "You've gone and turned philosopher while you were gone."

They were silent again, but this time the silence didn't seem as awkward. Nellie didn't usually enjoy quiet, but she'd learned it was a big part of life with Johnny Hagaman. Now she sighed deeply, letting go of her tension and the morose cloud that had been following her around lately.

"What?" he asked quietly.

She shook her head. "I wouldn't know how to explain it, Johnny. Sometimes it's just like I fall in a hole and I have to pull myself out of it."

"Are you sick?"

"No," she said, squeezing his fingers when they reached for hers. His skin was warm and soft. "Not sick in body so much. But sometimes I'm awful tired. And it makes me feel like I can't do anything right. My brain gets foggy and my heart's not in anything. I just want to sleep all the time."

His forehead crinkled with concern. "I didn't know that. Have you seen the doctor?"

"I have," she said, waving him off. "Here and in Missouri. They say I just have a delicate constitution. I think it's a nice way of saying I'm plumb crazy."

She expected him to say something, but he only watched her. Maybe he thought she was crazy too.

"What do your parents say?" he finally asked.

"Dad is concerned. I know he is. But he doesn't know what to do other than send me to another doctor. My mother believes I don't have enough faith to get well."

"What does faith have to do with it?" Johnny rubbed his thumb over the top of her hand, sending shivers down her back.

She laughed humorlessly. "I don't rightly know. I've seen my mother lay her hands on sick kids, and they immediately get well. My little cousin had leukemia before Mother healed him. But she's never tried to do that for me. I guess she has her reasons. Maybe I'm not good enough for God to heal."

"That doesn't sound like God, Nellie Mae. Not from what I've learned recently. God is love."

She shrugged and sighed again, staring at their entwined hands. She was peaceful. Calmer than she'd felt in weeks, really. The tension seemed to creep out of her pores the longer she sat there in the dim light with Johnny.

"If I were your husband, I'd make sure you got well."

His soft words echoed in her mind like he'd yelled them. She pressed her lips together. "Johnny, I'm a project, not a catch," she whispered. "You'd do better to find yourself a girl who will dote on you."

She was a dolt for saying it, she was sure. But he squeezed her hand.

"I don't want any other girl. You're the only girl I ever think of." He seemed like he was going to leave it at that, but he suddenly started talking and didn't stop. "I think of you when I'm exercising and when I'm at meals and when I'm jumping out of planes in the pitch black. You're the last thought before I sleep. You're my first thought when I wake up. I can't stop thinking of you."

She was breathless. Why in the world did he think so much about her? What was there to even think about? Was he blind?

152

"I don't know why you'd do that," she managed awkwardly.

He stubbornly shook his head. "You're worth the time. Trust me."

The night wore on and they talked of many things. Well, Nellie talked mostly, and Johnny listened. They sat together until the lights were turned off and they were shooed out of the building. Then they stood beside Johnny's car and talked long after Emma and Lola had gone home to bed. Nellie knew she had missed curfew, but she couldn't make herself care. Emma Jane would cover for her. She didn't want to break the spell of the magical evening.

She knew her mother would not approve of her behavior. Good Christian girls didn't stay out all hours of the night with boys. Dad would be disappointed that she wasn't honoring her good name. But she wanted to be with Johnny as long as she could before the war reached out and swallowed him back up. Before he was jumping out of planes and fighting enemies in a far-off place so mysterious she could hardly conjure up images.

"I should have taken you home a long time ago," Johnny said as he glanced at his watch. "I'm going to get you in trouble."

"I don't want to go home yet."

He smiled. "Me either." He took her in his arms then. She breathed deeply against his chest, smelling cloves and Old Spice aftershave.

"Your hair smells good." He sniffed her head. She giggled and leaned back, looking up into his eyes. It proved a dangerous move. He looked at her lips and she felt a wave of fear along with a good dose of anticipation.

"Has anyone ever kissed you before?" he asked.

"Just you."

"Honey, if I'd kissed you, I would have remembered," he disagreed.

"At the train station."

"That's not the kind of kiss I mean."

She blushed. "Then no. I mean, plenty of boys have asked, but my parents are strict about that and –"

He didn't let her finish her sentence. His lips met hers and for the first time Nellie Mae understood what it meant in books when the characters saw fireworks kissing their sweethearts. Her mind dazzled with a dozen different feelings as she leaned into him and did what seemed natural. He held her waist close and she could almost imagine them as movie stars in a picture at the closing scene.

"I love you," he whispered when he finally pulled away. She wanted to return the words, but something held her back. She smiled and patted his cheek.

"You're quite a guy," she said. He seemed to accept the words.

"I want you to marry me." His words came tumbling from his mouth, faster than he was thinking them, she thought. "I don't have a ring and I know I'm going off to war, but someday, I want you to be my wife."

She wanted to be exultant. She'd been waiting a lifetime to hear those words. But again, fear choked out any excitement she could feel at the prospect of being his wife.

"Let's get through this awful war first, Johnny. Then we'll talk."

His face fell at her answer. She put her hand on his chest and stared at the button on his collar, unable to meet his gaze any longer. "I think it's time you take me home."

He gave a silent nod and opened her door. They didn't say another word.

Twenty-Four

Emma Jane was waiting when Nellie Mae finally got back to the boardinghouse. She'd been waiting by the door to let her in.

"I was so worried," she said after they sneaked through the parlor and up the stairs to their room without waking anyone.

Nellie Mae wasn't in the mood for a lecture. Tension and anger built inside until she tore back the covers on the bed angrily and made a sound of frustration.

"You've no right to be angry at anyone except yourself. You know better, Nellie. If Mother finds out ..."

It would have been easy to respond in anger if Nellie hadn't known very well her sister was right. But who cared? Feelings bombarded her like the bombs falling on London an ocean away. Destroying the walls she'd put up to protect herself.

"Nellie Mae, were you compromised?" Emma Jane asked in a worried tone.

Nellie gasped and shook her head. "Of course not! Johnny's honorable. We just got to talking and lost track of time."

"I'll say." Emma glanced at the clock on the bedside table. "It's a quarter to two!"

Nellie Mae sighed and threw herself back on the bed. "He wanted me to say I'd marry him."

Emma Jane's entire demeanor changed. "Nellie Mae Thomas!

Why didn't you say so? Why in the world are you so down in the mouth if he was out there proposing to you? Isn't that what you want?"

Nellie Mae shrugged, staring at the ceiling. "He's too good for me, Em. I can't even think what he sees in me. I'd be a burden to him the rest of his life. I can't do that to him."

Emma Jane sat down on the bed and breathed a soft sigh. "Nellie Mae, what kind of funhouse mirror have you been looking into your whole life? It's like you can't even see yourself for who you really are."

Nellie Mae met her sister's baffled gaze. "I can. And it's not a pretty sight."

"You're beautiful. And not just on the outside, you have a beauty and vitality that just springs up out of your soul. You're so friendly … how many times have I been jealous of your ability to light up a room with your laugh and conversation? You put people at ease. Besides that, you're smart with numbers, well-read, great with little kids. What man in his right mind wouldn't want that?"

Nellie only shrugged again, determined not to fall for the lovely words her sister spoke. She knew the truth. She knew the darkness underneath the surface.

"I'm not joking, Nellie Mae," Emma said insistently. "I'm just about fed up with this hatred you carry around for yourself. I don't know where you picked it up, but you're believing lies. You're a good person. Better than me."

Nellie didn't answer. Eventually, Emma Jane lay down and fell asleep. But Nellie couldn't get her mind to settle. She thought about Johnny. About his proposal. She thought about the awful way she'd reacted to it. She considered what Emma Jane had said, over and over. It was hard to believe it was true. She wanted to – badly – but she was more than a little afraid of being disappointed to find out she'd been right about herself all along.

How was she supposed to look in the mirror and see anything but an awkward, homely girl with the gap in her front teeth and frizzy hair that refused to curl the way the girls in the magazines looked? And what about her ever-smudged lipstick and eyes too small for her face? She'd taken plenty of pictures on her little camera that Dad had bought her the last Christmas. They confirmed she didn't have much to offer in the way of looks.

But if Johnny wanted to marry her, maybe she shouldn't hesitate. Maybe he'd be sorry for asking later when he realized her true nature and how terrible she looked when she'd just gotten out of bed. But who knew? Maybe he'd stay blind his whole life. Maybe it would work out.

She would like to have a family. She loved children and she was good with them; she knew that, at least. To have her own children would fulfill one of her dearest desires. And Johnny would be a good father, wouldn't he? He'd teach his children how to fish and take care of animals and appreciate nature and learn to be quiet and hear God's voice. He'd teach them not to be afraid of anything but to run after their purpose. He was good with kids, too. He was kind to Harvey. And once she'd seen him kneel and talk to a little boy who'd lost his dog. He'd eased the boy's frantic crying and gone with him until they found the puppy exploring the woods nearby. Then Johnny had sat and played with that puppy for all of ten minutes before he remembered Nellie was waiting on him. She hadn't minded. She'd leaned against his car and watched with a smile the whole time. All the while realizing what a good father this man could be someday.

If the problem of her own dark side wasn't enough of an obstacle, Nellie Mae knew for certain relationships were hard. She'd been by Hodges' Mill in Willow Springs enough to know that some couples fought loudly and incessantly for the entirety of their marriage. She didn't want to live in constant conflict. Her spirit craved peace. She wanted to know that she could be herself and not have to constantly prove she was worth her skin. Did Johnny want that, too? Or would he turn out to be one of those smoking, drinking, beating kind of husbands like Hodges who took all their frustration out on their wives and children?

She didn't want any part of that. And who knew if Johnny would stay pleasant and mild as he got older?

It wasn't until five in the morning that she finally made her decision and fell asleep.

She'd meet him at the train before he left to return to Fort Bragg in the morning. Union Station was on the way from the boardinghouse to the RCA plant.

She'd say yes.

Johnny threw his pack on the pile with the other luggage to be stored below the bus. He hung back from the crowd that had gathered. Family members saying goodbye, soldiers kissing their girls, lone travelers waiting idly for the bus to begin loading.

He eyed the street in front of Union Station. He'd been trying to keep his mind off the sadness. He hated seeing Pete so broken up. The funeral had been one of the saddest events he'd ever attended. Beech Grove was a quiet place. A safe place. When he had occasion to pass the police station, the cops were always inside at their desk with their feet up, drinking coffee. Nothing bad ever happened.

In a way, his little hometown was a little like the world – suddenly going crazy. A woman just trying to bring home a few groceries thrown from the truck of a drunken man. Her skull cracked in just the right way to lose her life. Who'd have ever expected such a thing? It was unthinkable. And in a country across the ocean, a guy with an ugly mustache got it into his head that he could control everyone and everything and get rid of anyone different than himself. If a man walked up to Johnny on the street and said he was taking over the world, he would laugh at him. And yet here they all were – men from every corner of the world having to put their lives on hold, or even sacrifice their lives to put this man back in his place.

The world was a strange place. There was no denying it.

He glanced up and down the street again. There was a small part of him – okay, a rather large part – that hoped Nellie Mae might show up. She'd been unhappy when he'd dropped her off in the wee hours of the morning. Probably because of his lousy excuse for a proposal. He'd been kicking himself all morning because of it.

He checked his watch. The bus would leave in fifteen minutes. His eyes returned to the street. Right. Left. Nothing.

But suddenly from around the corner a familiar face flooded his view and his silly heart leaped for joy. But as the woman came closer, he saw it wasn't the one he'd been longing for. She didn't have the wispy brown hair or the teasing smile or the adorable red lipstick and high heels of the woman he wanted to see. Instead, Nellie's cousin Lola approached him.

He gave her a polite smile. Her hands were in her pockets as she glanced at him with a guarded expression. "Hello, Johnny."

"Hello, Lola."

He thought he should say something, but he wasn't sure what. Lola was a good kid. She reminded him of Nancy in some ways. They'd had some good times together back on Christmas break when Nellie was in Missouri.

"Why did you abandon me last night?" Her tone suggested she was teasing, but he couldn't be completely sure.

He shrugged, uncomfortable. "Hadn't seen Nellie in a few months. We were catching up."

"I thought we had something," she said, not looking him in the eye as she spoke. "But I understand. I see why you like her."

He felt bad as he watched her twist her handkerchief. "I didn't mean anything by it." He wanted to be honest. He could see she was interested. He should have figured a boy and girl couldn't be friends without complications.

She huffed quietly, but she didn't cry. Johnny gave her credit for that. "When you were coming around so often at Christmas, I guess I kind of thought you were interested. I should have known better, though. I'm a fool."

Johnny felt like the fool. "I'm really sorry. I didn't mean to give you the wrong impression. I guess I thought of you as a little sister. I'm older than you."

She regarded him with an even expression. "I'm not even a year younger than Nellie Mae."

She had him pinned in the corner. What else could he say? He hated seeing her upset because of his stupidity. He had been leaning against the bus, but he stood up and took a step closer to her. He took one of her hands. "I'm truly sorry, Lola. I think you're swell. I just …"

"You love someone else," she finished for him, resignation thick in her voice.

"You're going find a great guy, Lola. I know it." Johnny kissed her cheek.

She gave him a half-hearted smile. "Thanks, Johnny. Take care of yourself. Don't get killed."

"I'll do my best, kiddo."

She walked away. He watched her, thinking how her height and gait reminded him of Nellie. He smiled, feeling sad and contented and wistful all at once.

"Well of all the nerve."

He was instantly filled with joy at the sound of Nellie's voice behind him. He whirled around to see her in all her glory, complete with lipstick and heels. "You came!" He reached for her, but her stance was rigid. She had her fists on her hips and she was breathing kind of fast for a young, fit girl. If he didn't know better, he'd say she was angry. Really angry. But at him? Why? "What's the matter, Nellie Mae?"

She made a strangled sound of disbelief. "I came all the way downtown to say goodbye to you, Johnny Hagaman," she began in a hushed, scathing tone. "Even though I bet my desk at work will be ready to walk away, it will have such a load on it."

"And I'm awful grateful you came," he said hopefully.

"Could have fooled me! Here you are kissing my cousin! Not twelve hours after you asked me to marry you."

It dawned on him what it had looked like to Nellie. "No, you got it all wrong," he promised, reaching for her arms. "I was letting her down easy."

"I'll say," she said with ice in her voice, moving away from his reach. "I just can't trust you, Johnny. You've betrayed me."

She turned on her smart red heel and headed back the other direction, pulling her coat tightly around her even though the day wasn't too cold. Although it felt ten degrees colder in her wake.

He met the eyes of an older gentleman carrying a newspaper. The man shook his head. "Looks like you blew it. Never let them see you with the other woman."

Johnny sighed and watched Nellie go. He would run after her, but he couldn't miss his bus. The army didn't respond well to men coming back from furlough late. As much trouble as he was in with Nellie, he'd be in more with Uncle Sam if he didn't get on that bus.

He had to go. He had to go and leave his heart right there in Indianapolis.

Twenty-Five

In the months that followed, Johnny was plagued with constant restlessness. He stopped reading his Bible and praying. When the boys offered him a smoke, he took it. He especially went for those thick cigars. He imagined himself a man's man when he smoked them. The exact opposite of what Nellie Mae had made him feel like when she left him standing by that bus.

When the men went into town for drinking parties on the weekends, he joined them, even though a part of him was disgusted by the off-color jokes and rough language of his fellow soldiers. Johnny developed a taste for beer, enjoying the way his brain slowed and he didn't think so much about Nellie after he'd had a few. She'd disapprove of his behavior. He was sure God already did. But he was headed for war. There were precious few joys where he was headed. Didn't he deserve to have a good time once in a while? To forget what he was losing?

Soon enough, higher ups spoke of shipping out to England come the end of August. Johnny was actually relieved to hear it. He thought it might help to put more distance between him and his grief over all his recent losses and misses. That is, until Grovenburg pulled him aside during mortar platoon exercises.

"I pulled some strings, Hagaman. Got you one more leave."

"I just came back from furlough for my aunt's funeral. Said goodbye to everyone."

Grovenburg laughed like Johnny was missing something important. "The leave is already settled, so you have to use it. Why don't you go see your girl?"

"But I didn't request it." Johnny didn't want to disrespect Grovenburg, him being a sergeant, but he was annoyed.

"I heard you talking to Day," Grovenburg admitted. "This girl you've got – she sounds like a once-in-a-lifetime kind of special. I had a girl like that back home, and I didn't take the time to write her while we were at Curahee. When I got home in January, she'd already found another guy. I missed my chance. I don't want you to do the same."

Johnny considered the offer. "I don't think she's still in Indianapolis. School will be starting soon."

"Do you know where she is?"

"I have her address in Missouri." Johnny shrugged.

"Then go see her. Put it to rest, one way or another, so you can focus on the task at hand. I haven't missed your moping. You need to settle it."

Johnny nodded, but he wasn't sold on the idea. Avoidance sounded like a much better idea than meeting the problem head-on. "I don't know what I'd say. She was mad as a hornet when I left."

"Did she have a right?" Grovenburg asked.

Johnny shrugged. "She misunderstood."

"So go explain it to her. It's all you can do."

Johnny didn't know why Grovenburg was so interested, but now that the offer had been made, he was intrigued by the idea of seeing her one more time. Maybe they didn't have to end on such a sour note.

"It's different over there," Grovenburg said. He watched the second platoon go through their mortar exercises and frowned.

"In England?"

"Anywhere really, except here, Hagaman," the other man said. Though Grovenburg couldn't be too much older than Johnny, he seemed to have a store of wisdom not common for his age. Born of experience, maybe? Johnny wondered about his story. "You know, we're in this bubble here in America. I hear from the men who've already been in battle. We're headed to a terrible place. People are dying, and it's not just soldiers. It's women. Children. Elderly. I hear about some of the garbage the Nazis are doing to decent folk. I hear about all those little kids in London being sent away to the country because their homes are being bombed … I don't know. I just think we need to tie up all our loose ends before we go. To be prepared."

"You mean be ready to die." Johnny reached for the cigar Grovenburg offered him. The tangy smoke filled his lungs and satisfied something inside him. Maybe it dulled the fear a little. Made him feel more like a man.

"Not just ready to die. I think the worst would be having to live with whatever we see over there – if we survive."

Johnny hadn't considered that. Honestly, he had a hard time imagining war at all. He'd lived his life in the safe cocoon of the idyllic American life. He'd never been hungry without finding something to eat. He'd never been in a squabble with another boy and come out with anything more than a scrape. He had a head full of imagination, but no experience to go along with it. Part of him dreaded what might be in store. Part of him anticipated it.

Now, thinking about it, he couldn't help but wonder if war was going to change him into a completely different person.

For her birthday, Nellie went to the soda fountain with Martha, Bill and Henry. It was a spur of the moment arrangement set up by Martha when she discovered it was Nellie's seventeenth birthday.

"Did your mother make you a cake?" Martha sipped her soda. Nellie smiled at her friend. She wished she could be as petite and dainty as Martha. Everything about her was cute as a button.

"She told me to have a happy birthday as she was headed out the door this morning. Someone from church had a sick baby."

"Is she a doctor?" Martha asked.

"No." Nellie didn't explain. Henry and Bill went to church with her sometimes, but she was afraid Martha wouldn't understand if she tried to explain her mother laying hands on babies and praying for their healing.

Nellie didn't care about celebrating her birthday. They had never been a big deal in her home. She had no right to expect special treatment just because it happened to be the same calendar day she'd entered the world.

"Her mama's a preacher," Henry explained to Martha, to Nellie's chagrin. He was sprawled in the seat next to her with his long arm behind her on the booth. Something in his lanky mannerism reminded her of Johnny, which felt like a stab to the chest.

"I wouldn't exactly put it that way, and neither would she," Nellie replied, but didn't elaborate. "Now Bill, we're all dying to hear what you decided. Are you joining up?"

"As soon as I'm old enough." Bill shrugged. "Henry too."

Nellie listened while the boys launched into a discussion about the process of joining the service after high school. She was glad she'd shifted the conversation, but the topic left her with a dull sadness. She didn't like thinking of her friends heading off to a mysterious dark war. Maybe it was because she knew Johnny was headed there soon, if he wasn't there already.

"You're exceptionally quiet tonight, Nellie." When there was a break in the conversation, Martha pinned her eyes on Nellie and wouldn't let go. "What's the matter?"

A boy they knew from school who waited tables at the soda fountain brought over their hamburgers and fries, flashing Nellie and Martha a smile as his cheeks turned red. She made sure she heartily thanked him before he walked away.

"Well, Martha, not a thing in the world is wrong," she lied. "Let's dig in. I'm so hungry I could eat a horse."

Martha made an expression of disgust at the thought, but she didn't stop watching Nellie suspiciously, like she knew there was something Nellie wasn't saying. Nellie took a big bite of her hamburger and attempted to chew and swallow it without choking. As she did, a shadow fell across their table.

"Well, if it isn't Nellie Mae Thomas. Our paths just keep crossing."

For a fraction of a moment, Nellie was sure it was Johnny. She almost leaped out of her seat with joy. But when she turned to look at him, she recognized the smug smile right away.

"Oh, hello there, James William." She tried not to sound disappointed. He didn't seem to notice and put a hand on the booth behind her and the other on the table next to her so that she was pinned between his arms. He leaned too close.

"Who's this?" Henry asked. Nellie could hear the suspicion in his voice. Bill and Martha didn't say anything, but Nellie didn't miss the distrust in either of their gazes.

She felt defensive. She wasn't sure why, but it irritated her that her friends viewed James William as a threat, as if it were some grave error on her part for being acquainted with the soldier. She smiled up at him. "This is James William Liman. He's a soldier in the army. And we're thankful for his service," she said with a tone of admonishment. Martha and the boys seemed less than impressed.

Nellie looked back at James William. "When do you ship out?"

"Soon." His face was a smirk. "Why are you hanging out with the little kids, Nellie Mae?"

She laughed, thinking he must be joking, but no one joined her. "Beg your pardon?" she finally asked.

"Baby-faced boys who can't join up and defend their country yet. You could do better." He shifted his eyes to Martha, giving her form a perusal that made all of them uncomfortable. Martha glared back.

"Just who do you think you are?" Bill's face had gone red. Nellie prayed he wouldn't start something. She had a feeling James William would be all too happy to give him a lesson or two.

James William chuckled. "Meet me when you're done with the schoolkids, Nellie Mae." He stood up straight and headed to the counter where a couple other soldiers were waiting for their orders.

Nellie glanced at her friends, embarrassed by James William's arrogant behavior. What had gotten into him? "I guess he's a little too big for his britches nowadays, isn't he?" She sipped her drink and looked out the window. No one commented further.

Bill, Henry and Martha decided to go to Martha's house to play games, but Nellie begged out, saying her tooth was hurting. It wasn't a lie. It had been aching for days, but she hadn't said anything because she hated going to the dentist. Just the thought of it made her stomach roll with anxiety. The last time she'd ended up in that chair, he'd ripped out two molars. Her gums were still sensitive months later.

She sighed and headed the opposite way on the street, kicking at the gravel that spread across the sidewalk. She wished many things were different. She almost wanted to go back to Indianapolis, but a deeper part of her being was determined to finish high school. As long as she got that diploma, she'd be able to say she'd made something of herself, despite her roots.

It all went back to her family, didn't it? It wasn't that she was ashamed of them. Her parents were honorable and brave, and they loved the Lord. She couldn't ask for more. But she saw a different perspective than they did – a bigger picture of the world she wanted to connect with. She longed for people to see her as independent and intelligent. With her friendliness, people often got the impression she was nothing but a dumb blonde. She hated being seen that way. She was smart, and she wanted people to know it.

Johnny doesn't think of me as a dumb blonde. He treats me like I'm worth something.

"It's time to stop thinking on Johnny Hagaman," she said firmly under her breath. "He's long gone and as good as dead."

"Don't nail the coffin shut just yet," a voice spoke next to her, startling her. She gasped and looked up to see Johnny standing in front of her, right there on Main Street in her little hick hometown in the middle of nowhere. His hands were on his hips and he was smiling that lopsided grin under his tipped paratrooper cap.

"Why, Johnny!" she cried. "Whatever are you doing in Willow Springs?"

His face was lit with hope. She'd been supposing he hated her after that tense parting they'd had at the bus station. But his expression was open. Vulnerable.

He took his cap off and fidgeted with it as he spoke. "I'm shipping out in a few weeks. I wanted to explain before I go."

"Well, explain what?" She glanced across the street to the post office, suddenly remembering why she had been so icy at their last encounter.

"I'm not interested in your cousin," he said plainly. She watched him struggle to find words. Standing up for himself didn't come naturally. Either that or he was lying.

"Sure could have fooled me and anyone else standing around that bus depot." She stared down at the sidewalk. A dog approached them, and she nudged it away with her foot, disgusted by its muddy fur and strong smell. Not Johnny. He knelt down and gave the dog a good scratch behind his filthy ears.

"Hey, there, sport." His tone changed, like his words came easy when he was talking to animals.

She twisted her mouth. "Whenever you two are done talking, I'll be waiting here."

Johnny looked up at her. Did his expression flash to annoyed, just for a moment? He slowly stood up and stuck his hands in his pockets. "You aren't the center of the universe, Nellie Mae."

She felt the sting immediately, and the rage just after that. She wanted to think of herself as a victim. The girl who wasn't paid any mind by her own mother. Always called upon to put her plans on hold for the emergencies of others. Selfless to a fault, giving more than required, committed to following God's commands no matter what it took.

But even if all those things were true, what he was saying held merit as well, and she knew it. She could do all the right things and store up all the good works, but it wouldn't make her heart right before God.

She was back to that mirror to stare at her own ugliness again. She could try to cover that darkness deep down with a veil of goodness, sweetness and sugar pie, but God saw straight through her disguise.

And apparently, so did Johnny.

She was both humiliated and awed. She didn't want him to see her for what she really was. But she'd never had someone come close enough to see beyond the surface. It meant something to her she couldn't ignore.

She met his eyes, determined not to cry. "When did I ever say I was the center of the universe?"

He leaned back on the brick wall of the store, his hands still buried in his pockets. "There's a fella on the other side of the ocean who thinks he is. Lots of folks dying over his ignorance."

Nellie nodded. "You're right about that." She peered at her feet, feeling shame. Maybe she was just like Hitler.

She felt a finger under her chin. He made her look at him again. "I'm not saying you're Hitler. Just saying pride's an awful thing to let get out of hand."

She agreed with him. "Of course, Johnny." But she didn't like the conversation. Not a single bit. She wanted to escape, to get away from the light he was shining into her messy heart. "So you came all the way to Missouri to tell me that I'm an ugly, proud little girl who isn't worth your important time?"

His hands returned to his pockets and he gazed away from her, down the street. She hadn't intended her words to be so biting, but she couldn't take them back.

He twisted his mouth and gave a little nod and a sigh. "I never said either." He shifted. "You have a maddening habit of putting words in my mouth."

"Well, it isn't like your words are pouring forth as it is." She clenched her fists at the sides of her flowered sundress.

"Is there a problem here?" Another male voice spoke behind Nellie, startling her. She turned around and tried to smile. "Hello, James William. You remember Johnny Hagaman, of course?"

"Well, sure," John shook Johnny's hand. The three of them stood in silence for a moment.

"You shipping out soon?" James William asked Johnny.

"End of August. You?"

"Next week."

Nellie noticed James William was standing close to her. Close enough that her skirt brushed against his uniform. She saw a twinge of jealousy in Johnny's face, and felt some hope. Maybe he did care for her after all.

When Johnny didn't say anything else, which was not surprising in the least, James William spoke. "I'll be waiting by the grocery when you're done with your conversation." He held her arm so tightly that it began to ache. He leaned over and kissed her cheek with wet lips. She wanted to rub the moisture away as he departed, but she resisted the urge.

Johnny watched James William saunter away. His eyes were narrowed.

"What now? You don't like him either? He's a soldier, for Pete's sake." Nellie scoffed. "Maybe no one quite meets Johnny's standards."

Johnny looked back at her, the even expression on his face aggravating her. "That guy's no good, Nellie."

She laughed, but the sound was harsh instead of amused. "How could you possibly know that after a two-sentence conversation? I've never had the slightest notion about James William. He's friendly, he's brave, and he makes me feel like I'm worth something to him."

"Sure you are. A trophy." Johnny shrugged. "But you take it any farther with him, and you'll regret it for the rest of your life."

"How could you know that?"

Johnny glanced at the other man. "I just get a sense."

"Same sense that tells you I think I'm the center of the universe?"

Johnny met her eyes. She could tell she'd finally riled him. "Same sense," he said.

"I don't have to stand here and take this. I have nothing more to say to you. I don't care to hang around men who make me feel like I'm nothing. Just go off to your war and jump out of your planes and do what you have to do. I'll stay here and forget all about you. Just watch me – I will!"

Nellie spun on her high heel and stepped into the dusty street. She crossed to James William; her head held high. She didn't look back, even once, though she did immediately regret what she'd said. She wouldn't give him the satisfaction of knowing she was exactly what he'd accused her of being.

"Goodbye, then, Nellie Mae," she heard his soft answer.

She almost turned back. The words stuck in her throat and refused to be said. *I'm sorry. You're right. Be careful. Don't die.*

I love you.

Twenty-Six

Johnny's first time in New York City was marred by the memory of his visit to see Nellie Mae. While his fellow soldiers took part in the night life, soaking up all the attention they could before they boarded that boat waiting out in the harbor, Johnny moped. Kept to himself. Stayed in his bunk during free time to write in his journal or read.

August flew by. Before any of them could possibly be prepared for it, they were told to pack up their trunks and tidy up the barracks one last time. They marched together to the ship, heralded by thousands of family, friends and well-wishers. They waved handkerchiefs and called their thanks to the men. Johnny didn't glance at the crowd – even once. Nobody he loved was there to see him off. He didn't want to see all the fellows that had people – especially their girls – to send them off properly.

The ship was intolerably overcrowded. Johnny heard one of his superiors mention that the S.S. Samaria would extend its capacity by four thousand men during this trip. The cabins of the luxury liner had been converted into bunks upon bunks for the men. They stacked as many as four beds high in most of the sleeping cabins.

Johnny wasn't fortunate enough to get a cabin. He was assigned to the deck. He had a makeshift cot that scraped back and forth across the wood in response to the waves. It got sopping wet in storms, too. Especially the night the ship made its way through the leftover high winds and rain from a massive hurricane. It battered the ship until nearly morning. Johnny's insides rocked as much as the cot, and the smell of vomit and sea water almost did him in.

"I'll take jumping out of planes over this any time," he said to the men unlucky enough to be on the deck with him. They chuckled and agreed.

Johnny figured no one was as glad as he was to see the shores of England come into view September 15. It seemed like the last few hours were the longest of the entire trip. Thousands of soldiers crowded the decks, collectively trying to will the creaking, lumbering ship to make landfall by evening.

It managed to do so. Johnny was one of the first down the ramp to solid ground. He wobbled, unsure of how to stand on cement that didn't move beneath him. It felt surreal. He'd come to expect the unsupported gait of the ship's movements. He'd grown used to his stomach having to fight to keep down any food he ate.

But once he acclimated, he was amazed by the sights. He kept forgetting they were there to fight and kill. England was mysterious and captivating, covered in mist and gray clouds that argued with sunshine all day long.

Ancient structures and antiquated homes dotted the sides of the rolling roads. They rode in military trucks, unceremoniously jostled in even rows as they witnessed the apparent peace and safety of the idyllic life.

But he knew better. The people living in these dwellings were daily afraid for their lives. They hid in bomb shelters and wore gas masks. Johnny saw the same look in every face they passed. He wasn't in the safe bubble of American society anymore. He'd been thrown among the people enduring the ravages of war.

The consideration caused him guilt. He'd been living the life, dreaming all his dreams, complaining about his safe and well-paying job in the factory. He'd been bored. He had longed for adventure. Wasn't that why he'd come here to this dark place? To be a part of the action?

He had envisioned playing the hero, but he had never considered the prospect of being part of the misery and despair. He could sense it in the air. It lingered in the spaces between every person trying to carry on with the will to live, pretending hell wasn't descending all around them.

After they arrived in Ramsbury, England, his life centered on waiting. Always waiting to be told what to do. More than that, he came to expect that everything happened at night. They learned to take their rest in warm autumn afternoons and evenings because it was all too common to be awakened an hour after falling asleep. They were sent on mock missions and trained to locate their objectives. They were handed a compass and a map and ordered to stage a practice attack on a certain location. Johnny came to look forward to the missions once he learned he was pretty good at them. He had a knack for maneuvering in the dark and taking charge, and the other men in his unit let him. He was promoted to mortar gunner instead of munitions carrier. Grovenburg said more than once he was planning on bringing Johnny's name to the brass as a candidate for sergeant.

Johnny wasn't sure how he felt about being a sarge. He liked the missions. He felt alive when he was in the zone and focused on the goal, but he didn't really want to be responsible for the other men's lives. He'd never actually been in combat. Would he be able to take control over men's destinies, sending them on missions that led them to their deaths? It was a heavy burden to carry. He supposed it was something that stuck with a person his whole life. If they survived long enough, that is.

But it didn't matter how he felt about it. There was little choice in the service. If he was promoted, he would have to complete his duties without complaining. And he would. Of that he was determined.

He spent his free time in Ramsbury outside. It was like his best dream, walking along the bubbling creeks with rolling hills painted behind them. He watched animals go about their simple business of living. The English village and countryside were a beautiful substitute for home, and he couldn't find a single fault.

Thoughts of Nellie Mae became the standard for his mind. He brought her to his consciousness whenever he could. The picture of her he kept in his mind's eye was a surreal contrast to the bitter purpose of war. Never mind she had the ever present potential to be as mad as a dog who'd been in a tangle with a porcupine. Here, as his mind played the reel called Nellie, she was as tranquil as the countryside and its serene paths displaying their brilliant golden autumn foliage. She was as beautiful as his nature paradise. He envisioned her skipping along the path in the village, gasping in delight when she peered into shop windows. She would stop to talk to every person she met as if they were her new best friend. That was the essence of Nellie. Friendly, delightful, wonderful Nellie Mae with the face that shown like a beacon in the night when a soul needed uplifting.

But as much as he liked watching his pretend version of Nellie frolic in the English landscape, he couldn't forget for too long that she seemed to have a dark contrast of her own, somewhere just below the surface.

He'd spent a lot of time pondering just what it was that made the voice within Nellie tell her she wasn't good enough, and that she should distrust anyone who came near with affection or interest. It didn't seem like Nellie's mother was evil, so he couldn't really believe the problems came from their strained relationship. He could only guess it was the devil's work, trying to stamp out the light of one of God's beautiful souls.

Johnny loved watching her with children. She knew how to kneel at their level and smile. She listened to whatever they had to say and responded with a gentle voice. He could see her with a whole passel of her own young someday. But the thought of her marrying someone like Liman made him angry. So angry it felt like his blood was boiling inside his body.

That guy was no good. He had no right to take a girl like Nellie Mae. He'd break her. He'd make her miserable, expect her to slave for him even worse than her mother did. Nellie would never have her own identity or explore the things God had for her to do. She needed freedom, not restriction. She needed someone to let her fly, not clip her wings.

"What am I supposed to do with you, woman?" he said aloud, drawing the confused expression of a squirrel foraging for acorns near the tree he sat against. "How am I going to keep you safe?"

A few months later, after the cold, quiet winter passed, it would be time to ask the same question of himself.

Twenty-Seven

In March, there were rumors they would be heading to the front lines. Soon.

Johnny had already made his peace with the news. He was beyond ready. The winter had been a long routine of mock battles and artillery drills and practice jumps from C-47s at night.

Lots of soldiers had gotten injured in the night jumps. Some of Johnny's buddies landed on rooftops in Ramsbury, breaking arms or legs or both. A couple fellows hit their heads pretty hard on the cobblestone streets. He watched medics pack them up and carry them off to the field hospital while he meticulously folded up his parachute and packed it. He couldn't imagine being put out of commission before the fight even started. He thanked God for keeping him out of harm's way every time he came away from training exercises unscathed. It would be humiliating to be sidelined now. He'd never get over the guilt.

In early spring, several large-scale exercises were set up to mimic the invasion planned for early summer. Johnny was proud to be a part of it, but the early versions were fraught with obstacles and stalls. Not enough bathroom facilities, not enough transportation, poor communication in the ranks – it ended up being a frustrating and cold waste of time and resources.

By the time they got to Exercise Tiger, most of the wrinkles had been sorted out. Johnny felt a familiar sense of thrill as they prepared to set out. Supplies for the invasion, like meal kits, bedding, artillery and clothing, their *beans and bullets*, as LT said, were all bundled up and carried on their person. They included their parachutes, though they wouldn't be jumping this time.

All the boys grew restless waiting for the call. No one slept much the night before. Most expected they would be awakened in the middle of the night. They camped out under the stars on the Ramsbury hillside.

Johnny's squad consisted of eight men, led by Grovenburg. Johnny was the gunner for the 81 mm mortar platoon, and he knew his duties so well he could probably perform them in his sleep, if he could sleep. But the man who had taken his place as munitions carrier left something to be desired. Jack Mullet was young, probably younger than the eighteen years he'd claimed on his papers. It had become clear he was there for thrills rather than a sense of duty to his country.

"You'll straighten him out," Grovenburg slapped Johnny on the back when Johnny asked him about Mullet. "Why do you think I assigned him to you?"

Johnny wasn't so sure it was a great idea. Mullet was disrespectful and loud. He liked to sneak off to pubs and get drunk the day before missions, and he'd been found in a compromising situation with a Ramsbury girl just a few days before. When Johnny tried to talk to him about their duty to be sober-minded and represent their country well in the battle they were about to join, Mullet did the best he could to hide his scoff.

"What?" Johnny asked. "Go ahead and speak freely."

Mullet looked around like he was afraid someone would overhear his questioning a soldier with higher ranking. "Like you're so perfect. Tell me you've never had a few too many and done something you regretted."

Johnny almost argued with him, but in the end he couldn't. He'd drank his fair share of beer, though he'd never gotten dead drunk. Even so, he'd developed a taste for cigars. He usually passed off the cigarettes in his meal kits to other men or traded them for candy, but when he came across a fine cigar, he couldn't resist.

It was sobering to realize he wasn't really that different from the other men. What had happened to his big plan of going into the army to share the gospel he'd so freely and wonderfully received that night in the little church? Where exactly had he lost his passion to convert the soldiers around him running headlong into their deaths? Instead of him changing them, they had changed him.

He hadn't argued with Mullet. He had let it go. And now, watching Mullet laugh loudly and down a gulp from a silver flask he'd pulled out of his pocket, Johnny realized the man was getting worse. In fact, he'd probably kill their entire squad with his careless behavior.

Grovenburg had said it was on him. What was he going to do?

Mullet tucked the flask back in his pocket and reached into the front pocket of his pack he wore on his chest. He produced a pineapple grenade. Fear struck Johnny straight in the heart.

"Stop messing around," Johnny said firmly, sitting up slowly. If that grenade went off, they could all very well be killed. Everyone Johnny was supposed to protect. "You know better than to play with the weapons."

"Knock it off, Mullet," Day said, eyeing the grenade uneasily.

Mullet laughed. He was like a kid who didn't care whether the attention he got was positive or negative. Just so everyone was looking at him. And the fact that he was drunk made everything worse.

Johnny scanned the vicinity for Grovenburg or one of the other commanding officers, but no one was around. It was on him. He stood up and approached Mullet, extending his hand.

"Give me the grenade," he demanded, in a tone he would use if he were disciplining a child. He silently prayed the man handed it over without a fight.

"Why should I?" Mullet smirked, tossing the grenade from one hand to another. Before Johnny could stop him, Mullet tossed the weapon in the air. Johnny reached for it, but Mullet grabbed it back, laughing like they were playing a game. Then he tossed it higher into the air.

Then he pulled the clip.

Everyone jumped back out of the way. Everyone except Johnny. Everyone around that campfire had seen enough grenades go off to know that the only way to avoid certain serious injury or death was to jump out of the way.

Johnny stood his ground, staring Mullet down. "Put that clip back in and hand to me. Now."

Mullet chuckled, meeting Johnny's gaze with a look of smug challenge on his young, skinny face. "Maybe I don't wanna."

"Hand it over."

Mullet stalled.

"Alright, listen up. The rest of us don't want to die because you're acting like a stupid kid." Johnny's voice rose, because he was angry and also because he was hoping it would draw the attention of someone in charge. He thought about pulling out his gun, but Mullet would know he couldn't shoot him without causing the grenade to go off.

"Why don't you make me, Hagaman?" Mullet said.

The boys around them kept backing up, and he thought he saw

someone run off into the brush to find Grovenburg.

"Get out of there, Hagaman," Day called.

But Johnny's boots were rooted to the spot. He was sure in his bones he was making the only right choice to stay exactly where he was and get that grenade away from Mullet. He wasn't going to risk anyone dying because of Mullet's stupidity, even Mullet himself.

"Don't do this," Johnny said in a quieter voice. "Not on the eve of the most important training we've had so far."

"Listen to the big man," Mullet sneered, turning the grenade to right and then to the left. "You know how to do the fancy talk. You think you're so much smarter than me."

Johnny eyed Mullet curiously. Was the boy covering for a lack of confidence? Fear that he wasn't good enough or smart enough to be there?

But his curiosity was short-lived. Mullet took a step back to prevent Johnny from being able to reach the grenade, and in his drunken state he easily stumbled over a tree branch. The grenade tumbled from his hand, and both of them went flying for cover in the brief window of time they had before the thing exploded.

In the moment after, Johnny only knew pain. It seemed like he was sprayed with bullets, shredding his skin, leaving holes all over him. He touched the stickiness of blood; he smelled iron.

It was over. He was dying. And he'd accomplished nothing.

Twenty-Eight

Tell us, Johnny, do
Where all this long night you have been
What have you heard? What have you seen?
And Johnny, mind you tell us true.

Wordsworth

"Stay with us, Private," someone said in a hushed voice at the end of a dark tunnel.

"His eyes are opening. He's alive."

Johnny squinted against the flashes. Feminine voices spoke. They sounded like they were far away, but he smelled their flowery scent close to his nose.

"Am I dead?" he asked the women when he could make his tongue work again.

He felt a gentle brush of fingers against his brow. "You're not dead, Mr. Hagaman. You're still with us."

At her words, almost as if proving to him that he was indeed still among the living, his leg began to burn with the worst pain he'd ever felt. He heard a sound like an animal dying a slow, painful death,

183

and it took him a moment to realize the sound was coming from him.

Johnny had had burns, he'd broken bones, he'd done all manner of damage a boy could manage to do to himself, and so far, he'd never screamed like that before. But this was fire and torment and agony. He felt like he'd been ripped apart. Surely his knee must be lying on the bed in pieces. He tried to glance down, but the bright light above the bed kept him from seeing anything but a swirl of white uniforms and the deep gray he'd come to associate with the color red. Blood red. Everywhere.

"Now don't you worry," the nurse said in a soothing tone. "It looks worse than it is."

Johnny tried to make his eyes focus on her face. She was beautiful. She had black hair and dark lipstick, a white nurse's cap pinned neatly over her head. It had been a long time since he'd been this close to a woman. The English women flirted with the soldiers in the pubs, but he'd stayed close to home since they got here. Girls reminded him of Nellie Mae.

"You're the most beautiful woman I ever saw," he said before he thought better of it. He blushed with embarrassment.

She laughed, and it sounded like a tinkling bell. "That's the pain medication talking. Don't worry about it." She adjusted the tubes attached to his arms. "The doctor's taking a look at your knee right now. It's your worst injury, though there are others along both your legs, Mr. Hagaman."

"Johnny," he said.

"Johnny," she said with a smile. "He's going to try to save your leg. You must be brave."

Her words hit him like a pile of bricks. Was there a chance he'd lose his leg?

He breathed faster and reached up for the metal supports on either side of the bed. He'd show them. He'd stand up, and everything would be just fine.

"Hold him down," a man said, and the beautiful nameless nurse scooted closer and guided his shaking arms away from the metal. "Now, now. Tell me where you're from."

Johnny knew she was trying to distract him, but he answered anyway. "Indiana."

"Oh, how nice! I'm from Illinois, so we're practically neighbors. My name is Peggy. I'm going to stay right here with you the whole time, and Dr. Martin is going to do everything he can to make you better."

"But I need to get back," Johnny argued. "We've got the operation to prepare for. It's going to be soon."

If Johnny would have been more coherent, he would never have said such a thing. No one was to know about the plans. Not that he knew that much.

"What job did you have in Indiana?" Peggy asked as if she hadn't heard his statement.

"Drill press operator," he said, his words slurring. The doctor did something to his leg that made him cry out again, his mind going blank except for the white-hot sparks of pain.

"Tell me about it," she encouraged, holding his hand and squeezing tightly.

"It was a train station," he managed around the pain, holding her hand so tightly that he was amazed she didn't wince. "Most boring job you'd ever know. Wanted … adventure."

"Well, you certainly found that, didn't you?" She smiled. She glanced down at what the doctor was doing, then looked back at his face. "Do you have a sweetheart?"

Pain tore through him again. He groaned in agony. "Please don't make me talk about Nellie Mae."

She nodded and patted his hand.

"Where am I?" he glanced wildly around the room. It was well lit, for a tent, anyway. Curved white fabric joined together over

185

support beams, and the room was lined with beds, lamps and wheelchairs. Only one other bed was occupied that he could tell. It was a reminder to him that it wasn't time for a soldier to be injured yet. He'd failed before he even started.

"You're at the 40th General Hospital at Alfoxton Park." She gestured proudly to the space. Her face grew more serious. "I'm sorry to tell you that the other man who was injured in the incident didn't make it."

Johnny sighed deeply, thinking of drunken Mullet throwing around that grenade. Had he ever had a chance to talk to Mullet about God? Maybe he could have changed both their fates if he'd been willing to find a way to share the good news with him.

Another failure.

"I've messed up big time, Peggy," he said, shaking his head and staring up at the white canopy.

"That's not the way I heard it," she disagreed. "You were the only one brave enough to try to stop Mr. Mullet from handling the grenade. Everyone else ran."

"Maybe I was the only one stupid enough," he replied quickly. "How long till I get out of here? I need to get back to my squad."

She hesitated for a long time before she answered, and Johnny didn't like it. Not one bit. He gritted his teeth together and willed her to say what he wanted to hear.

She didn't. "You're going to be here for a long while yet, Johnny. I'm so sorry."

He didn't know what she meant by "a long while," but he didn't like the sound of it.

"I'll show you," he said. "I'll get out of here in no time."

As soon as that doctor stopped poking around his sore knee, he'd get up and walk out of the tent to show them he was just fine. He'd get back before the operation went down.

"Oh, now don't you rush. Besides, you'll like it here at

Alfoxton." Peggy was cheerful. Too cheerful to be ruining his day like this. "Did you know the poet Wordsworth lived here for a year or two? Wrote some poems right here on the property. I think he even wrote one about someone named Johnny." She smiled, but Johnny couldn't make himself return the gesture. She went on as if he had. "We'll still be here for at least a couple months, I believe. There's a nice mansion on the property and plenty of space to walk and enjoy nature."

"Is there a creek?" Johnny thought of Lick Creek back home, where he'd spent his childhood roaming wild and free with his best friend and more dogs than he could remember.

"Why, yes! Do you like to fish?"

"Sure do." But it didn't mean anything. Not when he was supposed to be in battle. He didn't have long to contemplate it. The doctor did something to his knee that hurt so awful Johnny passed clean out.

Twenty-Nine

Nellie glanced out at the assembly hall filled with people. All eyes were on the stage where she sat with the other members of the band. A hush fell over the room, besides the occasional cough. Somewhere out there, Dad was watching her.

Nellie held up the full weight of her bass violin, drawing the bow across the strings in what she hoped was the semblance of melody. She'd signed up for just about everything she could this year, including learning to play the largest musical instrument in the band.

She'd been practicing too. When her mother grumbled about how much time she was wasting on "that infernal thing," Nellie practiced louder and longer just to show her she meant business. Her teacher, Miss Morgan, had said that Nellie was the fastest learner she'd ever taught.

Mother wasn't happy about it, but Dad was proud of her, and he didn't mind saying so. He'd come to every performance so far, including this one. She'd seen him sitting on the edge of his seat before they got started.

In this particular concert, she'd been assigned to the back row, right next to the edge of the stage. She quickly discovered there wasn't enough room for her bass violin. She pushed her stage chair as far over as it would go, until her chair was pushed up next to the poor guy seated next to her, but still the endpin rested an inch or two from the drop.

As the music swelled, Nellie forgot her worry over her situation. She pulled her bow in the familiar pattern and moved her fingers to the correct positions, letting the music take her away. Her eyes closed and she let the sounds carry her away.

Her line of music took her to the lowest tones of the bass violin. It bolstered the other instruments, bringing them all to the culmination of the song. One moment she was exalting in the rich tones her instrument produced, the next … everything was falling.

Her bass's endpin had slipped from the edge of the stage and tumbled down with a guttural spurt of indignation that could be heard over all the other instruments. The music continued, though stunted by the surprise of the players. Miss Morgan was mortified as she watched Nellie attempt to wrestle the instrument almost as big as herself back into place.

When Nellie looked up, embarrassed and wondering how many people were laughing at her, she saw her father standing in his place in the audience. She could tell he was tempted to jump up on the stage and help her. And suddenly, seeing his fatherly reaction and her predicament, Nellie couldn't be anything but amused. She giggled.

And then so did everyone around her, as if her laughter was catching. Miss Morgan tried to get her students to finish the song, but a smile was pulling at the sides of her mouth as well.

"No one can resist joining in when Nellie Mae's laughing," she said afterward, and they all had another hearty laugh together.

But the joy of the evening was short-lived. When Nellie Mae arrived home with her father, her mother was holding an envelope in her hands. Mother's gaze was tentative as she stared at Nellie Mae.

"You've got some mail." She held out the letter. "From Indianapolis."

He's dead. She thought immediately. Her mind said the words over and over. *He's dead. He's dead. He's dead.*

"I've been praying," her mother started to say, but her voice faltered. And when Nellie saw the concern in her mother's eyes, she felt guilty for all the times she'd been convinced her mother didn't value anything Nellie Mae cared about.

Her father didn't say anything, but he put his hands on her shoulders.

Nellie Mae's breath came in little gasps as she tore open the paper and opened the letter. Her eyes dropped to the last lines where she saw it was from Johnny's sister, Rena. With a hot, dizzy feeling in her head and something nearly blocking her throat, she began to read the opening lines aloud.

Dear Nellie,

We've heard from the War Department. They sent a telegram only yesterday, the 24th of April. Johnny has been injured. They didn't provide any details, they only said he's in a hospital in England. I will write again when I know more.

Rena

The room was as silent as the grave.

"He's not dead," she finally said, as if she was trying to convince herself. What else was there to say? He was injured, on the other side of the world, and she'd rejected him.

"He's not dead." She repeated the words. In a strange way, they comforted her.

"We'll pray." Her mother stood up straight, resolutely hitting the weathered counter top with her fist. "We have the power of prayer on our side. Who knows but that the good Lord gave John an appointment with injury to save him from a certain death?"

Nellie Mae hadn't thought about it that way, but now that her mother had spoken the words, they seemed to take hold of her. God had spared him. He wasn't on the front lines any longer. He wasn't jumping from airplanes into war zones or shooting guns or dodging mortars. He was lying in a hospital bed, being cared for by doctors and nurses.

Nellie felt a calm seep into her spirit. She needn't fret. God himself was attending Johnny in his hour of need.

Thirty

When he came to, Johnny was exhausted. He felt like he'd been through the worst battle of his life. And lost.

The room was dimly lit and quiet. He figured it must be nighttime. Soft snores came from another patient down the row.

Johnny lay there for a few minutes before he had the courage to try to move. When he did, the inevitable wave of agony rolled over his body, originating in his knee. He couldn't help crying out. He bit his lip to keep from making more noise.

The nurse, Peggy, came into the room, headed his way. "Hello, Johnny," she said pleasantly, as if he hadn't just moaned in pain. Somehow her smile made it easier to manage. "How are you feeling?"

"I'm fine." He gritted his teeth and tried to pull himself into a sitting position. "I just need to get up and use the facilities."

"I'm sorry, Johnny," she said in a delicate whisper. "But you can't get up right now. Not for a long time yet."

"Why not?" Johnny couldn't fathom why they would keep him

from getting up. What else was he going to do? Lay in this bed for the foreseeable future? He had to rejoin his squad in Operation Tiger. The day of attack was looming close; he needed to be ready.

"Your knee is in pieces," she said simply as she tucked his blanket and sheet back around him. "You'll need surgery to put it back together. The grenade shrapnel entered on the top and the bottom of your knee. It's simply decimated."

The full weight of her words dawned on him. It was good she'd used a strong word like decimated, or he might have stayed in the dark by choice. After all, who'd want to hear that they were going to be lying in a bed for weeks or months instead of days? Even now, his mind couldn't fully accept her words.

"I gotta get back to the war," he said, his voice breaking a little. She sadly shook her head.

"You can't. I'm so sorry. Your soldiers will have to go on without you."

He shook his head, pushing himself into a more upright position, as if he was warning her he was about to get up and leave. "No, listen, I don't feel that bad. It hardly hurts."

In answer, his leg radiated indescribable pain.

"You are more comfortable because of the morphine," she said, pointing to his IV bag full of liquid.

Upon realization of the truth, he suddenly felt angry. Without thinking, he reached out and slammed the small lamp onto the floor. He heard the sound of glass breaking. He didn't regret it until he looked up and saw Peggy's fearful expression.

"You're wrong." He pointed at her so she'd know he meant it. "I'll prove it."

Peggy sadly went to get a broom to clean up the mess. "I'll get you a bedpan," she said quietly.

He felt his face go hot with rage. "I don't need one!" he called after her. He'd never been so humiliated. He would walk to that bathroom or die trying.

And try he did. He attempted to lift his left leg off the side of the bed, but a sharp, burning pain unlike anything he'd ever experienced trembled through his entire body like lightning. He cried out without meaning to, trying desperately to get his leg back where it had been and make the agony stop.

"Give him another dose of morphine," he heard the doctor say behind the curtained partition. "It'll knock him out for a while."

Peggy returned and wordlessly injected a syringe into his IV bag. He tasted metal in the back of his throat and his vision blurred. The room spun around him. He laid his head back and watched her walk away.

She looked back once, and he noticed the sadness in her expression. She was feeling sorry for him. Him! The man who jumped out of airplanes and ran up and down Currahee and crawled across forest floors with an armful of mortar supplies. But now he was helpless.

"I'm going back to my squad," he whispered before he lost consciousness again.

Days passed in an agonizingly slow procession until they formed into weeks. Johnny languished in his hospital bed. He had surgery to put his kneecap back together. The doctor was confident he'd keep his leg and even walk again.

"But it's never going to be the same," the doctor warned sternly. "I couldn't get all the shrapnel out. You're going to have it in your leg the rest of your life. You may not be able to play sports or do any strenuous activity."

Johnny couldn't even comprehend that possibility. He scoffed instead. "I will." He wouldn't let any old stuffy doctor say differently. A life without the ability to hike into the woods or climb along the creek bed or play baseball and tennis was no life he was interested in living.

"I hope you prove me wrong." The doctor nodded. "But I want you to take your recovery slowly. You're too injured to move right now, but in a few weeks, I'd like to send you home to convalesce in one of the state military hospitals. There's a new state-of-the-art facility in Galesburg. Illinois. You'll get better care there than here in a hospital always moving with the troops."

"I am part of the troops," Johnny said. "I'll stay. I'm going to rejoin them as soon as I can."

The doctor hesitated, as if he might say something else, but he sighed and moved on to his next patient.

When Johnny had been there three weeks, the unbearable monotony of his day was mercifully interrupted by the visit of his friend, Ken Day. He felt a shock of envy as Day stepped into the tent, healthy and whole and sharp in his freshly ironed uniform.

"Aw, Johnny, you look awful," Day said, but then he gave Johnny an apologetic look. "I'm sorry. I didn't mean it like that. You just look like you're in a lot of pain."

Johnny brushed off his friend's concern and asked for all the news from the front. He learned the men had completed Operation Tiger and were preparing for the invasion. Just another week or two, Winens kept saying.

"Rumor is we're headed for Normandy Beach," Ken said. Johnny thought maybe he saw the faintest hint of fear in his eyes. "We'll be dropped from planes by night. Going to take them by storm."

Johnny quickly calculated. "So around the end of May? I could be out of here by then."

Ken glanced at Johnny's immobilized leg, held up in traction to keep the swelling down. "I don't know about that, looking at you."

Johnny didn't realize how pathetic he'd sounded until he saw

Ken looking at his leg. How could a man who couldn't even lift his leg over the side of the bed expect to be dropping out of a plane and invading an army in a couple weeks? It was ridiculous to suggest it. Ken probably thought he was deluded.

"If I were you, I'd be saying the same thing," Ken said quietly. "I'm sorry about Mullet."

Johnny felt a sting of tears in his eyes but he wouldn't allow them. He was weak enough already without crying like a little girl. "I don't know that Mullet was ready to die. I never told him."

"Told him what?" Ken shifted from foot to foot, fingering his cap in his hands.

"Told him about salvation. About how we have to be saved if we hope to escape hell when we die. For us soldiers, that could be anytime."

Ken leaned back on the unoccupied bed behind him and didn't speak for a long moment. "You really believe that Johnny? You believe Mullet's in hell?"

Johnny couldn't tell if Day sincerely wanted an answer. "I believe the Bible," Johnny finally said. With his words came the sense of conviction he'd been missing in recent days. It surged through him like a strong wind blowing through a valley and nearly knocking him over. "I know my sins need forgiving. We all need forgiving."

He sighed. "I didn't speak up. And now you're all headed to war and nobody's ready to meet their Maker. I've failed, yet again."

"If you really believe Jesus Christ is the only one who can forgive our sins, what does that have to do with you? I suppose God is able to handle it without your help if he needs to."

Johnny was speechless. Ken shook his head and stood up. "I just came to say goodbye. You're a good soldier and we'll miss you on the front lines." He reached out his hand to shake Johnny's.

Johnny wanted to explain. He wanted to smooth it over so the awkward silence wasn't the last they ever would ever know of each other. He wanted Day to understand, but he couldn't think of anything to say to salvage the conversation.

"Goodbye, Day."

Ken walked out of the room before Johnny's tongue came untied. The black anger and bitterness surrounding Johnny's gut clenched tight. He hadn't asked for this. He wanted God to send him as a beacon into the night. He was going to win souls. He was going to fight for freedom and the safety of his country. He was going to give his children and grandchildren a safe place to live and a man to admire.

What would Nellie Mae think now? He'd tried a hundred times to write her, but he didn't want her to think of him this way. Not when she'd already rejected him twice. He didn't want her knowing how weak he was. It was a good thing she'd turned him down.

"You were right about me, Kit," he whispered. "You were right all along."

Thirty-One

June 6, 1944 came with a rush of terror as the morning headlines pumped out the truth of the Allied victory despite their heavy losses.

Johnny couldn't stop staring at the bold print and large letters on the front page of the British newspaper the nurse handed him.

INVASION!

His eyes shifted lower, catching on certain words or phrases. *The Battle of Normandy. Operation Overlord. 155,000 Allied troops on the beaches of Normandy in France. Push inland. Liberates France from Germany. Weakens the Nazi hold on Europe.*

D-day, they were calling it.

Later that day, the reports of the dead and wounded flooded the radios on the other side of the thin fabric walls. Most of the hospital staff had made the eight-hour journey to join the wounded on the front lines. The few that remained behind in the hospital stood next to the radio. Some of the nurses quietly sniffled.

Johnny was humiliated. He should have been out there bravely pushing his way into France to take back the world from the Nazis. It was his duty. Instead, he was the "goldbricker" sitting on a thin cot with his leg dangling in the air, nothing to do but think about what he might have accomplished if he hadn't gotten himself in this mess.

At supper, he told Peggy he wasn't hungry.

"You must trust the Lord," Peggy said, nodding toward the Bible he kept on the side table by his pillow, after his trunk was delivered to the hospital.

He scoffed. "I don't know if I believe in God anymore."

He was as shocked at his words as she was, but it was a relief to finally speak the truth. How could he believe in a God who loved them and had control over all things when everything was in chaos? When the ground was littered with dead bodies and evil men had a stranglehold on everything good? It seemed like the darkness was winning these days.

And why had God led him halfway across the world, after all the intense training, just to leave him languishing in a tent hospital in the middle of nowhere, draining military resources, not offering one single bit of benefit to this fight?

"Now, you don't mean that." Peggy gathered up his untouched tray and walked away, her shoulders sagging with the weight of his crisis of faith. She was a good woman. She deserved to have someone around that could cheer her up.

The next evening a list of casualties came. Peggy let him read it. He scanned the list of unfamiliar names until he found HQ, first battalion. Some he didn't know well, but many of the names belonged to men he had known. One name caught his attention and his throat immediately swelled with pressure. Lieutenant Colonel Turner was dead. He'd been wounded in the invasion and died the following morning in a hospital much like the one Johnny was in. Johnny saw the page with blurred vision after that. He imagined his name right where it belonged among the "H"s for Hagaman.

He continued to persist in his dark mood for days. With deep-rooted determination, he would beat the injury sidelining him. He seethed as he forced his legs to move, first to dangle on the edge of the bed, then to support his frame as he took a walker to the bathroom, then to carry him across the floor. He didn't care how much pain it caused him. His fellow soldiers were facing worse. He took every stab of pain as penance, his punishment for failure. He growled at Peggy when she tried to make him rest. He argued with the doctor when he suggested Johnny might need more time than he thought.

Before long he was rolling himself outdoors in a wheelchair. Peggy offered to push it for him, but he refused. He wanted to do it himself. Maneuvering the gardens proved more difficult than he'd imagined, but it only made him more determined to do it. He felt like a stubborn fool, but he couldn't seem to be anything else.

It took his restless, reeling mind a moment to notice the music. But when the sound filled his ears, he couldn't hear anything else. Rich melody and harmony easily danced together in peaceful tones that spread across the field to the patio where he struggled.

I am tired and weary but I must toil on
Till the Lord come to call me away
Where the morning is bright and the Lamb is the light
And the night is fair as the day.

There'll be peace in the valley for me some day
There'll be peace in the valley for me
I pray no more sorrow and sadness or trouble will be
There'll be peace in the valley for me.

There the bear will be gentle, the wolf will be tame

And the lion will lay down by the lamb
The host from the wild will be led by a child
I'll be changed from the creature I am.

No headaches or heartaches or misunderstands
No confusion or trouble won't be
No frowns to defile, just a big endless smile
There'll be peace and contentment for me.

Johnny's head came to rest in his hands. He didn't look out over the lawn and the people gathering there, offering a contemplative applause as the singers came to the final line of their beautiful spiritual.

I'm here, John. A voice spoke – a voice no one heard but the inside of Johnny's mind. *I'm not going to leave you. You are just where I want you to be. Don't be afraid.*

"You'll have to help me," he said in a faltering whisper, not caring that some of those on the edge of the crowd turned to see the crazy soldier in the wheelchair talking to himself. "I can't do it on my own."

I will never leave thee nor forsake thee.

"What about all the good men that died trying to make this world a little better? Why weren't you with them?"

I am with you always, even unto the end of the world.

"Why didn't I die, too? And why Turner? What if I could have saved him? I don't understand your plan here."

My thoughts are not your thoughts.

Johnny's arguments died away. He was nothing. He had nothing to offer. He was insignificant in the grand scale of God's work in the world.

But he could live his life in honor of the one who was everything good and important and true. If God had left him here on the earth, there must be a reason.

"Show me what you want me to do with my life." Johnny took a deep breath and sat up straight, staring into the clear English blue sky. "I'll do it."

Every week Johnny expected he would be sent back to the war. But every week the doctor came to evaluate his progress, and every week he said Johnny wasn't ready.

Johnny grilled the doctor on what he could do to heal faster. The doctor gave him exercises to make his leg stronger. Johnny did them, day after day, for hours, until the doctor told him he was straining his leg and slowing his recovery.

"I want to get back to the war," Johnny said again.

"I want you to get there, too, but you have to be patient."

Not long after the June invasion of Normandy, the 40th General Hospital packed up everything and moved to Paris. Johnny asked to go with them instead of going back to the States. He wanted to stay near the front lines. He made himself busy by helping nurses fetch things and sitting with men who had been wounded. He held some soldiers by the arm as their spirits slipped away. He pleaded in quiet whispers that they trust in the power of Jesus' name. He read Scripture to the discouraged. He prayed with some so traumatized they couldn't eat. He listened to many who just needed to talk.

In the serving and praying Johnny found a measure of peace for himself. Peace to live in the eye of the storm and be useful for God's Kingdom. He was where he was supposed to be, as frustrating as it was. God wanted him there. His little Bible had never had more use than it did in those months as Johnny stayed with the hospital and moved along the path of destruction – first to France, then on to Holland.

In September Johnny heard about Operation Market Garden from wounded soldiers coming into the hospital. He put together that the airborne soldiers were there to free several bridges from German control. It seemed straightforward enough, and all the commanding officers were confident it would be an easy task.

One morning in mid-September, Johnny looked up from his breakfast and saw Colonel Sink. He was shocked. THE Colonel Sink – who led the whole band of airborne troops – was in the hospital mess tent. Johnny had seen him in person several times, but never this close. He felt his mouth go dry and prayed he wouldn't be required to say anything. He'd be tongue-tied for sure.

Another man with the group of officials came toward Johnny.

"Lieutenant Winens!" Johnny recognized him. He was so glad to see him alive he forgot about his nerves. He pushed his hands against the arms of his wheelchair and tried to stand up on his good foot, ignoring the pain. He awkwardly saluted.

Winens smiled. "Private Hagaman, you may want to stay standing."

Winens helped him out to the aisle close to where the colonel and other officials stood in a rather intimidating line.

"Boys, we have a few awards to pass out today." Colonel Sink stood with his hands on his hips as another officer opened a mahogany box full of Purple Heart medals, or "slow-mover badges" as LT had called them. Johnny gulped, realizing he was about to be given one. He wanted to argue, to say he didn't deserve it. He hadn't been fighting the enemy when he was injured. He just wasn't able to do his job. The medals should go to the heroes, not to him. But he had no choice. He tucked his shirt more tightly under his belt and stood as best as he could at attention while balancing on one leg.

Colonel Sink proceeded around the room, bringing the medals to the men since most of them were weak and unable to walk. He neatly pinned the purple medal to their uniform shirts and thanked them for their duty.

Winens motioned to Johnny, and Sink came their way. "Private John Hagaman," Sink read his name from the list. "Thank you for your service." He pinned the medal to his shirt as Johnny continued to salute. His hand shook as he stared straight ahead. He could smell Sink's aftershave and see the individual hairs of his beard out of the corner of his eye.

"Thank you, sir," he managed to squeak.

Winens clapped him on the back as Sink moved on. "Good job, Hagaman," he whispered. "And word has it you may be in for a promotion."

Johnny wanted to ask him what he meant, but he knew it wasn't the time. Promotion? To what – head nurse? What could he accomplish that warranted a promotion?

He never had the chance to ask Winens. Exactly one week later, Lieutenant Winens gave his life for his platoon, throwing himself in the way of a mortar as his men escaped at the battle of Arnhem.

Johnny knew there were plenty of other soldiers who deserved the Purple Heart more than he did. He'd only managed to get himself sidelined from the real fight.

A couple weeks later, Johnny saw the very sight he'd started dreading. Ken Day was brought in on a stretcher, bloodied and screaming. His wounds bled freely as Johnny wheeled himself across the room to his bedside.

"What happened?" Johnny asked around the lump in his throat.

Day took several labored breaths. "They got me, Johnny. I'm scared. I'm so scared!"

Johnny swallowed hard. "I'm here, Ken. And Jesus is here. Trust him. Give yourself to him. He'll bring you home."

Ken looked straight into Johnny's eyes. He didn't speak another word. His breath expelled and he went still, his eyes still focused on

Johnny's face.

It was a sight Johnny knew he'd never forget as long as he lived.

Thirty-Two

Somehow Johnny survived the winter and then the spring. The Allied forces finally made headway in Holland and prepared to move to Belgium. While the hospital made preparations to move along with them, Johnny's doctor walked out to the edge of the woods where Johnny wheeled himself every day.

Doctor Dewey sat down on a tree limb next to him. He gave a great sigh, and Johnny knew what was coming.

"You're sending me home," he said without emotion.

The doctor looked at him curiously for a minute, then nodded. "You've been here for a year now, John. Your leg is healing, but you know it's slow going. Those bones of yours are still so fragile. There's no way they could support you out there in combat." Dewey folded his arms across his chest and stared across the stream. "Now if it were an arm, I would get you back there. But I can't in good conscience put you back in the war, Hagaman. It would be dangerous. Not only for you, but for the men who would be dependent on your ability to fight."

Johnny felt a bitter taste in his mouth. He stared hard at the rolling, gurgling creek he'd come to love. He heard the squirrels chirping overhead and chasing each other across the branches. They didn't know he was leaving. They just went on with their simple existence like it was any other day.

"I'm sorry. I know this isn't what you wanted. But I'm going to send you home on the next C-54 bound for America."

The doctor stood to leave. Johnny suddenly held out his hand to the other man. "Thanks, Doc. For taking care of me."

The doctor nodded and shook his hand. "You're a good man, John. You go live a good life. You've been spared by that injury, like it or not."

Johnny's airplane ride home was a much shorter trip than his boat ride to England. The Douglas Skymaster was comfortable, with ample room for everyone on board. Some of the men were being transported in cots, unconscious, badly injured or unable to walk. Johnny insisted on sitting in one of the chairs with the other stubborn men like him. The ones protesting being sent home in the first place. He sat up the whole way home, even when his leg swelled and ached.

The next few days proceeded in typical military fashion. No one told Johnny anything. He finally found himself standing in front of the newly built Mayo General Hospital in Galesburg, Illinois. From the moment he saw the place from the transport truck, he was in awe. Lines of freshly painted patient residences stood beside official administration and surgical wards. A lovely new chapel complete with spire and cross, an entertainment building, a mess hall and a library accompanied the other buildings. The hospital seemed to go on and on with no end in sight.

The truck drove down the long drive and arrived by the flagpole in front of the main building. They were assisted to their beds and treated to an assortment of items for their stay. Johnny was thrilled to see genuine American gum and candy, cigars by the boxful, crackers and peanut butter, packs of postcards, pens, stamps, notebooks, and lots of books to read. He felt like he must have died over in the war and now he'd been sent straight to heaven. The guilt hit him whenever he thought about Winens and Day.

In the months that followed he spent most of his time at the chapel and the library. When he wasn't trying to sneak off to find some woods or a stream, that is. He also made his daily trek to the Physical Therapy Department, staring down long rows of neat, white beds. He watched the clock on the wall count down the time as nurses and therapists worked on his leg. Gradually, it started to hurt less, to the point he could walk on it with only a slightly painful limp. And watching all the cute white-uniformed American nurses with their pink cheeks and shiny curls made him start to remember all the more another beauty he'd left behind.

She was only a state away. And now he wasn't planning on dying anymore.

Nellie Mae could feel the letter inside her desk even if she couldn't see it. She'd read it enough times to know what it said. A mixture of dread and anticipation welled up in her when she thought about the words she knew it contained:

Dear Kit,

Hello from the next state over.

I was wounded in England. I stayed in the hospital there for over a year, but I'm back now, in the Mayo General in Galesburg, Il. Word has it I'm headed for Camp Atterbury in Indiana as soon as my leg has healed enough. I'll be given a job to do to keep me busy and helpful and continue physical therapy on my knee.

I don't know how to bring this up delicately, so I'm just going to say it. I can't stop thinking about you. Ever since I found out I'm going to live through this war, I keep seeing my future and no matter what else happens, I see me with you, growing old together. I love you, Kit. I want to marry you. Do you think you could find it in your heart?

I sent a letter to your father a few weeks back, asking for his permission to propose. He wrote back and gave it.

I know you think we're too different. I know I don't deserve a lady like you. I know you're not perfect, but neither am I, and I think we're perfect for each other. Whatever hurdles exist, we could overcome together I would take care of you. I would spend the rest of my life taking care of you. It's all I want.

I've been doing some thinking about what I want to do. I think I'd like to go to veterinary school. As you know, I've always had a soft spot for animals, and I think I'd be good at it. I'm thinking of attending Butler next year and studying pre-med as a first step. I think I can get my drill press job back in the meantime.

I can't promise I'll ever be rich, and I can't tell you I'm the hero who saved you from the Nazis, but I can promise you I'll work hard, do my best, walk with God and take care of you every step of the way.

Please say yes.

Love,
Johnny

"Good morning, darlin'," Nellie's boss said as he came through the office door with his briefcase in hand. "I'll take my coffee black today."

"Yes, Mr. Goodall," Nellie said with a friendly smile. "Anything else?"

"Transcribe the notes from yesterday's meeting. And cancel my appointments for this afternoon. I have to go to the doctor."

Nellie dutifully asked him what was wrong as she went to pour his coffee, but she didn't listen to the answer. Her mind was only on the letter inside her desk.

Please say yes.

Please say yes.

She was finally starting to feel like her life was going somewhere. She'd graduated high school with her friends just two months ago. She'd secured a secretary's job in town before her mother could send her off on any more missions. Nellie was earning money. Of all things, who would have thought? Did she really want to give it up for an uncertain future with an injured young soldier who had only vague ideas what he wanted to do for the rest of his life?

Yet the thought of being his wife made her feel like she had feathers in her stomach tickling her from the inside. She wasn't sure if it was excitement, or dread, or both. She did want to be married – that was not in question. She came home at the end of her workday exhausted. She'd much rather keep house and have babies and let her husband earn the living.

But where would they live? How would he support them while he went to school? What if they had a baby right away? Would she have to work and give her baby to someone else to care for during the day?

Nellie felt a little panicked at the real possibility of being a mother in the near future. She'd always dreamed of it, but now that it was staring her in the face, would she be a good mother? What if she didn't know how to take care of a baby? What if she ended up like her own mother?

There were so many variables. She didn't feel equipped to make such a huge decision. Too much was at stake.

But at the very least, marrying Johnny was a way to ensure she'd never be under her mother's thumb again. And she did imagine she loved him enough to spend her life with him, through the ups and downs that would inevitably come.

When Mr. Goodall had disappeared into his office, she pulled out a sheet of stationary. She took her pen from the cup on the desk and only hesitated a moment before she began to write.

Dear Johnny,

Yes. I'll marry you.

Love,
Nellie

It didn't take long at all for Johnny to write back. She could tell even from his handwriting, usually neat and deliberate but now slightly rushed, that he was overjoyed. She wasn't sure why he loved her, but she believed he did. And it would be enough, wouldn't it? His love for her would sustain them. She had to believe it would.

Johnny went on about details, telling her he thought he'd be discharged from the army come the New Year, so they could marry any time after that. She wrote back to say that maybe they should give him some time to figure out where they'd be living and let him apply to college. He sent her a package in response. A beautiful gold band with a small diamond and two tiny diamonds on either side was set in a velvet box. She was sure he'd spent his life savings on such a lovely ring. It fit her finger perfectly.

She couldn't stop staring at it the first few days she wore it. She got plenty of attention, too. Martha swooned and jumped for joy as a best friend should. Mother was positively thrilled. At Nellie's "advanced" age of twenty, she'd already be six years older than Mother had been when she married Dad. Nellie received no shortage of reminders, either. Mother wanted her to have a big church wedding. Nellie didn't question it. It was the way it had been for her sisters and it might as well be the way it was for her as well.

In the next weeks and months, many letters were sent back and forth between the military hospital and Willow Springs. It was fun to plan and dream, wondering how everything might turn out. Nellie was curious as anything to know what it was like to be married. Specifically, what intimacy with a spouse might be like. Her parents were quite open with their affection and quite insistent that their children abstain until they had a spouse of their own. Naturally, Nellie was anxious to know what she hadn't been allowed to contemplate. Emma Jane had only filled her in on a few basic secrets after she had gotten married, which really only served to make Nellie more curious.

In the fall, Opal came from Springfield with her three children for a visit. She and Emma and Nellie had a time together, just like the old days. One day they fell exhausted and laughing into a booth at the soda fountain, tired from walking and shopping all afternoon.

"So we haven't seen you in a good year if it's been a day, Opal," Nellie said. "What's kept you away so long?"

Opal's smile slipped. She sighed and cleared her throat in that older sister way that told Nellie and Emma she wished she could protect them from the truth.

"I've been watching several children. Five extra, to be honest. I feel half worked to death some days, if I'm honest."

"What's the situation?" Emma asked. Nellie knew her sister wasn't surprised; neither was she. It was the way of their family to take care of the downtrodden, and surely there was a sad story to go along with it.

Opal hesitated, but she shrugged as if she was giving herself permission. "It's not a lovely story, I'll tell you that. It's downright scandalous to two young things like you. But the children's father is in the service. Navy, I believe. His wife got the notion into her head that he had been with other girls while he was away. She decided she was going to get even. She ran off with another man and left her little ones on their own. I wouldn't have known except I took a dinner over there, knowing she was feeling down with him being away."

Opal sighed and leaned back in the booth. "I found the kids – scared to death. Oldest one was only ten. He said their mama had left in the night and put a note on the kitchen table saying they were their daddy's problem now since she'd found herself a new man. Oh, dear, but those kids were scared spitless. I just gathered them up in my arms and took them home without a further thought for or against the idea. I knew it was what Mother would do."

"It's just what Mother would do," Emma Jane nodded. "What a big heart you have, Opal."

Nellie couldn't speak. Her face had gone hot and her throat was swollen with emotion. What kind of immature, flighty little backwoods woman ran off on her husband while he was away in the service? She wasn't even married to Johnny yet and the thought of cheating on him by even looking twice at another man was despicable enough to leave a bad taste in her mouth. Of all the nerve! She'd like to tell that hussy a thing or two…

"Nellie?" Opal took a sip of her soda. "You're turning purple. I knew you couldn't handle this story."

"I'm fine," Nellie lied.

"No, you're not." Opal set down her drink. "Listen – there are bad eggs in the world. We have to accept that. You're getting married soon. You're going to have to leave behind your notion that people are good and will always treat each other well, or you're going to spend much of your life disappointed. We have to be ready to clean up the messes of other people sometimes – without falling apart ourselves."

Nellie shook her head and seethed. It took her a moment to collect herself enough to speak. "I can't accept someone would do that to her own husband and kids. What is this world coming to?"

The words she spoke were not nearly enough to express the dark thoughts that swarmed in her brain.

Emma Jane patted her shoulder. "Don't take it personally, Nellie."

Nellie shook off her hand. "What if Johnny isn't what I think he is? What if he gets tired of my dramatics and realizes I'm not all I was cracked up to be? You know I'm a handful. I'm always tired and sometimes I lose it. I'd just die if I married him and he walked out on me. I just know it'll happen."

Opal grabbed Nellie's wrist from across the table, holding it firmly enough to get Nellie's full attention. "Nellie Mae Thomas, you stop spouting off that garbage right now! You know that man is decent. He's not perfect, but no one is. You can't expect perfection from a man, it just ain't realistic. We can't even expect our men to be as solid as Dad. He's special. We just have to trust the Lord to do with our husbands as he will and stay out of his way while he's working on them."

Nellie Mae stubbornly shook her head and clenched the tissue she had pulled out of her purse to wipe her eyes. "I won't do it. I won't take the chance. You're good. You don't fly off the handle and you don't fall into morose times where all you can do is sleep. There's something broken in me. I'll only drag him down. I'll make him leave me."

"That just isn't true," Emma Jane said softy. "You know it isn't."

But Nellie knew it *was* true. She clamped her mouth shut and didn't say another word, but when she got home, she went straight to her little desk in the room she shared with her sisters. She pulled out stationary and a pen, resolved to get it done while she had the determination to do so. Her handwriting was barely legible as she quickly wrote out the words of refusal. She dropped the ring in the envelope with the letter and sealed it. After addressing it, she ran all the way to the post office and tossed it in the bin before she could second guess her decision.

It just wasn't a good idea. She may be the only one who saw that, so it was her duty to be the strong one and call it off.

Thirty-Three

Johnny,

I'm sorry, but I can't see you anymore. We would never make a go of it. I know it's mostly my fault, but I can't help it. You'll find someone you really love and trust someday. I just know it.

Here's the ring. I know any girl would love it. Please go to church and find some nice girl and marry her.

I'll always appreciate your kindness.

> *Goodbye,*
> *Nellie*

P.S. Please forgive me for being so mean at times. Try to have a nice memory in your thoughts for me.

Johnny stared in shock at the words on the page, written in a hurried script, like she'd been angry when she'd written it. Had he said something or done something he shouldn't have? Something that would make her so mad she'd dump him so suddenly?

He let the ring fall from the envelope into his hand. It seemed so tiny and delicate next to his large fingers. Like her. So fragile her mood could turn on a dime.

Was this just a hasty rejection she'd regret? Did she really feel so strongly? He stood up, holding the tiny gold ring, staring at it as if it held the story of what he should do. He felt his chest tightening with panic. He realized just how much he'd come to like the idea of Nellie Mae being his wife. He didn't want to lose her, even if she was unpredictable. In fact, he loved that about her.

He loved *her*.

He thought about calling her on a telephone, but he was pretty sure her family didn't have a telephone and any others in town wouldn't be private. Not to mention the only telephone he had access to was in the middle of the lobby at the reception building, always full of activity. He ached to go to her, but his life wasn't his own. Not yet. He doubted he'd be granted a furlough just to go talk his fiancé off the proverbial ledge.

The words she'd written ate away at him for a few days. Finally, he was desperate enough to bring it up with his commanding officer, Lieutenant Biggs.

"You haven't taken a furlough since you were wounded, Hagaman. It would be good for you to get out of town for a few days. You're a good soldier, Sergeant. The theater will make it a few days without you. Go get your girl back."

Johnny was surprised by Biggs' kind words. The army in America was different than the army across the sea.

Johnny was also taken aback by his own reticence to leave. He had been promoted to Staff Sergeant and been put in charge of the motion picture operation at Camp Atterbury's theater. He liked his squad of recuperating soldiers. They manned the theater together, showing training films to groups of recruits coming through the camp. On weekends they played Hollywood films for the soldiers, and those nights always resulted in a packed theater.

It was a far different life than the dangerous existence the rest of the 101st continued to live in Europe, painstakingly freeing one little town after another from the Nazis. He knew his fellow soldiers didn't have even half the pleasantries Johnny enjoyed now. If he thought too hard about it, he felt guilty. So much, in fact, he had started to loathe talking about his experiences overseas, and about the war in general. It was easier to pretend it wasn't happening.

Johnny walked all the way out past the prison camp at the edge of Atterbury where 15,000 German and Italian soldiers were being held until the war was over. He stood on the banks of Nineveh Creek, surveying the fish darting just below the surface of the water. He'd give anything for his old handmade fishing pole and a few worms. And Peter, of course, sitting beside him and telling him what to do about his broken heart.

Being in nature, back in his element where he belonged, Johnny could almost make sense of it all. Almost. He sat down on the bank until the sun started setting.

When he knew he'd be missed in his barracks, he started back. He saw that the POWs were out for exercise inside their gated enclosure. He heard familiar shouts and hoots from young men, bored and stir crazy, razzing each other and shooting the breeze. Johnny didn't understand their words. He could only tell this group was Italian by their accent and Mediterranean features.

"Hey, soldier," one of them called from the fence in good-natured, broken English. "You look like you have had your heart ripped from your chest. By a woman, no doubt?"

Johnny didn't stop walking. "How would you know that?"

"Because I recognize the expression in the mirror." The man sighed and chuckled. "Ah, my Annamarie!"

Johnny didn't know why, but he found himself stopping and turning toward the soldiers with hands buried deeply in his pockets.

He determined to stay aloof, since he really shouldn't be talking to a prisoner. He wanted to maintain his good record.

The soldier spoke again. "Did she turn down your proposal?"

Johnny shrugged. "Nope. Got a letter saying she changed her mind. Sent me back the ring."

The man groaned with sympathy. "Oh, I know that smarts, my good man. Will you go and win her back?"

Johnny took a good hard look at the sky above. Pretty as Nellie Mae's cheeks when she was breathless and excited, even if he couldn't see the colors. "Thought about it. But maybe I'll just let it be."

"Oh, no," the soldier disagreed. "You must go after her. The women – they want us to prove we care. Chase them. Then she'll know for sure you love her."

"Don't know why she can't just believe it when I say it."

"Because that is merely words. She wants to hear the longing in your voice. See the desperation in your eyes. You must fight hard as you fight for lousy American freedoms." The Italian laughed.

Johnny could see his point. The hint of something he'd been thinking himself – deep down in that part of him that was too scared to take leave and go get her back.

"Nothing ever comes of a man choosing to be a coward," the man said, as if he'd read Johnny's mind.

"Maybe not," Johnny answered. He saluted the soldier even though they hailed from different sides of ideals. At the heart, every Italian, German, English and American soldier had the same things on his mind.

What will happen to me if I die?

Or in some ways the more troubling question, *what will happen to me if I live?*

He'd go. He'd go to Missouri and win her back. He'd convince her somehow they were right for each other. He'd promise her he'd always be there, even if she couldn't always love him the way he wanted or serve him as well as some other theoretical wife might. He'd love her even if she was tired or insecure, afraid or disillusioned, angry or ill, or any other negative emotion he'd see Nellie Mae Thomas come up with. He'd see her through, and when they came to the end of their lives, he'd still be by her side.

Johnny didn't often set his mind to things, but if he did, he would follow through. It wasn't in his nature to fail if he felt strong enough to try. A blasted grenade had ruined his plan to give everything he had to the fight against evil. He'd pin his faith to loving her instead. He had to find something to do with his life. Might as well be a pretty little thing with a delicate constitution and a fiery personality to keep him on his toes. Might as well be Nellie Mae.

He was consumed with consternation when he stood in front of Nellie Mae's door two days later, flowers in hand and the ring in his pocket. One of her brothers opened the door and snickered at him before he said a word.

"May I speak to Nellie Mae?" Johnny asked.

The boy smirked. "Neeeelllllllllie!" He called in a sing-song voice. "Your boyfriend's here!"

He heard her speak from the other end of the house. "How many times do I have to tell you Henry and Bill aren't my boyfriends? Get your sorry behind out and stop gawking at company." She came into the front room and slapped her brother on the shoulder. He turned around and jumped on her. They fell out of view, engaged in a rowdy tussle on the faded rug. Johnny stood awkwardly in the doorway, waiting while they laughed and carried on.

Apparently, Nellie won. She emerged at the door breathless, glancing back at her brother with triumph. "You're not big enough to hold me down yet, Punk," she mocked. Then she turned to face him. "Sorry to keep you waiting…"

Her voice trailed off. Johnny supposed she must have believed him to be either the Henry or the Bill she had mentioned. Her cheeks darkened like she was blushing. She covered them with her hands, which he noticed were suddenly trembling. "Johnny?"

He cleared his throat and shuffled from one foot to the other before he remembered to hand her the flowers. She hesitated before she took them. She stared hard at them, like she was trying to avoid looking at him instead.

"You shouldn't have come," she whispered. He wasn't sure how to respond. He scratched his forehead and shifted again. Finally, she seemed to snap out of it and turned to see if anyone was watching them. Johnny noticed a growing number of curious parties standing in the hallway.

"Oh, for pity's sake." She came out on the porch and closed the door behind her. "Can't get a moment's peace in this house. I'm so glad I'm headed back to Indianapolis."

"You're going back?" He felt a surge of delight. "To your aunt's?"

"No." She folded her arms across her chest. Her hair was still mussed from her wrestle with her brother. He wished he had the courage to reach out and push back the wayward strands. "Emma and I and another girl are going to get an apartment and work. I just graduated high school. Finally, considering I'm nearly twenty years old!"

"I'm proud of you." He really was. She'd been determined despite her parents being indifferent on the subject of education. Her mother seemed downright determined to turn Nellie into a one-woman traveling housekeeping and childcare service.

"Thanks," she said, and then they stood in silence for another long moment. She stared at the flowers again, and then at the worn floorboards beneath their feet. He looked down as well and noticed she wasn't wearing socks or shoes, just a pair of cozy looking booties. He wondered if she'd made them herself. The thought made him smile, but when she saw what he was smiling at, she groaned.

"I'm sorry. I shouldn't have come to the door like this."

"You should have," he disagreed. "I think you're cute."

She laughed, and the tinkling sound of it touched the deepest part of his soul. How he loved this little woman!

"I brought something that belongs to you," he said, his heart nearly pounding out of his chest as he fished the ring out of his pocket and held it out. Her smile fell as she saw it.

"I just can't, Johnny. Please don't put me on the spot. I haven't changed my mind. We're no good for each other, or at least I'm no good for you. I'll just drive you crazy and make you want to leave."

"I think I know my own mind well enough to say I'm willing to make it work," he answered. "I want you. Nobody else will do."

She sighed and shook her head. "I'll only disappoint you."

He shuffled on his feet and shrugged. "I'm sure I'll disappoint you, too. We're human."

"Johnny, you think more of me than you should. I'm not a good person. I'm downright broken."

He sighed. "You keep saying that, so I keep waiting for you to turn into this monster, and it hasn't happened. You doubt yourself; you have a sensitive conscience and a bit of a temper. But that's it."

A need to make her understand overtook him. He grabbed her hands and held them tightly. They were small and soft within his. "I can live with those things. I'm willing and able. I'll take care of you; just say you'll marry me. We can figure it all out later."

She dared to meet his eyes, obviously affected by his words. She caught the corner of her lip in her teeth as if she were deliberating.

"Please," he added. He could see she was on the cusp of changing her mind.

"But what if you stray?" she finally asked him in a voice so quiet he barely heard her. "And what if it makes me do something I'd regret?"

He chuckled, even though he knew it wasn't the best response. He couldn't help it. The idea of him breaking his vows was laughable. "It's not going to happen, Kit. Not in a million years. I promise. I'll never give you a reason to doubt. And you're better than you give yourself credit for. I trust you."

She stared at him for the longest moment. She stared straight into his eyes and down into his soul. She must have seen what she was looking for, because a moment later, she made him the happiest man on earth.

"Okay, Johnny. I'll marry you." She lifted her left hand, inviting him to slide the ring back on her finger.

He laughed and crushed her to his chest. He put the ring back where it belonged and gave her a kiss she wouldn't soon forget.

"I'll come back for you," he said as he hugged her again. "For a little while longer, I still belong to this country. But as soon as they let me go, I'm all yours."

Thirty-Four

Nellie Mae stayed on the porch as long as she dared. When Johnny finally walked away into the night, promising to write soon and make plans, Nellie sighed and steeled herself before she opened the door to her family.

A whole lot of noise greeted her. Her sisters hugged her and squealed. Her little brother teased her. Her mother immediately started going on about wedding plans in a sensible tone that nearly masked her emotion, save the unshed tears shining in her eyes. She caught her father's eye. He smiled and winked at her. Suddenly she felt peace she hadn't known before that moment. Maybe it would be okay. If Dad could smile about the whole thing, surely she wasn't making a mistake.

"Of course you'll have a church wedding just like your sisters," her mother said as she hurried to the kitchen "catch-all" drawer for a pencil and pad of paper. "We'll make you a lovely dress, won't we? We can use Emma Jane's and style it any way you like. It won't cost a penny."

Emma Jane joined her mother at the kitchen table. She'd only been married recently, but her new husband, Evan, was still in the service. She continued living at home until his time was up. She got letters from him nearly every day, sometimes more than one a day. It was part of the reason Nellie Mae had figured Johnny didn't care for her as much as she did him. The day she'd decided to end things with him, a full two weeks had passed without a word from him. Meanwhile, Emma Jane had two thick envelopes arrive just that day.

Nellie Mae shook her head as if to clear it of cobwebs. She couldn't keep second-guessing herself or Johnny, for that matter. She knew she could waffle back and forth 'til the cows came home if she allowed it. She needed to focus on something. Wouldn't wedding planning be good for that?

"Now what time of year you thinking, Nellie Mae?" Her mother was busily scribbling across the top of the paper.

Nellie Mae's Wedding

"Sure would be nice to catch my breath first," Nellie said, but she knew her voice lacked conviction. Her mother wouldn't be deterred anyway. She was a planner. Now was better than later. If someone was going to arrange all the details, Nellie Mae preferred it to be her mother. Nellie didn't know the first thing about weddings or what she even wanted at her own ceremony.

"Nonsense," her mother said with a short laugh. "Catch your breath a few years down the road when you've nothing to do but dishes and diapers. It'll come soon enough. Now, what about a spring wedding? When does John get discharged?"

"Um ..." Nellie realized she didn't even know for sure. "Early next year, I suppose he said."

"Spring might work, then."

"Actually, Johnny's saying he'd like to enroll in college in the fall. He might need time to get settled and find a job to keep us fed and clothed," Nellie said practically, thinking aloud. She wasn't sure of the rules of society. Was she allowed to work to help out?

"I'll have my job, of course," she said, to test the waters. Emma Jane nodded her encouragement, but Mother frowned.

"You don't want to give him the idea you're only there to bring home the bacon. If he's the right sort of man, he'll find a way to provide."

"Mother, he's been in the army for the past three years. He was only twenty-one and working as a drill press operator when he joined. He needs training before he can do what he wants to do with his life. If I can help, why not? Haven't you been telling me my whole life I need to make myself useful?"

Her mother seemed nonplussed by her arguments. "What does he want to do? And where will you be living?"

Nellie didn't know what to say. Honestly, they hadn't discussed a word of concrete plans. "I … I think he wants to be a veterinarian. He has a way with animals. He'd like to go to Butler for pre-med, I believe." Nellie hoped her information was correct.

Her mother neither tsked nor nodded any sign of approval. "It would be better for him to start out doing what he did before, working the drill press," she said as if she had some say in the matter. "It's work he knows, and it will provide for you. Didn't his father suggest that?"

Nellie shrugged. "How should I know what his father suggested?" Her mother narrowed her eyes. Afraid of a lecture, Nellie changed her tone. "Anyway, Johnny hates the drill press job. He says it numbs his brain. I don't want my husband being forced to do something he hates just so I can have food on my plate and a roof over my head."

Her mother set down the pencil. Apparently wedding planning had suddenly taken a back seat. "And just where do you intend to live while he makes his dreams come true? I'm sure you have no answer to that question, either."

Nellie did have an answer, but she was pretty sure her mother didn't want to hear it. "He said something about renting a small apartment. But if things are too tight, his mother has offered to let us live with them until we get on our feet."

"Oh, Nellie Mae," Her mother said with a sigh. Nellie felt like a silly child playing at being a grown-up. "That's no life for a newly married couple. Surely it won't come to that."

Nellie Mae didn't answer. Suddenly she felt a lot worse about the entire situation. She had been so concerned about the possibility of Johnny straying and her retaliating, she hadn't thought much about the practical details. She wondered if Johnny had thought about any of it. His only worry seemed to be that they get married as soon as he was discharged.

"Your father and I were married the summer after my fourteenth birthday," her mother began the familiar story.

"I know, Mother," she said dully. Emma Jane shot her a sympathetic look as their mother got up and went to the sink for a drink of water.

Beulah stared out the window as she sipped from the glass. "Your father only finished the fifth grade. But he was a hard worker. He went down to that mine every day so we'd have a home and food to eat. He hated every minute of it, but he didn't complain once. He knew the most important thing he could do was provide for his family."

"Mother, Johnny wants that too." Nellie sat up in her chair, determined to stand up for her husband-to-be. "But we aren't all called by the Lord to be miners and drill press operators. Or preachers, for that matter."

Nellie's voice was low, but her words made her mother turn and give her a reproachful look. "You are wrong about that, young lady. We are all called to preach the gospel. Wherever our path may take us."

Nellie didn't say anything else for a long time. It was so quiet in the kitchen they could hear the ticking of the clock on the mantle in the next room. "I don't have everything figured out," she finally admitted. "And neither does Johnny. But he's a good man, he trusts in the Lord and he loves me. Not only that, he's brave and true and the hardest worker I've ever known. He'll be a good husband. Just you wait and see."

She didn't wait to hear her mother's response. She went outside, letting the screen door fall back with a satisfying bang.

As she walked the path to Martha's to tell her the news, she tried to convince herself that her mother was wrong. This would work out just fine and it would be everything she had ever dreamed marriage could be. Johnny wouldn't fail her. She trusted him. She was going to throw caution to the wind and put all her faith in him. Everything would turn out just fine.

It had to.

Life settled back into routine, as it tends to when it doesn't know what else to do. Nellie wanted to think only of Johnny, but the simple truth was – he wasn't there. He wasn't part of her daily life yet. They wrote letters frequently, but it wasn't the same thing as living with a person.

She daydreamed about what it would be like to be married to Johnny. All of her woes would disappear, wouldn't they? She wouldn't be tired and unmotivated anymore, because she would be too busy loving her husband and meeting his needs. She had come to believe this was the answer to everything. Johnny was the answer.

In February, Johnny wrote to say he had been discharged and was back home in Indianapolis. He'd taken his old job for the spring and summer. Hopefully he'd have enough saved by the time school started in the fall to get a small apartment and a car.

Honestly, she didn't care about the money. Her family had never worried over finances, and the Lord always provided what was needed. She didn't expect that he would suddenly stop now. But

Johnny shared a piece of news that did worry her.

My mother is still offering to let us live with them. She's downright insistent, even, Johnny wrote. *There's plenty of room. Rena's gone to school so her bedroom is free. When she comes home, she can share with Nancy. So don't worry, sugar, we won't be homeless.*

Nellie did worry. She wasn't keen on the idea of spending the first year of her marriage under the constant surveillance of her mother-in-law. Picturing it bothered her so much she didn't answer his letter for a week.

Doubt ruled her mind. She had nightmares where Johnny left her and married someone else. Once she dreamed he left her at his parents' home and traveled the world with her cousin Lola.

Mother continued to make plans for a big church wedding with all the trimmings while Johnny continued to mention in his letters that he wouldn't mind a simpler affair. Eloping, even. His parents and sisters weren't going to make it to the wedding anyway. Why not just get married at her sister's new home in town rather than have a church wedding with so many people he didn't even know?

She wasn't sure how she felt about his idea. Wouldn't it look as if they were ashamed if they canceled the wedding? Didn't her family and friends deserve to celebrate with them? She'd be moving away, after all. It was as much a send-off as a wedding.

Not to mention her mother would be mortified if they were to elope.

Using the guise of her parents' home being too far out in the country to get to work every morning, Nellie found an apartment with a friend. They rented one of the bedrooms on the doctor's second floor. A schoolteacher and her sister rented the other room. The four of them had good times listening to Frank Sinatra records and laughing. She would remember those moments all her life. They helped her through the waiting and the worry and the unsettled dread that she couldn't name.

She knew it was ridiculous to be so out of sorts over a wedding. People got married every day without going on about it, and no one ever went on to have the perfect marriage. Well, save her parents, she supposed. But Johnny and Nellie were only human. There would be good times as well as bad times. Just as she had now. She knew somewhere deep down that it wasn't right to expect life to make a body happy all the time. Where in the Bible did God promise that? She'd take the joys with the sorrows and trust the path led to the right place. It was all she could do. She was so tired of worrying over it.

Even so, she continued to pray fervently that they weren't making the biggest mistake of their life.

Thirty-Five

December 26, 1946

Johnny couldn't help bouncing on the leather seat of his new car as he drove the highway between Indiana and Missouri. He couldn't quite grasp the thought that he'd be a married man in three days.

He felt more delight than nerves. Somewhere in the back of his mind he was reticent about the church wedding and all the talking he'd have to do at the reception, but he was willing to brave it with Nellie as his reward.

Another small part of him was just the tiniest bit worried Nellie Mae might back out at the last minute. He loved her with all his heart, but he knew by now she could be a bit of a powder keg. Something he meant in the very best way could easily be taken completely wrong, and he'd have a dramatic episode on his hands. She could also be given to icy silence when she was angry. He could imagine her calling off the wedding over something petty.

This is the woman you're choosing to spend your life with, his brain reminded him. Try as he might, he couldn't work up doubt that he should marry her, though. He didn't care if she was the most difficult little wife who ever walked the face of the earth. He loved her, he wanted her for his own, and he would dedicate his life to making her happy enough that she never needed to go silent.

Surely, he could be a good enough husband. He'd make it work.

He knew she suffered with health problems. Recently she'd had several teeth worked on and had become ill as a result. The doctor said she was anemic, and that was why she was always tired and cold. He suggested iron pills, which Nellie Mae dutifully took, but they made her vomit, so she'd had to give them up.

When she was his wife and they were living in the city he'd take her to the best doctor he could find. They'd get all of these issues sorted out. He thought maybe she wouldn't be so difficult if she were in good health. And if he could keep her happy, maybe she'd never be sick again.

He rehearsed his responsibilities silently. He'd gotten the marriage license and his mother's wedding handkerchief for Nellie to carry with her. He'd had his blood test over a month before in Beech Grove and the doctor had promised to send the results to the doctor in Willow Springs in plenty of time for the December 29 wedding. The doctor been surprised that it was necessary, thinking it an antiquated requirement, but when Johnny explained his fiancé was from Missouri, the doctor suddenly nodded in understanding.

Johnny had picked up his formal uniform from the cleaners before he left town, and his black shoes had been shined until he could see his face in the leather.

He was ready.

When he arrived in Willow Springs and pulled up in front of the doctor's house on Second Street, his heart was beating a mile a minute. For a moment, nothing happened. Everything went on as normal and no one paid any mind to the tall soldier with the protruding ears who stepped out of his shiny new Ford Deluxe.

Well, not new. Ten years old, actually. But new to him, and he'd waxed it until it looked brand new. Hopefully Nellie Mae would be impressed and not repulsed by it.

He needn't have worried. About fifteen seconds after he got out of the car, Nellie came running from the door, shrieking with excitement. She launched herself into his arms without even looking at the car.

The next three days sped by in a blur, filled with the ethereal moments of bliss he wanted to last forever. He reveled in the excitement of kisses, he tried to memorize how soft and lovely her skin, how shiny her brown curls. He listened to the lilt of her voice and how fragile it sounded on his ears. It made him want to keep her safe. Make her happy. Could he accomplish such a task?

In another sense, the days dragged. In the first hour he was there, he heard more than he ever cared to hear again on the subject of dresses and luncheons and cakes and guests.

"John, what color flowers do you favor?" His soon-to-be mother-in-law eyed him as if the entire future of mankind depended on his answer.

"Mother, he's colorblind," Nellie reminded her quietly.

There was a slight moment of uncertainty in Beulah Thomas's eyes, as if she was mortified at her blunder. Nellie's mother did not like making mistakes.

"Sunflowers," he said. "The yellow ones. I can see yellow."

"Yellow flowers it is," Beulah replied with a smile as she wrote it on her list. Johnny didn't ask where she intended to get sunflowers in December.

As the sisters conversed on the other side of the kitchen table that appeared to have lived a rough life, Johnny leaned close to Nellie's ear. "Sure you don't want to elope?"

She turned red and elbowed him. Hard. He must have found the strongest spitfire this side of the Mississippi.

At Beulah's urging, he went to the post office and the doctor's office every day to check for the results of his blood test. He didn't mind, since Nellie lived in the doctor's house.

Nellie had informed him all the way back in February when he was discharged from the army that Missouri still required blood tests prior to marriage in order to check for venereal disease and genetic disorders. Johnny had put it off, partly because he thought it was a ridiculous rule and partly because he was afraid if he got it too soon it wouldn't be valid by the time of the wedding, and someone would say they couldn't get married. But here it was, two days before the wedding and the final day mail would be received, and it hadn't yet come.

Johnny's first thought was to panic. Now they wouldn't be able to get married. The wedding would have to be postponed and Nellie Mae would surely say it was a sign they shouldn't go through with it. He paced outside the post office for a good ten minutes before the postmaster came outside to talk to him.

"You know, Mr. Hagaman, I couldn't help but notice you've been meeting the doctor's secretary here every day waiting for those results. Are you the soldier hoping to marry our Nellie Mae?"

Hoping. As in unsure. Johnny shouldn't have been surprised that the postmaster knew Nellie well enough to refer to her in a possessive way. There couldn't be a soul in Willow Springs that didn't love her, as friendly and relational as she was.

"I am, sir," he replied. He was hoping for good news. Maybe the postman had misplaced the letter and had just found it behind his desk or a mail slot. But his hands were empty.

"I'm certainly sorry your results haven't come. But I did want to let you know that Arkansas, just a short car ride away from Willow Springs, doesn't require blood tests. There has been a time or two when an impatient couple simply headed down to Mammoth Spring to say their vows."

"My parents had to do that when they tried to get married in Virginia," Johnny said, remembering the story he hadn't thought about in years. "They had to cross over into Tennessee."

"It's done all the time in these cases," the man said with a nod.

Johnny was both relieved and anxious at the news. He'd definitely prefer to ditch the wedding and head south. It would be an adventure. A story to tell their children and grandchildren. He didn't think Nellie would care so much, but Beulah might be downright heartbroken. She might even oppose by some Scriptural mandate he didn't know. Would Nellie's family consider them truly married if they didn't have a church wedding?

"Do you know where they head in Arkansas?" Johnny asked the postmaster.

"Come on in and take a look at the map." The man led him inside and unfolded the map of the United States. He flattened it out and perched his glasses on the edge of his nose. "Here we are in Howell County. If you follow Route 63 – used to be Route 7 – all the way down to the state line, the first town you'll come to is Mammoth Spring. It's a small town, but they have a City Hall."

Johnny studied the map, memorizing the route. It sounded easy enough. Route 63 would take them right where they needed to go. "Thanks. We'll see what she says." He shook the man's hand.

"We'll be sorry to miss your wedding," the postman said as they shook. "Everyone's been looking forward to it. But if it's the only way, then go for it, man."

Johnny thanked him again and left. Unfortunately, he'd have to convince more than the local postman. He'd have to convince Beulah Thomas.

"You just can't do that."

Johnny listened to the room go silent in the wake of Beulah's answer. He'd asked if they could call off the church wedding and hop on the road to Mammoth Spring.

"My parents did it, actually, when they found themselves in the same circumstance. And your postman said folks do it all the time."

Nellie Mae wouldn't look at him. She watched her mother without saying a word. But Johnny saw the argument sitting there on the tip of her tongue.

When she didn't speak, he continued. "I respect your concern, Mrs. Thomas. I understand it would be a great disappointment. But it may be our only choice."

"We always have a choice," she said firmly. "We don't need to rush into decisions. If the blood test hasn't arrived, maybe it's a sign from the Lord to wait."

Since Johnny had his eyes pinned on Nellie Mae, he could see the exact moment her resolve began to falter. "Maybe she's right," she said without looking his way.

"I don't see why anyone would think that," Johnny argued, standing up. "It could just as easily be a sign we shouldn't have some big church wedding."

Nellie Mae still didn't look at him. She took to staring at her hands in her lap with a sad expression.

Opal, Nellie's oldest sister, crossed her arms over her chest. "We've already made all the plans," she said sensibly. "Nellie has her dress ready. Folks are preparing the supper, flowers are being arranged, the minister is due to meet us at the church."

"But those things won't matter if the blood tests don't come in," Emma Jane offered. Her husband, who had just arrived home after his discharge from the army, stood next to her, staying out of the discussion.

"I don't see what the big problem is," Manny, Nellie's younger brother said from the couch where he was laid up with a broken ankle. His hands were propped up behind his head. He was only listening because he had nothing better to do. "Go ahead with the church wedding. Then wait for the blood tests to sign the license. No one would ever know the difference."

"I'd know. I'd hate that." Nellie Mae sighed. Johnny felt her melancholy rising. He was desperate to do something to make everything better. To get her to believe in their marriage again.

He had to get her away from the noise of her family. Especially her mother. Beulah stood in the center of the room with her lip quivering and her hands on the back of a worn kitchen chair. She wouldn't make this easy. She was a woman of strong convictions, and he couldn't see her giving in.

"Can I talk to you alone?" He said next to Nellie's ear. She raised her eyes and met his. He saw her focus switch to him and felt hope. She nodded and let him lead her outside. He closed the door firmly behind him, hoping it would dissuade anyone from following.

The family had recently moved to the house. Boxes and random pieces of furniture were piled on the veranda and the front walk. Even though Ollie had a new service station he'd built with his own two hands on the edge of town, the house was still way out in the sticks. Sometimes Johnny wondered what they were hiding from. But then again, he could also appreciate the idea of being alone in the middle of nature.

"I think I'd like to live somewhere like this," he said suddenly. She looked up at him, the shadow of a smile pulling at her lips.

"You've lived your whole life in the city," she pointed out.

"That's not true. I was born out in the middle of nowhere in Virginia. My dad loved the outdoors, and he didn't mind being as far away from civilization as possible. It was my ma who insisted on living in town when they moved to Indiana."

"So all these years later you're just trying to get back to your roots," she said ruefully.

He shrugged and smiled. "Look, sugar, I know your mother

doesn't want us to do this, but it could be for the best. She's got plenty to do here without worrying about all the wedding details."

Nellie Mae didn't answer for a long time. She walked, her arms pulling her sweater tight across her chest.

"You cold?" he asked.

The December day was seasonable. He hadn't thought about the fact that she'd probably be chilled. He put his arm around her and pulled her tightly against him.

"How can I disappoint them?" she said softly. "How can I run off and do this against their will?"

"What does your dad say?" he asked, wondering if Ollie had voiced any opinion.

She shrugged. "He's still at the station fixing it up. They open on Monday."

"What do you think he'll say?"

She considered his question for a long time. He took the opportunity to look down at her, noticing the pretty white blouse and light skirt she wore. Fashionable heels clad her feet even out in the middle of nowhere. He appreciated her looks until he remembered that soon he would be responsible to provide those things for her. Could he give her everything she wanted?

"I guess he'd say we have to do what we believe the Lord wants us to do no matter what anyone else says." She didn't sound convinced by the words.

He prayed for patience. "And what do you think the Lord wants us to do?"

She shook her head and sighed again. "I'm not a good person to ask, Johnny. I always second guess myself. It's hard for me to make decisions."

"Okay," he said, grabbing her hands and making her face him. "Then do you trust me to do what I know He wants?"

Nellie Mae stared at his face for a long moment. Finally, she gave him the faintest nod. "Yes."

He felt his heart soar. "Good," he tried to reign in his elation. "It's an easy answer for me. We go to Arkansas and get married before I have to be back in Indiana for school."

He expected her to argue. He expected more uncertainty and indecision, more family deliberation. But she stared straight into his eyes, and as she did, something changed in her expression. He saw that determination light. She seemed to throw all of her trust on him in that one moment.

"Okay. Let's go."

Thirty-Six

The moment Nellie Mae threw caution to the wind and put all her trust in Johnny, she knew freedom. She felt the thrill of adventure.

"I'll go pack," she said with a laugh of exhilaration.

"I'll talk to Evan. We can have him and Emma Jane come along with us to be our witnesses. They can take the bus back to Willow Springs afterwards. Bring everything you'll need in our new house, because we'll be driving straight through to Indiana."

She kissed him and ran inside to do what he'd asked. She'd already brought all her belongings from town, so she was surrounded by all her worldly possessions, which honestly wasn't much. But what should she take? She put her clothes in an old carpet bag of her mother's that didn't get much use anymore. She stuffed her notebooks and her Bible and her stationary in the bag on top of the clothes, along with her extra pair of heels and her makeup and hair curlers.

Her eyes fell to the shelf where her old camera sat, unused. It had been a while since she'd taken any pictures. In high school, it had been her and Martha's favorite pastime, walking around and taking pictures, but now that she was getting married and neither of them were in school anymore, she saw Martha less than she used to. It made her sad. She wished she could tuck her little friend in her pocket and take her along to Indiana, but she knew that wasn't the way of the world. Martha would find her own love and live her own life. Their time had come to an end. Nellie thought about all the things she'd never told her best friend and wondered if she'd ever have the chance again.

She ran her fingers over the cold, rough surface of the camera. She wished she could capture every space and every dear face that would stay here in Willow Springs as she ran off to her new life. She wished for an album of all her favorite things so she could look at them every day and never forget them. She wished whenever she opened it, the pages would transport her to that very moment, that very space, renewing the feelings and thoughts born in her spirit as each event transpired.

A tear slipped out of the corner of her eye. She was giving up everything familiar and safe to be with a man she didn't even know all that well. He seemed to like her, and he had a lot of plans for the future. Their future. Would she regret uprooting herself from her family and her life here to become a new entity – Mrs. J.H. Hagaman?

She gave a short laugh. The name made her sound old and stodgy. Not the vibrant, living being she wanted to be.

Her eyes fell upon the camera once more and she suddenly grabbed it. "I need to say goodbye to Martha," she whispered.

She packed the camera and the rest of her things. She dressed in her nicest Sunday dress and brushed her curls until they shone. She darkened her lipstick and slipped into her heels. Then she stared in the mirror, sure that the face looking back at her wasn't really hers. That girl looked confident. Ready to embark on a new life. Ready to face the future and be a wife.

"Goodbye," she said softly, touching the mirror.

She ran to the car. Emma Jane and her husband Evan were already in the backseat. She hesitated before she got in, but her eyes fell on Johnny's dear face and her heart jumped at his lopsided grin. He looked so handsome in his military uniform and cap.

She turned back and looked at her family. Her mother came to her, and Nellie was surprised to see tears in her eyes, along with uncertainty Nellie would never have expected to see there. Her father, who had arrived home, reached for her hands and squeezed them.

"Be a good girl, Nellie Mae," he said with tears in his eyes. "Read your Bible and pray. Honor your good name wherever your path takes you."

She nodded. How she would miss his calming, happy presence! "Thanks for always being there, Dad," she said through her own tears.

He smiled as he stepped back and allowed her mother to step forward.

Beulah didn't smile. She didn't gush or sob or say any of the lovely pleasantries a mother might say at the moment of a goodbye to her daughter. She cleared her throat and looked Nellie in the eyes.

"I know I've been firm with you," she said solemnly. "But I hope you know it was only ever because I care. And don't worry about the church and the dress and the cake. I'll take care of everything. Just get married by a minister. And respect your husband, no matter what happens."

Nellie Mae nodded. As she got into the car, she thought about her mother's words. Mother had never shown anything but the utmost respect for her husband. And Dad had always been worth every drop of it. Nellie didn't think it seemed like such a hard thing. Johnny would make her happy. He would be gallant and hard-working. He'd nurture her love for God and teach their children and their children's children to follow the Lord, wouldn't he? Why would her mother give her such a solemn charge when it would come so easily? Wasn't it supposed to, after all?

She shook off the doubt as she waved goodbye. She reached for Johnny's hand as he turned the key to start the car. It was only then she noticed the car. She should have said something. She opened her mouth to thank him, but something unexpected came out instead.

"I need to say goodbye to Martha."

Unquestioning, Johnny drove down the main road of Willow Springs until he came to the edge of town where Martha lived. He parked in the driveway and gave her an encouraging nod. "Take all the time you need."

Nellie nodded and ran to the door. When her best friend in all the world opened it, Nellie could hold back her tears no longer.

"I'm leaving," she said, grabbing Martha's arms and pulling her into a fierce hug. "I'm leaving right now to go get married in Arkansas, and then I'm going on to Indiana after."

"Oh!" Martha hugged her back, gasping in surprise. "But the wedding—"

"The blood test didn't come in." Nellie didn't want to talk about the particulars. She only wanted to soak in every inch of Martha's dear face. She didn't know when she'd see her again.

"Oh, we had such times together," Nellie squeezed her hands. And they had. They had shared their dreams and their laughs. Martha's mischievous, wonderful way had given Nellie peace in the darkest moments. She'd given her joy when she felt nothing but sadness and fatigue. How could she just say goodbye and leave?

"Write to me?" Nellie asked, her voice breaking.

"Of course," Martha said as she wiped a tear from Nellie's cheek. "And you'll write me. That's what friends do."

Nellie swallowed hard. "Martha, I … we talked about so many things. I told you all my secrets, and you told me yours. I know I'm not the best example, and I don't have everything figured out, but I should have said more about the most important thing in my life. I … I just want to make sure you know the Lord. He loves you so."

Martha shrugged. "I go to church, too, Nellie. I know God."

Nellie nodded and smiled, leaning over to kiss Martha's cheek. "I know. But it's not just about going to church, you know that, right? It's about Jesus and what he did for us that we couldn't do for ourselves. I just need to make sure you understand. Before I go."

Martha nodded, looking a little bewildered, but she still wore a smile. Nellie had a sinking feeling that she'd waited too long to bring up the conversation they could have had. Why had she been so selfish?

Martha patted her cheek and gave her a prim smile. "Don't worry none about me, love. I'll be just fine. You go on now and marry your sweetheart."

"I love you, Martha," Nellie said, squeezing her hand.

"I love you too, sweetie. We'll see each other again. You go on now."

Mammoth Spring was only an hour away, especially considering Nellie's soon-to-be husband's heavy foot on the accelerator. The ride went faster than she'd expected. Before she was ready, they were driving into the small town.

"What a beautiful little spot!" Emma Jane exclaimed as she looked out her window. A rushing spring made its busy way along the side of the main road in the town. Johnny pulled into the city park so they could get out and look at it.

"Can you imagine how peaceful it'd be listening to the song of that spring every day? I can't see how I'd ever find anything to worry about again." Nellie breathed deeply of the cold winter air. It wasn't cool enough to stop the rushing waters of the industrious spring. She was a little jealous. Oh, to have that much energy!

Johnny put his arm around her and kissed her cheek. His lips felt warm in the chilly air. He spoke next to her ear. "I'll see what I can do about finding you a spring."

She chuckled and put her arms around his waist. She leaned her head against his chest and listened to the steady beat of his heart. Emma Jane and Evan had wandered further down the path, hand in hand, talking in low voices.

"Guess we better go find the judge," Johnny said finally, when she was so relaxed, she was ready to drift off to sleep. "Wish we could get married right here in nature. Seems like the best place on earth to me."

Nellie glanced up at him. "You didn't want that old church wedding, did you, dear?"

He looked sheepish, but he admitted as much with a nod. "You got me, sugar. I'm not one for big to-dos."

Nellie stared back at the water. "Neither am I. But I'm also not one to go against my family. That was hard."

"They think we went against them?"

She shrugged. "I don't know. Maybe not. I hope they understand."

He quietly took her hand and led her down the path toward the main street of the town. He didn't say anything as he marched down the abandoned sidewalk. They came to an unassuming, newer square building in the center of town, just across from the police station and directly to the right of the public library. The front of the structure was made of the familiar Ozark masonry, large rocks of different colors plastered together with neatly painted white trim around the windows and doors.

"Looks like a giraffe," Nellie said, putting her palm on the thick sandstone arranged whimsically across the surface of the building.

"You only see this in the Ozarks," Johnny remarked as he

covered her hand with his own. He wound his fingers through hers and turned her to him, kissing the tip of her nose. "You ready?"

"Yes," she said immediately. Her certainty seemed to catch him off guard. "But it's closed, Johnny."

Johnny glanced down at the "closed" sign in the corner of the window. He slapped his hand on his knee. "It's Sunday! I didn't even stop to think that everything would be closed up tight."

Evan and Emma Jane had caught up to them. "We could get a couple rooms at the motel out by the highway and come back first thing in the morning," Evan suggested.

Nellie shook her head. "We've come this far. Johnny has to be back for school tomorrow."

"I can miss one day," he said. He frowned, and she wondered if he was feeling guilty that they wouldn't have a honeymoon. No wedding, no honeymoon. None of the things a groom usually offered his bride to ease their way into a marriage.

"It's alright," she assured him, squeezing his hand. "We'll get you back on time. We've got a whole lifetime of adventures ahead of us. We can have them on days you aren't due in the classroom."

"Good woman you've got there," Evan said with a grin, running his hands up and down his wife's arms in a gesture that seemed to say he knew he'd gotten a good woman as well. "Trait that seems to run in the family."

"Come on," Nellie said, starting off down the sidewalk, pulling Johnny along with her. "There's a church down where the road bends. Let's see if anyone's there."

Indeed there was a small gathering of the congregation seated in the pews, placidly listening to the tranquil voice of a man standing at the pulpit inside the little church building.

"Oh, the depth of the riches both of the wisdom and knowledge of God! How unsearchable are his judgments, and his ways past finding out! For who hath known the mind of the Lord? Or who hath been his counselor? Or who hath first given to him, and it shall be recompensed unto him again? For of him and through him and to him are all things: to whom be glory forever. Amen."

Johnny, Nellie Mae, Emma Jane and Evan all slipped into the back pew as quiet as could be so as not to disturb the serene group. Nellie Mae looked around, sizing up the church. Her church had strong opinions about other denominations. She had been given the impression that Baptists, Methodists or Presbyterians were "social clubs" where the truth of the Bible was not held up as the standard for life.

But this minister obviously revered the words on the pages of his worn Bible as he held it close to his chest, reveling in the words he had just spoken.

"Dear people, we must stop thinking we know better than God! We must believe him when he says he is in control of every detail of our lives, every ripple and effect. He knows what he is doing, and when it is all said and done, and the story of our lives is finished, he gets the praise. It's all about him, Christian, not about you. Do you wonder if you are making the right choice? Only honor him with your activities, and he will bless. Do you feel you failed? Let him pick you up out of the mire and set your feet on the rock of Christ once again. Do you worry about the future, about your relationships and your ministries? Give it all into his capable hands. He loves you. He will get the job done."

The pastor paused and turned a few pages in his Bible. His finger found its mark, and he read. "Being confident of this very thing, that he which hath begun a good work in you will perform it until the day of Jesus Christ."

The last of his words seemed to echo off the old stained-glass windows and the tall ceiling of the building. He closed his Bible and prayed. When he was done, his friendly eyes fell to the four who had recently entered the room.

"We have visitors with us," he said warmly. "Would you all mind standing and introducing yourselves? Tell us what has brought you here tonight."

Johnny froze beside her. He hesitated so long Nellie thought she might have to get up and explain in his place. She was taking a deep breath to do so when she felt the pew creak and shift as he stood, still holding her hand. She stood with him.

"We came here to get married."

Nellie Mae chuckled along with the other members of the congregation at his brief and terrible explanation. Everyone watched them, waiting for him to continue.

Nellie spoke with a cheerful smile as she met the eyes of the people around them. "Hello. This is Johnny, who has recently returned from the war after being injured during his service. I'm Nellie Mae. This is my sister Emma Jane and her husband, Evan. I'm here to tell you that was just the message we needed to hear! We're from Missouri, and we were supposed to have our church wedding today. One of our blood tests didn't come in on time, so we had to give up our lovely wedding my friends and family had planned. We came here looking for a justice of the peace but remembered it's Sunday and the city hall is closed. Seems like everything is against us getting married today!"

The group laughed and the pastor held out his arms. "Welcome. My name is Pastor Weaver. Our dear brother Lester Collins is the city clerk. I think he might be persuaded to open up the office long enough to fill out your paperwork. And I am not a justice of the peace, but I would be happy to marry you. This is a house of the Lord, so you need not even give up your church wedding."

The crowd gave a scattered applause as the four of them came to the front of the sanctuary. Pastor Weaver had Johnny and Nellie Mae join hands. He prayed a blessing over their marriage, then had them repeat simple vows.

Just like that, Nellie was a married woman. She stared into the eyes of her husband. He smiled his adorable half-grin and squeezed her fingers so tightly they went numb.

I'm Mrs. John Hagaman, she thought to herself, unable to grasp it. *Not a Thomas anymore. Everything is different.*

Johnny kissed her and Pastor Weaver dismissed the gathering. He introduced them to his wife and a daughter around the same age as Nellie. Then he introduced them to Mr. Collins and his wife and children.

The rest of the evening was a blur. They went to city hall and completed the appropriate documents, they had a nice dinner with the Collins family in their home, and then they drove Emma Jane and Evan to the bus stop.

Emma Jane grabbed Nellie's hands with both of hers as the men walked together to the ticket booth. Emma Jane's face was as red as a tomato.

"Don't judge things by the first night," she said cryptically after she looked all around to make sure no one was eavesdropping.

Nellie giggled and put her palm on her sister's face. "Thanks, sis. I wouldn't have had a clue."

Emma Jane sighed with relief. "I know Mama doesn't talk about it except to preach about purity until marriage. It would be nice if she talked a little bit about what you're supposed to do *after* the marriage part."

Nellie nodded. "That's for sure!"

She kissed her sister goodbye and hugged her as hard as she dared until the men returned, and it was time for them to board the waiting bus.

After they waved goodbye, Mr. and Mrs. Hagaman started out on the journey home to Indianapolis.

Thirty-Seven

Nellie Mae awoke with a start, not certain for a moment where she was. It was dark and chilly, and the hum of the car motor that had lulled her to sleep was now silent. Nellie Mae sat up and tried to gather her wits

"Sorry to wake you," Johnny said. "You were sleeping so peacefully, but I was starting to fall asleep, and I didn't want to drive off the road. Would you mind driving a while?"

She stared down at the stick shift in the console. She had no idea how to drive a stick shift, even though her brother had tried to teach her. She was a dunce at it. But she didn't want her new husband to know, so she nodded without a word and switched seats with him.

Johnny tried to sleep, but it didn't take too long for him to realize by the constant shifting and stalling that Nellie had no idea what she was doing. Her face burned with embarrassment as he chuckled and had her pull over to the nearest parking lot.

They were in the parking lot of a motel.

"Do we have enough money?" she asked, thinking better of her words only after she'd spoken them. He hesitated. She was fairly certain he hadn't appreciated her doubt.

"I have enough for a night."

He went to get the room while she waited in the car. She shivered in the cold December night air and pulled her coat tightly around herself. He eventually returned with a key and pulled the overnight bag from the trunk of the car. He came to her door and opened it for her.

"Thank you," she said, trying to sound cheerful. She followed him down the long sidewalk outside the quiet motel. The rooms were all dark and silent, a testament to the very late hour. Nellie felt awkward and wished he would say something. But she was learning not to expect much conversation from her new husband.

He stopped in front of a door and put the key into the lock. The door swung open with a creak.

Nellie Mae wanted to think of some romantic thought – something about how she would enter the room a girl, but leave a woman, or something silly like that, but she didn't feel sentimental. Truth be told, she was as scared as a gopher caught outside his hole. She had always thought getting married would somehow make her more mature. Capable. Confident. But she was the same backwoods girl she'd always been. Johnny was going to figure it out sooner or later and be a good sight disappointed.

If only he'd say something.

She finally spoke as they stood inside their room, surveying the meager surroundings. "I'm not sure what to say. How to act." She chuckled with uncertainty as she took off her coat.

Her vulnerability seemed to crack the resolve of his silence. He reached for her and pulled her close. "I just want you to be Nellie Mae. Nellie Mae Hagaman." He kissed her, and the icy chill that had clung to her began to melt, if just a little.

"I don't know how to be her," she joked. "She's a whole new woman."

"I guess you'll figure it out." He smiled at her and held her close again, driving away the rest of the cold. It was the first time she'd really ever felt warm – truly warm.

The next morning Nellie awoke with a start, surprised to find Johnny's side of the bed empty. She heard the water running in the bathroom on the other side of the thin wall.

She sat up as it struck her anew. She was a married woman. That man was her husband. Her *husband.* Never again would she have to obey her mother's instructions. Never again would she share a room with her sisters. Never again would she have to endure a lecture for being too friendly with a boy. She could get as friendly as she wanted with her husband. She laughed out loud at the thought.

"What's so funny?" Johnny stuck his head out of the bathroom. He was dressed in his white undershirt and his pants. Without a belt they hung low on his slender frame. She was tickled by his disheveled, boyish appearance.

"I was just thinking how we're married. We're married, Johnny! Free!"

He smiled, but he didn't appear as taken with the thought of freedom as she was. He came to her and kissed her, embarrassing her because he had freshly cleaned teeth and she had morning breath.

"Sky's the limit, Kitten," he said in a low voice that made her insides feel like they were melting. "As soon as I get done with school, I'm going to build you a house. Your own house with two bedrooms and a bath, a kitchen and a front room. And it'll have a nice creek nearby and no neighbors for miles."

She felt her excitement deflate a little. It wasn't exactly what she had in mind. She had seen them in a posh apartment for the foreseeable future. At least until they had children. Then she'd seen them buying one of those modern pod-type homes with a green lawn and neighbors up and down both sides of the street. They'd be the enviable contemporary family.

"Hopefully a few neighbors," was all she said, working to keep her cheerful tone intact.

"Well, sure," he said, but he hesitated first.

A thought occurred to her in that moment. The same thought that had been occurring to her over and over, along with many other thoughts and questions she'd been too nervous to bring up before. But she supposed they had to discuss things sooner or later.

"Johnny, where are we going to live when we get back to Indianapolis?"

His smile dropped and he stood up straight. "I wasn't able to find a thing. We'll have to stay with my parents for a little while, just until something comes up."

The news hit her like a ton of bricks. She'd thought for sure he'd find something. Who wanted to bring their new bride home to live with their mama? She shuddered involuntarily as she thought about it.

He gave her a look before he returned to the bathroom. She followed him, watching as he lathered his cheeks with shaving cream. The rich, familiar smell reminded her of her father. Good old Dad. He'd never made his bride live with his mother. Not even when he was a sixteen-year-old groom. He'd made a way to provide for her.

"Nellie Mae, you said you'd be okay if we had to live with my family for a while."

His voice was stern, and she felt an inner switch flip at the sound. Her throat went tight and her eyes burned. She was angry, and it seemed the only thing to do was to let off the steam building up inside.

"I never said so!" she shot back. "I said I hoped it wouldn't come to that, but it was very nice of her to offer. That was the polite way of saying I don't want to live with your parents!"

It seemed obvious to her. How could he ask such a thing? Not ask, even, but demand! She breathed deeply through her nose, feeling her cheeks go hot.

"What do you want me to do?" he asked, his shoulders drooping. She saw the flicker of disappointment in his eyes, followed by irritation. He finished shaving and rinsed off his face. As he pressed a clean towel to his damp skin, he turned to her. "I have to finish school before I can get a job. Do you think someone is going to give us an apartment for free?"

"I can work." She crossed her arms across her chest.

"I don't want you to do that." He quickly went to pack the suitcase, nodding at the bathroom to indicate she should do what she needed to do because they were leaving. "If we leave now, I can still get to my first class on time."

She angrily grabbed her dress from the chair and her small toiletry case. She went into the bathroom, slamming the door behind her.

She didn't speak to him for the rest of the day. Not as they drove back to Beech Grove. Not as he parked the car in the street and opened her door, carrying their things up to his parents' front porch. Not as he knocked on the door. She wouldn't even look at him as he presented her to his parents and younger sister, or as he carried their things to their tiny bedroom off the living room, or as he dressed for class and kissed her on the forehead.

"Goodbye, Nellie Mae," he said, his tone resigned. He left her in the room by herself.

She threw herself down on the bed and sobbed until her heart had spent its frustration and sorrow.

She wanted to go home.

Thirty-Eight

May 30, 1947

Somehow Nellie Mae survived five months in her in-laws' home. Five long months.

It had taken her at least a week before she could even look at Johnny without being angry. Then she chose let it go and accept her fate. She left as early in the morning as she could for her job – which she insisted on taking even though Johnny protested – and came home as late as she could at night. Dinner time was the worst part of the day. Her mother-in-law's bland cooking and the constant arguing amongst the family members, especially the elder Hagamans, left her frazzled.

Her mother-in-law wasn't cruel, but she wasn't kind, either. Nellie Mae knew where she stood in the home the first week they lived there. They'd been sitting down for dinner, and Nellie had asked if she might pray over the food. The Hagaman family was not in the habit of praying before meals, so they all exchanged rather uncomfortable looks. But of course, they agreed.

"Sure, Nellie Mae," Mr. Hagaman said. "Why don't you go ahead?"

So Nellie prayed. She prayed for the same things she prayed for

255

at home: that they would honor their good name, work hard, be thankful and love each other. She had opened her eyes and reached for her fork only to discover Mrs. Hagaman was glaring at her. She tried to ignore it, but Johnny had noticed first.

"What's wrong, ma?" He dug into his mashed potatoes.

"Why would you say that?" Mrs. Hagaman directed her question toward Nellie. "Do you think this family doesn't love each other?"

Nellie glanced at Johnny, shocked at her reaction to such a generic prayer. "Course not, ma'am. That's just what I always say."

"Just because we aren't as affectionate a family as yours, just because we don't hold hands and pray and gush over each other doesn't mean we don't love each other. Don't ever say such a thing again in this house."

Nellie looked to Johnny to defend her, but he made sure his mouth was full and he couldn't speak. She gave a little inward sigh before she pasted a smile on her face. "I'm so sorry, Mrs. Hagaman. I promise you I did not intend to offend. I would have prayed the same thing in my own house." Nellie Mae tried to force a bit of contriteness in her voice for the sake of peace, though she wanted to get up and yell.

"I don't think the girl meant anything, Helen," Mr. Hagaman said impatiently. "Just eat your dinner."

"I won't have her putting our family down." Mrs. Hagaman took her fork and began to eat, spending the rest of the dinner in silence.

Nellie looked again at Johnny, who continued to shovel food into his mouth as if he hadn't eaten in days. He didn't look at her. She realized she was to have no heroic rescues in this house.

Nellie excused herself as soon as it was justifiable to do so. She didn't feel the least bit guilty when she made no offer to help clean up. She went to the solace of her little room and stared out the front window to the quiet street for a long while.

She'd always thought her own home was too rigid. She'd

thought of her parents, or at least her mother, as distant and downright tyrannical. She'd chafed under their thumb.

But now she could see she'd had it all wrong. Her home was a happy one. It was a place where folks were free to speak their mind and wrestle on the floor and play practical jokes. How could she have thought of that warm environment as a prison? Had she no sense at all?

Later, when Johnny came to bed, he put his arms around her and kissed her neck. "I'm sorry about that, Kit."

"Why didn't you stand up for me?" she asked. She sat stiffly in his embrace. "Did you think I was putting your family down, too?"

He didn't answer immediately. In fact, she got to thinking he wasn't going to answer at all. "It wasn't what you said, Nellie. It was just because it was you saying it."

She turned around to face him. "What's that supposed to mean?"

He hesitated again. "I don't think my mother and sisters are hard on you because they look down on you. I think they're jealous of you."

She laughed, because she honestly thought he must be joking. But he didn't laugh, and she realized he meant it. She mulled over his words. "What in tarnation could they be jealous about?"

It was his turn to laugh. "Nellie Mae, look in the mirror! There are movie stars who aren't as pretty as you. Plus, you're the friendliest person I've ever met. And you have my heart. That's plenty to make them jealous."

His words bolstered her confidence a little. Somehow, knowing he supported her, she made it through the next few months. She'd take a deep breath and remind herself of what he'd said every time someone shot sharp words her way or made a point to exclude her from family life. Without that glimpse from his perspective, she might have made a run for it. Gone back home. Back to the people who loved her.

One night five months after they moved in, she came home from work exhausted. She was ready to put up her feet for a few minutes before dinner. The only thing that kept her going as she walked up the steps and through the front door was the thought of her pillow and her bed.

She knew why she was so tired. She'd gone to the doctor that day on her lunch break. He'd confirmed what she suspected. She was going to be a mother.

She hadn't expected a baby so soon, but she was happy to hear the news. She knew her family would be over the moon when they heard. However, she was concerned about Johnny's reaction. He would worry about money. She dreaded having to tell him.

As she headed toward the bedroom, she was suddenly filled with resolve. *I'll just tell him and get it over with*, she decided.

Lost in her thoughts, she didn't see her mother-in-law come around the corner until she was standing directly in front of Nellie and Johnny's bedroom door. Nellie stopped short in surprise.

"Johnny's sleeping," Mrs. Hagaman said firmly, crossing her arms across her chest like a sentry guard. "He needs his rest."

Nellie Mae was so angry she saw spots. A hundred biting remarks were on the tip of her tongue, but she was so mad she couldn't speak a word of them. She summoned all the control she could muster and pushed past her mother-in-law without knocking her over. She slammed the door behind her, hearing a gasp from Mrs. Hagaman that satisfied some of her rage.

Johnny was startled awake by the bang. He sat up, bleary-eyed, trying to gather his wits as she stood over him with her hands on her hips.

"Do you know what she just said to me?" Nellie Mae said in a loud whisper.

He rubbed his face with his hands. She was reminded that her husband was genuinely tired. He'd been working and going to school from sunup to sundown. But it only irked her more to think that her mother-in-law may have been right.

"I have to talk to you." She was sullen, but she tried to inject a note of contriteness into her tone. She sighed and threw her sweater across the back of the chair in the corner.

"Go ahead."

She wasn't sure how to tactfully or gently share her news, so she just said the words. "I'm going to have a baby. I'm due in January."

He didn't answer. She sat down on the chair in front of the mirror and stared at her appearance. She picked up her brush and tried to sort out the tangles in her curls as she waited for him to answer.

"We need to get our own place."

Johnny's words were like a balm for her cloistered soul. She jumped up and went to him, climbing into his lap and putting her arms around his neck. "Oh, Johnny, do you mean it? Can we afford it?"

He put his arms around her waist and leaned his head against her chest. "We'll make it work. It will have to be small. It's not going to be anything fancy. But we can't stay here if a baby's on the way."

She suddenly felt nothing but the utmost compassion for her hard-working husband. She was also quite tickled with the little one growing within, since the child had managed to set Nellie free from her prison. She kissed Johnny and wrapped her arms around him.

"I love you, Johnny. I'm sorry we fight so much."

"Me too," he said with a sigh.

To her great relief, the following week Johnny found a tiny apartment in the not-so-safe area of Beech Grove. There was no heat save a fireplace, the water only worked certain times of the day and the electricity routinely went out for days at a time, but Nellie Mae loved her newfound independence. She reveled in the ability to come home from work and make dinner for her husband. She decorated with what she had on hand and made sure their little nest was comfortable and clean.

One night she hid in the pantry and waited until he came through the door. He called for her, searching the three rooms before he came near enough. She jumped out of the pantry and scared him so much he yelled. Then he laughed.

"Now this is marriage," Johnny said, catching her around the waist. He kissed her as he twirled her around the room. "You know I'm going to have to get you back for that."

"I'd like to see you try!" She laughed and wriggled away from him, giggling when he came after her.

Her energy level gradually continued to decrease as her abdomen grew. In some ways, the pregnancy made some of her fatigue and sadness easier to bear. But her anemia only got worse. She had to boil nails in the kettle and drink the rusty water, but it only helped a little. When she climbed the stairs to their apartment after work, her feet felt like lead bricks and her lungs burned. Once she blacked out at the top of the stairs. A neighbor helped her inside and called the school to find Johnny.

Johnny resumed his welding job at the train yard and saved enough money from his military salary and Nellie's salary from her secretary's position to purchase a rural piece of land with several acres of creek and woods. He said he was going to build his own house.

"Are you sure you know how to do it?" Nellie was skeptical. He'd never built a house before. She could see he was bound and determined, though, so she tried to talk him into buying a precut model from Sears. They had some they were trying to get rid of for just six hundred dollars. He could pay as little as fifteen dollars a month.

But he wanted to build the little house from scratch. He set to work on the design and gathered materials he would need on the land. Every moment of spare time was spent at the site, hammering away at the structure. It quickly took shape.

Nellie Mae had seen the building of a few houses in her day. She came to the site with him and watched him work, but his methods were far different than the standard. When he went to work digging a foundation after the skeleton of the house was already built, she put her foot down. She stood over the hole he was scraping out.

"That's not going to work," she said, over and over. "You can't just move a house on top of a foundation. Who ever heard of such a thing?"

He didn't argue with her. He just kept working, digging one day and shingling and siding the house another.

"You can't build a house this way," she continued to protest.

"I can," he replied more than once. It was his only defense.

She continued to badger him about all the things that could go wrong. Weeks passed, and cicadas began to buzz and summer nights grew shorter. Still, he dug the foundation and built the house separately. Still, she fussed.

"What do you think you're going to get me to do differently at this point?" He tossed down the shovel one evening and turned to her, his hands on his hips. "Even if it wasn't going to work, it's too late. This is the way that made sense to me, and this is the way I'm going to do it. So, unless you plan to take over from here, you might as well go back to the apartment."

She sniffed and held her abdomen as if she were protecting their offspring from their father's unwholesome words. "It's not the way you build a house, Johnny. I hate to see all that money wasted for nothing. You know I worked for it every bit as hard as you did."

He didn't seem to appreciate the reminder that she'd earned a good portion of the money he was spending. But her contributions to the finances were about to end, anyway. After Christmas, she could hardly move, she was so tired and swollen. She quit her job and took to her bed for the last few weeks while Johnny fought the elements to finish digging out the cellar in the new house.

One January morning, a morning as cold and icy as they come, Nellie woke up to realize she was freezing. The fire had gone out in the grate and her clothes and sheets were flooded with frigid liquid.

"Johnny," she said, sitting up straight in bed and shaking him hard. "The baby is coming!"

Thirty-Nine

Johnny's young wife sat on the soaking wet bed next to him, stunned. With her face cleansed of makeup and curlers in her hair she seemed much younger than her twenty-three years.

He had no idea what to do. The realization hit him that no one had prepared him to take care of his wife and baby. Either that or he'd forgotten everything.

He sat there for a long time staring at her. Finally, he worked up the nerve to ask. "What do we do?"

He almost cringed, waiting for her to hit him or scream at him, but she surprised him by chuckling.

"Well, I'm going to get up and put my face on," she said lightly. "You can put in a call to the doctor, get the suitcase in the car and get ready to take me to St. Francis."

He was relieved to have instructions. A plan. He'd sort of expected Nellie Mae to fall apart when the time came. As she calmly began removing the soiled bed sheets, he headed for the door.

Johnny called the doctor's number on the black rotary phone in the living room. The doctor asked him questions he had no clue how to answer. Instead of trying to decipher what he meant by "pinkish tinges" or "gushing waters" or "contractions," he simply told the doctor in hardly more than a whisper that the bed was soaked and Nellie Mae said it was time to go to the hospital.

The doctor let him off the hook. "Bring her in. I'll make sure the nurses in the maternity ward have her room ready."

And so it was that early in the morning as the sun was just beginning to rise on their frozen town, Johnny bundled his wife into the car and set off for the hospital.

When they arrived, things began to happen faster than Johnny was prepared to handle. Nellie Mae was whisked away on a wheelchair without a chance to say goodbye. A nurse pushed papers and a pen into his hands. He watched Nellie Mae as a nurse pushed her through a door. Her face was as white as a sheet.

He wondered if he should ask to go with her, but he couldn't bring himself to say the words. He'd never heard of a man joining his wife in the delivery room, and he had no interest in finding out what went on there.

The nurse directed him to a table where he could sit and fill out the papers. "She'll be fine, now. Don't worry."

"How do you know for sure?"

She must not have received that response often, because she stared at him in surprise. Then her eyes narrowed. "Because they almost always are. We go to great lengths to keep our mothers and babies safe. We employ the most modern practices known to medicine. We keep our maternity ward completely disinfected, and all of our policies are meant to keep your wife and baby safe."

Johnny didn't know enough about it to argue with her. But his mother had been talking to Nellie Mae lately, and he'd overheard some of the conversation. She'd said Johnny wouldn't have made it without her constant care. Mrs. Hagaman had continued to tell Nellie horror stories about the maternity wards of city hospitals.

"If I'd gone to a hospital, they would have tied me down to a metal device and given me medicine that would make me hallucinate and writhe in pain during my entire labor," Mrs. Hagaman explained. "And I wouldn't be able to complain about it afterwards, because I wouldn't remember a moment of it."

She paused to allow her words to sink in. "Afterwards, Johnny would have been taken away from me and put in an incubator. He wouldn't have survived. He was too tiny. The only thing that made him stronger was my warmth and constant nursing. Just like a mama cat taking care of her newborn kittens. All I did for the first week of his life was nurse and hold him close to me. If you let nurses have your baby, they will try to keep you from nursing. If you insist, they'll control how much and when. That baby needs to start right away and keep going as much and often as they want."

Johnny's father had been irritated by the story. He'd shaken his newspaper in agitation. "Now how can you know any of that nonsense when you were never in a hospital? Let her be before you scare her half to death."

"I'm only trying to help," she'd shot back.

Johnny knew Nellie had been listening. Intently. But he didn't see any animosity in his mother's eyes. She wanted the best for them and for the baby. She was just convinced the best would not be found in a maternity ward.

Since that conversation a few weeks before, Nellie had been reading up on labor and delivery in a hospital, and asking her friends about their experiences. She'd told him she was worried city hospitals were in some sort of conspiracy against mothers and babies. But when she'd asked Johnny if she could have the baby at home, he couldn't agree to it.

"What if something went wrong, Kit?" He'd held her hands gently, kissing them. "What if being in the hospital saves both your lives?"

She'd sighed and hadn't answered. He'd taken that to mean that she agreed with his reasoning. But it had been clear she didn't like it.

He'd been satisfied with their decision then. But now, sitting out in the stark waiting room while his wife faced whatever waited for her behind that door, he wasn't so sure. Both Johnny and Nellie had been born at home with a midwife in attendance. Johnny accepted the fact that if his mother had gone to the hospital, he probably wouldn't have survived. He figured she'd kept him alive by sheer will. How would they take care of their baby if nurses whisked him away and wouldn't let them see him? He knew it was a valid concern, but he didn't know the right answer.

Johnny remembered the words from a pamphlet Nellie had asked him to read. *To lessen baby deaths, let us have more mother-fed babies. You can't improve on God's plan. For your baby's sake, nurse it.*

It made sense. Who better than God would know what an infant needed for nutrition? After a few calls, Nellie reported to him that she would be required to stay seven days in the hospital. She was worried they would give her drugs so she wouldn't remember having her baby or be able to bond or nurse.

"Johnny, when I was born, my mother couldn't stand to even look at me. I reminded her of her little stillborn daughter who came before me. I've always wondered if all my problems were because I was taken away from my mother those first days. I don't want that to happen with my baby."

He'd told her that she was worrying for nothing, that she was going to be the best little mother a baby had ever had, but now Nellie's words haunted him.

He went back to the nurses' station. "She wants to be awake." He looked the nurse in the eye and tried to be severe. It must have worked, because he saw her resolve falter.

"The doctor will know what's best. You need to trust him."

"Nellie Mae wants to remember the birth," he said stubbornly.

"You get that message to him. And you tell them she's going to be nursing her baby."

She made a face of disgust. "That's not sanitary. The milk we will provide will be rich and formulated for the baby."

He started to argue, but she interrupted him. "And even if it were your concern, we don't allow mothers to nurse for twenty-four hours after the birth, so there will be plenty of time to –"

Protective anger surged within his chest. He should have never brought Nellie Mae into this building. "It *is* my concern. That's my wife you have in there. Tell the doctor she wants to be awake and nurse her baby right after the birth. Go."

The nurse stood up quickly and backed toward the door. "Yes, sir."

The nurse reported back a few minutes later that Dr. Rhea had heard his concerns and was willing to comply with his instructions as long as everything went the way it should. Johnny was relieved. Until he had spent four hours wearing a hole in the thin carpet of the waiting room. He supposed it was a long four hours for the admitting nurse as well, whom he glared at the entire time.

In the army, no one left their comrades alone. Ever. They stuck together as a group no matter what happened. He felt guilty. He should be in the trenches with her, though no part of him desired to see what happened in a birthing room. He hated the feeling of helplessness. It reminded him of being in that hospital bed, unable to go on with his unit, unable to protect his squad. Now it was Nellie lying there, all on her own.

After five hours, he had run out of patience. He went to the desk. "What's taking so long?"

"These things take time, sir. You should sit down and get some rest. We have magazines, and there is a cafeteria downstairs."

"I don't want a magazine; I want an update."

He refused to walk away from the desk until she obliged him, so she stood with a barely concealed sigh and walked through the mysterious white door. In the seconds it was open, he heard yelling.

He knew the tone of that yell anywhere. His wife was screaming. He ran behind the desk and tried to open the door but it was locked. He considered breaking the lock, but even if he could get back there, he would have no idea what to do.

The nurse returned within a couple minutes, disapproval on her face when she saw him behind the desk. "Please return to the waiting room, sir."

"I heard her."

"Sir, please remain calm. Look at the other husbands sitting patiently in the waiting room. This is a normal process. We do it every day. Your wife is progressing as expected. No one has given her any medication to make her sleep, and the attending nurse knows your wife would like to nurse her baby. Everything will be fine. Please go sit down."

"If everything is fine, why is she screaming?"

"Because this is childbirth," another, older nurse said as she stepped into the room by way of the white door. She came to Johnny and put her hand on his arm. "It's part of the curse of sin. It's a tremendous amount of pain and work. And your wife has chosen to experience it with eyes wide open. She is doing what she believes is best for your child. Trust her. Trust God. Pray for your family. That's how your time can best be used right now."

Johnny had needed to hear the advice. Armed with something to do, he gave the woman a grateful nod before he headed back to the seat closest to the nurse's desk. "Just tell me if there's any news."

"Of course," the older nurse said with a nod.

Sometime during the day Johnny fell asleep praying. The next thing he knew, a nurse was shaking him.

She smiled. "You have a daughter. Would you like to see her?"

He jumped out of his chair, grabbing her arm without thinking how rude it must be. She laughed though, especially when he gasped the same time he laughed and nearly choked to death. A couple men in the waiting room chuckled, and one handed him a wrapped cigar.

"Congratulations," he said, shaking his hand.

Johnny followed the woman down the hall where tightly shut doors and eerie silence reigned. None of the other women that must be laboring made the noises he'd heard from his wife earlier.

"We don't usually allow fathers back in this area." The nurse gave him a stern look, but he thought he spied a bit of admiration as well. "You may only stay a moment. Your wife insisted you be allowed to meet your baby girl before we take her to the nursery."

"Will Nellie Mae be alright?" Johnny's eyes narrowed as he fumbled with the brim of his hat in his hands.

"Oh, yes!" she answered brightly. "She'll be just fine, don't you worry. You have quite the spunky little wife."

Johnny grinned. "You don't have to tell me."

When he turned the corner and entered the room, his eyes went wide at the sight of them laying there on the bed. He felt lightheaded at the tender, fragile scene. Nellie Mae was white as a ghost, and her usually carefully kept hair and makeup were a mess. But he'd never seen her more radiant. She cuddled their baby close to her chest.

"There's your daddy, little girl. Your wonderful, strong daddy who is going to take good care of you, even when your mama has a bad day. You're blessed by the Almighty, baby, since you've got the best daddy in the whole world."

Johnny's eyes stung with tears he tried to blink away. The nurse tapped her watch.

"Only a moment, now."

He nodded as she turned and left the room, her sensible heels tapping smartly as she moved. He took a couple steps toward the bed and bent over so he could get a better look at both his girls.

"Oh, Kitten," he said softly, suddenly overcome with love he hadn't expected. "She's just beautiful."

He meant it. He'd always thought newborns were the ugliest things, all red and wrinkled and angry-looking, until now, laying eyes on his own little angel. He stared at her in amazement, daring to reach out and touch a tiny finger with his own. This little bit of flesh was his very lifeblood. She'd come from him. This little girl was part Nellie, part Johnny, and all herself at the same time.

"What are we going to call her?" His heart seemed to wring in two when her little fingers caught his and held on for dear life. He laughed, surprised at her strength.

"Might we call her Linda? Like Linda Darnell? And maybe her middle name could be Rhea, after the doctor who delivered her," Nellie said softly.

He smoothed back her damp hair and laughed at her apparent newfound affection for the doctor she'd mistrusted only hours before. "Honey, we can call her Billy the Kid if you've a mind. You deserve it after what you've been through to get her here," he said as the nurse came back in and gave him a knowing smile.

Nellie was mortified. "Did you hear me yell?"

He chuckled. "Only once for a moment when the door was open."

"We thought he might break down the door," the nurse said as she brought a clean blanket out of the drawer.

"Oh, dear," Nellie Mae said in consternation. "I just couldn't help it. I tried so hard not to make a peep but that once the scream just came right out of me without my permission."

"Perfectly normal," the nurse assured her. "Now off with you, Daddy. Go have something to eat and a nap while we get these two situated."

The walk to the cafeteria was a blur. Johnny had been a great many things in his life. He'd been a son. A cousin. An employee. A Christian. A soldier, a sergeant, and then a husband.

Now he was a father.

Let me be a good one.

Forty

At the hospital, Nellie Mae never felt right until one of the nurses brought her little Linda. The other mothers in her recovery room were friendly, and it was nice having all her meals brought to her, but she couldn't escape the feeling that she and her baby had ended up in some kind of prison rather than a maternity ward.

Johnny was only allowed to visit for an hour in the evening. And the times he was permitted to see her never seemed to be the same time Linda was with her, so he had to be content viewing her through the glass window of the nursery as a nurse with a surgical mask held her up for him.

Nellie was glad he was taking so well to being a father. Many men weren't fond of babies. Her own father had loved his children, though, from the very moment they were born. She remembered her dad holding her younger brothers even more than her mother did.

"I've got a surprise for you," Johnny said on the fourth day she languished in the hospital. "I moved our things out of the apartment to the house."

"I'll be …" she breathed in surprise. "When did you manage to finish the house? And how on God's green earth did you get it over the foundation by yourself?"

"I had help," he admitted.

She shook her head. "I'm speechless. I thought it'd never work."

"You mentioned as much." He raised an eyebrow.

She felt her cheeks warm. "I shouldn't have doubted you. I'm looking forward to seeing it."

"It's not quite finished," he said, playing with the rim of his hat. "There are a couple rooms not plastered yet, but it's close enough we can live in it."

She eyed the nurse who was coming to dismiss all the husbands from the room. "Do you think you could spring me out of this joint a couple days early?"

He didn't answer, and he seemed reticent.

"I'm going crazy not being able to see her. And I just lie around all day with nothing to do. Please take us home."

Johnny's doubtful answer didn't give her much hope, but he must have changed his mind. The nurse came to tell her the next morning that the doctor was discharging them early. They could leave the hospital as long as they came back at the first sign of trouble in either mother or baby.

The day the nurse handed her the baby and shut the car door was Nellie's best moment of motherhood so far. Finally, no one would come to take her daughter away or make decisions on their behalf. She couldn't believe she was free, and that the little bit of warmth in her arms was really all hers now. She'd show them. She'd keep everything clean and warm and Linda would never be sick. Nellie would be the best mother to ever walk the face of the earth.

Johnny started the engine and drove the car out of the parking lot. He drove all the way to their new home on the outskirts of Beech Grove. He drove down the long icy path until they got to the house.

"Oh, Johnny, it's just beautiful!" She'd never felt her heart beating so hard with happiness. "It's perfect."

And it was. The house was small with plain white siding and

green shutters. It had a protruding gable that dipped down the front of the house almost all the way to the ground, giving the structure a quaint, old-world feeling. It boasted cedar shingles and ornamental iron hinges on the door. The property Johnny had found was lovely. The house was nestled just in front of a backdrop of mature trees leading to woods behind. Nellie had seen him digging the cellar, but she hadn't been able to picture the final result until she was standing there looking at it.

"How did you get it on the foundation?" she asked in wonder.

He shrugged, like it had been nothing. "Put the whole thing on pipes and rolled it over the hole in the ground. Then I pulled out the pipes."

Nellie laughed in amazement. "We'll if that doesn't just dill my pickle!"

He chuckled.

She got out of the car, holding Linda easily on her arm. "I'm just speechless!"

She wasn't, though. She approached the house, bouncing the baby in her arms as she giggled. She pointed at details and exclaimed over every little thing she noticed.

"We have a home! Our own little house in the woods!"

Joy welled up within as she came to stand at the threshold. Johnny reached for the baby and hurried to open the door to invite her in. She stepped inside the vestibule, her mind turning so much she felt dizzy. She envisioned a sweet little coat stand just inside the door. And they'd get a sofa for the living room eventually. Maybe even a chair and a television someday.

Next to the front room a door led to a tiny bedroom. Johnny had already set up their bed and the crib, so there was hardly room for anything else. She came back through the door and went beyond the front room to the narrow kitchen. It led to a back porch, which was no more than a stoop leading to the backyard and the trees beyond.

A small stove graced the wall to the right of the window, while a sink with storage underneath sat directly under. She had a small work counter with simple cabinets overhead. The back door had a west-facing window, so she'd see the sunset each night as she made dinner. A table had been pushed under the other window by the wall, graced by two rickety chairs and a high chair. She ran her finger along the cool white enamel of the table and imagined sitting with Johnny, reading her Bible and sipping coffee. They'd stop and join hands so they could pray together.

"It's just perfect," she said again. She went to her husband and hugged him, making little Linda squirm between them. "I'm so happy. So very happy. Our life together is just beginning."

For a while, things were very nearly perfect. Johnny went to school in the mornings and work in the afternoons and came home in time to eat dinner just as she set it on the table. She spent her days trying to get her baby to nurse. When she wasn't working on that project, she attempted to disinfect and wash and set up her new house. She bundled up and walked with the baby through the snow up to the front of the long dirt road and back to get the mail. She wrote letters home and made out a budget so she might save money for furniture and other household items.

For the first time in her life, she felt as if she were in control of her destiny. She didn't have to follow anyone else's plan for her days. She spent them alone with her baby. Johnny had requests, but he was always polite and sweet when he asked her to do things. She wished those peaceful winter days would last forever.

But they didn't.

As spring barely began to tease, Nellie and Johnny woke early one morning to the sound of little Linda struggling to breathe. She coughed and sputtered as she tried to cry. Nellie rushed to her side and picked her up. Her mind flooded with a hundred different illnesses her baby could have. She'd had a little cold in the past few days, but nothing serious. She'd been getting better. But now Nellie could feel the heat of her fever through her clothes.

"Johnny, she can't breathe!"

He jumped out of bed and took the baby, staring at her for a long moment. He held her to his shoulder as he walked up and down the length of their small bedroom, patting her back.

Nellie spied Johnny's Microbiology and Pathology textbook, one of his pre-med classes, and grabbed it, opening it and scanning the index. None of the words were familiar, but Johnny saw her with the book and it must have jogged his memory.

"I just read about pneumonia," he said, causing her heart to constrict in fear. "It starts as a cold sometimes, but it progresses, either by bacteria or a virus."

"What do we do about it?" she asked impatiently. Desperately. "Please, Johnny!"

"We'll call the doctor," he said, setting the baby in her crib and pulling on his clothes that he'd set on the chair the night before. "He'll test her and find out what's causing it."

They called Dr. Rhea immediately and were instructed to hurry to the office. As the sun rose, they sat in the waiting room listening to Linda struggle. Finally, Dr. Rhea came through the door. He ushered them back to the examination room.

After listening to her lungs and checking her ears, nose and throat, he checked her temperature. He set down his stethoscope and shrugged. "She seems fine. Just a bit of a cold."

"She was much worse when she woke up this morning," Nellie replied quickly.

Dr. Rhea gave her a patronizing smile, which rubbed her the

wrong way. She felt a stab of irritation with the doctor she'd respected and trusted.

"It's normal for new mothers to be overly concerned," he said.

Nellie felt hot anger. How dare he belittle her concern for her daughter? She'd named the child after him, for Pete's sake!

Johnny took her and Linda home before he went to school. For the rest of the day, she fussed over Linda. She listened to her baby's labored breathing and worried over her loss of appetite and lethargy. Johnny's new puppy, a brown and white terrier named Monkey, watched her with curiosity as she fumed.

"I think I should know if something is wrong with my own child," she assured the dog. He only cocked his head and studied her with a confused expression. He wagged his tail in good-spirited support.

By the time an exhausted Johnny arrived home, Nellie Mae had worked herself into a frantic state. She paced over the floorboards, bouncing the unhappy baby.

"Something is wrong," she insisted. "The fever is back and her cough sounds worse."

"We'll see how she is in the morning," he said as he slipped off his shoes and rubbed his tired feet. "I hate to take her out in the cold again and be sent home."

Nellie Mae was past caring what the old fuddy-duddy doctor thought of her mothering skills. She only wanted Linda to be well. But she let Johnny sleep a few hours as she held a vigil by the crib.

At daybreak, she insisted they call the doctor again. He told them to meet him at his office.

"He seemed annoyed," Johnny said as he held up the phone.

But this time, as soon as the doctor stepped into the examination room, he donned a worried expression. He listened to the baby's chest and glanced at Nellie and Johnny.

"What?" Nellie cried as Johnny put his arm around her in

support. "What is it?"

"I'm sure she'll be fine, Mrs. Hagaman, but please take her to St. Francis. I'll call ahead. She's much worse today."

They rushed the baby to the hospital. Nellie Mae was unprepared for the events upon their arrival at the hospital. A nurse came from behind a door and took Linda back. Nellie and Johnny were told to sit and fill out papers.

"I want to go with her!" Nellie insisted, taking a step toward the door.

"Visiting hours are only on Wednesday and Sunday evenings," the nurse said pleasantly. "The doctor will come and talk to you after he examines the baby."

"I need to nurse her," Nellie said, tears stinging her eyes. She stared at Johnny, begging him with her eyes to do something. He shrugged helplessly. He didn't seem as surprised at what was happening.

"I'll talk to the doctor," he promised. And he did, within an hour. A good-natured doctor assured them he would put Linda on a list of critically ill children whose parents were given the right to unlimited visiting privileges, as long as they stayed out of the doctors' and nurses' way.

"Critically ill?" Nellie felt faint and stumbled. She would have fallen to the floor if Johnny hadn't held her up.

"I'm not going to lie to you. Your baby is very sick," the doctor said. "But I have every hope she'll recover with special care."

Nellie cried. Johnny held her and practically carried her through the door and down the long white hall. They followed the nurse into a room where many babies in cribs either cried or slept as nurses tended them.

Nellie's eyes found her baby immediately. She went to Linda and picked her up, trying to soothe her fussing. Tears fell down her cheeks. She was a terrible mother. She couldn't even keep her precious baby well for the first four months of her life. Not only that, but her determination to nurse was dwindling. She had less milk every day, even as Linda demanded more and more.

Maybe if Mother was here … Nellie thought wistfully. Maybe her mother would be able to tell her what she was doing wrong. Nellie only had strangers telling her nursing was unsanitary, no matter how diligently she washed her hands and body and disinfected everything in sight.

It's my fault. I made her sick with my own stubbornness.

Johnny had been quiet from the moment they'd entered the room. He watched her carry the baby and sob. He wore a terrified, stunned expression on his face that would have worried her if she weren't already consumed with worry over the baby.

"If something happens to her, we'll never have another one," he said suddenly.

She gasped. "Why on earth would you say such a thing?"

He shook his head, staring at the floor, a haunted expression on his face. "It's my fault."

She didn't tell him she'd already claimed that responsibility. "How could it possibly be your fault, Johnny?"

"It's the house," he said. "It's drafty. She caught a chill."

Nellie Mae laid Linda in the imposing metal crib and went to her husband, wrapping her arms around him. "It's not your fault. It's just the way these things go. We'll pray, Johnny. We'll pray and she'll be alright."

Johnny didn't respond. He turned and left her standing alone in the ward.

She swallowed back her disappointment as she realized she'd have to do her praying on her own.

Forty-One

Johnny was up before the sun every day to work on finishing the house, and he didn't stop working until the sun went down. He was determined to complete it before summer was over. There was no way his own flesh and blood was going to get pneumonia and die because he'd been too lazy to get the work done.

Linda recovered. The doctor called her a fighter with plenty of grit. In the months that followed, Linda had become a happy, contented baby. She was already scooting around and getting into things at only six months. She copied the sounds of their words and laughed when they laughed. He supposed they couldn't have asked for a nicer disposition in a baby.

But his wife wasn't faring quite so well. He had no idea what to do to fix her. After Linda had come home from the hospital, with Nellie already in a state, there'd been a letter waiting from Willow Springs.

Punk is gone, her mother had written. The words on the page seemed cold. Harsh. Nellie's younger brother, Manny, had set out for war as soon as he turned eighteen, even though the fighting was nearly over by that point. He'd been overseas, but it wasn't long before they were bringing the troops home. Nellie couldn't have been the least bit prepared to hear the tragic news contained in the letter.

His plane went down over the ocean. There were no survivors.

How many times had he been in those same planes and never given his safety a second thought? He'd jumped out of them with no hesitation. How could a young man just starting his life die coming home from war? It wasn't fair.

Nellie cried, and he wondered what to do with her. She told him her mother had prayed for Punk every day he was gone to war. Every day, on her knees, pleading with God to keep him safe. The only day she hadn't prayed was the day he flew home.

"How is that fair, Johnny?" Nellie cried. "Why would God allow such a thing to happen to us?"

They went to the funeral. It seemed to help soothe Nellie to be with her family for a time. After they came back to Indiana, she didn't cry anymore, but she carried the letter around in her apron pocket. She took long walks and didn't speak unless he spoke to her. It was unlike her to be so quiet, but he wasn't sure what else he could do for her.

Over time, little by little, she began to return to life. The first day he heard her musical laugh again, directed at something Linda had done, he had hope she was coming around. By Christmas, she seemed nearly back to her old self. And by Linda's first birthday, she had lost most of her anxiety and sadness.

Johnny, on the other hand, felt more anxious than he ever had in his life. He didn't like his pre-med classes, and he wasn't at all convinced he wanted to be a vet. He liked animals just as much as he ever had, and he enjoyed studying them, but the thought of dealing with sick animals bothered him. Would he be able to comfort sick and dying pets and the families that brought them in? But what else could Johnny do now?

Not too long after the baby's first birthday, Nellie asked if they could travel to Willow Springs so Linda could spend some time with her family. Johnny was happy to make the trip. But when they arrived, they'd hardly stepped through the door before Beulah told Nellie she had a last-minute mission for her. Nellie's face fell, but she bravely forced a smile.

"There's a wonderful girl who teaches the Meadows school out in Taney County. She sent word this morning that she was at the school and awful sick. I wouldn't ask you right when you get here, Nellie, but I just can't enjoy you and the baby knowing she's miserable. Would you go relieve her till the end of the school day?"

Johnny, seeing that his choices were to remain with his mother-in-law and attempt conversation or go with his wife, decided that he would join her. They drove out to the school together.

His eyes were opened as soon as they stepped into the one-room schoolhouse. Nellie didn't seem surprised at all by the small room or the variety of ages and education levels that had gathered in one room, but he was floored.

Johnny watched his wife teach those kids with all her heart. She took the little ones in her lap without hesitation while they said their alphabet and numbers. She did arithmetic on the board with the older kids and listened to the grammar and vocabulary of the biggest ones. When Nellie dismissed the kids for lunch, Johnny was sure of two things.

His wife had a gift for teaching children.

He wanted to be a teacher.

For the first time, he could see a place for himself somewhere. He was needed. The usual teacher of that little school was a teenager who only had an eighth-grade education. She was the only one available and willing to teach the kids, who mostly came from poor rural families. He saw so many obstacles in the way for those children. He envisioned they would end up in the same cycle of poverty as their parents. What if he could teach and bridge the gap, even just a little bit? What if he could inspire kids like these to reach their full potential and go on to do more with their lives?

As soon as the thought occurred to him, he could think of nothing else. He breathlessly told Nellie Mae his decision.

"I think I'll be a teacher," he said, wondering at the words as he spoke them aloud. "A good one, hopefully."

Nellie smiled, hoisting Linda on her hip and watching him curiously. "Well, I think you'd be a wonderful teacher, honey. But have you ever taught before?"

"No," he admitted. "But everything we do, we have to do for the first time at some point."

She shrugged and gave him a devilish grin. "I suppose you better get started right away. Kids will be back in ten minutes."

He caught the dare in her eyes and realized she wasn't just teasing him. She was giving him the opportunity to prove he was serious. He'd prove it.

And all afternoon he did just that, right up until the end of classes when he took all the kids down to the creek and taught them the science of the ecosystem.

That night as they got into bed, Nellie reached for his hand. "I'm right proud of you, darling. I never saw you so alive as I did today."

"Things are looking up," he said quietly, staring up at the water stains on the old ceiling. "Life has been hard, there's no doubt. But I think things are starting to turn around for us."

Nellie didn't say anything for a long time. When he thought she'd fallen asleep, she gave a small sigh. "I hope so."

Johnny wasted no time in changing his classes to major in

education. He dove in with gusto. A year later, he had jumped far ahead. In no time, he'd be a teacher. Maybe a science teacher. It would be the best of both worlds.

Nellie fared better those days, too. But she took her newfound peace and used it to begin pressuring him. She'd been attending a Nazarene church with Linda every Sunday, and he had yet to join them. She made it her one duty to remind him of this fact. Constantly.

He shrugged off her concern. "That's not my kind of place," he said, knowing full well it was an excuse as much as anything. "I worship God better standing alone by a stream with a fishing rod in my hand."

She'd scoffed off that notion. And she didn't let it go. She nagged and threatened. He started spending more time by the creek, avoiding the house and her reminders that his eternal soul was at stake.

One day when he was rifling through some old papers in his desk, he found the cigar the man had given him after Linda's birth. He looked around and made sure Nellie was gone. When he was satisfied that she and Linda were truly absent and at the grocery store, he took it out back and sat on the lawn to smoke it. Nellie would never be the wiser.

He was mistaken. As soon as she walked into the kitchen, she inhaled deeply.

"You've been smoking!" She was horrified. He might as well have been with another woman for all the fury of her reaction. Or have murdered someone. He pushed past her and went to the bedroom.

She followed. "John Hagaman, what is wrong with you? You won't go to church, you ignore your family all day and now you take up smoking? You've gone off the deep end!"

"It was just a cigar, Kit. Everyone smokes."

"I can't think of a single person at church," she countered. "It's a godless thing to do."

He didn't answer her. And his silence made her angrier. Every day after that she cajoled him, worried about his soul and prayed that he would "turn from his backsliding and be saved."

He didn't feel like he wasn't saved. He just had a wife trying to control him, and he didn't much like it. And to show her that he could be a Christian and enjoy an occasional cigar, he bought an entire box and brought it home, placing it prominently on the dresser in their bedroom.

He expected her to react poorly, but he almost gave in when he saw the disappointment in her face. Regardless, he stubbornly stuck to his guns. He was going to show that woman he was the boss if it was the last thing he did.

The next evening when he finally came home, he found her standing in the middle of the tiny living room. She was holding one of his cigars.

"What are you doing with that?" He hung his coat on the stand by the door and eyed her apprehensively. Whatever she had planned, he knew he wasn't going to like it.

"If you won't get rid of them, I will. I'll eat them." Her cheeks were red with anger. He took one look at her expression and knew she wasn't kidding.

But his pride wouldn't have it. "If I want to smoke in the house I built with my own two hands, I will," he retorted, stepping by her and praying silently she was only bluffing.

She wasn't. She put the wretched thing in her mouth and started chewing.

"Of all the foolish things you could do, Kit," he said, but she wouldn't put it down until he chased her down and wrestled it out of her hand.

He spent the rest of the night caring for her as she shook with tremors, vomited repeatedly and cried in pain until the wee hours of the morning.

That was when he promised her he'd never touch a cigar again.

Forty-Two

Lord Jesus, I need to talk to you.

Nellie Mae sat on her bed, her hands spread over the white chenille bedspread Johnny's mother had given them for their wedding.

She paused, listening to the quiet. She heard the soft, sweet sound of her baby's breathing, slow and steady as she napped in her crib. Johnny's dog, Monkey, lifted his head from his place in the corner as if he was waiting to hear what Nellie would say.

What would she pray? The words were hard to form on her tongue. They were words she didn't want to admit. She didn't want to speak them aloud. Doing so made her fears more real in a sense.

My husband has backslidden, she prayed silently. Urgently. *He's run away from you. I fear he's lost.*

Even as she thought the words, the passage she'd read in Psalms that morning returned to her mind. "The Lord redeemeth the soul of his servants: and none of them that trust in him shall be desolate."

My husband has trusted in you, but now he acts like he's of the world. He doesn't read his Bible or pray or come to church with me. Maybe he was lying to win me over. Maybe he changed his mind.

A feeling, freeing and comforting, came over her, and she

prayed aloud in a whisper.

"But you have not changed your mind, Lord Jesus. You have not changed your mind! What you have started, you will finish. You will get the victory!"

She dropped to her knees and rested her forehead on the bedspread that retained the faint scent of her husband – that of Old Spice and cut grass and motor oil. She breathed deeply of the smell, overwhelmed with the power of love she felt in that moment, both for her Savior and for her husband.

"Lord," she continued in her softest voice, though her mind shouted the words. "I've seen you work before. I saw my mother pray and heal the sick. She always said 'The Lord will work when nothing else will.' Nothing else will work. I've done everything I can think to do. I've warned and pleaded. I've tried to make an impression. I've not accomplished a single thing but to push him further away. You have to do this. It has to be you. I see that now."

She looked up into the silence of her bedroom, hearing nothing but the faint ticking of the alarm clock on the bedside table. "I'll keep on asking until you do."

Nellie allowed her daughter to consume her days. She watched with joyful anticipation as the little blonde-haired baby transformed into a precocious toddler. She was ever on the move. She crawled and then walked long before Nellie expected she'd have to clear things out of the way. Linda loved the dog, Monkey, and followed him everywhere, much to the dog's chagrin.

It didn't take her long to figure out how to get out of the house. Linda loved being outside. One morning Nellie didn't take her out because she was mending a dress. Linda made it her business to get the door open. It took her a long time to piece together what didn't work and discover the mechanics that would result in her freedom, but she finally succeeded.

Nellie looked up from her mending when the silence became suspicious. She rushed to the back door and saw it standing open. Linda wasn't sitting on the floor with her blocks where Nellie had set her. Hadn't it only been a moment ago?

She ran outside, calling for the baby. She checked the cellar. She came to the front of the house and surveyed the landscape. She gave a great gasp of relief when she saw the familiar little dot of pink against the green of spring grass and purple crocuses blooming along the gravel road.

She kept a closer eye on the doors and watched her daughter more closely after that. She didn't lose vigilance even when she found out she was expecting again and spent her mornings hovering over the toilet as she lost her breakfast.

Johnny was excited when she told him she was going to have another baby. The news almost pulled him out of his funk, if only for a while.

In the time Nellie waited for her second baby, she began to chafe at her rural home setting. She loved their little house, and she loved being with Linda, but she did long for friendship. She'd always been a social butterfly, never one to go off by herself for very long. This life was Johnny's preference, not hers, and he wasn't even around to experience it most of the time. Shouldn't the homemaker be able to decide where she kept her home?

She wrote long letters to Martha and her family and sent them pictures of Linda she'd taken. But writing wasn't the same as talking to someone made of flesh and blood.

She soon discovered that one should be careful what they wish for – or pray for – when her cousin Lola, now married herself with a baby of her own, decided that she and her husband, Bill, would build a house of their own next door on isolated Hagaman Lane.

At first Nellie was glad to have family so close. The babies were the same age and enjoyed playing in the sunshine together or romping with the dogs while Lola and Nellie sipped lemonade and gossiped about family or folks in town. Bill and Johnny hit it off as well, taking on building projects together in their spare time.

But as time went on, Nellie felt that same unnamed discomfort she'd known when they lived with Johnny's parents. It wasn't so much that Lola did anything overtly negative. And Nellie remembered Johnny saying the faults she found in others were only her imagination, products of her own negative self-view. Perhaps he was right.

Whatever they were and wherever they came from, a subtle weed of contempt sprung up not long after they moved in. When Lola found out Nellie was pregnant again, she came over every day to help out. She'd do the chores at her own house in the mornings and come to Nellie's to cook and clean for her as well.

Nellie knew it was silly, but she couldn't help feeling a white spark of rage at her cousin. What kind of person was Nellie to secretly loathe someone just for trying to help? But the other side of her spoke different words into her heart – words she couldn't forget.

She thinks you don't do a good enough job.

She thinks you aren't taking care of Johnny and Linda.

She's putting you down as a mother and housekeeper.

If you let this continue, Johnny won't respect or love you.

Nellie didn't speak a word of her dark thoughts aloud, so every day Lola came and cleaned. She played with Linda. She made supper. And every day Nellie Mae pretended to be fine. She joked that she had done the same for many other mothers for years before she was married, so now she was receiving her reward. But inside, her bitterness grew stronger and wilier. It wound around her heart and squeezed so tight Nellie's joy vanished.

She didn't speak a word of her secret thoughts until late in her pregnancy. One night Johnny came home, exhausted and quiet as usual, which annoyed her until she could stand it no more. She slammed the bowl of mashed potatoes on the table in front of him.

"Johnny, talk to me! You can't leave me out here in the middle of nowhere all day by myself and then come home and say nothing. I can't stand the quiet. It's driving me crazy!"

"Lola comes over every day," Johnny reminded her as he took a helping of potatoes for himself. He sipped his milk as he waited for her to bring the pot roast Lola had put in the oven before she left that afternoon.

Nellie fumed as she brought the steaming, perfect roast to the table. She set it down rather hard on the table. She began to cut Linda's food as the baby babbled and giggled, unaware of Nellie's foul mood.

"What's wrong?" Johnny sighed, as if he didn't want to ask and didn't want to know. He eyed his newspaper rolled up beside his plate.

"Why did they have to move next door?" Nellie sniffed back tears as she fed the baby. "We were doing just fine."

"I thought you just said you were lonely." His voice was calm. Calm enraged her further.

"I wasn't lonely for her! Why would I want someone to come along and make me feel useless as a housekeeper and mother? I wanted a friend!"

Johnny stared at her evenly. "She's just helping. You're expecting. You say all the time you constantly feel cold and tired. I think you should be grateful for her, Kit."

She knew the pet name was added to soften his words, but it only made her angrier. "I don't want her here. She thinks I can't clean my own house or take care of my baby or make supper for you. She makes me feel worthless."

He chuckled. The man actually sat in front of her and laughed at her vulnerable words. "I've never heard her insult you. Lola looks up to you."

Nellie Mae scoffed loudly. "Fiddlesticks," she spat around a mouthful of green beans. "You're too much of an oaf to see it, but she tries to make me look bad. Always pointing out my flaws. How dare you take her side?"

Johnny sighed again, very long and deeply, as if he were too tired to discuss it further. He set down his fork and rubbed his eyes. "Can't you just try to get along? Maybe things will get better."

"They won't," she insisted.

Linda screeched and attempted to insert her childish opinion. Nellie stared at the little blue-eyed beauty, wishing she was in the right frame of mind to enjoy the treasure of her daughter.

"I want to move," Nellie said impulsively.

Johnny stared at her in disbelief. "You can't be serious. I built you this house from scratch."

She held her chin in the air. "I don't care. She's ruined it. I want to move to town and have friends again."

He stood up abruptly and shoved his chair into place with a loud clatter. "Fine."

He left the room quickly. Too quickly for her to apologize. To say she didn't mean it.

Johnny came home the next week and told her he'd found a little house on Main Street. They'd be moving that Saturday, so she better pack her things.

Nellie knew she'd driven a wedge between herself and her husband. Now she'd be doing the same with her cousin and her family. She was sorry. But stubbornness, pride and embarrassment kept her from making things right.

Every time she tried to speak words to mend her relationships, her mouth went dry and her voice wouldn't work. So she said nothing. And little by little, it was easier to justify staying quiet.

Forty-Three

Nellie would never forget the day. And not just because it was her first baby girl's eighth birthday.

A dozen little girls sat in their party dresses around the kitchen table as Linda opened her gifts. Linda's younger sister, Teri, sat next to her. She exclaimed over a pogo stick and hula hoop as Nellie leaned back against the kitchen counter and opened her *Look* magazine that had come that day in the mail.

She smiled at the pretty teenage twins on the front cover. Their red lipstick and rosy cheeks reminded her of simpler days. Of Martha and Bill and Howard and all the folks back home. Of Punk, her little brother, lost in an airplane crash on his way home from the war.

She quickly shifted her thoughts from the sadness. She imagined the next few years. As she glanced up at her darling daughters, she realized for the first time that Linda didn't look so much like a little girl anymore. She wasn't nearly a young woman yet, but Nellie could see her small child was only a memory. And it wasn't only her looks. Linda was responsible and smart, and had long since proved herself a mature young lady.

Nellie didn't want to think of her babies becoming women. It only seemed like yesterday they'd been born. Her own childhood had dragged on for ages, so she had assumed her daughters would take just as long to grow up. Instead, the days, the months, the years flew by.

Nellie wondered what in the world she would do with herself when her girls were grown and no longer needed her. She had wanted more children. Had begged for them. She'd cried on her knees night after night, promising God anything if he'd only give her another baby. She'd lamented to John as well.

"I always wanted a bunch of kids," she told him. "At least six, anyway. I never thought I'd only have two."

"Maybe it's a good thing we don't have more," was his short answer. She hadn't wanted to hear that. It reminded her how far out of line her husband's ideals had become. He had attained every goal he'd gone after, becoming one of the best teachers Indianapolis' school system had ever seen. He loved his students and went the extra mile to make his classes inspiring. His interests had undeniably passed down to his daughters. Linda and Teri had been delighted when he brought home a baby alligator he'd found and taken to his science class at school. Nellie had wondered what they'd do with the thing when it wasn't a baby anymore, but fortunately, it escaped. John assured them it had probably made itself a home in Lick Creek, over by the old house.

Yes, John had become all he'd imagined. He always did. When that man set his mind to something, whether it be war or recovery from injury or getting the girl, he always got what he wanted. And he had wanted to be a respected and memorable teacher.

But it had been years since her husband had mentioned God. It had been years since he had attended the church she attended with the girls every week. It had been years since he'd read his Bible or prayed, at least as far as she knew. She kept her Bible on the kitchen table and read it every day, praying for her girls and her husband, trying to be a good example, but all the while, feeling like she was never quite good enough. Maybe all her prayers were for nothing. Maybe God wasn't listening to someone as average and uninteresting as she was.

His distance and her doubts strained their relationship. She was ever determined not to allow it, but it was difficult to relate to someone who had such different values. He taught the girls to love nature, taking them fishing or horseback riding, camping out under the stars on weekends. But he never spoke about the one thing most important to Nellie Mae. She felt deflated of hope and faith. Had she made a mistake marrying him? Had she been too hasty? Too wishy-washy to realize he wasn't a good choice?

It was as these thoughts plagued her that a new difficulty arose. One day Nellie answered the phone and discovered her husband already on the line with a woman. It was his secretary.

"I just called to tell you something," the woman said in a soft voice Nellie immediately recognized as intimate. Too intimate. "I have feelings for you. I have for a long time. I'm just now brave enough to say something," she'd said in a vulnerable tone. Nellie's face had gone white hot with anger. How dare she?

Nellie knew the woman. And she'd never liked how she acted around John. Nellie waited, breathless, hoping he'd put her in her place.

"Thanks for calling," John had said before he'd hung up. No word of how inappropriate she'd been to call him. No stern rebuke for her unbecoming behavior. The more she thought about it, the more convinced she was that he'd even liked her calling him like that.

Hoping to get his attention, she had declared she was leaving him. She had packed up the girls and her belongings and called her brother to come and get them.

It had been a month before John came to Missouri for them. He gave no words of regret, no remorse, no promise of better behavior. He wore a lonely, sullen glint in his eye. But she could easily see it wasn't good for Johnny to be alone. So she had relented and returned to Indianapolis.

There was nothing to be done now except to grin and bear it. She did the best she could. She tried to swallow back her nagging comments and complaints. She tried to fill up the silence with small talk and pleasantries. Even if he wouldn't talk, she was plenty good at it. She talked about the girls. She talked about the Lord, about church, about the Bible. And she talked about the children she wanted. A little boy at least, to carry on the family name.

"You should have a son named John," she insisted over and over, though he never agreed with her.

"The fates don't agree," he said absently from behind his paper, his black-rimmed reading glasses a tell-tale sign that age was slowly creeping up on them.

Now, as the birthday party continued, Nellie turned the pages of her magazine, half interested in the girls around the table, half-interested in the wanderings of her mind. But when she turned the page and saw the familiar face staring back at her, her blood suddenly felt like ice. The whooshing sound of her heartbeat filled her ears as she tried to comprehend the features of the older-but-still-recognizable face in the photograph.

Her eyes quickly went to the title of the article.

The shocking story of CONDONED MURDER IN MISSISSIPPI

Her breathing became labored, and the happy sounds of the girls faded away. She read frantically, trying to understand what the strange title had to do with the face of her old beau, James William

MY GOOD NAME

Liman.

True account... slaying... fourteen-year-old youth named Louis Little... Anita's husband, James William Liman... "I'm going to make an example of you, just so everybody can know how me and my folks stand" ... "just whip him, and scare some sense into him," ... barb-wired the gin fan to his neck, rolled him into twenty feet of water...

Nellie dropped the magazine, holding her hands over her face. The girls stopped talking and looked at her.

"Mother, what's wrong?" Six-year-old Teri came and squeezed her hand.

"I'll get Daddy," Linda said.

When John came in, he helped Nellie to their bed and told her he'd watch the girls, that she should take a nap.

When she woke several hours later, he sat on the chair next to the bed, his elbows resting on his knees. She saw the magazine she'd been reading rolled up in his hand.

"Where are the girls?" she asked.

"They're in bed." He regarded her evenly.

She gulped as the story and the images came back to her. "Johnny, he murdered a boy in cold blood. James William killed a child just for mouthing off. How could I not have seen his character?"

John didn't answer. She knew why. She knew that he had seen it all along, and he was trying to be polite and not tell her he'd told her so. She moaned and pinched the bridge of her nose. "What if I'd married him? What if I'd married a murderer?"

"You didn't," he said simply. "That's all that matters."

"How can you say that when a boy is dead?" Nellie cried. "Why do people hate others just because they're different? Why are people so full of infernal pride? I don't understand how a man who went to war to fight for his country could go home and slaughter a child.

298

What kind of world are we living in?"

John sighed and didn't say a word. Nellie listened to the familiar silence, longing for an answer to soothe her troubled soul. "Jesus, may that boy rest in your peace," she prayed softly.

John watched her. "I'm sorry, Kit."

"Me too," she said. She reached for his hand and took her comfort. "He isn't even in prison. They let him go. Said there wasn't enough evidence, even though he outright admitted with pride he did it!"

John nodded. "I read it."

"I'm ashamed of us all." Nellie reached for a tissue and blew her nose. "This'll break Dad's heart. He'd hoped things were changing in the South. He's always tried to help folks get along and treat each other as they'd like to be treated."

"Good advice. It would be a better world if it were so."

Nellie Mae wondered if John even knew the "advice" was the very word of Christ. But she didn't say it. She sat up in bed and reached for both his hands. "I haven't been fair to you, sweetheart." She squeezed his hands as more tears squeezed from the corners of her eyes. "Not at all. You're a good man. I'm glad you're my husband. I know we have our differences, and I know I've tried to change you so many times, but I'm glad God gave you to me. You're hard-working, you're so smart, and you're a loving father."

John's eyes lit with surprised appreciation. She felt guilty that she'd been so hard on him.

"I know I've been a disappointment," he said quietly.

She started to argue, but he held her hands tighter, silencing her words.

"I don't know why I keep pulling away from you," he said. "I want to be everything I should be. But I guess I'm afraid to fail. Our girls are beautiful and kind ... so much like you. I've failed all of you."

"You haven't," she started to protest, but he shook his head and pushed her hands aside.

He stood up and walked to the small window that overlooked the street below. "I've got to do better."

She didn't answer. But the smallest speck of hope filled her with a reason to go on. A reason to believe, to try, to pray.

"I'll do better, too," she promised. And she meant it.

Forty-Four

September 30, 1957

John walked the halls of the elementary school to his office. He glanced in satisfaction at the nameplate on his desk. *John Hagaman, Principal.*

He'd done it. He'd accomplished every single thing he'd set out to do. He loved his job. He enjoyed teaching and interacting with his students. His colleagues had given him glowing recommendations that ultimately led to him being made the principal of his own school that year. His space science demonstration had made an impression on his students. One had decided as a result to pursue astronomy and become an astronaut.

He was making a difference. He was appreciated. He had his life figured out, and no one was going to take away the satisfaction he felt over it.

But then he thought of his wife.

She seemed to be the only person in the world that could reduce all his accomplishments to ashes. She didn't care how far he'd come. She didn't care that he'd jumped out of planes and taken a grenade to the knee. She didn't care that he'd become the best teacher and principal possible. None of it mattered to her.

Why don't you go to church with us, John? Why don't you read your Bible? Why don't you pray with us? She didn't even have to say the words anymore. They were written all over the grim set of her mouth every time she looked his direction.

The truth was, he had no idea why he was so opposed to doing those things. Maybe it was because he didn't feel it. If he didn't feel something, he wasn't moved to act, and he didn't plan on being a hypocrite just to make his wife happy.

But he hadn't forgotten what it had been like to meet the Lord for the first time. He'd never forget that night with his cousin at the little church where he first heard Jesus loved him and wanted a relationship with him. What Jesus had done for him to make that possible. He'd needed to know that they were settled up before he'd gone to war.

But now, with a steady job and a house, and with a wife and two daughters as near to perfect as a father could hope, he didn't feel the need to be a fanatic about religion. Nellie did enough of that for both of them. He hadn't stopped believing in God, and he knew he had a peace in his heart that Jesus was his Savior, no matter how many times Nellie tried to make him doubt it.

But he didn't know what to do next in his journey of faith. So he did nothing.

Night after night, she made no secret that his smoking in the garage and his avoidance of church and the Bible was aligning him on the wide path of destruction.

"How do you think Linda and Teri will feel when they come to rest in heaven one day and you aren't there? How can you do that to them? To me?"

He tried once or twice to explain things, but she didn't want to listen. He tried to tell her he didn't feel comfortable at her church. It wasn't his style. But she'd called his bluff and began attending a new church. It was the same little Baptist church in which he'd first found the Lord.

Still, he didn't go more than once or twice a year. He didn't know why.

He did pray, in his own way, when he was alone. Never aloud. But he breathed silent words to God as he drove to or from work, or when he needed patience during one of Nellie's lectures.

"Answer me!" she said often. "Please, just say something. Anything!"

"You don't want to hear what I have to say," he reminded her.

Now he shuffled the papers on his desk and surveyed his office, content in the comfortable silence. Nobody talking his ear off, breaking his concentration away from his thoughts. He took a stack of tests out of his briefcase and started grading.

"Mr. Hagaman?" the school secretary stood in the open doorway with a pleasant smile. The woman had told him once a while back that she had feelings for him. He was flattered, but he avoided her like the plague now. Nellie had been furious when she'd overheard the conversation on the phone. She'd left him. He'd had to go back to Missouri and grovel to take his family home.

No, it would lead to nothing good if he encouraged the flirtatious behavior. Unfortunately, the woman only seemed more interested after his rebuffs.

"Your wife called," she said. "She'd like for you to meet her at the doctor's office."

He frowned. "Did she say why she was there?"

"No, sir," she replied and left before John could question further. He sighed and began to pack the tests and his other things he'd need. He turned off the light and regretfully left the stillness of the office.

He worried all the way across town. Nellie's teeth had been plaguing her. He hoped she didn't have another infection. She had womanly problems as well, which had kept her from having more children after Teresa. Nellie was only thirty, not too old to have another child, but so far, she had not had success. He wondered if it was the nature of the doctor visit. He didn't like discussing these things with strangers. It made him feel inadequate as a husband.

When he arrived, the receptionist greeted him and sent him back to the room where Nellie was waiting. She was wearing a white hospital gown and footies, which made her seem younger and more vulnerable than she usually allowed herself to look in public. He smiled and took her hand as he leaned down to kiss her forehead. "What's going on, Kit?"

She didn't seem troubled. In fact, he was fairly sure she was about to burst with joy. Her eyes shone as she stared up at him. "I'm going to have a baby."

His first reaction was total shock. After nearly eight years, he hadn't considered it a possibility. But he knew how badly she wanted more children. He should be glad for her.

"That's wonderful news," he said with a chuckle.

"I wouldn't have made all this fuss, but the doctor said to call you over. He wanted to discuss something."

John saw her tension then. She was worried. A foreboding chill crept over him as he cleared his throat and squeezed her hand. "Did he ask you anything?"

Her forehead creased in concentration. "Just the standard questions. I don't know what could have been so concerning. He said I was healthy. Even starting to show a little. Two and a half months along." She smiled, though apprehension hid behind her happiness. "The baby is due in the spring. Maybe he'll come in April on your birthday."

John felt a well of unexpected emotion, both at the thought of having a baby born on his birthday and the idea of possibly having a son. A myriad of images cascaded through his mind. Taking his boy fishing in the still waters of Lick Creek. Showing his boy how to sleep under the stars. Roasting squirrel and mud-baked potatoes over the fire. Smoking Indian cigars. Presenting his son with his first puppy to train and raise himself.

He was still trying to clear out his throat when the doctor came into the room. John's dreams died when he saw Dr. Rhea's expression. The images popped like soap bubbles as quickly as they had formed.

The doctor shook his hand and offered a polite word of congratulations. Then he opened the file in front of him and pretended to be focused on the words of the page rather than their faces.

John felt prickles of fear. "Is she okay?" he asked abruptly.

"Oh, yes," the doctor said. "Your wife is in good health."

"So what's the problem?"

The doctor nodded as if acknowledging that John was not one to play games and had ascertained there was something amiss.

"I am concerned about the baby."

Nellie gasped, causing John to wince. If there were something wrong with this baby, it would destroy her. Would he lose his wife to insanity if she were pushed too far? He should have done something to prevent this. It was all his fault.

"She mentioned having a slight rash and fever a month ago, after one of your daughters came down with a case of German measles."

"I was fine," Nellie said. "I hardly even noticed being sick."

"I understand," the doctor said in a gentle tone. "Three-day measles is usually very mild. But this disease, known as Rubella, can be devastating for babies in the womb at least half the time an expectant mother catches it. We call it Congenital Rubella Syndrome."

John felt Nellie's hand tighten around his fingers until they went numb.

"Normally in these cases, I use a wait-and-see approach. But when I listened to the heartbeat today, I noticed a slight abnormality. In a couple months, when the baby is more developed, I'd like to do an x-ray of your unborn child to see if I can see any damage."

"Why?" John asked, hearing the harsh tone of his voice, but suddenly unable to speak civilly. "What can you do about it? Nothing. You can't change it."

"What have I done to my baby?" Nellie put her hands on her abdomen. John had the instinct to hold her and tell her it was his fault, but instead he turned on the doctor.

"What can you do? What would be the point of an x-ray?"

"Well, it may show us a perfectly healthy baby, and you'll have peace of mind. But if there is something wrong, at least you can be prepared."

The doctor shrugged, irritating John so much he wished he could take a swing at the man sitting on his stool with his white coat and dark glasses and ridiculous mustache.

The doctor, unaware of John's raging emotions, went on. "If it were me, I'd want to know what I was in for."

John felt an urge to attack he hadn't felt since he was a soldier thinking about the enemy in battle. He was about to turn down the x-ray when Nellie spoke.

"I'd like to have the x-ray," she said in a soft voice, still staring down at the small mound of her abdomen. Her hands rested on either side of it.

"It won't do any good, Nellie," he said. "There's no point in worrying yourself."

"I want to see him," she said, her voice faltering.

They spoke no more of it in the days that followed, but John felt the tension there, just under the surface. It reminded him of the land mines back in the war. If you put enough pressure on a live one, it would blow your head off.

That's how he felt about the unspoken grief in his family.

Forty-Five

John would forever wish they could have avoided that x-ray. It didn't do any good at all to know their baby was going to be born with severe handicaps. That if the baby even lived, he would need special care his entire life.

He felt like a failure as a father. He hadn't kept that baby safe. Just like he hadn't been able to keep his men safe back in company HQ. He'd been disqualified by a stupid accident before he even laid eyes on the enemy. Why did everything he worked so hard to achieve end up a joke?

After the appointment with the doctor, John took Nellie home and left her sobbing on their bed. He gave the girls something to eat and read them a story before tucking them in.

"Be good and let your mother rest," he told them as he kissed them goodnight. "Daddy's going out for a little while."

They both stared up at him with wide eyes. He knew they were afraid. More afraid than they had been taught to express.

"What's wrong with Mother?" Linda asked. He hated the tremor in her voice. His Linda – even tempered, always smiling, always sensible and fearless. She had a knack for animals just as he did, always and forever asking for a horse of her own. He knew she took after him in so many ways. He wished he was the kind of father who

307

took his girls into his arms and kissed all their fears away so they could sleep soundly and never be afraid of anything. He wished he was the kind of man to be humble enough to get on his knees beside their beds and pray with them when life was painful. But he just wasn't. He would only fail if he tried.

He drove around for a long time, smoking the cigars he kept hidden in the garage. It calmed him some. Numbed the pain somewhat.

It had been a long time since John had allowed himself the indulgence of cigars. He had learned to avoid them for the sake of peace. But in his state, he believed it was worth it. He deserved it, didn't he? He'd earned it by being dealt such a harsh hand by the Man upstairs.

Finally, he drove home and sat in the car in the driveway for a long time, staring at the paint peeling off the garage door.

"Why, God?" He leaned his head against the steering wheel. "Why do you let these bad things happen to us? I thought you were supposed to be loving. This doesn't feel like love."

There was no answer in the dark silence. He sighed and climbed out of the car. He planned to open the back door as quietly as possible, but the key refused to go straight into the lock. Another blow from a supposedly benevolent God? Suddenly, it opened without his help.

"What in the world do you think you're doing at this hour?" Nellie Mae stood in the doorway, disbelief and fire mingled in her expression, making quite an affect.

"I just went out for a few minutes," he said sullenly. "Needed to clear my head."

"Ha!" There was no humor in the sound of her reply. "You don't clear your head by smoking yourself to death. What could possibly warrant smoking and probably drinking and staying out all hours of the night?"

He decided honesty was his best option at this point. "Because it was a blow, Nellie. That news was a blow. You're not the only one hurting."

Her feature softened, if only a little. She crossed her arms over her chest. "I may be hurting, but at least I'm committed to this baby come what may. What kind of father will you be to him if you're good-for-nothing? If you even live that long, driving around town drunk as a skunk."

"I'm not drunk, Nellie. I didn't have anything to drink." John sighed and came through the door. He threw his keys on the table and leaned back against the oven.

She folded her hands in front of her. "It will all get easier after the baby comes." Her tone softened.

He shook his head. "I don't want this baby."

He hadn't meant to say the words, but it was a relief to say them. She didn't speak for a long time. He could tell she was angry.

"This is a helpless baby," she finally whispered. "What kind of person are you?"

"It's a helpless baby, and it'll always be helpless. Do you understand what that means for us, Nellie?"

She was not impressed by his words. "I understand I'm married to a heartless fool. I'm amazed you have the gall to come back here with smoke clinging to your clothes. Do you think your children will soon forget this?"

He waved off the words. "They're asleep. I put them to bed myself."

Nellie Mae said nothing, but she moved to the side so he could see both girls standing in the kitchen doorway, holding hands.

"Daddy?" Linda asked tentatively.

John swore under his breath, but not quietly enough. Nellie gasped and went to gather the girls.

"Don't bother coming up to bed," she said as she shooed the girls up the stairs.

It was three weeks before Nellie would talk to him again. He tried flowers and chocolates for the first few days, then he tried apologizing. Finally, he lapsed into silence and let her be. There was no sense making a fool of himself.

One night after tossing and turning on the couch, he heard a soft sound from the bedroom above. He went up to see if one of the girls needed something, but realized it was coming from Nellie's and his bedroom. He leaned his ear on the door and listened to his wife's whisper as she prayed.

"Lord Jesus, I beg you to change his heart! I beg you to convict him and make him care again …"

Her voice trailed off and her prayer went on in silence. He wondered if she was crying. How many tears had his wife shed in secret on account of his foolish actions or words? Part of him wanted to open the door and go to her. Make it right somehow. Do whatever it took to have peace between them. But how could he do that and still be a man in her eyes? He'd be whipped. Everyone would think it.

Nellie spoke again, and this time her voice sounded different. Stronger, though it was still barely more than a mumbling. It didn't sound like his wife talking anymore, but rather the rising spirit of One greater than either of them entering her body and speaking on her behalf.

"I am asking now in the name of the Lord Jesus Christ who died on that cross and rose out of that grave to act on my husband's behalf. Do whatever it takes to get a hold of him, Jesus. Do whatever it takes."

Her voice dropped to whisperings and murmurs, but he heard the phrase several more times. "Whatever it takes…"

A strange feeling came over him – one he couldn't shake off. He felt a heat in the pit of his stomach. He'd only felt that once before. The first time he'd jumped out of an airplane.

He knew in that moment without even a hint of a doubt that God would answer that prayer. And somehow, somewhere deep inside of him, he knew he would regret the things he was saying and doing right now. More so – the things he wasn't doing. Saying. This attitude he'd had about a baby he didn't know and didn't want, even though it was his own child.

But he also knew he had no ability in himself to deal with these problems they were facing. He couldn't fix it. He couldn't pull himself out of the pit.

And though he was fearful of God answering that prayer in His time and way, he was also grateful. Grateful for a wife who wasn't afraid to pray for God's extraordinary grace to be poured out into their life.

Even more – grateful for a God who was sure to answer.

Forty-Six

March 30, 1958

What started the brush fire that night – the fire that set off a sequence of events that forever changed their family? Was it a flicked cigarette from a passing motorist? Or did a divine hand set the scrub ablaze in a similar manner as Moses' burning bush?

After that night, hearing Nellie pray on his behalf, she'd become a different person to him. Like night and day, really. Her coldness, her worry, it slipped away and she became peaceful. As if resigned to and even welcoming whatever God was going to do in their lives. She took care of her family with a pleasant, kind manner. She welcomed him back to their bedroom. It was as if her prayer had erased all of her turmoil, and she'd been granted perfect trust.

Often, she held her abdomen and closed her eyes, as if in prayer for the little one growing beneath her fingers. Once he saw her smile.

"How can you be so happy?" he asked before he thought better of it. He could hear the tone of his voice and hated himself for thinking it, let alone saying it. But the words had to be spoken. Reason trumped emotion, didn't it?

At first, he saw the flash of anger and expected a sound rebuke. But it passed and she sighed. She absently rubbed her stomach with a slow, soothing motion.

"How could I not be happy about our child? The life God created from you and me?"

He shook his head, unable to answer. She watched him thoughtfully for a long moment.

"My daddy taught me that all life matters. Whether it be a person of different color, or age, or size, level of education, or faith … or disability. There isn't a single soul on God's green earth that matters more than any other. And God can use a little one with challenges as much as he can use the strongest man. Maybe more."

John didn't believe it. Not in this case. He could accept that no person was more important in God's eyes, but down here on earth, some people were definitely more of a strain on finances and family life. He didn't want that for their family. He didn't want others to look at him and only see his handicapped child in the wheelchair, draining them of their time, resources and energy. He'd be embarrassed. He'd feel like less of a man. And their family would have nothing left.

But he couldn't say those thoughts out loud. Nellie had the "godlier" response, and it would be silly to argue. Better just to leave it as it was.

He was envious of Nellie's calm assurance. He wished he could pray like she did and see results. When he prayed it felt like he was talking to a brick wall. He had asked God to change his wife and not let the baby have birth defects. He'd asked God to make him the leader he should be. Yet still he just felt like he was spinning his wheels in the most important areas of his life.

So he avoided the issues. He didn't go to church, even on Christmas when Nellie asked several times if he might join them. Linda and Teri asked too, but he told them he was making a surprise for them, which seemed to distract them from pestering.

He stopped praying. It wasn't doing him any good, and he didn't like doing things without results. He figured he'd just let his wife do the praying. Anyway, her prayers had only worked for her. God hadn't done anything to him as he'd expected after her powerful words. The first few days he'd been bracing for the lightning strike, but it never came. Life proceeded as normal. Now it had been months, and things were settled. His life seemed almost peaceful, especially with such a docile and compliant wife for the first time in their marriage.

It was just enough time for him to work up quite a false sense of security.

It had been the usual quiet Sunday. He'd worked in the garage while the girls and Nellie went to Sunday school and church. When they came home, they ate the roast Nellie had put in the oven before she left. After a cozy afternoon nap, Nellie sat at the sink and did the dishes while the girls played *One Potato, Two Potatoes* on their skipping ropes in the kitchen.

"Girls, please play outside," Nellie said, cringing a bit and holding her abdomen. John wondered if she'd had a contraction, but it was too early for the baby to come so he dismissed the thought. She seemed to recover and return to work, apparently lost in her thoughts as she plunged her gloved hands into the steaming water for another fork or spoon resting on the bottom of the sink.

"It's cold outside," Teri complained.

"Well, aren't you just a city girl?" Nellie joked. "It's not that cold. It's a nice spring afternoon. Put your coat on."

The girls stopped skipping and watched their mother. "We wanted you to watch us skip rope," Linda said, disappointed.

Nellie smiled. "All right. Play your game."

They went back to skipping, but the small kitchen wasn't the best place for it. The ropes kept hitting the table, which frustrated the girls.

John had sudden inspiration. "Let's go for a drive. I heard there was a little air show at the airport this evening. We could see it." He put down his newspaper.

The girls jumped in excitement and ran to get their jackets. Nellie smiled at him and pulled out the stopper to let the water out of the sink.

"You don't have to go if you're too tired," John said, putting a hand on her shoulder.

"I'm fine. It sounds nice," she said, standing and taking off the gloves and apron. "Let's go."

And so they got in the car and set out. John drove as Nellie and the girls called out the first signs of spring.

"I see purple flowers!" Teri called.

"Those are crocuses. Soon enough the tulips will be up, too," Linda said in a knowledgeable tone.

"New life," Nellie mused, more to herself than anyone else, John figured. "God always makes a way, doesn't he? No matter what we do to mess it up."

John nodded, feeling the statement was strong enough without comment from him.

Later, after the air show, they got back in the car.

"You should wear your seat belt, you know," Nellie said mildly with a smile. She said it every time they got in the car, and every time he reminded her it was the only seat belt in the car.

"Why should I wear one if you aren't?" he teased.

John drove down Post Road and began heading south in the direction of Beech Grove where they lived. The girls sang a song they'd learned that morning in church, and Nellie hummed along, glancing back at them with a motherly smile. John came to a stop at the intersection and looked at her, suddenly struck by her beauty. She'd been a looker at sixteen when he met her, but now, at thirty-two, with that rosy glow of pregnancy on her cheeks, she was downright breathtaking.

"Daddy, the light is green!" Linda laughed. "Did you not notice because you're colorblind?"

He made a face at her. "I saw it." He smiled at her in the rear-view mirror. He put his foot on the accelerator, moving the car forward into the intersection.

It would seem afterward that the Oldsmobile came out of nowhere, appearing as suddenly as a phantom. Afterward, John would be asked if he had heard the constant blaring of the car horn, but he simply hadn't. There was no explanation.

John slammed on his brakes, but neither car could stop fast enough. He saw the large features of the headlights and the front fender as a face laughing at him, smashing into his car and his family.

Somewhere in the back of his mind he processed the sound of screeching tires, screaming from his girls, the force of metal scraping the side of his leg from top to bottom.

In the next moment, he was powerless to do anything as the car skidded sideways along the road. He felt his body being thrown from his door, which had been jarred open. It was an odd sensation, not unlike the feeling of jumping out of airplanes. He could do nothing to keep Nellie from flying out after him. One of the girls tumbled into the front seat, and his throat ached as he tried to cry out, unable to stop her from hitting her head on the steering wheel.

He felt the gravelly pavement, cold and harsh beneath his palms. He tried to lift himself off the ground, but the wind had been knocked out of him, and he could barely breathe. Across from him, laying haphazardly with her arm splayed behind her at an awkward angle, Nellie lay on the asphalt with her eyes closed. She didn't move.

She's dead. I've killed her.

A horrible dread filled him as he crawled toward her, calling her name in a broken voice he didn't recognize as his own. Behind him he could hear one of the girls crying for her mother. He thought it was Linda.

The man in the other car jumped out and limped toward the wreckage. John glanced at him and saw that he was hardly more than a kid.

"I'm so sorry!" the man called in an anxious voice. I tried to stop, honest I did! Didn't you hear me honking?"

"Kit!" he moaned, dragging his leg along behind him as he moved toward his wife. He finally reached her side and took her gingerly into his arms, cradling her motionless head in his lap. "Kit, talk to me!"

She didn't answer. Her body was completely limp. He leaned close to her mouth and thought he felt warmth from her breath. Hope ignited.

"Call for an ambulance!"

A woman stopped her car next to them and got out. He saw her rush to the mangled car and help the girls step out of the driver's side door and over their mother. They cried as she led them across the street to the gas station. Teri held her head as it bled freely.

"Is she okay?" John called desperately to the stranger who might as well be an angel for all he knew.

"Yes!" the lady called back. "She's coming around. We'll call for an ambulance!" She moved the girls toward the door to the service station.

John had no idea how long he sat on the road with his wife's head in his lap, staring at the cut gushing behind her ear, feeling the growing bump on the back of her head, begging her to wake up. He heard the young man try to explain to the deputies what had happened as they all waited for the ambulance. The policemen tried to ask him questions as well, but he only shook his head. All he could think of was Nellie.

When the ambulance finally arrived, John stared at the white Cadillac wagon and saw a hearse. All the memories of his aunt being thrown from that truck and dying from the head trauma she received returned to his mind with a vengeance. But his aunt had died before the ambulance arrived. Nellie was still breathing.

The driver quickly loaded their family into the vehicle. Nellie was strapped to the stretcher while Linda sat on it with her, and John held Teri in his lap.

"I hope this is a nightmare!" Teri cried as blood trickled down her face. "Please let it be a nightmare!"

The car raced to St. Francis. John knew would be about ten minutes before they arrived at the hospital. He reached back and clung to his wife's limp hand as he held on to Teri.

John tried to make sense of his families' injuries. Linda held her shoulder and whimpered, but John could tell she was holding back her emotions. Being strong. Teri had been knocked unconscious when she hit the steering wheel. He'd never seen a goose egg as big as the one on her forehead. He realized with a sickening feeling in his stomach that if he'd only put that seat belt on like Nellie had said, none of this would have happened. He would have broken Nellie's and Teri's falls.

He wanted to tell them it would be okay. He wanted to say their mother would wake up and everything would be just fine when they got to the hospital, but he knew it wasn't true. Somehow, he knew everything was changing.

Lord, do whatever it takes. His wife's words haunted his mind.

As the ambulance raced along past ambling cars and slow traffic, it came upon the busy intersection of Emerson and Randall. John gripped his children and his wife as the ambulance driver suddenly cursed loudly and slammed on his brakes. He honked the horn loudly at a car who had pulled out in front of them, nearly giving them a second crash.

"It's only a nightmare!" Teri cried again.

Forty-Seven

Once at the hospital, nurses quickly whisked Nellie away, promising to return when there was news. John stood in the middle of the waiting room, stunned. Could life change this quickly? Could his entire sense of self and security be placed in complete upheaval in the very space of an hour?

A nurse took Linda and Teri away to be seen for their injuries. Another came to John, pointing at his torn and bloodied pant leg.

"Please, sir, let the doctor look at that cut," she said, motioning back to the door that had just swallowed up his whole family.

He glanced down at the jagged edge of his ripped pants and the blood soaking through, but he shook his head. "I'm staying here till there's news."

The nurse tried to change his mind, but he wouldn't budge. "I'm not going anywhere until I hear how my wife is doing," he insisted. Finally, a nurse brought him a clean section of bandage to tie around the gash and slow the bleeding.

The other man involved in the crash was taken back as well, so John was left alone in the waiting room. The silence quickly left him reeling from the loud roar inside his mind.

"Jesus," he prayed without thinking. Without remembering they weren't on speaking terms. But he didn't know what else to do. "Jesus." His voice broke.

Memories flooded his mind as tears filled his eyes. He recalled the first time he'd laid eyes on his beautiful wife in her vibrant yellow dress. Her smile had been so easy, her friendly manner would light up a room. Her petite little form somehow seemed larger than life when he got to know her and saw the fire in her spirit. He didn't want to live in a world without Nellie. He'd give anything to have her standing next to him now, pestering him about his awful driving and shaming him for putting her girls in danger.

When will you learn, Johnny? she'd say, shaking her head in irritation and punching him in the arm hard enough to make him wince.

"Jesus," he said again, sinking into a chair and covering his face with his hands.

At some point, the girls were returned to him. Linda had a splint for her shoulder. Teri carried an ice pack for the bump on her head.

"You have strong little girls," the nurse patted their shoulders. "And your older daughter held that strap so tightly she sprained her muscle."

"That's what Daddy told me to do if there was ever an accident," Linda explained. "Hold on for dear life."

The nurse nodded. "Quite so, dear. You're a good girl."

John tried to contain his emotions. He told the girls to sit and read magazines. Teri couldn't concentrate on hers and kept saying her head hurt. All three of them glanced up at that door often.

Eventually, the fireman's wife came into the room, panicked and asking for her husband. When the nurse said he was being seen, the woman nearly passed out. As she was led to a chair, John realized the woman was with child and near her due date. Just like Kit.

He approached her. She was trembling. "He was all right when they took him back, ma'am," he said. "I'm sure they're just making certain."

Her eyes fell immediately to his bloodied pant leg and she

gasped. He was sorry he'd come over to her. He limped back to the other side of the room with the girls. But the woman turned around to look at him.

"Thank you," she said, sniffling.

Nearly three hours passed before anyone came to speak to him. The fireman and his wife had long since gone home. Night had fallen and the murmurs of nurses and the receptionist at the desk were the only sounds.

Jesus… Jesus… Jesus…

"Mr. Hagaman?" A nurse stepped into the room, her uniform crisp and white and her hair as neat as a pin. The opposite of how he felt.

He jumped to his feet. "Is she okay?"

The nurse didn't answer his question directly, which worried him. "She's just woken up. She's rather inconsolable at the moment, I'm afraid. She is demanding to see her children so she'll know for herself that they are unharmed."

John almost smiled in spite of himself. It sounded like his wife, for sure. "But how is she?"

The nurse gave a little sigh and shook her head. "It's simply too soon to know, Mr. Hagaman. Please bring the girls through. We'll say a quick hello and then you can bring them back here while the doctor looks after your wife."

He nodded, glad for even just a moment's glance to see for himself that Kit was alive and awake. He followed the nurse, holding his daughter's hands tightly as they sniffled and tried to be brave.

The girls walked before him into the room. He saw their eyes go as wide as saucers. He steeled his jaw and followed them in, prepared for whatever sight would meet him. Nellie seemed so small, lying on that table with blood staining the pillowcase and sheets. She reached feebly toward the girls.

"Mother?" Linda said in a tiny voice, her lip trembling.

"Oh!" Nellie said in a weak voice. "You're okay. Praise the Lord!"

"I bumped my head," Teri said, showing her mother the ice pack. "It hurts."

"Oh, my baby," Nellie cooed softly. "Mama's sorry you're hurt. And Linda, your arm…"

"How are you?" John asked. The words seemed hollow. Insufficient to everything he wanted to say – everything he wanted her to understand. He wished he could express his thoughts.

I love you. I always have, I always will. I love your spunk when you preach at me and your fire when you pray. I love your mischievous smile when you jump from behind the door to scare me. I can't imagine ever loving anyone else as much as I love you, and I don't want to be without you. Please be okay. If you're okay, I'll do anything. I promise. Anything.

"I'm afraid we'll have to cut this visit short," the doctor said sternly. "Mrs. Hagaman needs to save her strength."

John gulped back all the words that wouldn't go past the lump in his throat. He ushered the girls out of the room. Teri began to cry and call for her mother. John picked her up and carried her down the white hall to the waiting room. Linda followed, silent and stoic. Like her father. So very much like him. He wondered if her world was falling apart inside her like his was. He wished he knew how to ask her the right questions. Assure them both. But the words were stuck in his throat.

"Daddy?"

He looked down, seeing Linda's pixie face staring up at him. Her eyes were large and solemn.

"Daddy, would you pray?"

He stared at her, shaking his head. He didn't have any right to pray with them. "Why don't you pray, honey? Pray for Mother."

Linda refused. "I want *you* to pray, Daddy."

"I do, too," Teri said with a loud sniff.

He looked at them. It was one of the longest moments of his life. He thought of the words of the hymn. They bubbled up out of his soul as if they had been waiting for their moment.

Come home, come home
You who are weary come home
Earnestly, tenderly, Jesus is calling,
Calling, O sinner, come home.

"Dear Lord," he prayed aloud, before he could second-guess himself. In that moment, surrender hit him like a tidal wave. "Please let her be okay. I'll do anything."

"Me too," Linda prayed.

"Me too," Teri echoed.

Forty-Eight

John lifted his wife from the car and carried her into the house as the girls followed along behind him. It was after midnight. They had to be as tired as they had ever been in their lives. Teri had fallen asleep in the taxi on the way home. John was worried about that lump that was still growing on her forehead.

"Help your sister to bed," he told Linda. She took Teri's hand and led her into the house and up to their room, where she took their pajamas from the drawer and helped her sister get dressed and into bed. As he passed by their room, he heard them saying their prayers together.

Ah, but his girls had their mother's faith.

Nellie drifted in and out of consciousness as he helped her get ready for bed. She moaned and held her head as if it ached. When he tried to get her to walk across the hall to the bathroom, her knees gave out and she started to fall. He caught her and carried her the rest of the way.

"Everything hurts," she cried as he helped her use the toilet. He took a washcloth and wet it, wiping away the crusted blood on her face and head as best as he could. He dressed her in her nightgown and lifted her into bed. He laid down beside her, but sleep wouldn't come. The events of the evening replayed in his mind, over and over like a record needle stuck in a groove of the vinyl.

He eyed the protrusion of Nellie's abdomen under the blanket, thinking about the last thing the doctor had told him before they left.

"We can't find any sign of life from the baby, Mr. Hagaman. I'm sorry, but I don't think your child survived the accident."

He could only think of the grief his wife would surely bear. "Does she know?"

"I tried several times to explain it to her," the doctor said. "Her concussion is causing marked amnesia. She doesn't remember the accident and she can't remember anything we've told her about the baby. Perhaps she is simply not prepared to deal with the loss."

John closed his eyes and shook his head.

"Her body will most likely detect that the baby is no longer alive and she will go into labor to expel the dead child. This can take a few days or a few weeks. When it happens, bring her back to the hospital. We'll give her medicine to make her sleep so she doesn't remember the event. I would prescribe a drug to speed up this process, but she is so weak from the accident, I don't want to further tax her system right now. She should regain her strength first."

John glanced at his sleeping wife. Her features were dimly lit by the nearly full moon that shone through the window. He'd forgotten to pull the shades. She usually did it.

How much could one woman take? Why hadn't God protected her from flying out onto the pavement? It should have been John instead. He was big and strong, and he would have been alright. How many times had he hit his noggin in army training and not suffered a single lasting effect?

"Jesus," he whispered, looking out the window into the night sky full of stars. "Show me what I should do."

It was hard to imagine God in here, with them in their bedroom, present in the storm they were weathering. God must be far away. He must be looking the other way. Surely if he had seen, he would have kept Nellie safe.

John stayed home from school the next day and kept the girls home as well. He told them to stay in bed and play quietly so they could rest and recover. Teri slept much of the day, but Linda sat on her bed, trying to read or work on the schoolwork their teacher dropped off after school. She found it hard to concentrate.

"Will Mother be okay?" Linda asked when he brought their lunch tray.

He wanted to assure them their mother would be fine. But was it fair to promise if he wasn't sure? "I think so, Linda. I hope so. Keep praying."

"What about the baby in her tummy?" Teri asked sleepily.

John scratched his forehead and stared hard at the floor. "The baby went to heaven, girls."

They didn't say anything for a long moment. "Does Mother know?" Linda finally asked.

"Mother loves the baby, Daddy. She'll be so sad," Teri said mournfully.

"I know. She can't remember right now. When her mind is strong again, I'll tell her."

Linda looked down at her book, her eyebrows drawn together. "Why did God let this happen?"

John could tell she wasn't angry. She was simply voicing the question he'd been asking himself all night. The one that didn't have a single good answer.

"Only God knows, I guess," he said. "Mother would say we need to trust him."

"That is what she would say," Linda agreed, nodding firmly. "So that's what we'll do."

John returned to school the next day. Teri went to her class as well, but Linda stayed home to take care of Nellie. He felt guilty leaving his ten-year-old daughter to care for her mother, but he couldn't miss any more work. There would be medical bills to pay. Linda had shown no fear, though. It seemed to relieve her to have something helpful to do.

"How is she?" John asked as he came in the door. Linda was standing at the counter with her mother's apron wrapped around her waist. She was studying a recipe with furrowed brow.

"She won't eat. I was going to make her favorite fried chicken and mashed potatoes, but I'm not sure I can do all of this."

His heart went out to his daughter. "We'll figure it out together."

He went up to see Nellie. She was lying down, facing the window. She glanced at him with a confused expression.

He sat down beside her and kissed her forehead. "How are you?"

She took her time answering. "The baby isn't moving. I didn't want to scare Linda, but I think something is wrong."

"Do you remember what the doctor told you?"

She looked at the floor as if she were trying to calculate a complicated math formula on it. She finally shook her head. "I don't recall …"

"What's the last thing you remember?"

She thought again. "Church. Sunday morning. We sang my favorite hymn, *In the Garden*."

"Do you remember me saying we should take a drive to the air show?"

She hesitated, then nodded. "Yes. But I don't remember the drive."

He nodded. He took a deep breath and held her hands tightly, wishing for a doctor or nurse to come and do the explaining now. But he was the only one there. He'd have to break the news. "Kit, we were in a car accident. You were thrown from the car and hit your head. It knocked you unconscious. It's why you're having trouble remembering."

Her eyes grew wide. "But what about the baby?"

He swallowed hard before he answered. "The baby didn't survive the crash. They couldn't find a heartbeat."

She gasped and cried out as if he'd struck her. "No! No, Lord, please," she prayed.

"I'm sorry," he said, trying to think of something to comfort her distress. "But maybe it's a blessing in disguise."

She yanked her hands away from his and held her stomach protectively. "How could you say that? This is our child!"

He didn't answer. He dropped his arms to rest on his knees and folded his hands together, staring out the window.

"You're glad. You're glad the baby's dead."

He heard her harsh tone, and it felt like a knife to his chest. "Of course not."

"You're not glad," she admitted, her voice lowering. "But you're relieved."

He didn't answer, because in all truth, she was right. He was relieved his child wouldn't live a life of suffering, and their family would be spared the burden. He was relieved, but he wasn't about to admit it to her.

The months that followed were the hardest of John's life. Harder than war. Harder than injury. More difficult than anything he'd ever experienced before. It wasn't long before he reached the end of his ability and endurance.

Nellie suffered daily with headaches. She closed the shades and curtains in every room of the house. She groaned as she moved, the stiffness and pain in her knees and ankles lingering weeks after the accident.

She carried her dead child in her womb for another couple

weeks. It was pure torture. He frequently found her curled in a ball, crying as she held her abdomen. Sometimes she woke in the night, frightened at the thought of the dead baby trapped in her body. She would panic and pace the room, mumbling disjointed prayers. He didn't blame her. He couldn't imagine what it must be like to walk around with a dead human being inside. The very idea was abhorrent.

Finally, her body responded and began the process of labor. He took her to the hospital immediately, where he waited once again in the familiar waiting room. Hours later, a nurse came to tell him the baby had been delivered and his wife was waking up.

Nellie asked for the dead baby after John came into the room. When the nurse told her it had been taken away, Nellie cried. John's heart twisted inside him at the sound.

"Please just tell me if it was a boy," she begged, but the nurse shook her head and shrugged before she made a quick exit. Nellie turned to him. "I just wanted to hold him."

John didn't know what to say, so he said nothing.

"I just wanted to hold my own baby," she said again as she leaned back on the pillow, completely spent.

John was glad he wouldn't have to see the child's face. He didn't want to see their features on the little face. He didn't want to have to live with that picture in his mind for the rest of his life. But Nellie was stronger than him when it came to love. She could love fiercely, even in unbearable pain. Even if she could barely stand. Even if her emotions were as delicate as tissue paper. She could love harder than anyone he'd ever met.

"Your wife needs to eat," the doctor said to him in the hallway as he left later that evening. "She's down to ninety pounds. I'm sure you know just by looking at her she's far too thin. If she's going to build up her strength again, she must start eating."

John shifted uncomfortably. "She doesn't have much of an

appetite." He felt like a failure for letting her get into such a state. "I try to get her to eat, but I'm not the best cook, and she says nothing tastes right anymore. She can't smell things like she used to, either."

"That can happen after a head injury," the doctor acknowledged. "I can't guarantee it will get better, though it might. She will need to learn how to feed herself even if food doesn't taste or smell the way she remembers it."

John determined he would talk her into eating again.

Time wore on in a slow and painstaking path of briars and thistles, so it seemed. John became like a machine, performing his duties and calling the day successful if he'd completed all his tasks. *Go to school. Get through classes and meetings. Get home soon after the girls. Make dinner. Sit with Nellie. Get her to eat. Look over the girls' homework and talk about their days. Put girls to bed. Sit with Nellie. Get her to eat. Let her talk or cry. Get to bed no later than midnight.*

He read all the information he could find about head injuries. He took every suggestion in medical journals and took Nellie to doctor appointment after doctor appointment. He was ever engaged in the search for something beyond the familiar "rest and wait for time to heal her injury."

Nellie developed infections after the stillbirth. Some days she would rock back and forth in her bed, fighting severe pain in her head and abdomen. She began to react to the traffic noise outside the window. She would gasp or cry out every time someone honked a horn at the stop light in front of their house. She refused to get in the car to go anywhere.

The girls missed going to church. John rallied himself and took them. He sat in the back of the church he'd attended first so long ago as a young man with stars in his eyes, headed off to war to be a hero. How much had changed. He had changed, and not for the better. He wished he could recapture that faith and emotional high he'd felt that Sunday so many years before. He figured that, along with everything else, was long gone by now.

Forty-Nine

After the service, Pastor Grayson stopped John on his way out the door with the girls. "How is Mrs. Hagaman? We miss her so much. Our children's classes haven't been the same without her."

"She's fine," John started the polite response, but something in the pastor's expression stopped him. He looked down. "She's in a rough spot, to be honest. She had a bad concussion and a miscarriage. She hasn't recovered well from either."

"Oh, she lost the baby? I'm so sorry to hear that." The pastor seemed genuinely dismayed at the news.

"Thank you for your concern," John mumbled. He motioned the girls to the door. But suddenly, his feet stopped moving. He didn't know why, but his legs just wouldn't work. Try as he might, his brain could not convince them to move any further.

After an awkward pause, Pastor Grayson came to his rescue. "Mr. Hagaman, would you like to meet in my office for a few minutes? My wife would be so happy to spend some time with your girls."

John opened his mouth to decline. He meant to say "no, thank you," but instead he heard a "yes" come out of his mouth.

He followed the pastor back to his study, cursing his now-compliant legs. As he sat down in the office, he wondered what he was going to say. The pastor saved him again by speaking first.

"We're honored to see you here today, John. We've been praying for you."

John shifted. "I know you probably wonder why I don't come more often. Nellie acts like I'm a backslidden heathen standing on the brink of hell's door."

"Your wife is zealous," Pastor Grayson said with a knowing smile. "But I can assure you she only speaks highly of you in our midst. I can tell she admires you very much."

The words surprised John. They fell upon his wounded soul like a salve. All he'd ever wanted was for his wife to be proud of him. Had he missed the fact that she already was?

"Nellie's changed," John said, suddenly wanting to tell this near-stranger everything. "She has trouble remembering. And she's so nervous, especially about the traffic. She hardly eats, and her head and stomach always hurt."

Grayson nodded. John saw the concern in his gaze. This man didn't feel pity, but he felt their pain alongside them.

"Head injuries are difficult to predict. It could be years before she completely returns to her old self. Some things might never improve," John explained. "We've seen so many doctors and they just don't help her. It's been months we've been living like this. I've had to be both father and mother and work to provide at the same time."

"Do you resent that?" Pastor Grayson asked. His tone was not judgmental, only inquisitive.

John considered the question. "I don't resent Nellie. She didn't ask for any of this." He suddenly chuckled. "Well, maybe in a way she did. But she couldn't have known how it would have all played out."

"What do you mean?" the pastor asked as he leaned back in his chair and folded his hands in front of him.

"I overheard her once a few months back. She was praying. She asked God to do whatever it took to get me to come back to church."

Grayson's eyebrows raised. "I guess you have a mighty prayer warrior on your side, John."

John could only nod and twist the edges of his hat in his lap.

"It sounds like God is pursuing you. I guess the question you have to ask yourself is whether you are willing to let him catch you. To surrender your will to him."

"But I did," John argued, leaning forward with his elbows on his knees. "Before I went to war. I asked Jesus to be my personal Savior. Right out there in that very pew where I sat this morning."

The pastor nodded. "And he heard your prayer, of course. But we can push even our personal Savior away. He will not force us to live for him. It is our choice. The only thing is – and I think you're realizing this – he will come after us if we belong to him. He'll put people in our lives, just like your wife, who are willing to sacrifice themselves on our behalf. He'll do whatever it takes."

John felt tears sting his eyes without warning. He'd been thinking of it all wrong. He'd been thinking of himself as the sacrificial one. He was doing all the work, wasn't he? Bearing all the burden? But now he saw a different perspective. Nellie had done the hardest job. When she'd gone flying out of that car and smashed her head against the pavement, she'd been doing just what Jesus did when he went to the cross.

Whatever it cost.

In that moment, he was overcome by love for his wife. And love for Jesus. A great, overwhelming shame came over him like a dark cloud as he thought of the way he'd been running from God for so long. He stared hard at the old linoleum tile on the office floor.

"John," Pastor Grayson said softly. "You can always come home."

John knew what he meant. He could return to church. Be involved in the lives of others and grow as a believer in Christ. He could put his selfishness and his sinfulness behind him for good. He could let go of the vices and his pride. And in that moment, how he wanted to do all those things! He wanted to let it all fall and run back to that place where he'd started so many years before.

There was a long silence in the room. Longer than was comfortable. But John couldn't make another half-hearted decision and later go back on it. It had to be everything this time. Nothing held back. And he didn't know if he was capable of that.

"John, the Bible says in the second chapter of Revelation: *I have somewhat against thee, because thou has left thy first love. Remember therefore from whence thou art fallen, and repent, and do the first works.* It means Jesus is waiting for you to come home. He is merciful, and he will forgive. What's stopping you? What questions remain?"

John considered the passage the pastor had quoted. "I guess I just don't have it all figured out yet. Sometimes I don't understand God. I wonder why he lets bad things happen. Why he allowed a war as terrible as the one we just fought, for instance."

The truth of it hit John in the gut like a sucker punch. He inhaled quickly and clenched his fists tightly. "Why all my men died over there, but I came home before I even saw a real battle. Why my wife's teenage brother crashed while he was flying home from the war he had survived. Why the car accident happened and my wife lost the baby she loved. Why would he let all these things happen to Nellie? Sometimes it's hard to trust God."

The pastor nodded. "You aren't the first to voice those questions. I give you credit for having the courage to speak them. But remember, the Bible says God's ways are not our ways. His thoughts are beyond knowing. He's so much bigger than us, our minds can't comprehend what he's up to. I guess the question is, are you willing to let him be big? Acknowledge that you are weak and you need his help? Are you willing to throw caution to the wind and trust him, just like you put all your trust in that parachute when you jumped out of those planes in England? Nothing less than that kind of trust will last."

John could see what the pastor was saying. Pieces of the puzzle in his mind linked together. The pastor's answer voided all the other questions he had piled atop one another.

"*He must become greater, I must become less,*" the pastor quoted. "John the Baptist said that. Your namesake."

John nodded with a small smile. "I guess he did."

"Are you ready for this, John? Are you ready to give your whole self to the Lord and hold nothing back? To repent and walk humbly in his ways from this day forward?"

John didn't have to think about it. His heart had already decided. "I am."

"Let's tell him." The pastor bowed his head.

From that moment on, John's world changed. No, things didn't necessarily improve. Nellie Mae continued to suffer the effects of her head injury. In fact, she would carry the wounds for the rest of her life, though God was gracious to her. It was John's heart that changed. He no longer feared living for God. He no longer had interest in those silly cigars or avoiding church. In fact, he began to read his Bible and pray every morning. He eventually became a deacon and led a men's Bible study.

John never spoke much of the war or of the early struggles in their marriage, but he spoke in other ways to his family and his church. He took care of his wife for every last day he had breath in his body.

Nellie eventually went back to church and even began a Sunday school ministry that continued long after she'd become a grandmother. She never had another child of her own, but they gave foster care to two troubled teenage boys.

God surprised her later in her life, not only with two godly sons-in-law, one a pastor and the other an evangelist, but also with nine grandchildren. And she gave her whole heart to every one of them. When they were grown with families of their own, she held her great-grandchildren in her arms, long after the time she should have carried any baby around, never mind that she couldn't remember even half of their thirty names.

John read a verse in the Bible that stuck with him. *So I will restore to you the years that the swarming locust has eaten*, God had said to the prophet Joel. And John figured that's what God did for Nellie and him, too. There were plenty of hardships to face in their later years, especially as Nellie's health and memory declined, but John never once doubted in the goodness of his God. Ever.

February 14, 2008

Fifty years passed by in a heartbeat. John was old. Old and tired. He didn't want to give in to the fatigue, but he was exhausted. Cancer had a way of doing the worst to a body. Maybe tomorrow he'd get out there and ride his bicycle. Wouldn't that make Nellie's eyes shine with pride? Show her what her husband was still made of?

He fell asleep, transported to the belly of a Douglas DC 3. He sat up with a start. The plane rumbled beneath him, riding the waves of the night air. He squinted at the dim light. He could only make out the yellow flashing lights.

None of Company HQ accompanied him on this mission. He was alone in the plane. He stood up, feeling the cool metal of the seat beneath him and the familiar disorientation. He planted his boots on the floor to keep from swaying or falling over.

Captain Wilson appeared at the doorway. He was somber, his

forehead creased and his brow furrowed. He was watching the night sky. John could see it was full of planes and bombers headed for the shore.

"I'm here," John said in surprise. "I made it to the war."

Captain Wilson quickly turned and stared him straight in the eye. "It's hell out there, Hagaman. I don't suggest jumping tonight. But it ain't up to me. We're taking orders from the Big Man."

Johnny gulped, but he swallowed back his fear. He reached up and hooked his pack to the line.

There's no one to check my pack, he worried. *I'm alone. We aren't supposed to jump alone.*

"It's time, Hagaman," Wilson stepped back and motioned John forward. John felt the wind stir up at his feet.

"Out you go," Wilson said, slapping his rear as the usual sign that time was up.

Johnny gave him one last look before he jumped. Before he could check his parachute. Before he could figure out what he was supposed to do when he landed. Where he'd go. How he'd find his platoon.

He felt a sudden stab of pain and looked down. His leg was shattered by the grenade. Blood ran everywhere. He tried to look up to see if his parachute was opening, but he could only see night sky and the smoke of a hundred planes. He felt the force of the wind and knew he was falling faster and faster, hurtling toward earth in a mad frenzy.

"I can't do this on my own!" He yelled at the top of his lungs, hoping someone would hear his cry. "I need help!"

Just as the ground came into view and the dark waters of the ocean were reaching up to grab him and pull him down into the depths, he felt arms go around him. Strong, familiar arms he recognized immediately. He felt absolute relief.

"I've got you," a kind voice spoke. He could tell the man was smiling. "And I'm never going to let you go."

In that moment, John Hagaman, the man who had spent so much of his life trusting only himself, trying to control the events of his life, trying to make everyone he loved proud of him for being brave and strong … let go.

And he fell headlong into the unfathomable grasp of a Savior who had pursued him down every course, every pathway, every tragedy and triumph of his life.

He was finally home.

Epilogue

June 26, 2010

Light play danced on the wall as chimes tinkled somewhere just outside the door. Nellie shook her head slightly and opened her eyes. She hoped to sweep away the cobwebs tangled in her mind. She couldn't imagine why she'd be napping in the middle of the day. She searched the room for something tangible on which to rest her gaze.

Her eyes found his face in the picture frame. Tears sprung up, blurring the lines of his beautiful face, his dear smile. In a moment, she was home again. In a heartbeat, she was his.

"John, honey?" she called, her voice catching on the silence and falling flat. Surely John was just in the next room. Maybe he was sleeping in front of the tennis game on television. Or perhaps he'd gone out to mow the lawn. He'd be back soon.

"He'll be wanting supper," she reprimanded herself, startled by how tired her voice sounded.

With great effort she pulled her aching body from the couch, trying to remember what in the world she'd done to be so sore and unsteady. She hobbled awkwardly toward the window and looked out, searching the far field. Had John said he was going to mow today? She watched hopefully for his tall form perched atop his riding mower. How she loved catching a glimpse of him when he didn't know she was watching! She chuckled at the thought.

"Dinner," she reminded herself again. She tore her eyes away, focusing on the familiar little kitchen they shared instead. He'd like some leftover fried chicken. Maybe some beans. And a tall glass of buttermilk, of course.

She rummaged around, frantic upon discovering no sign of the creamy milk in the fridge. How could she have let it run out? She'd have to make a trip to the store.

She set out his tray and continued her preparations. Folded napkin, just so. Fork, knife. All the while her ear listened for the familiar slam of the screen door on the porch.

A touch on her arm almost sent the tray flying. She put her hand over her racing heart and tried to steady her breathing. "Well, I'll be …" Nellie turned around to see her grown daughter standing behind her. "What in the world are you doing here?"

"I brought your dinner, Mother," her daughter said kindly, eyeing the tray in Nellie's hands with a contemplative glance.

"Well, now, I can make my own dinner." Nellie was sorry her busy daughter had gone to the trouble. "I just got Dad's tray all set up. I'm expecting him any minute."

The mournful expression on her daughter's face made something deep within, something dark and sad and too awful to think about start to swirl just below the surface of her consciousness. She tried to shut it out. Nellie closed her eyes and thought of Johnny and his capable, steady ways. He could fix anything. He was always there for her, no matter what. He wouldn't abandon her when she needed him. He'd promised he'd always be there to take care of her. What would she do without him, for goodness' sake?

"I'm sorry, Mother." Teri said the words even as Nellie silently begged her not to. "Dad's gone."

Nellie nodded, swallowing back the lump in her throat that

confirmed her daughter's statement. "Oh, yes," she said softly. "He's gone to church. Or to play tennis with Wade ..."

"No, Mother. He passed away two years ago. He's gone."

Gone. How could her world be gone? But in that moment, she remembered everything. The funeral. The family gathered around her, grandkids and great-grandkids laughing and running the aisle in their pretty dresses and church clothes. Her daughters on either side of her, holding her hands. Looking up at the front of the funeral home and seeing the vacant body of the dearest form on earth. Knowing he was forever silent this side of heaven.

She hated how easily she forgot. Hated it as much as she was grateful for it. Her memory had started slipping long ago, after the car accident. Her mind struggled for focus. Her tongue stalled as her brain tried to keep up, to recognize all the dear faces surrounding her.

Now she looked back at the picture. She wished fiercely she could turn back the pages of time. John's smile almost taunted her under his tilted paratrooper cap. It seemed if she just reached far enough and high enough, she might slip her hand through the years and rest her fingers against his familiar face.

"Oh, my Johnny," she breathed as a lament. She looked at her daughter. "I'm sorry. I can't seem to remember things like I used to."

Her voice trailed off and her eyes remained glued to the picture. *I want to come home.*

"Come sit, Mother."

Her daughter helped her to her bed. She lay back on the pillow and closed her eyes, reaching her hand out into the darkness. Slowly the sounds of cars going by and a television somewhere in the distance and children laughing in another part of the house faded. Everything became still. Everything but the voice, quoting Scripture. The book of First John, wasn't it?

If anyone acknowledges Jesus is the Son of God, God lives in them. We rely on the love God has for us. We love because he first loved us.

She strained her fingers as far as she could reach. Searching. *I rely on your love, Lord. I know it was never my place to try to earn it. Thank you for all you did to save me, despite my sins. My pride.*

Suddenly a strong grasp caught her hand. Pulled her up. She gasped and opened her eyes to infinite light.

"Welcome home, Nellie Mae," he said with a smile. "We've been waiting for you."

Acknowledgments

This book would have been impossible without John and Nellie's daughters guiding the process of writing it. I didn't realize what I was asking when I first came to them with this idea – or how strange it would be for them to see their early life as fiction on a page. I'm so grateful to my Aunt Teri for sifting through her memories and conversations with my grandma and providing me such a detailed recounting of this story. And then, to carefully read the manuscript multiple times to ensure all the holes were filled in correctly and adjustments were made to make the story shine. Likewise, I am thankful for my mom, Linda, who provided her own perspective of the same events, which added another layer, making it richer and fuller. Together, your stories made this book come alive. I'm also thankful to their cousin, Karen, for providing her own thoughts.

I would also like to sincerely thank Martha, my grandma's best friend in high school, for being willing to share her stories over the phone. It was a delight to speak with her and it brought tears to my eyes when I heard her voice, which sounded so much like my grandmother's slight southern lilt. Her willingness to send me their high school yearbook and pictures meant more to me than I can express. With her help, I was able to piece together the timeline of my grandmother's early years and see the big picture with a little more clarity. Martha, one day I hope to be able to put my arms around you in person. I can see why my grandma loved you and spoke so highly of you.

As always, my editor, Tanya Dennis, makes this all possible. I am indebted to her careful, honest, creative talent for seeing the book that should be among the chaos I present her. Check out her services and ministries at tanyadennisbooks.com.

I also want to thank my daughter, Hannah, for posing as her great-grandmother for the cover!

Author's Note

Sometimes truth is stranger than fiction. Interestingly enough, the connections I have made to historical figures did happen mostly as I describe them in this story. My grandma's father was a friend of Harry Truman and corresponded with him for a time by letters after they met. My grandmother did have a connection to a well-known murderer (names were changed for this book) before his infamous story unfolded. My great-grandma's brother did take care of a drunken Red Skelton on a few occasions.

There was divergence over was whether or not my grandpa received a Purple Heart. Family records show that he did, and family legend claims it was stolen. Unfortunately, the official records were destroyed in a fire in 1973, and the criteria that Purple Hearts be granted only in enemy combat changed the same year Grandpa was injured. So in the interest of full disclosure, I don't know whether he received it or not.

But however it happened, my grandparents lived in an interesting time with interesting people, and their families weren't afraid to be involved in their culture. It makes it easier for me to tell the story of their world. I'm thankful they didn't hesitate to go outside the bounds of the normal and expected life.

I write their story to keep them alive just a little longer. They are still here, though they have long been in the presence of their Savior. I see them in a mannerisms of one of their grandchildren or great-grandchildren. I see their physical features in their descendants. In their interests and passions that somehow continue on in their offspring after two generations. Most of all, I see their heart for Christ continuing in the lives of those they left behind. John and Nellie taught us how to love Jesus. I am eternally grateful to them for that legacy of faith.

When I was sixteen, I sat my grandma down at her kitchen table late one night. With a notebook I've since lost and plenty of snacks and nail care supplies, I asked her to tell me the story of her life. I told her I wanted to write a book someday, because the parts I'd heard were good fodder for a story, and I needed to know what was most important. What were her strongest memories? What were her deepest regrets? If her life had a theme, how would it go?

I don't know exactly what prompted this late-night conference. At the time, I was convinced God wanted me on the stage singing about Jesus to full arenas. I saw writing as a personal quirk I should keep hidden. Along the same lines as a weird mole. Maybe at some point I'll time travel back to my sixteen-year-old self and tell her what to ask. However it happened, I grabbed the opportunity and even managed to ask a few of the right questions.

My grandma acted a bit uncharacteristic that night as well. Oh, don't get me wrong, Grandma was outgoing and fiercely loyal to her family, but she tended to present the best version of herself to her grandkids. I had a different, but deeper appreciation for my grandmother after that night. She was honest with me. She told me how it really was. She told me how she felt left out and forgotten as the middle child of so many siblings and a busy preacher mama. She told me about posing for photographers and romping with friends and taking care of her aunt's children in a different town where she happened to catch the eyes of a tall, quiet soldier with protruding ears, soulful eyes and a big grin. She beamed when she mentioned that she didn't know if that soldier liked her back until he kissed *her* goodbye instead of her pretty cousin.

But as we talked, her tone became more reflective, her stories more personal. She spoke of regrets. What she didn't get right. The choices she made as a younger woman that affected her relationships and hurt people she loved dearly. I heard the wistfulness in her voice. *If I'd only done it differently*, her spirit said to mine. *Maybe if I'd learned I can't make people change, there would have been less hurt. More happiness.*

Please don't misunderstand me. The grandmother I had known for sixteen years had never given me the impression she had ever done me wrong, besides an occasional grumpy word I probably heartily deserved. I knew beyond a shadow of a doubt she loved me furiously and would have done anything for me, and that she felt the same way about the other eight grandkids as well as her daughters and sons-in-law.

That night, I realized my grandma was human. She was flawed. She had made mistakes, some of them grave. And it only made her more interesting to me. What had led her from the person she had been at sixteen to the person she was at sixty-four?

She stopped talking and looked at me in a sort of bewildered surprise. "Why am I telling you all of this?" I didn't answer, hoping she wouldn't stop. I was hungry to hear more, but as conversations late at night tend to, it ended and we went to bed.

Now I know why she told me. I know why I asked, as determined as I was to hide my writing disease from everybody. Because God wanted this story to be told.

And so I tell it in my imperfect way, through my imperfect lens. Some may have told it better. All of those who loved Johnny and Nellie Mae would have told it differently, as I learned when I went back as an adult to ask their daughters and grandchildren to tell me what they remembered.

I can't promise every word of what I wrote in this story really happened. There are too many holes that had to be filled. Too many details lost to the past. Inevitably, they will be orchestrated by my personality.

But when all was said and done, I did my best to recapture the dear departed spirits of my grandparents. To wrestle them back to the land of the living for a time to gaze once again on the faces that have disappeared. I want those of us who loved them to remember why it mattered. I want those who didn't know them to be amazed at the way God works for good in the lives of those who belong to him.

He doesn't let us go, dear reader. If we belong to him, he holds us fast and never lets go for a second. Even if we wanted to, we couldn't hope to escape the powerful grip of his love. He gets the job done. He finishes what he starts. And he'll do the same now, in 2019, that he did way back in 1946.

If you're reading this book and you're realizing you don't know if you belong to him or if you are captured in his grip of grace forever, Grandma and Grandpa would want me to tell you three things:

- **Believe you are a sinner.** *Romans 3:23: All have sinned,* *and fall short of the glory of God.*

- **Ask Jesus to forgive you and cleanse you**. *Romans 6:23: For the wages of sin is death, but the free gift of God is eternal life through Jesus Christ our Lord. Ephesians 2:8-9: For by grace you are saved, through faith, and not of yourselves, it is the gift of God, not of works, so that no one can boast.*

- **Turn from your sin and follow him**. *2 Corinthians 7:10: Godly sorrow brings repentance that leads to salvation and leaves no regret. Matthew 4:19: "Come, follow me," Jesus said.*

I'm happy to report (for their sake, not ours) that Johnny and Nellie Mae only endured a brief separation before they were reunited in eternity. And now they are the best versions of themselves, without the limitations of sin. And they're with Jesus. It doesn't get any better than that.

Praise God for happy endings.

About the Author

Miranda Shisler grew up in a pastor's household. She inherited a love for writing from her father and began writing as a way of thinking from an early age. She attended Cornerstone University to study vocal music and music education, but after marrying her love and becoming a mother, she clearly sensed God's call to write.

These days, when not writing or reading, she can usually be found serving in the music ministry of her church, leading women's Bible study, gardening or homeschooling her four children.

Connect with her online!

mirandashislerbooks.wixsite.com/mirandashislerbooks
facebook.com/authormirandashisler
pinterest.com/mirandashisler/ (See the *My Good Name* board!)
goodreads.com/mirandashisler

Please remember this is an Indie project so you can have the best reading experience. You can help (far more than you might think) by leaving a review for *My Good Name* on Amazon and Goodreads today!

Meet the Inspiration!

The real Johnny and Nellie Mae

Nellie Mae, circa 1941

John and Nellie with Linda and Teri, c.1955

John in his uniform, 1943

John and Nellie, circa 1946

John and Nellie, circa 1970

Nellie's friend Martha

My grandparents as I remember them, 1991.